W9-BJI-488

Selected praise for
The Tales of Five Hundred Kingdoms series
by *New York Times* bestselling author
MERCEDES LACKEY

"Wry and scintillating take on the Cinderella story...
Lackey's tale resonates with charm as magical
as the fairy-tale realm she portrays."
—*BookPage* on *The Fairy Godmother*

"This Tale of the Five Hundred Kingdoms novel is a
delightful fairy-tale revamp. Lackey ensures that familiar
stories are turned on their ear with amusing results."
—*RT Book Reviews* on *The Snow Queen*

Selected praise for
The Chronicles of Elantra series by
New York Times bestselling author
MICHELLE SAGARA

"Intense, fast-paced, intriguing, compelling and
hard to put down, *Cast in Shadow* is unforgettable."
—*In the Library Reviews*

"Sagara swirls mystery and magical adventure
together with unforgettable characters
in the fifth Chronicles of Elantra installment."
—*Publishers Weekly* on *Cast in Silence*

Selected praise for
The Underworld Cycle series by
CAMERON HALEY

"Fast pacing, pungent wit, surprise twists,
thoughtful discussions of morality, and escalating,
cinematic battles keep the pages turning."
—*Publishers Weekly* (starred review) on *Mob Rules*

MERCEDES LACKEY

is the acclaimed author of more than fifty novels and many works of short fiction. In her "spare" time she is also a professional lyricist and a licensed wild bird rehabilitator. Mercedes lives in Oklahoma with her husband and frequent collaborator, the artist Larry Dixon, and their flock of parrots.

MICHELLE SAGARA

has written more than twenty novels since 1991. She's written a quarterly book review column for the venerable Magazine of Fantasy and Science Fiction for a number of years, as well as dozens of short stories. In 1986 she started working in an SF specialty bookstore, where she continues to work to this day. She loves reading, is allergic to cats (very, which means they crawl all over her), is happily married, has two lovely children and has spent all of her life in her native Toronto—none of it on Bay Street.

CAMERON HALEY

Since graduating from Tulane University, Cameron Haley has been a law school dropout, a stock broker, an award-winning game designer and a product manager for a large commercial bank, but through it all has never stopped writing. An active member of Science Fiction and Fantasy Writers of America, Cameron is hard at work on the second book in the Underworld Cycle. Cameron lives in Minneapolis. For the latest dirt, visit www.cameronhaley.com.

HARVEST M##N

NEW YORK TIMES & USA TODAY BESTSELLING AUTHOR

MERCEDES LACKEY

NEW YORK TIMES BESTSELLING AUTHOR

MICHELLE SAGARA

CAMERON HALEY

LUNA™

If you purchased this book without a cover you should be aware that this book is stolen property. It was reported as "unsold and destroyed" to the publisher, and neither the author nor the publisher has received any payment for this "stripped book."

LUNA™

Recycling programs
for this product may
not exist in your area.

HARVEST MOON

ISBN-13: 978-0-373-80334-7

Copyright © 2010 by Harlequin Books S.A.

The publisher acknowledges the copyright holders
of the individual works as follows:

A TANGLED WEB
Copyright © 2010 by Mercedes Lackey

CAST IN MOONLIGHT
Copyright © 2010 by Michelle Sagara

RETRIBUTION
Copyright © 2010 by Greg Benage

All rights reserved. Except for use in any review, the reproduction or utilization of this work in whole or in part in any form by any electronic, mechanical or other means, now known or hereafter invented, including xerography, photocopying and recording, or in any information storage or retrieval system, is forbidden without the written permission of the editorial office, Worldwide Library, 233 Broadway, New York, NY 10279 U.S.A.

This is a work of fiction. Names, characters, places and incidents are either the product of the author's imagination or are used fictitiously, and any resemblance to actual persons, living or dead, business establishments, events or locales is entirely coincidental.

This edition published by arrangement with Harlequin Books S.A.

For questions and comments about the quality of this book
please contact us at Customer_eCare@Harlequin.ca.

® and TM are trademarks of Harlequin Books S.A., used under license. Trademarks indicated with ® are registered in the United States Patent and Trademark Office, the Canadian Trade Marks Office and in other countries.

www.LUNA-Books.com

Printed in U.S.A.

CONTENTS

A TANGLED WEB

Mercedes Lackey

It was the usual perfect day in Demeter's gardens in the Kingdom of Olympia. Birds, multicolored and with exquisite voices, sang in every tree. Flowers of every sort bloomed and breathed delicate perfumes into a balmy breeze that wandered through the glossy green foliage. It would rain a little after sundown, a gentle, warm rain that would be just enough to nourish, but not enough to interfere with anyone's plans. The only insects were the beneficial sort. Troublesome creatures were not permitted here. When a goddess makes that sort of decision, you can be sure She Will Be Obeyed.

Now and again a dramatic thunderstorm would roar through the mountains, reminding everyone—everyone not a god, that is—that Nature was *not* to be trifled with. But it stormed only when Demeter and Hera scheduled it. Everyone had plenty of warning—in fact, some of the nymphs and fauns scheduled dances just for the erotic thrill of it. Zeus enjoyed those days as well, it gave him a chance to lob thunderbolts about;

and the other gods on Olympus would be drinking vats of ambrosia and wine and encouraging him.

Meanwhile, on this perfect afternoon of this perfect day, in this most perfect of homes in the center of the most perfect of gardens, Demeter's only daughter, Persephone, stood barefoot on the cool marble floor of the weaving room and stared at the loom in front of her, fuming with rebellion.

There was nothing in the little weaving room except the warp-weighted loom, and since you had to get the light on it properly to see what you were doing, you had to have your back to the open door and window, thus being deprived of even a glimpse of the outdoors. It was maddening. Persephone could hear the birdsong, smell the flowers, and had to stand there weaving plain dyed linen in the dullest of patterns.

Small as the room was, however, Persephone was not alone in it. There was a tumble of baby hedgehogs asleep in a rush-woven basket, and a young faun sitting on the doorstep, watching her from time to time with his strange goat-eyes. There were doves cooing in a cornice, a tumble of fuzzy red fox-kits playing with a battered pinecone behind her. Anything Persephone muttered to herself would be heard, and in the case of the faun, very probably prattled back to her mother. Demeter would sigh and give her The Look of Maternal Reproach. After all, it was a very small thing she had been tasked with. It wasn't as if she was being asked to sow a field or harvest grapes. It wasn't even as if she was weaving every day. Just now and again. Yes, this was all very reasonable. There was no cause for Persephone to be irritated.

Of course there was, but it was a cause she really did not want her mother to know about.

Persephone wanted to scream.

She had the shuttle loaded with thread in one hand, the beater-stick in the other, and stared daggers at the half-finished swath of ochre linen before her. Oh, how she loathed each. Not for itself, but for what it represented.

I love my mother. I really do. I just wish right now she was at the bottom of a well.

Persephone took the beater-stick and whacked upward at the weft she had created. Of all the times for her mother to decide that the weaving of her new cloak *had* to be done…this was the worst. In fact, the timing could not *possibly* have been worse. She had spent weeks on this plan, days setting it up, gotten everything carefully in place, managed to find a way to get rid of the nymphs constantly trailing her, and now it was ruined. Stupid Thanatos would probably drive the chariot around and around a few dozen times, forget what he was supposed to do and head back to the Underworld; he was a nice fellow, but not the sharpest knife in the kitchen. Well, really, how smart did you have to be to do the job of the god of death? Just turn up at the right time, escort the soul down to the Underworld, and leave him at the riverbank for Charon. Not something that took a lot of deep thinking.

And poor Hades—oh, wait, *Eubeleus,* she wasn't supposed to know it was Hades—would spend half the day questioning him until he finally figured out what had happened. It had to be Thanatos, though, that was the only way this would work. Otherwise, things got horribly complicated.

She wasn't supposed to know she was going to be carried off to the Underworld, just as she wasn't supposed to know her darling wasn't a simple shepherd. She was supposed to be "abducted" by "a friend with a chariot." But she had known Hades for who he was almost from the beginning, and given that her darling *was* Hades, who else would drive his chariot? Not Hypnos, that would be incredibly foolhardy. Certainly not Charon. Minos, Rhadamanthus or Aeacus? Not likely. First of all, Persephone had the feeling that the former kings and current judges intimidated Hades quite a bit, and he wasn't likely to ask them to do him that sort of favor, never mind that he was technically their overlord. And second, she had the feeling that he was afraid if one of them *did* agree, he might be tempted to keep her for himself. Poor Hades had none of the bluster and bravado of his other "brothers," Poseidon and Zeus. He second-guessed himself more than anyone she knew. That was probably another reason why she loved him.

Of course, Hades didn't realize she knew the *other* reason why the abductor had to be Thanatos, because he didn't know she knew—well, everything.

We can set it up again, she promised herself. It wasn't the end of the world. She was clever, and "Eubeleus" was smitten. Even if she hadn't met all that many men— *thanks to Mother*—she could see that. His feelings went a lot deeper than the lust the nymphs and fauns and satyrs had for each other too; the way he had been so patient, so careful in his courtship, spoke volumes. He was willing to be patient because he loved her.

And she was smitten in return. She didn't know why no one seemed to like the Lord of the Underworld. It wasn't as if *he* was the one who decided how long your life would be—that could be blamed on the Fates—and he wasn't the one who carried you off; that was Thanatos. He was kind—it was *hard* being Lord of the Dead, and if he covered his kindness with a cold face, well, she certainly understood why. No one wanted to die. No one wanted to have everything they'd said and done and ever thought judged. No one wanted to leave the earth where things were lively and interesting when you might end up punished, or wandering the Fields of Asphodel because you were ordinary. And everyone, *everyone,* blamed Hades for the fact that they would all one day end up down there.

The Underworld was not the most pleasant place to live, unless you were remarkable in some way. From what she understood, on the rare occasions when she'd listened to anyone talking about it, Hades didn't often get a chance to spend time in the Elysian Fields where things were pleasant—he mostly got stuck watching over the punishment parts. If he was very sober, well, no wonder! He needed a spot of brightness in his life. And she would very much like to be that spot of brightness.

Besides being kind, and patient, and considerate, he never seemed to lose his temper like so many of the other gods did. He was also quite funny, in the dry, witty sense, rather than the hearty practical joking sense like his brother-god Zeus.

She had started out liking him when they first met and he was pretending to be a shepherd. And as she revisited the meadow where he kept up his masquerade many times, she found "liking" turning into something much more substantial rather quickly. They'd done a lot of talking, some dreaming, and a fair amount of kissing and cuddling, and she had decided that she would very much like things to go straight from the "cuddling" to the "wild carrying-on in the long grass" that the nymphs and satyrs were known for. But he had been unbelievably restrained. He wanted her to be sure. Not like Zeus, oh, no! Not like Poseidon, either! They'd been seeing each other for more than a year now, and the more time she spent with him, the more time she *wanted* to spend with him. Finally he had hesitantly asked if she would be willing to defy her mother and run away with him, and she had told him yes, in no uncertain terms whatsoever.

He never seemed to have even half an eye for anyone else, either. And not many males paid attention to little Persephone—though it was true she didn't get a chance to see many, the few times she had been up to Mount Olympus with her mother, she might just as well not have been there.

It would have been hard to compete for the attention of the gods anyway. She wasn't full-bodied like her mother—face it, no one was as full-bodied as her mother except Aphrodite. She didn't make men's heads turn when she passed. By all the powers, men's heads turned when just a whiff of Demeter's perfume drifted by them! Aphrodite might be the patron of Love, but Demeter was noticed and sought after just as much. Zeus even gave her that sort of Look, when he thought Hera wasn't watching; Poseidon would always drop leaden hints about "renewing the acquaintance."

Not that *she* noticed. She was too busy being the mother of everything that wandered by and needed a mother. Demeter, goddess of fertility, was far more of a "mother" than Great Hera was. Hera couldn't be bothered. Demeter yearned to mother everything.

Oh, yes, everything. As Persephone grew up, she had resigned herself to being part of a household filled to bursting with babies of all species. Fawns and fauns, nests full of birds, wolf-cubs and wild-kits, calves and lambs, froglets and snakelets, mere sprouts of dryads; if a species could produce a baby and the baby was orphaned, Demeter would take it in. Very fine and generous of her, but it meant that even an Olympian villa was filled to the bursting, and Persephone shared her room with whatever part of the menagerie didn't fit in anywhere else. She might have a great many playmates, but she *never* had any privacy.

Or, for that matter, silence.

Demeter sailed through it all with Olympian serenity. After all, she was a goddess—granted, a goddess of a tiny Kingdom, one you could probably walk across in three days—but still, she was a goddess, and a goddess was not troubled by such things.

Her daughter, however…

Her daughter would like a place and a space all her very own, thank you, into which nothing could come unless she invites it. Is that so much to ask?

The fox-kits had gone looking for more adventures, but there were still four of the foundlings here in the weaving room, ensuring she didn't have any privacy. Not counting the hedgehogs, the faun was still in here, now there was a nymph sorting through the yarn to find something to use to weave flower crowns with, and there were a couple of sylphs chatting in the windowsill, for no other reason but that the windowsill was convenient. Unless, of course, Demeter had sent them to keep an eye on her. Persephone threw the shuttle through the weft again, trying not to wince at the noises the little faun by the door was making, trying to master his panpipes for the first time.

If Demeter had her way, Persephone would be the "little daughter" forever. Though nearly twenty, she'd aged so slowly that her mother was used to thinking of her as too young for any separate life. She'd never be alone with a male, never have an identity of her own. There was no doubt that Zeus himself was infatuated with Demeter, though he would never say so to his wife, nor probably even to Demeter herself. After all, Demeter was in charge of marriage vows, so she would take a dim view of *that.* But that was why it was no use complaining to Zeus. He would just pat her on the head, call her "Little Kore" (Oh, how she hated that childhood nickname!) and tell her that her mother knew best.

And Hera would take Demeter's side too, as would Hestia. Aphrodite would probably take Persephone's part, if only for the sake of mischief, but having Aphrodite on your side was almost worse than having her as your enemy. Whatever Aphrodite wanted, Athena would oppose. And any god who wasn't infatuated with Demeter would still side with her, because she controlled the very fertility of this Kingdom. No god wanted to risk her deciding that nothing would grow in his garden…or that his "plow" would fail to work the "furrow" properly…

Bah!

The loom rocked a little with the vigor of her weaving, the warp-weights knocking against each other as she pulled the heddle rod up and dropped it back again and beat the weft into place with her stick. She hated the loom, she hated standing at it, she hated the monotonous toil of it, and hated that although her mother considered it to be a proper "womanly" task, she was not considered to actually *be* a woman.

She luxuriated in her grievances for a good long time, until she had actually woven a full handbreadth of cloth. But she could never hold a temper, and once she started losing the anger, what Hades called her "clever" self came to the fore, and she found herself thinking... *But on the other hand...*

Oh, the curse of being able to see, clearly, both sides of everything! That was why she could never stay angry, no matter what, no matter how aggrieved she felt. And no one knew Demeter better than her own daughter did.

Could she really blame her mother for wanting her to stay a baby forever? Every single baby creature that left this household, Demeter watched go with sorrowful eyes. Sometimes she even wept over them. She hated losing them, hated seeing them go out into the dangerous world, even though their places were immediately taken by yet more foundlings. After all, the dangerous world was why they were foundlings in the first place.

Demeter's heart was as tender as it was large. It was impossible, when she looked at you with those enormous, loving eyes, not to love her back. Persephone knew, beyond a shadow of a doubt, that her mother loved her. Not as a little image of herself, not as a shadow, and not as a possession. Loved *her*. And wanted to keep her protected and safe forever.

But...being manipulated by love was still being manipulated. How long would it take before her mother allowed her to grow up and leave, as she did everything else in this household?

Or was she a special case who would never be allowed to grow? Her temper flared as frustration took over from understanding.

Persephone threw the shuttle again, beat at the weft with angry upward strokes, and the warp-weights clacked together.

Demeter glanced in at her daughter at the loom and sighed. There was no doubt that she was angry, probably at being sent to work when what she really wanted to do was be with her playmates, lazing about in the meadow. But the nymphs had tasks of their own to do today, and Demeter was not going to allow her darling to wander about unescorted. She had tried to explain that, but Persephone was hardly in the mood to listen. There were times when Demeter wondered if she would ever grow up.

But more times when she dreaded the day when she did. That would mean losing her, and things would change between them forever. Little Kore would vanish, and someone else would take her place, a stranger that Demeter might not recognize, someone who would have ideas of her own, and no longer have to listen to her mother's wise words. Demeter absolutely hated the idea that one day she would lose her little girl…if only there was a way to keep her little forever! But there was no doubt, given Kore's budding body, that even if it were possible to do so, the time to do so was long, long past.

She wished, sometimes, that she had the instincts of a mother animal. Animals knew that there is only room for one adult in the territory—and eventually even the most devoted mother animal drives her own children away. It would be easier to feel her love turning into irritation—easier than the pain of knowing that one day Kore would grow into her given name and no longer depend on her mother for anything.

There were other issues at hand; this was not a good time for Kore to assert her growing womanhood. There simply was no one suitable for her to assert it with. It troubled Demeter deeply that there was no one among the Olympians that she thought was a decent match for her daughter, and a mortal—well, that was just out of the question…the loves of gods and mortals were inevitably tragic. Zeus was out of the question, Poseidon was her father…maybe. There was some confusion over those things. Apollo never even gave her a second glance. Hephaestus never looked past Aphrodite. Hermes? Never! Other, lesser gods? Not one of them was a fit husband for the daughter of Two of the Six. *Perhaps a new Olympian will join us, one that is worthy of being her consort. One with real power, but even more important, one that won't treat her as Zeus treats Hera. One who will be devoted to her and not wander off to the bed of any female that catches his eye.* With an effort of will, she reminded herself of what the Olympian gods truly *were.* Their numbers were added to—albeit slowly—all the time. And even though the tales of the mortals made them all out to be brothers and sisters, or at the least, closely related—that wasn't actually true.

Which was just as well, considering how Zeus hopped beds. On the other hand, perhaps one day that bed hopping might produce a male that was as unlike his father in that way as possible. Demeter would be willing to welcome the right sort of part-mortal for her girl. Someone faithful, intelligent, and able to think beyond the urges of the moment.

If there was a drawback to being a god, it was that so much power seemed coupled with so little forethought.

Forethought.... *Prometheus?* No, she had to dismiss that, though with regret. The Titan was currently in Zeus's bad graces, and she wouldn't subject Persephone to the results of that. Besides, Prometheus, unlike his brother, had never shown much of an interest in women.

Then, again, finding a man in Olympus was never easy.

Demeter reflected back to the early days of her existence. Kore was the result of one of those early indiscretions on the part of Poseidon (although now they said her father was Zeus), though truth to be told, Demeter had quite enjoyed herself once she realized what the sea-patron was proposing. It wasn't as if she'd had a husband or he a wife in those days.

Things would be different for Kore. There would be no flitting off to some other light of love. Kore would never know the ache in her heart of watching the male she adored losing interest in her. Not if Demeter had anything to say about it.

Perhaps, Demeter reflected, she had sheltered the girl too much. She just seemed so utterly unprepared for life. There was nothing about her that said "woman," from her short, slender figure, to her mild blue eyes that seemed to hold no deeper thoughts than what color of flower she should pick or what dinner would be. And Demeter despaired of her ever attracting the attention of a man; charitably one could describe her hair as straw-colored, but really, it was just a yellow so pale it looked as if it had faded in the sun, her eyes were not so much light-colored as washed out, and no amount of sun would bring a blush to her cheek. And one had only to walk with her to see how the eyes of men slid over her as if they did not see her. Poor child. It was utterly unfair. Demeter could not for the life of her imagine how two gods as robust as she and Poseidon had managed to produce this slender shaft of nothing.

No, she was not ready for life. Demeter sighed and resigned herself to that fact. Kore needed nurturing and cultivation still. There was no one, god nor mortal, who was more adept at both than Demeter. Perhaps in another year, perhaps in two, she would finally begin to bloom, those pale cheeks would develop roses, and she'd ripen into a proper woman by Demeter's standards. Then Demeter could educate her in the ways of man and woman, give her all the hard-won wisdom she had garnered over the years, and (yes, reluctantly, but then at least the child would be a woman and would be ready) let her go.

Until then, she was safest here, at her mother's side.

Brunnhilde stretched in the sun like a cat, all her muscles rippling, and those gorgeous breasts pressing against the thin fabric that left nothing at all to the imagination. Leopold reflected happily that she looked absolutely fantastic without all the armor.

She looked good *in* it; in fact, she would look good in anything, of course, but Leopold was a man, after all, and he preferred his wife without all the hardware about her. In the gowns of his home, in the more elaborate gowns of Eltaria—the Kingdom where they'd met—in a feed sack, even. He had to admit, though, he liked her best of all in the costume of this country, which seemed to consist of a couple of flaps of thin cloth, a couple of brooches and a bit of cord. Marvelous! Her golden hair spilled in waves down to the ground, actually hiding more than the clothing did; her chiseled features seemed impossibly feminine when framed by the flowing hair. Her blue eyes had softened under the influence of this peaceful place, and her movements had taken on a grace that he hadn't expected.

Maybe it was being without armor. The armor made you walk stiffly, no matter how comfortable it was. And the gowns of his homeland and of Eltaria seemed to involve some female underpinnings that were almost as formidable as armor.

She had the most wonderful legs he had ever seen, and it was nice to see them without greaves, boots, or skirts getting in the way of the view.

"So what is this place again, and why are we here?" he asked, lazing on his side with his hand propping up his head and a couple bunches of luscious grapes near at hand. Oh, what a woman! One moment, she was right at his side, joyfully hacking away at whatever monster it was they had been summoned to get rid of—the next she was gamboling about in a meadow as if she had never seen a sword. This was the life. It was fantastic to be doing heroic deeds together, but it was equally fantastic to have this moment of absolute indolence too.

Brunnhilde finished her stretching and began combing her hair, which, as there was rather a lot of it, was a time-consuming process. "Olympia. They don't have a Godmother because they have gods instead." She frowned. "Which is not altogether a good idea. I mean, look at Vallahalia."

Leo picked a grape and ate it, still admiring the view. The sweet juice ran down his throat and at this moment, tasted better than wine. "I have to admit I am rather confused about that. If Godmothers are so good at keeping things from getting out of hand, why are gods so bad at it?"

"I'm not sure." Brunnhilde paused, and put the brush down on her very shapely knee to regard him with a very serious and earnest gaze. "The ravens told me once that gods are nothing more than another kind of Fae, who get power and shape from worship and the mortals who worship them. So I suppose it's because we are made in mortal image? Formed the way that mortals would choose to be themselves, if they had godlike powers?"

"Hmm, awkward," Leo acknowledged. "Given that every man *I* know would think he was in paradise if he could carry on with women the way the gods do. And given that gods don't seem to suffer the sorts of consequences from that sort of carrying-on the way mortals do."

"And other things. Mortals, given the choice, would rather not think too far ahead, or even think at all. So— the gods they worship don't, either." Brunnhilde nodded, and took up the brush again. "Then, of course, because awful things happen, the logical question becomes *Why didn't they see this coming?* and then the mortals make up all sorts of excuses for why infallible gods end up being very fallible indeed. Like Siegfried's Doom. Then they make us live through it. Ridiculous, really. I wish that there were no such things as gods. I'd rather be a nice half-Fae Godmother, and be on the side of making The Tradition work for us, instead of on us."

"But if you had been, I would never have met you, and that would be a tragedy." Leo grinned at her. She twinkled back at him.

"I don't think Wotan likes the idea of the others knowing about our true nature," she observed. "He'd rather we all believed the creation stories, which, even before the ravens told me about being Fae, I didn't entirely believe. My mother, Erda, told me there was no nonsense of me springing forth fully formed from Wotan's side, or his head, or any other part of him. I was born like any of the others, I was just first." She sighed. "Poor Mother. The shape and fate The Tradition forced her into was rather…awkward."

"Your mother is very…practical, and she seems to have done the best she can with her situation," Leo said, doing his best to restrain a shudder at the thought of that half woman, half hillside, who had done her awkward best to make polite talk with her new son-in-law without lapsing into fortune-telling cries of doom. "I was going to say 'down-to-earth,' but that is a bit redundant."

Brunnhilde barked a laugh. "Since she *is* the Earth, I would say so. It's a shame that the northlanders are so wretchedly literal minded."

Her nephew Siegfried's escape from *his* fate had seriously disturbed the northlanders' unswerving view of The Way Things Were, and had shaken them all up a good deal. Having Brunnhilde take up with a mortal, and an outsider, had shaken them up even more.

That just might be all for the best. If it shakes them up enough to start changing how The Tradition works up there, everyone will be better off.

Once they had left Siegfried and Rosa, Queen of Eltaria and his new bride, Leo and Brunnhilde had worked their way up to the northlands to break the news of their marriage to Brunnhilde's mother in person—in no small part because they weren't sure Wotan had done so. It had been an interesting meeting, if a bit unnerving. He'd sensed that Erda hadn't really known whether to manifest as a full woman and offer mead and cakes, or manifest as a hill and leave them to their own devices. She'd opted for a middle course, which made for a peculiar meeting at the least. He'd ignored the beetle and moss in his mead and brushed the leaves from his cake without a comment, and tried to act like a responsible son-in-law.

"My mother is delusional, as they all are," Brunnhilde responded dryly. "I'd come to that conclusion once I saw what life was like outside of Vallahalia, long before you woke me up, you ravisher."

Leo raised an eyebrow and smirked a little, since the "ravishing" had gone both ways. "You promised me you were going to explain why you seemed to know all about everything when I woke you."

She laughed. "You see, while Father was planting me in meadows and on rocks across half a dozen Kingdoms, he forgot that I would see what was going on around me in my dreams. It's something the Valkyria can do—we get it from Mother. She sees everything going on around her, no matter what state she's in. I might not have been trudging through all those places afoot the way Siegfried was, but I learned a lot. Probably more than he did, because I wasn't having to do anything but watch and learn, while he was trying to keep from starving to death or being hacked up."

Leo blinked. He tried to imagine what that must have been like, and failed. "Well, that must have been useful."

"Useful enough to know when you came marching across my ring of fire I had a good idea of exactly what

I wanted." She winked at him. He grinned. He hadn't awakened her with just a kiss, and they had very nearly reignited the fire ring all by themselves.

"At any rate, unless the mortals of our land manage to actually learn to think, now that my sisters have told Wotan what he can do with his magic spear and flown off, what will probably happen is that he'll seduce Erda all over again. She'll have another litter of daughters, Wotan will create another swarm of Valkyrias. Then, not having learned his lesson the first time, he'll philander with another mortal, produce another set of twins-separated-at-birth, another dwarf will steal that damned Ring from the River Maidens, and it will begin all over again." She sighed. "Stupid Tradition."

He echoed her sigh. Godmother Elena, Godmother Lily, Queen Rosa and King Siegfried had carefully explained The Tradition to both of them before they left Eltaria. It seemed prudent to all of them, given that Leo was a tale just waiting to happen and Brunnhilde was a goddess. It had left Brunnhilde nodding, and Leopold outraged, but with no target to be outraged with. Just some nebulous force that was going to make him dance to the tune it piped unless he learned how to avoid it or manipulate it himself.

"Well, maybe we can find it a whole new path," he replied. "We've got time to think and plan. Well, you do." He felt a moment of melancholy. That was the one fly in their soup of happiness. He was mortal. She wasn't.

"Well—it just might be that *we* do," she replied, her blue eyes going very serious indeed as her brush stopped moving. "I asked Godmother Elena's dragons about other places with gods, and they knew all about this one, and what is more, they had some interesting things to tell me about The Traditions here. This Olympia is just *stiff* with ways for mortals to become immortal. That's why I brought us here."

He sat straight up, grapes and melancholy forgotten. He was hard put to say whether he was more shocked, delighted or terrified. Probably all three at once. "You—what?" he gasped. "You mean—"

She nodded. "We'll have to be really careful, though. Some of the ways for mortals to become immortal are not pleasant. For instance, becoming immortal but continuing to age. Or becoming immortal as a spring or a rock. Or a constellation of stars. Not the sort of thing I want to see happen to you."

He thought about the first, and shuddered. A bit of waterworks or a rock would be far preferable, and still not something he wanted to think about.

"So how do you go about it without nasty consequences?" he asked. "Or have you found that out yet?"

"Nothing that will work yet, but I expect to. Either we'll find a god-tale, or we'll go introduce ourselves to the gods here and ask. Right now, all I know are the things that come to me in my sleep—when you let me sleep—" she began with a grin.

And that was when the ground opened up behind her with an ominous rumble.

It really *did* open up; there was a sound like thunder, the earth trembled, a crack appeared and the ground rolled back as if two giant hands had pulled it apart. Steam issued from the opening. Leo nearly jumped out of his skin, and both of them leapt to their feet, seizing the swords that were never far from their hands.

A chariot pulled by four magnificent black horses rumbled up out of the chasm; the chariot was black without a lot of ornamentation; the horses were huge things, very powerful; snorting and tossing their heads as they plunged up the slant of raw earth. The chariot was driven by a man in a long black cloak with a deep hood, who reached up with one hand and threw back the hood of his garment on seeing the two of them there. Leo hesitated; the man was unarmed, and looked absurdly young, barely more than a stripling.

"Well, *there* you are!" the fellow said crossly as his eyes lit on Brunnhilde. "You went to the wrong meadow, *just* like a girl. I've been looking all over for you!"

"I—what?" Brunnhilde stammered, for once speechless. "I think you must have mistak—"

Too late. The man jumped from the chariot, seized Brunnhilde and tossed her into the chariot as if she weighed nothing. She shrieked with outrage and tried to scramble to her feet, but he leapt back in, grabbed her around the waist with one hand to keep her from jumping out, and wheeled the horses with the other hand. Before Leo could do more than take two steps and Brunnhilde start to fight back, the chariot plunged down into the chasm, which promptly closed up behind them, leaving Leo to claw frantically at the earth, shouting Brunnhilde's name.

When Persephone finally had woven enough to satisfy her mother, the sun was going down and she practically flew to the meadow on the chance that Eubeleus would be there. Her mother, thank all the powers, had gone off to round up some of her foundlings and had not given Persephone any orders. Persephone didn't wait for her to change her mind. She didn't even stop to snatch something from the kitchen for supper, afraid that her mother would invent some reason to keep her indoors until nightfall. And by nightfall, her beloved would certainly have left the meadow.

She'd forgotten her sandals, but that hardly mattered, this was Olympia and the paths were thick with soft moss wherever her feet touched them. Neither Persephone nor Demeter would *ever* suffer a bruised foot within her walls. Like the magic that kept the carnivorous foundlings from snacking on the rest, Demeter's magic kept all harm at bay.

Wonder of wonders, her love was still in the meadow, looking altogether forlorn as he perched on a rock with his hands clasped between his knees.

She whistled like a boy, and he looked up, startled, to push off the rock and race toward her. He was quite tall, but it would be difficult to tell how tall he was, since he habitually slouched, as if he carried all of the troubles Pandora had allegedly let out of the box on his own back. His hair was as black as Zeus's but fell about his face in unconfined ringlets, since he never wore the royal diadem of the gods in her presence. People forgot that he was as much a warrior as his brother-god Zeus, but the simple, one-shouldered garment of linen he wore showed off his muscles rather nicely, she thought, especially when he was running. Of the three original male gods, he was really the cleverest, too, though she suspected if she told him so he would just mumble a little and blush.

It's just as well he got the Underworld, I suppose. Zeus would have made a dreadful mess governing it.

Only someone who actually knew him would see the Lord of the Underworld in this sad-faced shepherd, who looked gratifyingly lovelorn, and whose face lit up in a way that was even more gratifying as she ran toward him. Oh, how she loved seeing his dark eyes shine when they met hers!

They met in an embrace that threatened to become very heated indeed.

He broke it off, not she, but kept his arms around her as he looked into her upturned face. "I was afraid you had changed your mind."

Persephone snorted. "No, it was Mother. She decided that today I needed to weave. I'm sorry I was too late to be abducted. I hope your friend didn't get too bored. Where is he?"

Hades frowned. "Actually, he drove off, saying he was going to look for you, but he's never seen you, has he?"

"I don't think so." She shrugged. "There can't be that many blond-haired, blue-eyed immortal maidens hanging about in meadows on the slopes of Mount Olympus. Not that there aren't a lot of maidens, or at least young females, and if they are nymphs or dryads or sylphs, they might very well be hanging about in meadows, but there are not many blondes. Most of them are brown- or raven-haired. I hope he comes back here instead of going back to the stables. We could still go through with this if he does."

"I suppose you are right. You generally are. But hoping that Tha—my friend does something practical is hoping for a lot. He doesn't think much past his job, which isn't exactly hard." Hades's brow creased with thought. "Is there any real need for us to go through that entire abduction business?"

She looked at him quizzically. "What do you mean?

I thought it was Traditional, and it would make it harder for Mother to demand me back." She did not mention the other part, which she was not supposed to know but had deduced.

"Well, yes, but—" Hades waved his hands helplessly. "Why not? You were ready to go, why not just come with me? We might not get another chance. Especially if Demeter finds out about me." He looked at her with pleading eyes. "We've been tempting the Fates, dodging anything that could tell her. We can't have good luck forever. And I don't want to lose you."

She didn't have to think about it very long. A solid afternoon at that loom, while Demeter kept popping in "just to see how you are doing," while that wretched little faun-baby made the most appalling sounds on his flute, was more than enough to convince her that if she didn't get out of that house soon, she would probably be a candidate for the Maenads.

And she didn't want to lose him. Not ever.

"It's a wonderful idea," she said warmly. "Let's go."

Obviously, Persephone had never been to Hades's Realm before. The passage in proved to be surprisingly uncomplicated, since she was with the Ruler. The most complicated part was when Hades decided it was time to Reveal His True Self.

Hades found a cave, and led her inside, that was when he held up his hand and made a ghost-light. The little ball of light drifted just over his palm, and reflected off his face. She could tell he was working his way up to the Revelation. "Um," he said awkwardly. "I—uh—I'm not really a shepherd…"

She stood on tiptoe and kissed the corner of his

mouth. "I know you aren't, silly. You're Hades. And the friend who was supposed to abduct me is Thanatos."

His jaw dropped. He stared at her for a moment.

Now in this position, Zeus would have spluttered, and Poseidon just stared dumbly. But Hades was made of better stuff. After a moment, he began to chuckle.

"How long have you known?" he asked.

"Since about a month after we first met," she replied, holding tight to his hand. "I knew you weren't mortal. And I knew there were only a limited number of gods you could be. Eros is in love with Psyche, Zeus wouldn't dare come near me for fear of Mother, Poseidon smells of fish no matter how much he washes, Apollo is too arrogant to disguise himself, Hermes could never control his need to pull pranks, Ares is…" She rolled her eyes, and he nodded. "And besides, he's besotted with Aphrodite. Hephaestus is besotted with Aphrodite too. Who did that leave? You or Dionysus. And you always left part of the wine in the jar when we picnicked."

"And you don't mind? I mean…I'm old…" But the eyes he looked at her with were not old. They were as young as any shepherd lad with his first girl. That look only made her love him the more. "Old enough to be your father, surely. And my kingdom isn't the loveliest place in the cosmos, either. Well, with you in it, it would be, but…" He stammered to a halt.

"We're *immortal,*" she reminded him. "It doesn't matter how old you are, you'll still look like you do now in a hundred years, and then the difference between us will be insignificant. And anyway, it's not as if you were like Zeus, chasing after…well…."

"What do you—oh," he replied, and a flush crept up his dark cheek. She giggled.

"Maybe I'm *not* old," she said, "but I am fairly sure that I love you, whatever you call yourself. And I think you are certainly old enough to be sure you love *me*."

"Oh, yes," he said fervently, and if it hadn't been that this was a cave, the floor was cold and not very pleasant, and neither of them wanted Demeter to somehow find them before they got into his realm safely, they might just have torn the chitons off each other and consummated things then and there.

But Hades was not Zeus, and after breaking off the fevered kiss in which tongues and hands and bodies played a very great part, he stroked the hair off her damp brow, smiled and turned toward the back of the cave. With Hades holding her hand, a door appeared in the rock wall, as clear and solid a door as any in her mother's villa. It swung open as they approached, then swung shut behind them.

"Are we there yet?" she teased.

He laughed. "Almost. But Demeter can't follow us now."

There was a long, rough-hewn passage with bright light at the end of it, which brought them out on the banks of a mist-shrouded river.

It was a sad, gray river, with a sluggish current, and had more of a beach of varying shades of gray pebbles than a "bank." Mist not only covered its surface, it extended in every direction; you couldn't see more than a few feet into it. Tiny wavelets lapped at Persephone's bare feet. The water was quite cold, with a chill that was somehow more than mere temperature could account for.

"The Styx!" Persephone exclaimed, but Hades made a face.

"Everyone makes that mistake. It's the Acheron. The river of woe. The Styx, the river of hate, is the one that makes you invulnerable. When you see it, you won't ever mistake the one for the other. Look out—"

The warning came aptly, as a flood of wispy things, like mortals, but mortals made of fog, thronged them.

Spirits! Persephone had never actually seen a spirit, and she shrank back against Hades instinctively. There must have been thousands of them. They couldn't actually *do* anything to either her or Hades, but their touch was cold, and Persephone clutched Hades's comfortingly solid bicep. "What are they?" she asked, her voice dropping to a whisper—but still loud enough to sound like a shout over the faint susurrus of the voices of the spirits, too faint for her to make out anything of what they were saying. They tried, fruitlessly, to pluck at her hem, at her sleeves, to get her attention. "Why are they here?"

"They're the poor, the friendless. They're stuck on this side of the Acheron. Charon charges a fee to take them over, everyone knows that. You're supposed to put a coin in the mouth of the dead person when you bury him so the dead can pay the ferryman's fee. It's not much, but if they don't have it…" Hades's voice trailed off as she gave him a stricken look. She glanced at the poor wispy things, and their forlorn look practically broke her heart.

"I have my standards, you know." The sepulchral voice coming out of the mist made her jump and yelp, and the poor ghosts shrank back from the river's edge. Hades turned toward the river in irritation.

"I've asked you not to do that, damn it!" Hades snapped. "Don't just sneak up on people, do something to announce yourself when you know they can't see you!"

A boat's prow appeared, poking through the mist, and soon both the boat and its occupant were visible. The ferryman plunged his pole into the river and drove the boat up on the bank with a crunch of pebbles against wood. He had swathed his head in a fold of his robe, and bowed without uncovering it.

"As you say," the ferryman intoned, pushing his boat closer to the bank, so that it lay parallel to the beach. With his foot he pushed a plank over the side to the dry beach. "Do you need my services, oh, Lord?"

"No, we'll just walk across," Hades replied with irritation. "Of course we need your services!"

"Wait a moment." Persephone was pulling off her rings, her necklace, her bracelets, even the diadem in her hair. Gold all of it, and pearls, which Demeter thought proper for a maiden. She'd put them on this morning on a whim, thinking it would be nice to be married in them. She offered all of them now to Charon. "How many will these pay for? To go across?"

The hooded head swung in her direction. Slowly Charon removed the covering, revealing his real face. He was exceptionally ugly, with grayish skin, a crooked nose and very sad eyes. "I—uh—" The dread ferryman appeared unaccountably flustered. "I mean—"

Hades brightened. "Give her a discount rate," he said with a low chuckle. "After all, she's buying in bulk. It's the least you can do."

The ferryman swiveled his head ponderously, from Persephone's face, to her hands full of gold, to the suddenly silent throng of spirits, and back again. "I—uh—I am not accustomed to—uh—" The ferryman gave up.

"All of them," he said, sounding frustrated, and a bony hand plucked the jewelry from Persephone's hands.

With an almost-silent cheer, the spirits flooded into the boat. Although, as far as Persephone could tell, they were insubstantial and weighed nothing, the boat sank lower and lower into the water as they continued to pour across the little gangplank. Finally the last one squeezed aboard—or at least, there were no more wisps of anything on the shore—and with a sigh of resignation, Charon pushed off.

"Don't blame me when Minos gets testy about all the extra work—my Lord," Charon called over his shoulder as he vanished into the mist, poling the boat to the farther shore.

"And that is why I love you," Hades said, pulling her into his arms for an exuberant kiss that was all out of keeping with the gloom of the place. "You see what needs doing, know I can't do anything about it, and deal with it yourself. What a woman you are!"

His arms about her felt warm and supportive, a bulwark against the dank chill of the mist that surrounded them.

She flushed with pleasure. "I know they'll only start piling up again," she said apologetically when he let her go. "But I just couldn't stand here and do nothing about them."

He considered this. "Perhaps something can be worked out," he suggested. "Put a definite end to their time of waiting. Shorten it if the living will do something for them. Sacrifices or…something. Maybe even pay ahead of time when they are still alive." He pondered that a moment. "I shall put that into the minds of the priests and see what they come up with."

They watched the mist for a while, listened to the wavelets lapping against the stones at their feet. This was a curiously private, if chilly, space—the most private time they had ever had together. When they had met in the meadows it was always possible that someone would stumble upon them, or her Otherfolk friends would come looking for her. And it occurred to her at that moment that this was as good a time and place as any to ask some rather troubling questions. The most pressing of which was—

"Are you really my uncle?" Persephone asked suddenly, to catch him by surprise.

"Wait—what? No!" He looked and sounded genuinely shocked. Persephone sighed with relief. That was one hurdle out of the way, at least.

"Then why do all the stories say you are?" she asked with an air that should tell him she was not going to accept being put off, the way Demeter always tried to put off her questions.

He groaned, and shook his head. "Mortals. And that damn Tradition. And—it's a long story."

"We have time," she pointed out. "Mother never tells me anything. She always says she will, later, but she never does."

He looked a little aggrieved, but then visibly gave in. "All right, I'll start at the beginning." He pondered a bit. "The truth is, gods are just—immortals that mortals *say* are gods, or at least, that's what *we* are. We're half-Fae, the offspring of Fae and mortals. I don't know how it came about, but there happened to be a concentration of us here in Olympia. Some of us eventually became the gods, and some became the Titans."

Persephone nodded, and waited for him to continue.

She had never actually *seen* any Fae, only Otherfolk, but she knew they existed, if only because the Otherfolk talked about them a great deal. She had the impression that the Fae were, more or less, keeping a watchful eye on Olympia to see that the gods didn't get themselves into something they couldn't get out of.

"The original six of us—me, Zeus, Poseidon, Demeter, Hera and Hestia—fought and confined what the mortals decided to call the Titans, which were also half-Fae, but were mostly from Dark parents..." He paused. "They were making life pretty hideous for the mortals here. Rounding them up and using them for slaves, and even eating them, like cattle, for one thing. You do know that not all Fae are particularly pleasant, right?"

She nodded at that as well.

"Well, someone had to put a stop to that, and we decided that we would. Besides, it was only a matter of time before they ran out of mortals and came after us." He gave her a wry smile. "Not all of the Titans were bad, of course, and the ones that sided with us as allies didn't get imprisoned. In fact, Zeus—"

He stopped, flushing. She squeezed his hand. "No surprise that the ones that sided with you were mostly female?" she suggested. "The only ones I can think of that are male are Prometheus and Epimetheus."

"Uh—er. Yes. Zeus can be very—persuasive." He hastily continued. "We built ourselves a nice little complex of palaces and villas up on Mount Olympus, flung a wall around it to keep mortals from straying up there uninvited and thought that was the end of that. Then— the first of the Godmothers, the fully Fae ones, had started turning up, and Zeus suggested we study them and see if we wanted to do what they were doing, you know, steering The Tradition and all that. It seemed like a good idea."

"Well, I don't know what else you could have done, really," she replied as an eddy of mist wrapped around them. "Someone had to, right?"

"We all thought so. The thing is…we were used to thinking in Olympian time." He laughed ruefully. "We thought we had plenty of time to figure things out, what to do, who would deal with what, you see. But the mortals here have particularly strong wills and good imaginations, and before you know it, I literally woke up down here as Lord of the Underworld, Poseidon found himself in a sea cave and Zeus woke up alone except for the women, and there was an entire Traditional mythos built up around us and compelling us to do what it wanted." He sighed. "Which ended up with poor Prometheus on that damned rock. How fair is that? Bloody-minded mortals. And, of course, every time another half-Fae turned up, the mortals dreamed up some role for him that fit into the mythos and the family."

"Or not," Persephone said sourly.

"Or not," Hades agreed. "There are some wretched bad fits. I wouldn't be poor Prometheus under any circumstances. So no, the long and the short of it is, I am not your uncle. Poseidon is your father, not Zeus, no matter what the mortals say. And none of us are Demeter's brothers by blood. Not even half brothers."

"That's good, because I wouldn't want our children to have one eye or three heads," Persephone replied, hugging his arm and patting his bicep admiringly. He flushed. "There are more than enough Cyclopses about, and your dog is the only three-headed creature I would care to meet."

"Oh, he's a good puppy." Hades softened. "I suppose since you guessed who I was, you've already figured out why I wanted Thanatos to abduct you, right?"

She nodded with enthusiasm. "And it's horribly clever. Thanatos is the god of death, and if he takes me, I'm dead and belong here, right?"

"Exactly." He actually grinned. "Well, you'll have to help me figure out some other way to keep you here. I'm sure that between us we can do it."

"I wonder, why doesn't every one of the Olympians know that they're really only half-Fae? The 'gods,' I mean, not the Otherfolk and the mortals." To her mind that was a very good question. Of course, she knew very well why Demeter wouldn't have told her—Demeter always assumed she "wasn't ready" anytime she asked a tricky question, and this was certainly the trickiest of all.

"Ah, good question. Two reasons, really. Well....two and a half." He nodded gravely. "The first is the mortals and their Tradition, as I said, it is very strong, and once a role has been picked out for you, it becomes harder and harder to remember that this role wasn't always what you were. You really have to work at it. Some of the Olympians aren't comfortable working at it and would really rather just fall into the role."

"Like Zeus?" she prompted.

"Ah, that is where the half part of the two and a half reasons comes in. Over there—" he waved his hand vaguely at the mist "—I have two fountains. Lethe and Mnemosyne."

"Forgetfulness and Memory?"

He nodded. "I, for one, take great care to have a drink of Mnemosyne whenever I feel my memories of what

I really am start to slip. Zeus, on the other hand…" He paused. "In fact, one of these days we'll be going to one of Zeus's feasts, and when we do, at some point Hebe will ask you if you want the 'special cup.' That's ambrosia mixed with Lethe water. Drink that, and all you'll remember about yourself is what The Tradition says you are."

She shuddered. "No, thank you. Do the others know this?"

Hades nodded. "Or—well, they know it before they take the first drink. After, it hardly matters, does it? I'll say this much for Zeus, he will generally explain it all to the newcomers before they are offered the option. I'm just not sure he'll explain it to you, especially not if your mother—" He broke off what he was going to say.

"That's a good point." Persephone scuffed her bare toe into the pebbles. "I can't always predict what Mother will think, and I honestly don't know what view she'd take, whether it was better for me not to know, or better for me to know and fight what I don't want this 'Tradition' to do to me." She heard a splashing—it sounded deliberate—and looked up to see something out there on the water. "Oh, look, there's Charon."

A dark shape loomed out of the mist, resolving into the boat and the ferryman. "Well," Charon said, sounding a tad less lugubrious, "that was interesting." He toed the plank over the side, and it slid onto the gravel.

"Good interesting, or bad interesting?" Hades asked, handing Persephone into the boat, which was surprisingly stable.

"Good, I think. Minos is going to have his hands full for a little." Charon chuckled. "I confess I am rather

surprised that I carried over quite a few who are neither destined for Tartarus nor the Fields of Asphodel.
The friendless and poor on earth may not be such paltry
stuff after all. In fact," he added thoughtfully, "a good
many of them are, in their own way, heroes. Leaving
them on the bank is doing them a grave—" he chuckled
again at his own pun "—disservice, perhaps."

Hades looked to Persephone. "We might be able to
think of something," she said, in answer to his unspo-
ken query, as he handed her into the boat. "We were
just talking about that, in fact." Hades got into the boat
beside her, which rocked not at all under his weight.

Charon poled them through the mist to the opposite
shore. It wasn't as far as Persephone had thought, and
yet it was very difficult to tell just how much time actually had passed; Hades remained silent, and Charon
wasn't very chatty.

On the other side…if Persephone had thought that
the banks of the river were crowded with souls, here
there were shades in uncounted thousands.

As far as she could see in either direction, a thinner
mist hung over endless fields of pale blossoms. The
shades wandered among them. They seemed particularly joyless as they gathered the white flowers of the asphodel, marked with a blood-red stripe down the center
of each petal. They did not seem sad, just…not happy.

Until the fields themselves hazed off into the mist,
the asphodel blossoms waved, pallid lilies standing
about knee-high to the shades. They seemed to have
no other occupation than to pick and eat the blossoms,
showing neither enjoyment nor distaste.

This apparently infinite stretch of ground, flowers
and mist, she knew already, was the part of Hades's

realm called the Fields of Asphodel, where the souls of those who were neither good nor evil went. In a way, the penalty for being ordinary was to be condemned to continue to be ordinary. Every day was like every other day; the only change was in the comings and goings of new souls, and the Lords of the Underworld.

Charon pushed off once they had gotten out of the boat; there were always new souls to ferry across, it seemed.

The mist still persisted everywhere, making it impossible to judge distance properly, or to make out much that wasn't near. She and Hades made their way on a road that passed between the two Fields, and the shades gathering and eating flowers paid no particular attention to them. But as they traveled, hand in hand, she saw that there actually was a boundary, a place where the Fields ended. The asphodel gave way to short, mosslike purple turf, and like two mirrors set into the turf, she saw two pools, one on the left of the road, and one on the right. The one on the right was thronged with more shades; only a few were kneeling to scoop water from the one on the left.

"Lethe is on the right," Hades said, and sighed. "The ordinary choose to forget."

She nodded, and the two of them stepped a little off the road, which now passed through a long span of the dark purple mosslike growth. It actually felt quite nice on her bare feet. The road itself was crowded with shades, waiting in line. Eventually Persephone made out three platforms ahead of them, each platform holding a kind of throne. The closer they got, the more details she was able to make out.

The three platforms stood in the courtyard of an

enormous building, which, at the moment, was little more than a shape in the mist. There were three men there, one enthroned on each platform, and Persephone already knew who *they* were. They were the judges of the dead, who had been three great kings in life, well-known for their wisdom. Minos was the chief of them, and held the casting vote, if the other two disagreed.

Hades led her past them with a wave. Minos, in the center, shook a fist at him, but with a smile.

Hades chuckled. "Minos would rather have more to do than less," he explained. "Despite what Charon said."

The judges held their tribunals in the forecourt of what proved to be a great palace, which, as they approached and details resolved out of the mist, was not what Persephone had expected. She had thought it would be gloomy and black, forbidding, bulky. It was, in fact, all of white marble, and as graceful and airy as anything built on Mount Olympus. Waiting there impatiently in front of the great doors was a young man holding the reins of four black, ebon-eyed horses hitched to a black chariot. There was a bundle in the chariot that moved and made ominous and threatening noises.

"By Zeus's goolies, it's about time you got here!" the young man said, indignation written in every word and gesture. "I thought you said the wench was going to come willingly! I finally had to gag and bag her! If I can't father children, Hades, it'll be all your fault!" Then he stopped, and stared at Persephone. "Who," he said slowly, "is that?"

Horror crossed Hades's face. "This is Persephone. We decided to forgo the abduction and figure out some other way to keep her down here. Maybe arrange for my priests to have some dreams about her or something—"

Thanatos went pale. Which was quite a feat for someone already as white as the marble of the palace behind him. "Then who have *I* got?"

"That is a very good question," Hades replied in a flat voice.

All three of them stared at the moving bag. The sounds it was making were very ominous indeed. And very, very angry.

By the time Leo had dug out a pit the size of a shallow grave, he had to give up. He sat back on his heels and restrained his first impulse, which was to scream imprecations at the heavens. His tunic was plastered to his body with sweat and dirt, there was dirt in his hair and dug under his fingernails. And he didn't care. All he wanted was Brunnhilde back.

Screaming wasn't going to do any good. This was either the work of a very powerful magician, or—possibly one of the local gods?

Leo clenched his fists and tried to remember what the charioteer had said. *"I've been looking all over for you."*

He ran a grimy hand through his hair, thoroughly confused now.

Think, Leo. Think this through. The man shows up coming up out of the ground, and the ground closes up behind him. He says, "There you are! I've been looking all over for you!" And I've never seen him in my life.

Could the man have been looking for Brunnhilde?

If it was someone from the northlands...maybe. He was dressed like a local, not like one of the gods or mortals of Vallahalia. He'd never seen a chariot that looked like that in Vallahalia, and anyway, the only chariot

there was one pulled by goats. The rocky terrain of the
north wasn't very good for chariots.

And he was dark, not blond; virtually every north-
lander he'd seen was either blond or red-haired. No, he
looked like the people around here.

They didn't know anyone local.

"There you are! I've been looking all over for you!"
The man certainly thought he knew Bru; Bru had certainly stared at him without any sign of recognition at
all.

The only way he could have known her was if someone local had been scrying them—but if so, why would
he say, "I've been looking all over for you"? If he could
scry them, he would have known exactly where they
were, and he wouldn't have had to go looking for them.

He couldn't have been looking for *Bru*.

If he hadn't been looking for Bru, he must have been
looking for someone *like* Brunnhilde.

What else had he said…? *"You went to the wrong
meadow, just like a girl."*

"You went to the wrong meadow"?

It not only sounded as if he was looking for someone, it sounded as if he was looking for someone who
was expecting him.

And it must have been someone he had never actually seen.

So he *had* been looking for someone *like* Brunnhilde.
It was a case of mistaken identity.

It would be hard to mistake Bru for anyone else, if
you knew her. Even someone who had only been scrying them from a distance would have a hard time mis-
taking her for anyone else.

Conclusion: the man *had* to have been going from a description, and not a very good one, either.

And that meant another question. Man, or *god?*

Leo didn't even have to think twice about that. Only a god would be so sure of his own power that he would simply appear and abduct a complete stranger without thought of consequences.

All right. Assume that it was one of the local gods. That put Leo up against a god. With all the power of a god, who could probably squash him flat without thinking twice about it....

To hell with that!

He lurched to his feet, feeling rage surge through him. So what if they were gods? They were pretty damned small gods, and he was *married* to a god, and he was going to get to the bottom of this and get her back no matter what it cost him!

He caught up his discarded sword and headed for the Vallahalian horses at a grim trot. Damn if he was going to bother going through an intermediary; let the natives putter about with priests. After all, he'd been presented to a goddess of the *earth* as her son-in-law, and faced down the All-father. In a Kingdom where the gods were real, physical beings, he might as well go straight to the top.

Or wherever he needed to get to in order to confront them directly. And he had a pretty good idea of who could get him there.

The two big bay horses—well, they weren't just horses, after all, they could stride through the air, you never had to worry about them straying off and they always looked magnificent—were still where he and Bru had left them. They weren't happy though; they were prancing and pawing the earth, looking every bit as agitated as he was.

And now, if ever, was the time to find out just *how* different they were from "horses."

He seized the reins of the horse he had been given on either side of the bit and looked into its eyes. "Do you know where the gods of this land live?" he asked it. On the surface of things, such a question, put to a horse, might have seemed insane, but these were horses that had served the Valkyria, were bred in the pastures of Vallahalia, and he wasn't inclined to put anything past them. One of Brunnhilde's sister-Valkyria had given her mount to him, saying with a laugh that it made a fitting "dowry" for him, and that this way he wouldn't have to ride pillion behind Bru. The other Valkyria had found this hilarious at the time.

Since then, his mount, named Drachen, had done literally anything he asked of it. The only "supernatural" ability it had displayed so far was the ability to fly—or rather, to run through the air. It had a doglike loyalty, was a cherub to him and Bru, and a devil to anyone else. He'd suspected it had a very high level of intelligence, and perhaps a lot more than that, but hadn't had a chance to ask Bru.

The horse looked at him measuringly, and then slowly bobbed its head up and down.

"Was that a god who took our lady?" he asked it fiercely.

Drachen snorted, as if it thought the answer to such a question was so obvious the question didn't even need asking, but again bobbed its head up and down.

He didn't ask any further questions. He threw himself into the saddle and took up the reins—but left them slack, because clearly, he was not going to be the one in charge on this ride.

"Then let us go to these gods and get her back!" he growled.

Both horses threw up their heads and trumpeted agreement. Leo's mount reared up; its forefeet found purchase on the air through whatever magic it used to run, and they were off. Both of them plunged up toward the sky as if they were running on a hill. Powerful muscles drove them upward at a pace that far exceeded that of a flesh-and-blood horse.

Once they were well above the level of the treetops, it was pretty clear where they were heading; a cloud-capped mountain loomed in the middle distance, and looked to be exactly where one would want to set up housekeeping if one happened to be a god, at least in Leo's mind. And as they headed upward, Brunnhilde's horse cast a glance over its shoulder at him…and snorted.

"What?" he shouted at it. He got no direct answer. But his horse swerved a little and made a beeline for a patch of dark clouds. Before he got a chance to object, both beasts plunged in, and a moment later he found himself in the middle of a rainstorm.

When they emerged again on the other side he was spluttering and soaked. But clean.

His hide and the little one-shouldered excuse for a tunic he wore in imitation of the locals were both dry long before the slopes of the mountain and the buildings there were clearly visible. And if he hadn't still been so angry he was quite ready to set fire to the entire mountain, he would have been enchanted by the view.

The lowest slopes, mostly forested, were dotted with

flowering meadows where flocks of sheep and goats grazed, or little isolated structures of white marble rose. A little higher, as the trees began to thin, there were more substantial buildings, about the size of one of the manor houses that he was familiar with, also of white marble. Halfway up the slope, a line of clouds formed an unmoving ring around the mountain; so far as Leo could tell, this ring would make it impossible for anyone on the ground to see what *he* saw from his vantage in the air.

With its base rooted in the top of the clouds, a massive wall stretched around the mountain itself, not at all unlike the wall around Vallahalia, and probably erected for the same reason. The gods were not inclined to permit just any old mortal to come walking up the front path. There was a gate in this wall, and it was closed; not that this mattered in the least to Leo.

Behind the wall, and crowding up to the summit, were more of the white-marble manors, surrounded by terraced gardens. As Leo's mount galloped above the wall and these buildings passed beneath him, he saw the occasional person in the gardens or on a terrace gaping up at him. All the buildings had a kind of inner glow, like light shining through translucent porcelain.

He ignored the people below him. The gods were like anyone else; the most important personage lived at the top, and that was where he was heading, to a single enormous, colonnaded structure ornamented by heroic statues of men and women.

The horses seemed to take on fire and life as they neared this building; and rather than feeling intimidated, Leo experienced a surge of energy and strength, as if he had opened up some sort of heroic spring inside himself that he had never known was there. His anger stopped being all-consuming, and became focused; Brunnhilde had been taken, and there was nothing on this earth, above it, or below it, that was going to keep him from getting to her.

Beneath him, his horse began to shine with an unearthly, golden glow, just as the buildings here glowed, but brighter. He took heart from that; these beasts were the mounts of gods themselves, and if they felt he was worthy of being carried up here, then who were these upstarts in their draped sheets to stand between him and his mate?

The horses trumpeted a challenge as they landed in the forecourt of the chief building; their hooves rang on the pavement as they touched down, now blazing with golden light. Leo jumped out of the saddle without even thinking about it, pulling his sword from the sheath at the saddlebow. He was barely aware of half a dozen people in robes and tunics staring at him dumbfounded; he had eyes only for one. That one sat on what looked like a throne at the center of the forecourt; a man with the physique of a fighter, long, curling black hair and beard, and some of that same golden glow about him. Like the others, he wore one of those draped garments, but at least this man imparted the ridiculous swath of cloth with a sense of dignity.

Even with his mouth hanging open.

Leo stamped toward him. Evidently these gods were so convinced of their own power and invulnerability that they had nothing whatsoever like guards. But—anger didn't kill caution; Leo stopped a good twenty feet away. Just in case.

While the man still stared at him, Leo pointed at him with the sword he still held in his hand.

"You!" he roared, his own voice echoing at such a volume that he himself was startled, though he took care not to show it. He swept the sword point around in an arc. "All of you! *What have you done with my wife?"*

Demeter examined one of the trees in her orchard with a critical eye; like all the trees, it had buds, blossoms, green and ripening fruit on it all at the same time. She wondered if perhaps she should have some of the insects eat a few of the blooms so as not to overburden the tree unduly. While there were the strange cycles known as "seasons" outside Olympia, here there were no such things as set times to blossom and ripen or lie fallow; there was planting and harvest, of course, but no particular time for either. That was because of her; beneath her care, every plot and field in Olympia flourished, and year-beginning to year-end marked not so much a cycle as a progression.

Care had to be taken, though, to make sure the soil stayed fertile, the trees and bushes were not stressed. Demeter spent a great deal of time among the mortals, speaking through her priestesses, schooling them in husbandry, and spent almost as much time in her own fields and orchards, seeing to it that what she tended personally served as an example of perfection rather than neglect.

She directed a beetle to snip off a particular bud and drop it into a swarm of waiting ants, when she felt a tremor pass through her—and a sensation as if something had just been cut off from her as that bud had been cut from the tree.

Bud? she thought, and then, in something like Panic fear—*Kore!*

She whirled and ran as she had not run since she was a child herself, in that long-ago time when she played in the fields with the sheep tended by her shepherdess mother—ran back to her villa, and stopped, panting for breath, hand pressed against her aching side, in the door to the weaving room.

The loom was unattended except for a kitten playing with a ball of yarn and a faun curled around a basket of sleeping hedgehog babies, poking at them with a curious finger to see them stir.

"Where is Kore?" she demanded of the hooved child, who looked up at her with startled eyes, his mouth forming a little o.

"M-m-meadow?" he stammered.

Demeter ran to the meadow where Kore was used to playing. There was nothing there, nothing but a scatter of blossoms.

Nothing at all.

Gingerly, Hades approached the squirming bag. The very fabric looked angry. "What did you do, Thanatos?" he demanded.

"I did what you asked me to do," Thanatos replied, looking indignant and sullen at the same time. "I looked for an immortal maiden with yellow hair in a meadow. I found lots of maidens in meadows, not many with yellow hair, and only one immortal. So I took her. You said she wouldn't fight me, that she was expecting to be abducted, but she fought like five she-goats! I'm bruised all over!"

"You're a god, Thanatos, heal yourself," snapped Hades. "Who did you rape?"

"I didn't *rape* anyone!" Thanatos yelped.

"You know what I mean! Who's in the sack?" Hades bellowed.

"How should I know?" Thanatos shrieked back.

"Oh, for—" Persephone pulled the little dagger she used to cut fruit out of her belt, stalked around them and went straight to the bag. She bent over and cut the rope holding it shut, then leapt back with the grace and agility of a young doe.

The bag writhed, a pretty foot and a long, strong leg emerged with a vigorous kick, then the rest of the young woman fought free of the fabric, with only a momentary glimpse of something the lady probably would not have wanted strange men to see. A pair of extremely blue eyes beneath a mass of tumbled golden hair blazed at all of them, and it was only Hades's quick thought to cast a circle of magic around her that saved them all from the tiny bolts of levin-fire those eyes shot at them.

Thanatos yelped again, jumping back automatically.

"Well," Hades said slowly. "Definitely god-born."

Persephone approached the circle slowly. "One woman to another," she said, getting the captive's attention. "There has been a dreadful mistake. I'm going to cut you free now so we can explain it, all right?"

The woman glared for a long, long moment, then slowly, grudgingly, nodded. Persephone glanced at Hades, who dismissed the magic circle with a little twirl of his fingers. Then she knelt beside the woman and first cut her wrists free of their rope, then handed her the little knife so she could get rid of the gag herself.

When the woman untangled herself from ropes and

sack, she stood up, rubbing her wrists. She did not give back the knife.

She was taller than Persephone by more than a head; she was nearly as tall as Thanatos, and he was not small by either mortal or godly standards. As she glared at them all, he stopped sulking and began gawking.

Then the gawking took on a bit of a leer.

"Well," he said, looking aslant at Hades, "if this one isn't yours, can I have her?"

The words hadn't even left his mouth before he was dancing in place as levin-bolts peppered the area around his sandaled feet. She was tossing them this time; they looked like toy versions of Zeus's thunderbolts. Fascinated, Persephone wondered if one day *she* could learn to do that.

Persephone clasped both hands over her mouth to restrain her laughter, as Hades merely folded his arms and watched. Eventually the woman wearied of tormenting Thanatos and allowed him to stop capering to her crackling tune. She stood with her fists on her hips and looked them all over, ending with a glare at Thanatos.

"I'm no one's property, god or mortal. And I'm married," she said shortly. "Another suggestion of that sort, and I'll aim higher. And maybe with the knife, too."

Hades gave her a short bow, equal to equal. "Your pardon, sky-born," he said so smoothly that Persephone could only sigh and admire his manners. "The gods of Olympia are…somewhat free with their favors, as often as not."

The woman raised an eyebrow. "Some wouldn't consider that a 'favor,'" she retorted dryly. "Now, what, exactly, am I doing here, and where is *here* in the first place?"

Hades and Thanatos began speaking at once, and the stranger's head switched back and forth between them to the point where Persephone feared she was going to get a cramp. "Wait!" she cried, holding up her hand. Both men stopped. Hades bowed.

"My name is Persephone. I am the daughter of the goddess Demeter. My mother is—" she made a face "—overprotective. This is Hades, the Lord of the Underworld, where the dead go."

"Ah!" The woman's eyes brightened with understanding. "Like Vallahalia. Go on."

"You are actually in the Underworld now, to answer your second question," Hades put in. She nodded.

"I managed to catch sight of this lovely maid, and—" Hades reached for Persephone's hand. She let him take it, blushing. "I asked the king of our gods, Zeus, for permission to wed her. He agreed, but cautioned me that her mother would never let her go."

Persephone nodded. "She thinks I am still a child," the girl said sourly.

The stranger nodded, sighing. "All mothers are like that, I think. I begin to get the shape of this. I take it that you decided to abduct her?"

Hades hesitated. "Not—exactly. That is more in Zeus's style than mine."

"He courted me!" Persephone said proudly. "And as if he was nothing more noble than a shepherd's god, or one of the minor patrons of a brook or grove, so I wouldn't feel as if I *had* to yield to him!"

Now it was Hades's turn to blush, as she squeezed his hand.

The stranger's cold eyes warmed a little. "I begin to favor you, god of the Underworld. So. This still begs the question of why I am here."

"My mother is the Earth goddess, Demeter. Fertility," Persephone said pointedly. The woman's eyes widened.

"Aha! So you complicate things by sending another in your place to take the maid. So that she does not know who to curse, and you may garner more allies to soothe her before you reveal the truth."

"Exactly." Hades beamed.

"And because he did not know the maid—" she eyed Persephone "—there cannot be many yellow-haired wenches among your people. You are the first I have seen in this place. I can see where there would have been a mistake." She nodded, satisfied. "Well, with that settled, I forgive you. You can take me back now and in return for this insult you can help me and my Leopold with a problem of our own."

"Uh…" Hades bit his lip. "This is where things become…complicated."

"Complicated?" The woman's expression suddenly darkened. "What do you mean by complicated?"

"Thanatos is the god of death, you see—" Hades gestured helplessly with his free hand at the hapless Thanatos. "That was why *he* was supposed to take Persephone. She'd be dead, and have to stay here, you see—"

"But I am immortal!" the woman shouted, making them all wince.

"Well, er, yes. But gods can die—" Hades freed his hand from Persephone's and it looked to her as if he was preparing to cast another protective circle.

"I—!" the woman roared—and then suddenly fell

silent. "Damn it," she swore. "We can. Baldur did. And I was supposed to die to bring about the fall of Vallahalia—"

"So...er...you can't leave. I mean, I just can't let you go, you see." Hades gestured apologetically. "It would be a terrible precedent. People would be coming down here all the time, demanding that I turn this shade or that loose. You see?"

"Yes, damn it all, I do." The woman gritted her teeth. "But I am *not* staying here. If I have to, I will fight my way out."

Hades and Persephone exchanged a long look. "I think she would," Persephone whispered.

"I have no doubt of it," Hades responded. He ran a hand nervously through his dark curls. "I think we need to figure a way out of this."

"Yes," the woman said sharply. "You do."

Demeter stood in the middle of the open meadow with both hands clenched in her hair and her heart torn with anguish. Of all of the things that could have befallen her daughter, *this* had never, ever occurred to her. That Kore might, in some childish fit of pique, run away— yes, that she had thought of, and put barriers around her own small domain so that Kore would be turned back from them if she tried to cross. She had carefully kept Kore out of sight of the other gods once she began to mature, so that none of them would have been tempted to steal her away. The lesson of Hebe was plain there; Zeus had fancied the child as a cupbearer, and whisked her off before her mother could say aye or nay.

So who, or what, had stolen her child? Where had she been taken?

She did not stand in anguish for long; if there was a

single being that knew, or could find out, everything that went on between heaven and earth, it was Hecate. Hecate was one of only a few Titans who had been permitted by Zeus to retain her power. To Hecate she would go, then.

With her thoughts in turmoil, and her heart in despair, she did not even notice that in her wake, the growing things were beginning to fade and droop.

She paused only long enough in her kitchen to gather up what she would need; the roast lamb from the supper Kore would not now eat, poppy-seed bread, red wine and honey. She caught up three torches and sped to the nearest crossroads, a meeting of two paths that her flocks and their shepherdesses used. With a flat rock for a table, the three torches driven into the ground around it and lit, Demeter laid out the meal, and waited, slow tears tracing hot paths down her cheeks.

As darkness fell, she heard the slow footfalls of three creatures approaching; two four-legged, one going on two feet.

Through the trees, a golden glow neared; as Demeter waited, holding her breath, the light took on the shape of a flame, the flame of a torch held high by a figure still obscured by distance and the intervening foliage and tree trunks.

Soon, though, that dark-robed figure paced slowly and deliberately through the trees; on either side of her was a huge dog. As she drew near, the stranger slowly removed the veil covering her head, revealing that she was a gravely beautiful woman of indeterminate age, taller than Demeter. It was Hecate. Demeter's mouth was dry, and she could not manage to speak for a moment.

"What means this, sister?" Hecate asked. "Why do you invoke me as if you were a mere mortal?"

"I did not know how else to call you quickly, elder sister," Demeter whispered, and her voice broke on a sob. "Oh, Hecate, it is my daughter, my Kore! She has been taken from me, and I do not know where nor how!"

Hecate blinked with surprise. "This is a grave thing that you tell me," she replied. "And a puzzling one, for I know you fenced your child about with great protections. Tell me what you know."

While Demeter related the little that she knew, Hecate listened carefully. "I think," she said at last, "that we should go to Mount Olympus. If there is any being who would have seen your daughter stolen, it is Helios, and as the sun has set, he will be with the other gods, feasting."

She held out her hand to Demeter. "Come. If Zeus has been up to some mischief, or countenanced it, he will not dare to deny the both of us combined."

Demeter took Hecate's hand, and Hecate passed the torch in front of her from left to right. The world blurred for a moment, and when it settled, they stood in the forecourt of Zeus's palace.

But Zeus and the other gods were already occupied—with one very angry, and seemingly very powerful, mortal.

"What have you done with my wife?" Leo shouted again, holding down his sense of shock and surprise that no one had struck him dead with a thunderbolt yet. On either side of him, the Vallahalian horses pawed the marble, striking sparks with their hooves, tossing their heads and snorting.

"Ah…" The fellow on the throne looked down at the tip of Leo's sword, which was unaccountably glowing. "We haven't done anything?" He glanced around at others of his sort who were gathering in the twilight, while torches and lamps lit themselves. "At least *I* haven't. Have any of you lot been stealing mortals this afternoon?"

A chorus of baffled no's answered his question. Leo wasn't backing down. "We were minding our own business, when someone came up out of the ground in a chariot drawn by four black horses," he thundered, taking full advantage of the fact that his wrath seemed to have taken them all aback. "He said something about 'I've been looking all over for you,' grabbed my wife and dragged her underground. If that *wasn't* a god, I'm a eunuch, and *you* are the only gods hereabouts, so *what have you done with my wife?*"

"Impeccable reasoning, Father," said a rather stern-looking young woman in a helmet and metal breastplate in addition to the usual draperies. In her case, the draperies covered a disappointing amount, from her collarbone down to the ground.

His conscience chided him for that thought; he put it aside. Besides, she was carrying a spear and looked as though she knew how to use it.

"Four *black* horses? Then it can't have been Helios or Apollo," the young woman continued. "It's unlikely to have been Hephaestus. That leaves only one possible candidate."

"Two, if you count Thanatos. Hades lets him drive, sometimes," the man on the throne corrected with a sigh. He turned his attention back to Leo and was about to say something, when there was a soundless explosion of black smoke, and two *more* women appeared at the edge of the courtyard. One, dressed in a dark blue drape, was visibly distraught. The other, dressed in black and carrying a torch, with a huge dog on either side of her, looked sterner than the young woman in the helmet.

"Hold, Zeus!" the black-clad one intoned. "Hear now the pleas of Demeter, whose daughter has been foully riven from her this day!"

"What, *another* one?" exclaimed a young man, who was dressed in sandals with wings on them and not much else, exclaimed. "There hasn't been this much excitement around here since Zeus turned into a swan!"

The man on the throne colored, and the oldest-looking of the women glared metaphorical thunderbolts at both of them.

"Or was it a bull?" mused the irrepressible young man, glancing slyly at the chief of the gods.

"Hermes!" the young woman in the helmet hissed at him. The oldest woman glowered.

The woman in dark blue—Demeter—wept. Leo shifted his weight uncomfortably, but—*damn it, I was here first.* He firmed his chin and stood his ground.

But at this point all the gods started talking at once. The males were adamant that whatever had happened to Demeter's daughter, *they* had nothing to do with it. The females had started to group themselves around Demeter and the other one. Clearly, this was turning into a potentially ugly situation.

It was broken up when two literally radiant young men appeared in another explosion of smoke, this one white instead of black. "Hail Zeus!" said the handsomer of the two. "Ha—"

He did a double take.

"What in the name of heaven and earth is going on?" he demanded.

The gods all started talking again. Finally the young woman in the helmet silenced them all by pounding the butt of her spear on the marble, which rang like a gong.

Leo blinked. *That* was certainly an interesting trick. And effective.

"Hail Apollo," the young woman said, with no hint of mockery. "This mortal came before us on god-horses, making a claim that one of the gods falsely stole his wife away. He had not done making his testimony when Hecate appeared with Demeter, saying that Persephone was also stolen. That is the long and the short of it. However, now that you are here, you—or rather, Helios— are in a position to answer both those accusations, for Helios sees all things."

"Most things, wise Athena," said the other young man with a slight bow. "In the matter of Persephone..." He hesitated.

"Speak, Helios!" the woman in black commanded him sternly.

Helios sighed. "Much as I hate to break a mother's heart, I did see Hades take Persephone. But it looked to me as if she went willingly."

Demeter let out a wail that woke tears in Leo's eyes, and at least half the gods' as well. "No, great Zeus, this cannot be! Hades? Lord of Darkness and Gloom and Death? He is no fit mate for my golden child!"

Helios coughed. "Ah, gracious goddess, I hate to contradict you, but Hades is ruler of the Underworld, the third part of creation, and is the brother-equal to Poseidon and Zeus himself. If *he* isn't worthy, no one is."

"Then I shall linger here no longer!" Demeter let out

a heartbroken cry and fled, vanishing among the gardens and marble edifices below. The woman in black watched her go, broodingly, then turned to Zeus.

"I would learn the truth of this myself, Zeus," she declared.

"By all means, Hecate, do as you please," the man on the throne said weakly. "Don't mind me, I'm only the king here."

With a sardonic smile, the woman in black vanished in another poof of black smoke.

Now Helios turned to Leo. "As for this mortal…" he said, his brow wrinkling thoughtfully. "Ah, yes. It was Hades's chariot that took his golden mate. But it was Thanatos who took her."

A leaden silence fell. It was the woman in the helmet who broke it. "Mortal, what was it you said that Thanatos called out?"

Leo licked lips gone dry. Whoever this "Thanatos" was—the gods thought the situation was very serious indeed. "Uh—he said, 'Well, there you are! You went to the wrong meadow, just like a girl. I've been looking all over for you!' Then he grabbed her and vanished into the earth."

"Oh, dear." The silence grew even heavier. "Mortal, I am sorry. Given that Hades was seen to leave with Persephone—who is a golden-haired maiden—and given that Thanatos, Hades's servant, was driving Hades's chariot—I believe your wife is the victim of a case of mistaken identity."

Zeus looked unhappily down at the helmeted woman. "Do you think?"

She nodded. "Aye. I think he sent Thanatos to fetch Persephone, so that her mother would have no way to take her back. But Thanatos had never seen the girl, and took the first woman that matched her description. This mortal's wife." She turned to Leo. "Mortal, I am sorry. There is nothing we can do for you."

Leo's anger erupted again. "What do you mean, there is nothing you can do for me? He's one of you, isn't he? Order him to bring her back!"

"Mortal—" The oldest woman stepped forward, a sympathetic and sorrowful expression on her face that filled him with dread. "Mortal, even the gods are subject to rules. Thanatos took your lady. Thanatos is the god of death. Not even we can take her back from him. That is why Hades must have sent Thanatos to take Persephone." She shook her head. "I am sorry. But we are as helpless as you."

"Is there a precedent for getting someone out of here?" Brunnhilde demanded.

"Well…" Hades paused.

"I didn't actually *die,* you know!" she snapped. "I was kidnapped by your dim-witted flunky!"

"Hey—" Thanatos objected weakly.

"She has a point," Persephone said patiently. "Just because Thanatos took her doesn't mean she actually died. He took her body *and* spirit."

"It's a technicality, but it's the technicality we were going to use to keep *you* here," Hades pointed out.

Brunnhilde's eyes darkened dangerously. "Do you really *want* to get into a battle between my people and yours?" she asked, her voice low and menacing. "You wouldn't like that. We're not civilized." She moved very close to Hades and narrowed her eyes. "We *live* for fighting. We *thrive* on doom. My father actually *tried* to bring on Ragnorak. He'd be overjoyed to find a way to destroy not just one, but two entire sets of gods. If only to get away from his wife."

"What's Ragnorak?" Thanatos wanted to know.

"Never mind. I don't want to know." Hades waved his hands frantically. "No, we have to work together to figure out a solution. There has to be an answer."

A puff of black smoke erupted next to Hades's throne. "By Gaia's left breast, Hades, you really are a moron," said a sardonic female voice from inside it. The smoke cleared away, revealing a handsome dark-haired woman with a torch in one hand, accompanied by two dogs. "I cannot believe what a hash you made of this business. And you're no better," she added in Thanatos's direction. She looked down at her dogs. "You two, go run and play with Cereberus." She stuck her torch in a nearby holder, and the dogs, suddenly looking like perfectly ordinary canines, yipped and ran off.

She turned to Brunnhilde. "I'm Hecate. You must be the abducted barbarian."

Brunnhilde nodded, and drew herself up straight. "Brunnhilde, of the Valkyria, daughter of one-eyed Odin, king of the gods of Vallahalia, and Erda, goddess of the Earth."

"Or, in other words, half-Fae like all the rest of us." Hecate did not quite smile. "When we choose to remember it, that is. Bah! A fine mess this is."

She sat down on Hades's throne. Hades didn't even bother to protest. "All right, first things first. Persephone, I assume you're here of your own free will?"

Persephone looked ready to burst. "Aunt Hecate, I am *sick to death* of being treated like a toddler! I love my mother, really, I do, but she—"

"Was smothering you, as I told her a dozen times in the last year alone. You, Hades. Is this some enchantment or some other trick?" The gaze she threw at Hades would have impaled a lesser man.

Persephone answered before he could, proudly detailing how Hades had met her as a simple shepherd-god, much her inferior, and wooed her gently and with humor and consideration. Brunnhilde caught Hecate's lips twitching a little during this ebullient tale, as if the goddess was having trouble keeping her expression serious.

"All right, all right," Hecate said when Persephone paused for breath, before she could start in on another paean to her love. "I'll take that as a no. And I suppose Athena was right—you intended to have Thanatos take her so you'd have the rules on your side to keep her here. Right?"

Hades confined himself to a simple "Yes, Hecate."

"By Uranus's severed goolies, this is a mess. Let me think." Hecate drummed her fingers on the marble arm of the throne. Her nails made a sound like hailstones. "Persephone, keeping you here should be easy enough. Eat. Eat something that was grown down here."

Hades grimaced. "Ah…not…that…easy. The only thing that grows here is the asphodel—and that only nourishes spirits. We bring all the food we eat from Olympia. There just aren't that many of us that need real food."

"Try the Elysian Fields, at least there's light there," Hecate suggested. "Persephone, there has to be some of your mother's powers in you, go coax something to grow, then eat it. That will make you part of this realm. That's what works for the Fae realms, and The Tradition should make it work here." She pointed a thumb at Brunnhilde. "Now, you, and your mate. What is it, usually, Hades? Nearly impossible tasks?"

Hades nodded. "As few as one, as many as seven."

Brunnhilde quickly saw where this was going, and nodded, though not with any enthusiasm. "And a year and a day, usually," she said with resignation. "Damn."

"Hades, you figure out some tasks for the barbarian woman. I think the best thing to do with the man is to set him to guard Demeter so she doesn't manage to get herself abducted by something nasty, or fall down a well, or something." Hecate pondered. "I'll manufacture more tasks for him if I need to. Or who knows? He might just fall into some, thanks to The Tradition. Let's see if we can't get this happening sooner than a year and a day, or everyone and everything in Olympia is going to starve to death."

She got up and reached for her torch. "Wait!" Brunnhilde said.

Hecate paused.

"This was all *your* fault," Brunnhilde said, pointing at Thanatos. "I want something in exchange for going along with this and *not* just summoning my father and giving him an excuse for a war of the gods."

Hecate raised one eyebrow. "She has a point. And I'm a goddess of justice, among other things."

Hades nodded. "All right." He sighed. "What is it you want?"

Brunnhilde smiled in triumph. "I want you to make my husband an immortal."

So this was Elysium.

It was certainly pretty. Flowers, flowers everywhere,

underfoot, overhead in the trees, clouding the bushes. But not a hint of fruit. Nothing like a vegetable garden. No fields of grain.

Which, all things considered…was not at all surprising. Everyone here seemed to be blithely uninterested in the humbler tasks, or indeed, in work of any sort. Well, it wasn't as if they *had* to work; they were spirits after all, they didn't eat, or drink, they had everything provided for them. But it made her feel just a little impatient, looking at them lolling about, doing nothing but exercising, having games, discussing ridiculous things like "How do I know the color blue is the same to you as it is to me?"

Hecate was at least right about one thing. Elysium did have light. It had its own sun, and its own stars, which were in the heavens at the same time. She had gone to it by means of an imposing gate in an otherwise blank wall; here the gate stood, quite isolated, in the middle of a field of—yet more asphodels. She had the feeling that she was going to be very, very tired of asphodels after a while.

Perhaps if this experiment worked she could get other flowers to bloom in the gardens of Hades's palace.

There was none of that all-enshrouding mist here. Aside from the extraordinary sky—in which the sun, as near as she could tell, did not move, but simply winked out from time to time, making "night"—it was rather like the slopes of Mount Olympus, minus the animals and birds. No flocks of sheep, no songbirds, no insects. Hmm. And no bees.

Which means I am going to have to pollinate whatever I am trying to grow by hand.

But it wasn't wilderness. It was all very tame. Mannered groves, manicured meadows big enough to conduct games in, hills with just enough slope to make a good place to watch, rocks where they were most convenient to sit on, small, "rustic" buildings or miniature temples dotted about.

And everywhere, people. Which she ignored, because she was trying to figure out what, if anything, she might be able to get to bear fruit, and why there was nothing bearing fruit here now.

Finally she gave up trying to reason it out herself, and went searching for someone who could tell her. Most of those she asked looked at her askance, and said they hadn't really thought about it. A couple groups actually turned the topic of their debate to whether or not there *should* be such a thing as planting and harvesting here.

Well, it was no worse than the "color blue" question.

Finally she was sent to the ruler of Elysium; the former king Rhadamanthus, who was the son of a Titan. Or, as she was well aware now, at least half-Fae.

She found him arbitrating a dispute between two philosophers, but once he caught sight of her, he seemed more than pleased to tell them they were *both* wrong, dismiss them, and go to greet her.

"So, this is 'little' Persephone." The king chuckled. "I must say, I envy Hades. Perhaps Thanatos can find me another like you?"

"Oh, he already did, and you wouldn't want her," Persephone replied, thinking about the rather formidable war-goddess she had left stewing in Hades's care. "Cross Athena with Ares's temper, and throw in a bit of Bacchus's madness, just to keep things uncertain—" She explained to Rhadamanthus what had happened as briefly as she could. "So the problem is," she concluded, "since Thanatos didn't abduct me, I have to find another way to keep Mother from getting me back. Hecate says the only way she can think of is for me to eat something grown down here. But it has to be real food, apparently, flowers won't qualify, or I would already have had a salad of asphodel."

"Well…that is a problem. The definition of Elysium is that it lies in eternal spring—not a good time to produce anything edible." Rhadamanthus pondered this for a moment. "Well, if you have any of your mother's power…"

She sighed. "Hecate said the same thing."

"There might be one place where you can succeed. Come with me."

She followed Rhadamanthus, for quite some time. He proved to be an excellent conversationalist and told her many valuable things about Hades's moods and personality. It was only when he took her through a very precipitous cleft that she noticed that this part of Elysium was a bit different than the rest. Drier, not so lush, and at the moment—warmer.

On the other side of the cleft was a tiny valley. It was not a particularly fertile valley, either. But there were three stunted pomegranate trees here, with a few blossoms on them.

"I really don't know why this part of Elysium is resistant to the eternal spring we have everywhere else," Rhadamanthus mused. "But it is. No one but myself ever comes here. *I* only found the place by accident. I've seen fruit start—I've never seen one ripen, but I have seen them start. If there is anyplace in Elysium where you can succeed, it will be here."

Persephone stared at the unprosperous-looking trees,

and for a moment was ready to give up completely. This was ridiculous. The trees were warped by drought and deprivation, the soil was poor, and in any event, pomegranates took five months from blossom to fruit! By that time, Demeter would surely track her down and demand her back!

"The Tradition does demand the almost impossible in order for the Hero to succeed," Rhadamanthus said, as if he was reading her thoughts.

She almost groaned, but he was right. This was exactly the sort of thing that The Tradition required.

It seemed she was going to be growing pomegranates. Hopefully, at an accelerated pace.

Hopefully, her mother's power actually *was* in her.

Leo had more than a few choice words for the Olympians, and he was delivering them when Hecate returned. This time the billow of dark smoke sprang up between him and the others, so that Hecate was in an excellent position to interrupt them all when she stepped out of it. "Your woman seems to be fine, mortal," Hecate said, cutting his tirade short. "And she's no better pleased with this than you are. I pledge you that Hades has no intention of holding her if there is any way we can work out a solution for this predicament he and Thanatos managed to muddle into."

Leo frowned, and was about to demand what she meant by *if,* when she held up her hand, forestalling him. "However, if you'll give me the favor of holding your tongue for a moment, Olympia has a much bigger problem to deal with here than just one separated couple, and unfortunately, this is one that won't wait."

"Just what would that be?" Leo asked angrily.

Hecate's somber face made him pause. "Demeter is the goddess of fertility," she said slowly and deliberately. "And the goddess of fertility has just abandoned her home and run off into the wilderness and beyond. I would not in the least be surprised to discover that she has abandoned her duty and fled past our borders as well. The Tradition has put her firmly in charge of the magic that keeps Olympia fertile and growing, and there is no way to replace her. And we have a country populated by mortals who have no concept of 'seasons,' and no reason to store food, since Demeter has insured that things ripen all year long."

Athena was the one who grasped the gravity of the situation about the same time that Leo did. She gasped and paled, understanding that Hecate meant the country was about to plunge into starvation as the last of the food was eaten and there was nothing growing to replace it. Leo's first reaction was another flare of anger. These people had made their bed, so to speak, let them lie in it! What did he have to do with them, or the troubles they brought on themselves? He only wanted Bru back!

But then…

Then something else cooled the anger as quickly as if he'd had a bucket of water thrown over his head.

He couldn't let that happen. The mortals of Olympia were innocents in this, and what was worse, the gods could probably hold out and it would be the innocent mortals that would suffer.

He could not let that happen. Not and still be himself.

He was Leopold, the People's Prince, who had fought a city fire in his shirt and breeches like everyone else, passing buckets and setting the firebreaks among the homes of the great that saved the greater part of the capital. He was the Prince who had joined in with his own two hands while the citizens rebuilt.

And now, he was…well, if he wasn't quite a Hero like Siegfried, he was still the Prince who fought dragons and tyrants in lands not his own. And while he *claimed* that he did so because it was exciting and dangerous and therefore a fantastically amusing thing to do, down deep inside he knew that he did it for the same reasons Siegfried did. Because it was the right thing, because The Tradition, and magicians and powerful creatures and people, all conspired to make misery of the lives of ordinary people, and someone had to help them. He was a Prince. Noblesse oblige, that was the concept that his own father had taught him, and it wasn't just a nice phrase to him.

It was an obligation and one that, despite his outwardly cavalier attitude, he took seriously. He and Bru had talked about this at some length just before they crossed the border into Olympia, and it had been an interesting conversation.

At first, when he and Bru had embarked on this life of adventurers, Bru had been rather like a child let loose in a circus. While her fighting ability was both inherent—because she and her sisters were, after all, minor battle-goddesses—and instinctive, she had never actually *used* her weapons much. Like her sister Valkyria, her main tasks had been to fetch the heroic dead from the battlefield and take them to Vallahalia, and it was a rare occasion when she even brandished her spear or sword, much less used them. She and her sisters sparred, and that was about the extent of her opportunities to fight. She had the spirit of a born warrior, and to be finally able to go up against creatures and people that were clearly evil and best them in combat had been, for lack of a better term, exhilaratingly *fun* for her. She'd really not taken any thought for anything but the sheer excitement of pitting herself—and him—against them.

But it had been a brief visit to Siegfried and Rosa that had opened her eyes to the other side of the situation. They had just had a very odd encounter with another dragon, one who agreed to come guard Eltaria, but only if they could beat him in combat. After their victory, it seemed rude not to drop in on Queen Rosamund and King Siegfried.

After the initial greetings were over, Siegfried had asked casually if they wanted to come along and lend him a hand with a "wild bull problem." The Tradition was making things lively within Eltaria since the King was a genuine Hero. While the presence of guardian dragons on the border was keeping armies at bay, this did nothing to stop the country itself from presenting the new monarchs with all manner of Traditional challenges whenever things started to look a little too peaceful.

And Siegfried was very much a Hero King in the style of his native land. Which meant that he turned up wherever there was a problem, without fanfare or escort (other than the Firebird, his constant companion), talked to the locals, then dealt with the situation, or sent the Bird for some reinforcements. Usually (he said) he didn't need the reinforcements, and having seen him in action, Leo could well believe it. Besides, he was a Hero—and a Hero, Traditionally, was supposed to get rid of such things single-handedly. Siegfried had it down to a kind of routine now. Once he had the measure of the situation, he'd dispatch the menace in question, then allow the locals to make a great victory fuss over him, and depart.

"It's useful," Siegfried had pointed out. "I'm a foreigner, after all. Most of them expect me to turn up wearing nothing but a lion pelt or a bearskin, waving a club and grunting. They get a good look at me, I prove I'm dedicated to protecting them, and everyone feels better when it's all over."

In this case, however, without even going to the village being threatened, Siegfried already knew he would need a little help. This bull was a monster, powerful and preternaturally fast, very crafty, and he would need a team to tease and distract it until one of them managed to kill it.

"The Firebird could help," he had told them, "but she doesn't have the agility she did when she was just the little brown forest bird. A slash with a horn at the wrong moment—" He'd shaken his head. "I won't risk her. But the three of us are good enough to keep anyone from getting hurt, I think."

Leo and Bru were both more than willing to help out—and this was where Bru had gotten her first taste of what Leo and Siegfried both felt. That noblesse oblige, though if she had said anything at the time, Siegfried would just have shrugged and said, "But that is what a Hero does."

They went to the village, which was nearly on the eastern border, and saw at firsthand how the Black Bull had actually smashed cottages unless they were made of stone. She was at first impatient as Siegfried listened to the stories of his people and soothed them. She didn't see why he needed to talk to them. After all, Siegfried already knew the Black Bull was a monster, and that he needed to kill it because it had done dreadful things, he was king, and it was his job to remove such dangerous creatures. He didn't need to listen to story after tearful story. All he needed to do now (in her mind) was find out where it was so they could kill it.

But then she started to pay attention. Leo knew the moment when she understood that these were *people* to him and Siegfried, and not just warriors. He could see in her eyes the moment she stopped feeling impatient with what she had probably initially thought of as their "whining," and began to empathize with them.

The fight had gone as planned; the Black Bull, a creature easily twice the size of a farm cart and as vicious a beast as anything Leo had ever seen, was no match for three fighters, two of whom were as fast and deadly as it was, and the third, who, while not as fast, could take an astonishing amount of punishment. They had killed it, the villagers descended on it, and them, and there was a great feast. Siegfried had been genial and gracious, Leo had played the madcap "best friend," and Bru had watched them both as they filled the roles that the villagers expected, watched as the villagers took this "barbarian King" to their hearts and accepted him as their own.

It had been a good visit, if short. Gina, another of the Dragon Champions, had dropped by, and Bru had had a long talk with her that had led to them coming to Olympia.

For the entire visit, Brunnhilde had been very thoughtful, watching Leo and Siegfried as if she had just discovered something about them that she had never expected. That was when they'd had that talk, and it had been hard for her to articulate some of what she felt, but from that moment, their adventures had become something more meaningful than just another exciting battle for her, a chance to test her strength and skills. He could tell that her attitudes had changed. She was a protector, a defender now.

And so was he. They fought for more than adventure and glory. They fought to keep ordinary folk from extraordinary harm.

In a way, he suspected he had always felt like this. He might have cultivated a devil-may-care facade, but under that facade was a deep drive that was not unlike that of a fierce guard dog for its master.

Which was why, when Hecate had said what she had, he knew very well that he couldn't just let these people wallow in the crisis they had made for themselves. Once again, unless someone stepped in, it was the poor mortals who were going to suffer. The common folk. And as far as he could tell, these gods were about as useful in this situation as a lot of gawky adolescents. He was going to have to do something about it.

"How much food do you think is stored?" he demanded of the dark goddess. "Obviously the mortals are going to have no idea what is going on when winter falls on them, and they won't have prepared for such a thing, so how long do you think it will be before conditions get dire? A week? Less? More?"

"For the humans, a week, perhaps two." Hecate nodded. "They will be frightened within a few days when blossoms wither and fruit and vegetables do not ripen. For animals, the grass-eating ones at least, it will take a bit longer before they begin to starve. For the Otherfolk...I am not sure."

"Who's in charge of wild animals?" he demanded, looking around at the bewildered deities. "You're all gods, so presumably you have the duties and patronage all divided up. At least, that's how things usually go."

"Ah, I suppose that would be me," replied a young woman in an abbrieviated tunic, her hair cropped short, with a bow and arrows on her back. "And Pan, perhaps. Crius is in charge of domestic animals. I'm more of a huntress, but I'd better work with Pan to be sure he doesn't get distracted and forget what we're supposed to do." Her brows furrowed. "So what *are* we supposed to do?"

By this point all of the gods had gathered about him and Hecate; it was very clear that while they were completely willing to do what he told them, none of them had the faintest ideas of their own. At least they'd all seen the gravity of the situation at once. They could very well have taken the attitude that "what happens to the mortals doesn't concern us, there will be more along soon enough if this lot dies."

"You'll have to come up with some sort of way to awaken the wild things' instincts about winter," he told her. "Maybe you can borrow the memories of animals from outside your borders where there are seasons, but it has to be done if you don't want all your wildlife dying off. Can this be done by means of a spell or something?"

He looked to Hecate, who nodded.

"I think I can do that, with Pan and Artemis taking part in the ritual," she replied. "And I will tell Crius that we must do—what, with the flocks and herds? The pasturage won't last long once the grass stops growing."

"Let me think…" He massaged his temples with his fingers. He considered himself a quick thinker, but this was a bit like being thrown into the deep ocean and told you were going to have to reason your way to land. "Your neighbors…are they friendly?"

"Mostly absent," Zeus answered immediately. "The lands around Olympia are largely wilderness. Not nearly as lush as our land, nor as fertile, so mortals who are near the border tend to decide to join us," he added with great pride—but then his face sobered as he remembered who was responsible for the lush fields.

"As your land *was*. It won't be in a few weeks. Well, that is perfect. Tell Crius he must speak with the herders—and with the herds to get them to cooperate with their keepers. Some sort of pronouncement from the clouds or something outrageous to get the attention of the mortals. The point is, they need to be impressed with the urgency of this situation and begin to move the herds of this land across the border until you have gotten Demeter back to her duty." He spoke, and suddenly realized that he didn't sound like himself at all. His air of authority, his steadiness, were not like careless Prince Leopold, but rather like his father…

Hell. I'm turning into Papa.

"It will take time, of course," he added, quickly driving that uncomfortable thought out of his head, "but they can afford to go slowly, and take what grazing they can find until they reach a good place to stop. It's late spring out there, so they'll be all right for several moons. Let us hope this situation doesn't persist until winter."

Instinctively they were *all* turning toward him, as to the only person who seemed to have any ideas about what to do in this situation. Even Zeus. *I am standing here giving orders to gods…* It would have been a heady thought, except that this lot of "gods" seemed to be as feckless as a lot of young squires.

"As for the inhabitants of Olympia, I suggest you inform those creatures that are not mortal to seek the Fae realms for now, unless they want to begin starving. They can come back once Demeter returns." He made a wry face. "I don't suppose any of you have Fae allies? Or still are in contact with your parents?"

Zeus flushed, a few of the gods looked puzzled, as if his words made no sense to them. It was Zeus who answered.

"We…" He coughed. "As a whole we have tended to avoid the Fae."

"*You* have," Hera replied tartly. "Not all of us are so shortsighted." She turned to Leo. "Would you have us seek out our relatives, mortal?"

He nodded. "You're going to have to get food from somewhere. In the short term, see if you can find some Fae to supply something that mortals can eat safely. They're Fae though, they won't have the patience to put up with this for too long, you gods are *supposed* to be taking the place of Godmothers, not mucking things up. The good ones will wash their hands of you pretty quickly. The bad ones…well, I understand you fought them once already. So you know they'll take advantage." He rubbed his temples again. "You are going to have to find a way to buy food from outside your borders. And transport it."

"I can help there." The lively fellow with a look of mischief and little wings on his sandals and odd flat helmet had lost his smile, trading it for a look of determination. "I am the god of merchants as well as speed.

I myself have never bargained before, but you might say it is in my blood."

"I'll bring that out in you with another spell, Hermes," said Hecate. "And I am sure Hephaestus can come up with all manner of things you can barter with. Gold certainly."

"We can get the Giants to help with moving the food you buy." The speaker was a voluptuous woman that Leopold was resolutely *not* looking directly at. The moment she had joined the group, he'd had to keep himself under very tight restraint, because it was pretty clear what this lady was the patron of. "They won't say no to me."

"Nothing male will say no to you, Aphrodite," Hera replied with a touch of venom. Aphrodite just smiled lazily.

"And right now," she purred, "even you will admit that is a very good thing."

Leo decided that he had better get between the two of them before something erupted that would distract all of the gods. "All right then. The sooner you get going, the least harm will come of this," Leopold interjected. He gave Zeus a look. "And your king and I will sit down and work out more detailed plans, while the rest of you take care of the immediate situation."

Zeus nodded. "Winter…we just never had to think about such a thing before," he said weakly. "Demeter always kept things under control."

"If I have learned one thing in my short mortal life, King of the Olympians, it is that nothing lasts forever," Leo retorted. "And if I have learned another—it is that those who rule a land are *responsible* for it. Especially when things go wrong."

"You should be a philosopher," Zeus said glumly, and motioned for him to follow.

Demeter had experienced many emotions in her long life, but *grief* was new to her, and so painful that it overwhelmed her in every possible way. And now she was so lost in her grief that she was not sure where she was going, only that she needed to leave Olympia, for it had become a terrible and alien place to her. The other gods, who should have been her allies, were clearly not going to help her get her Kore back. Zeus had probably been in favor of this from the beginning!

Her grief was deepened by that betrayal.

She could not believe that her golden girl had gone with grim Hades of her own free will. He *must* have bewitched her somehow, and they were unwilling to admit it. Perhaps some of them had even helped him—she wouldn't have put it past Aphrodite to work her magic just for the sake of the mischief it would cause.

And as soon as Kore was carried beneath the earth, such enchantment would never last. How could Kore, who loved to laugh and frolic in the sun, ever find Hades and his sunless realm attractive, even under the most persuasive of Aphrodite's magics? She had never seen Hades so much as crack a smile in all the years she had known him. Surely once the magic wore off or was broken, he would terrify her poor child. And as for his realm, his "third of the earth"—

She shuddered. Oh, the Fields of Elysium were all right, but he would never allow an attractive girl like Kore to go there, populated as they were with all manner of the shades of the so-called "Heroes." Most of those "Heroes" were as lascivious as Zeus, and most of them regarded women as disposable playthings—no, Hades wouldn't allow his stolen bride anywhere near *them*. So Kore would find herself mewed up in Hades's gloomy palace in the Asphodel Fields, without sun, without music or laughter, where nothing grew except the lilies of the dead, and nothing moved but the shades in their dull, bleak, never-changing afterlife, condemned to be bored in the netherworld because they had been boring in their mortal lives. Not that Demeter had ever been there herself, since only Hecate, Hermes, and the gods of the Underworld could journey there, but Hades had complained about it often enough in her hearing.

By now, surely, she was learning the truth of this; by now she must be weeping with fear and loneliness, and longing desperately for her mother and home!

Demeter's throat closed, and her tears fell faster at the thought. How did mortals bear this dreadful emptiness, this aching sorrow? She was consumed with it, swallowed up, until grief was all that there was. And it was all the worse for being sure that Kore was wrapped in the same agony.

The Tradition held that a goddess was not bound by the restrictions of mortals or even Godmothers; she did not need a spell or magic sandals to make the miles speed beneath her feet. As Hecate did with or without her torch, Demeter only needed to desire to be somewhere—or away from somewhere—and it was so. So her feet took her, as only the feet of a goddess could, across the breadth of the Kingdom in moments; she rejected the fields of Olympia, and the gods that had been her companions, and her feet bore her swiftly away from their knowledge. The gods had not helped her, would not help her, and the fields that no longer would be the playground of her daughter could wither for all she cared. She suffered—so let all of Olympia suffer with her! She mourned—well, all of Olympia, if it would not mourn *for* her, let it mourn *with* her.

She knew, though, the moment when her path crossed the border. Behind her, the land was already showing the signs of her sorrow and neglect, as flowers faded and died, fruit dropped unripened and ripe fruit withered. But here...

Here there was something Olympia never saw.

Spring.

Confronted with this living exemplar of the renewal of life, Demeter sank to the ground beside a pure spring that welled up out of the greening earth, sobbing, grieving. As she grieved, she deliberately threw off her beauty and ripeness, transforming herself into the likeness of a barren old woman, withered without, as her heart and soul were withered within.

She cried until her eyes were sore, wept until her voice was no more than a hoarse croak, and thought, *Let it be so.* When she heard footsteps approaching, and the soft laughter and chatter of young women, she did not even look up.

The chattering suddenly stilled, and silence took its place. Finally, Demeter *did* look up, to see four pretty young maidens with bronze pitchers in their hands, clustered together and looking at her with faces full of pity. Their clothing was not unlike that of the mortals of Olympia, but they wore wool rather than linen, and were wrapped in the rectangular cloak as well, to keep off the chill in the spring air. They reminded her, in their grace and charm, of Kore, and she was about to burst into tears again, when one of them stepped forward.

"Old mother, we see that there is great sorrow in your heart," the pretty thing said as the others filled their pitchers. "Why do you lament beside the spring, alone with your grief, when there are many houses in our town that would welcome you, and many who would help you with your burden of tears?"

Demeter listened to the maiden's words with a faint sense of astonishment. Was *this* how mortals coped with loss? By sharing it? Was that even possible?

But her heart warmed a very little, because they were so young and pretty and so like Kore, and spoke out of hearts that were clearly kind. "I should not be welcome in your town, dear children," she replied. "My people are far away, and there are none who would care to be near me in my loss."

The maiden shook her head. "You are gentle of speech, old mother, showing a noble heart and birth, and clearly rich in experience. If your own people would not welcome you in their houses because you mourn, then the more shame to them. We honor the wisdom that comes with age, and cherish those who achieve it. There are Princes in this land who would be glad of one such as you as nurse to their child, and help you to temper your grief with the joy of an infant's smile." The maiden offered a shy smile of her own. "Indeed, my own father, Celeus, would gladly give you hearth-room for such a cause. My mother, Meitaneira, has given us a new brother, and she would rejoice to find such wise help with Demophoon. I feel sure that your heart would grow lighter with him in your arms."

It took Demeter a moment to realize that the girl was, essentially, offering her a *job,* that of nursemaid to a young Prince. And rather than feel offended, as

Hera might have, she actually did feel a little of her grief pass from her. They meant it kindly; the girl who had spoken had understood, instinctively perhaps, that having an infant in her arms again might well be the balm that Demeter needed to keep from going utterly mad with grief.

So Demeter bowed her head a little. "I am called Doso, maidens."

The four girls named themselves to her: Callidice and Cleisidice, Demo and Callithoe, who had spoken to her first.

"I thank you for your kindness," Demeter said gravely. "And I shall follow along behind, for I would have you ask your mother if she would indeed find me suitable as a nurse. Not that I doubt your honesty, but perhaps your hearts are a little more open to a stranger than hers." She choked back her grief. "Mothers are wise to protect their children, for the world is not all a kindly place, and disaster can fall upon the trusting and unwary."

But Callithoe only smiled. "We will run ahead, Mother Doso, but you will find that our mother will welcome you as warmly as ever you could wish."

With that, the four girls ran back up the path they had taken to the spring, with Demeter following.

"I don't know what to do," Persephone cried into Hades's shoulder as Hades comforted her. "I barely got the poor thing to get me half a dozen fruits, and now there are only three left, and they don't look as if they'll live to ripen! I've done everything I could think of, everything anyone in Elysium has suggested…I can't think of anything else!" She buried her face in the shoulder of his tunic as panic rose in her chest. Unless she could get something she could *eat* to grow here, her love for Hades and his for her was doomed.

"If it were dead, I would be of more help, my love," Hades replied, stroking her hair. "The asphodel might as well be weeds—nothing that happens to them ever seems to kill them, and they are the only plants I have any experience with. All I know is that you are doing your best."

Persephone sobbed into the smooth, dark fabric. Hecate had borrowed Hades's helmet, which granted invisibility, and followed Demeter to keep an eye on her. They both knew that things were getting rather dire in Olympia, because of the reports that Hecate brought them regularly. Demeter had left the realm entirely, and was playing nursemaid to a mortal king's child under the name of "Doso," which meant "to give," which was certainly an accurate description of her now-neglected duties as the goddess of fertility. From what Hecate said, she was pouring all her thwarted maternal energy into this child. For a little while, Persephone had hoped this would solve their problem; Demeter would be willing to let Persephone go and lavish her attentions on this mortal Prince. But her hopes were soon dashed; Demeter did not return to her duties, and Olympia continued to fail. For once, all the other gods were working together to keep the realm alive, but it was clear that what was needed was for Demeter to return to her duties.

But then something changed. Demeter was doing more than merely playing nursemaid; Hecate got very tight-lipped about it when Hades probed. From what Hecate did *not* say, Persephone suspected she was pouring something else into him, too.

Immortality.

Of all the gods, only Demeter knew the secret of how to give a mortal true immortality. Aphrodite had tried, and failed, with more than one of her lovers. Many of the others had done likewise. Demeter held the transformation as a closely guarded secret, and if her new charge was supposed to be a substitute for Persephone, it would make sense that she would make him immortal. And again, that seemed a cause for hope.

But once again, that hope failed.

The child's mother interrupted whatever it was that Demeter was doing, and although Hecate did not elaborate, it was clear that any hope Persephone had that the little Prince Demophoon would take her place were gone forever. Demeter forgave the king and his family because they immediately turned one of their palaces into a temple dedicated to her, but she did not return to them. Instead, she blessed his fields so that his land, at least, would still bear fruit, but she withdrew entirely into her new temple and did not even appear to her new priestesses.

And conditions were still dreadful in Olympia; from being one of the most lush lands in all the world, it had now become a wasteland. The climate was not as harsh as it was farther north—all around Olympia, the season of "winter" only meant that one needed a fire and a cloak to keep warm, and change the usual sandals for boots or shoes. But the last grain and vegetables had dried up without ever producing much in the way of seed, nothing that had been sown since had even come up. Fruit and vegetables that had been half-ripe when Demeter abandoned her post had rotted or withered on the branch or in the ground. Grass had stopped growing; the only things that *would* grow were weeds that not even goats would eat. All the flocks had been moved elsewhere; even the wildlife had abandoned the forests and meadows and fled over the border to territory where, if they did not live as well as they had before, at least they would not starve to death. Olympia was a realm of rock and dust, withered trees and rank weeds. Even the mortals were starting to abandon the realm.

If it had not been for the warrior-woman's mate, and Hecate, who had foreseen the disaster that Demeter's defection would mean, things would have been much worse than they were—but they were bad enough. Yes, food was coming in, but for how much longer? As mortals left, their belief in their gods waned, and the gods themselves lost power. Of course, they still had their inherent magics that they had as half-Fae, but they were losing the great powers they possessed as gods.

It wasn't bad *yet,* but it could become very dangerous indeed. As the gods lost power, their old enemies could rise to challenge them anew. Fortunately, the Titans and their king, Kronos, had been cast into Tartarus, and so far, it seemed, the one god who was not losing even a little of his powers was Hades. People still believed fervently in the Underworld and its king, it seemed, even when their belief in Zeus and the rest faded. So Hades was able to keep the worst of the gods' enemies safely bound here. And he was reinforcing that by sending the barbarian woman down into the pit to remind them that he still had the power to hold them.

But the rest would not be content to reign over a desert with no more power left to them than a common mortal wizard. It could not be too much longer before the other gods would give in to Demeter, beg her to come back and give in to her demand. Which would, of course, be that Persephone leave Hades.

Hades knew that as well as Persephone did. Unless she could somehow manage to get something growing here that she could eat, she would have to give in to her mother and leave him, since it was clear that there was no chance at all to get her to behave rationally about this.

All he could do was hold her.

Demeter would never, ever believe that she *wanted* to be with him—

This room in Hades's palace was quiet, dark, but comforting rather than forbidding. Hades's sturdy presence was just as comforting. She clung to his tunic with both hands. "Your mother…your mother has never been in love," Hades said slowly. "I have known her since the beginning, you know. From the very beginning, Zeus and Hera were bound. For all her jealous rages, Hera truly loves Zeus—when he's not letting his goolies lead him about, he really does love her…your mother never had that."

"Zeus…couch hopping. Isn't that as much the fault of The Tradition as it is of his own nature?" Persephone ventured.

Hades nodded. "Which is why Hera keeps forgiving him. And why she has remained faithful to him despite everything."

"But why doesn't Mother understand if she can see that?" Persephone tried very hard not to sound as if she was wailing.

"That is why she does not understand Aphrodite, who is often genuinely in love, if only briefly. Again, I suspect part of that is the fault of The Tradition. Aphrodite is a little minx, but mortals seem to think that the goddess of love should have the morals of a she-cat, so…" He shrugged.

Persephone sighed. She actually rather liked Aphrodite; because Hades was right, she did love very genuinely.

"The one I feel sorry for is poor Hephaestus. His situation is pure tragedy. If I were Zeus, I'd damn well hold him down and pour Lethe-water down his throat until he forgot Aphrodite." There was heat in Hades's voice that Persephone had rarely heard. Then he shook his head. "Not that it would do any good. The Tradition again. We're puppets to it. But I am sure that when Demeter thinks of Aphrodite and Hephaestus, she thinks you must feel the same as Aphrodite does for her husband. She doesn't believe in love, and she assumes you must be as revolted by my looks and manners as Aphrodite is by Hephaestus's crippled legs. That is why she cannot understand why you would wish to be with me of your own free will." He cupped his hand under her chin and raised her eyes to meet his grave gaze. "She has reason for this. On the whole, she has always been carelessly treated by men. When we came into the power granted to us by The Tradition, the men received theirs first, and most of us acted like the foolish boys we really were. Selfishly, taking no thought for anything but the pleasure of the moment, and thinking we deserved whatever we cared to take as a reward for ridding this realm of Kronos and the marauding Titans. After all, we were not being cruel, only enjoying ourselves."

He sighed. She smiled tremulously. It was so like him, to be able to see all sides to something.

"I would have thought you would be furious with

her," she replied. "She prides herself on being the mother of all things, and yet look what she does to her 'other' children in her quest to get a single one back! If I acted like she is right now, she'd say I was having a tantrum, and I promise you, I would be eating dry bread and water until I stopped acting like a petulant baby."

"But you are the only child of her body, my love." She hoped that he would kiss her, and as if he had read her thoughts in her eyes, he did. He broke it off before she would have liked, however. "As lord of the dead, I see people at their best and worst. I do not *like* how she is acting—how could I, when she wants to force us apart? But I understand it. What a mother feels for her child is not rational, especially not when she thinks her child is threatened. In a way, this is Demeter acting as we all did when our powers were new and we were drunk with them, thinking only of what she wants, and feeling only her own pain. And I can understand that. I do not like it, but I can understand it."

He kissed her again, and this time did not end it too soon. Persephone reveled in the bittersweet joy he gave her, knowing that their loving was going to be ended too soon, unless she somehow worked a miracle.

He picked her up in his arms, but just before he turned to take her into the inner chambers, he paused. "I have a thought."

Her arms tightened around his neck. "I know—"

"Not that sort of thought. I set the warrior-woman to chastising some of the inhabitants of Tartarus who had been giving trouble, but…perhaps that does not qualify as an impossible task. The Tradition is more likely to help us if what we ask her to do is something that seems to be outside of what she is good at. Well, look at what

her mate is doing! He's giving Hermes a challenge with
his bargaining and negotiation skills, and Zeus is acting
as *his* assistant in organizing the food distribution. He
and she were acting as Heroes or Champions, not as
administrators, so this should have been an impossible
task for him, and The Tradition is rewarding him with
success I would never have predicted."

"She is very good at breaking skulls," Persephone
agreed, repressing her sigh that this was interrupting
their pleasures. Hades would not have said anything at
this moment unless it had a bearing on *their* predicament.
"So…you think you should find her something that she is
not good at?" Suddenly it dawned on her, what Hades's
thought must have been. "Do you really think she has
any idea of what to do with a tree besides sit under it?"

"I don't know, but I think I will tell her she must help
you," he said, firmly. "It may be she has some skills, but
they are not obvious, so by definition, that is an impossible task. And thus, by the rules of The Tradition, having
her help you makes it *more* likely that you will succeed."

Persephone blinked. The twisted, inverted logic
made her head ache, and yet, instinctively, she felt sure
he was right.

"I think you are a genius, my husband," she replied,
feeling hope once again. "I think you are more clever
than Hephaestus, wiser than Zeus, and have deeper understanding than Athena."

A slow, gratified smile spread over Hades's face.
With an exuberant step, he carried her off to their couch,
and proved just how gratified her praise had made him.

Brunnhilde regarded the death god with a curious
gaze. He had laid out what he wanted from her, and

why, with all the skill of a master craftsman. "This is not the sort of thing I know," she replied. "In my land, I served as a sort of Charon on the battlefield, and as a cupbearer in the High Hall. Outside my land, I am better at breaking heads than nurturing much of anything. But I can see your point." She pondered for a moment more.

She had to give Hades this much; he was patient. He was perfectly prepared to let her think things through on her own time with no sign that he was getting irritated at how long she was taking.

"It is true that it seems absurd to set a warrior to making a tree grow," she said at last. "And thus, it *is* the sort of impossible task that The Tradition so loves. It further seems absurd to send someone from the snows of the north to tend a summer fruit. And likewise, to set a battle-maiden of death to bring something to life. I think I see a pattern of three, here, and a pattern of three is likelier to bring success than not." She thought a bit more.

There were things Hades could not know, of course, because she had told him as little as possible about herself. She wanted to hold on to every advantage she had. She was fairly sure, for instance, that Siegfried, Rosa and Lily knew something of what had happened to her. After all, they had promised to keep an eye on Leo and herself through their mirrors. She was also fairly sure that if she really put her mind to it, she could either fight her way out of here, or summon help from Vallahalia—not a battle of the gods, perhaps, but something smaller, a sudden raid by her sister Valkyria.

But this would turn things upside down here—and while she had been breaking heads down in Tartarus, she had gotten the measure of the things that were imprisoned down there. It was only Hades's strength, backed by The Tradition, that kept them chained. If she did *anything* that muddled The Tradition or weakened Hades—

Kronos and the Titans would break free, and bring with them an unpleasantly large number of monsters. The battle that followed would ravage this land, and if Kronos won, she didn't think he would care to rule over blighted Olympia. He and the others would look elsewhere.

She was *not* going to have that on her conscience.

Finally she nodded decisively. "I like this plan of yours, death god. Summon your mate, and she and I will go to look at this poor little tree. I will see what I can make of it."

What she did *not* say aloud—because Lily, in educating her and Leo about how The Tradition worked, had been very emphatic that when you had an edge over The Tradition, it was wise not to voice any part of that edge out loud—was that it was not as absurd for her to tend a plant as it might appear to be on the surface of things. Yes, she was a minor goddess whose main tasks had been to fetch and entertain the worthy dead. Yes, she was, indeed, better suited to wielding her sword than figuring out why a plant would not bear fruit to ripeness.

But despite that, her father Wotan's wife was the rather formidable Fricka, and despite that she had been known to refer to Fricka as "mother," in actual fact, her mother—as all of the Valkyria—was Erda, Goddess of the Earth. And unless Bru was dreadfully mistaken, she had the feeling that there was more than a little of her mother's power in her.

Certainly Bru was reasonably acquainted with the

husbandry of a land where there was no goddess meddling with the passing of the seasons, and where it took sweat and hard work to wrest food from the ground. Poor Persephone had likely never even seen a plow in action, much less gotten any notion of what a plant needed; Bru might not have been a patron goddess of farm holders, but she had watched them at work and admired their skill. Maybe farmers in the north didn't get carried off to Vallahalia when they died—but without them, the warriors wouldn't have the strength to fight, and certainly there would be no mead or beer in the festive drinking horns. Bru paid more attention to some of these small things than her father did, and often rewarded some of these fellows with spoils from the battlefield so that they could make themselves new tools and plows out of them.

"Excellent!" Hades beamed. "If you would wait here, I shall find her and send her to you."

Bru was not loath to take a seat on one of Hades's fine, comfortable couches that were placed about the courtyard. She would have expected stone, but instead, there were things more suited to indoors rather than out. Then again, there was no weather here. She rather liked the style of this place. If she and Leo ever were to settle down, she thought she'd get some furnishings made in this measure for their Hall.

Persephone looked both dubious and hopeful when she came out of the great palace to join Bru in the mist-wreathed courtyard. "I hope this Elysium of yours is more pleasant than Tartarus," Bru told her by way of preamble as she stood up to greet the young Olympian. "While I enjoyed thumping skulls, I didn't enjoy doing

so in a pit so dank and dark it seemed as if night itself
would have found itself groping in the darkness."

"I have not been there—" Persephone said doubt-
fully.

Bru shook her head. "Trust me, you won't miss anything if you don't go down there. Your mate asked me
to explain to some of his old enemies just how ill ad-
vised their attempts to escape were, so admittedly, I was
in the deepest part, where the monsters and the creatures called Titans are, but in a way, the region where
mortals are punished is just as bad." She motioned to
Persephone to take the lead, and the pretty little creature nodded and struck off in a purposeful manner.
The girl had become very much a woman over the last
several—weeks? At least. Maybe months. It was hard
to tell time down here, when there was no day or night,
and she slept when she was exhausted enough that even
the ache of being without Leo was dulled. No matter
how long it had been, that ache had not lessened in the
least, and only the prospect of seeing him made as "immortal" as herself could have allowed her to endure it.
"The darkness is bad enough, but the despair would be
enough to make the Fenris-wolf howl with grief." That
despair had come close to infecting her. She'd only kept
it away by giving vent to a full-on rage. Tartarus was a
dangerous place for someone in her position.

She was glad that Persephone knew where to go;
within moments of leaving the courtyard, the two of
them had been engulfed in mist. There did seem to be
some sort of path there, though; a bit of moss winding
through those ever-present white lilies.

Persephone shivered, as a dark shadow loomed ahead
of them, and Bru wondered what was casting it. "I have

enough despair of my own," she replied. "I don't need to seek any more out. Here we are."

What Bru had thought was a shadow turned out to be a sheer cliff face; in the midst of the rock was a plain wooden door with a simple bronze handle.

"This leads to the Fields of Elysium," Persephone explained. "It's where the worthy dead go."

Bru blinked as she took that in, then frowned. "Oh, no. You mean Heroes, don't you?" She sighed. "Which means we'll be wading through a sea of hearty bone-heads who think they have the right to grab anything that takes their fancy."

Persephone paused with one hand on the door. "Not…entirely. You have to be *interesting* to go to the Elysian Fields, not just heroic. There are a great many philosophers there. Rhadamanthus says that there are a few women, poets mostly, though I have never seen them. But…yes, some of the men are quite rude."

Bru smirked as she remembered that she was not subject to the same rules here that governed what she could do in Vallahalia. "Oh," she said with a certain relish. "I certainly do *hope* so."

Persephone gave her an odd look, then shrugged, and opened the door.

The bright light of Elysium was always a little bit of a shock after the mist of the Fields of Asphodel. As Persephone let her eyes adjust to the light, the warrior-goddess stared about her with an air of relief. "If I had known this place was here, I'd have been less testy," she told Persephone. "I've been going half mad for a bit of sun."

"It's not a real sun," Persephone felt impelled to point

out. "It doesn't move. When night comes, it just winks out."

"Yes, but there's real light here, and none of that confounded mist." The woman stretched her arms up toward the sky, as if she was reveling in the bright air. "If I'd known your tree was in a place like this, I'd have come *offering* to help instead of you having to ask. Speaking of which, where is your tree?"

"It's a long walk," Persephone began, apologetically.

"Not for me," the woman replied with a grin. "We Valkyria are a sturdy lot. Lead on. And you might as well call me Bru. I might still want to thump that numb-skull Thanatos, but you and your mate have been doing your best for me, and I appreciate it."

Persephone winced a little as she led the way to her pathetic little trees. "If it wasn't for me, you wouldn't be stuck here. I know I would be going half mad if I'd been taken from Hades. I don't know how you stand it."

"It hasn't been good. Believe me, I have been well employed taking out my frustrations in Tartarus," Bru said darkly. "I have to get fighting mad to keep from blubbering like a puling infant. Still...I *am* getting the chance to earn immortality for Leo, and that in the end is going to be worth all of this."

Persephone decided not to say anything about her mother being the only person who knew how to bestow true immortality. After all, there was no telling how Demeter would regard these two when it was all over. She might well decide to go along with the decision to reward them.

Still...better make sure that no one but she and Hades knew Bru was helping him to keep Persephone here.

The warrior had been badly treated, and she deserved to get the reward she wanted.

As they followed the path to the half-barren spot where the stunted trees were, they began to collect quite a crowd. Word spread quickly that a woman who was *not* Persephone had turned up in Persephone's company, and predictably, every Hero in Elysium had to come and have a gawk.

It quickly became evident that not all of them were inclined to restrict themselves to a gawk.

At first they limited themselves to posing and posturing. When Bru ignored that, they seemed to take it as a challenge, and called out to her, lewd comments that quickly went far beyond mere "suggestions" of what she could expect from an hour or so in their company. Persephone was soon scarlet with embarrassment, but Bru continued to act as if she couldn't even hear them.

But then one of them got bold enough to make a grab for her.

Persephone didn't even see what happened. One moment, the overly muscled oaf was reaching for her arm. The next, he was on the grass, gasping in pain. Persephone stopped cold, staring. So did the others. Bru looked down at her victim dispassionately.

"In my land," she said without any inflection at all, nor any sign of even minor annoyance, "the man who tries to force himself on a woman counts himself lucky to get off with only *temporary* pain. I suggest that you lot go back to what you were doing, and leave me and Hades's wife to get on with our work."

The stunned silence, punctuated only by the whimpers of the "hero" curled in a ball on the ground, was broken by the sound of solitary applause.

Persephone looked in the direction it was coming from, and spotted Rhadamanthus standing at the top of a bit of slope, looking down on the path.

"Well said, barbarian," he called out. "You've saved me from having to chastise these fellows, and possibly even banish one or two for being *ordinary*. There's certainly nothing *worthy* about behaving like he-goats in season. You are acting worse than centaurs who've gotten into the wine. Even satyrs have more sense than you lot are showing right now."

The expressions on the faces of the men surrounding the two women were as varied as the men themselves. Chagrin, guilt, annoyance and alarm predominated. Alarm, because of Rhadamanthus's threat—no one wanted to be banished to the Fields of Asphodel, or worse, Tartarus.

The annoyance, of course, was because, like rude boys, they had been caught.

But the expressions directed toward Bru were all alike—respect. Wary respect. Maybe a touch of fear. Aside from Athena, Persephone had never heard of any female warriors in Olympia, and a woman who looked like Bru and fought like a she-cat crossed with a snake was a new thing to these shades.

Well. Rhadamanthus definitely had the situation well in hand, so Persephone decided to let him deal with it. After all, he was their "king," and they were his subjects. She turned back up the path and struck out again, Bru following. As soon as they were out of earshot, she turned to her companion.

"Was that true?" she asked. It seemed incredible; even in relatively idyllic Olympia, even her mother could fall prey to the whim and will of a more powerful male god. And had. "Are women really treated with such respect where you come from? Are they all taught to fight like that?"

"No, actually," came the cheerful reply. "I was lying through my teeth. But now they'll think twice about giving me anything other than a polite greeting. I intend to come here on my own for some sun every day, and I *don't* feel like having to run a gauntlet every time I do so. How far are we now?"

"Not far," Persephone assured her, and pointed up to the cleft they were heading toward. "See that? It's on the other side."

Bru quickened her pace, until Persephone had to run to keep up with her. They came out into the sad little clear area with Bru well ahead; Persephone caught up to see her looking at the poor little trees thoughtfully.

With despair, Persephone saw that yet another of the fruits had withered and fallen from the branch.

"I just don't know what I can be doing wrong!" she cried. "I water them, I tend them, there are no insects here to trouble them, and I even found scrapings of bird dung to feed them with!"

"Huh," Bru said after a moment. "I'll be damned. I know just what your problem is."

Persephone stared at her.

"Or actually, two problems, but the ground is both of them." Bru knelt down, pulled a little knife out of the sheath at her belt and prodded at the ground beneath the tree. "Look at it! Hard as flint. You're watering the poor things, yes, but the water just runs away. And the other problem is there's no…sustenance in this ground." She chuckled mirthlessly. "There's *one* way to provide it, but that's a bit nasty, and there is a danger of damaging the tree by giving it too much of a good thing, so I think I'll go around to the kitchen—I know you have a kitchen—and claim some vegetable scraps. Meanwhile, you and I have some digging to do. This ground has to be cultivated and carefully, so as not to damage the roots." She examined the last three fruits carefully. "It's going to be touch-and-go, but I think we can count on getting you one all the way to ripe."

Persephone almost danced with joy.

By the time Bru declared the ground "fit," however, she was aching with exhaustion—not just physical exhaustion either. Both of them had concentrated all their will on the tree, coaxing it to flourish, as they had worked. Persephone was familiar enough with this sort of thing; this was how she had managed to save three of the six fruits in the first place. It was very hard work, and by the time they were done, they were both drained physically, mentally and magically.

When she realized that they were going to have to do this day after day, until one of the pomegranates ripened, she groaned.

"I know, I know, it's harder than breaking skulls," Bru said, helping her to her feet. "Just keep remembering that the harder it is, the more likely we'll succeed. I wouldn't even mind having to fight my way here every day, just to make sure the job is difficult enough."

"That might not be a bad idea…" Persephone said slowly. "If you are really willing."

The warrior-woman snorted. "Child, I would do more than that to drop more weight on our side. Who would we see about setting up some opposition? Your husband?"

"Rhadamanthus. The one who was applauding you."

Bru smiled. "Good. Let's not waste any time in finding him."

The scene had all the air of a carnival. The cleft that led to the pomegranate tree was blocked by no less than twenty strong men. Rhadamanthus, who was supervising the gauntlet and set the rules of the contest, had decreed that the fight would be in full armor, which in the case of the Olympians was not much, and in Bru's case, it was quite a bit. Then again, she was outnumbered twenty to one.

He had also decreed that while he would arrange for wounds to heal instantly, the combatants would still feel the pain of their injuries. That hadn't stopped the Olympian shades from lining up to try themselves against the Valkyria.

But far more of the shades gathered as spectators—roaring, betting, cheering and jeering spectators. Hence the carnival atmosphere.

"Ready?" Bru asked. Persephone nodded. The warrior-woman took a deep breath and flung herself on the waiting throng.

A roar went up from the crowd as Bru vanished beneath a pile of bodies. A moment later, she emerged, with four men lying on the ground, groaning with the pain of healed-but-fatal wounds. The remaining combatants circled her warily, and Persephone averted her eyes. Even though no one was permanently hurt, she couldn't bear to watch. Bru would eventually clear the way to the trees; all she had to do was wait. The disadvantage in numbers was more than made up for by the advantage of her armor and her skill. Even fully armored she was much faster than any of the shades.

"You can look now," Rhadamanthus said quietly in her ear. When she turned to look at the field of battle, she saw that, once again, Bru was triumphant, grimacing with pain, her hair plastered to her head with sweat, but taking the congratulations of those losers still able to stand through their pain. Rhadamanthus had ensured that the contest was fair by ensuring that the pain of the wounds persisted until the competition was over and the losers had all surrendered.

Now he waved his hand, and they straightened or pulled themselves to their feet as their pain vanished.

Bru turned to the cleft, without waiting to see if Persephone was following. Persephone hurried to join her as she stumbled to the tree in exhaustion.

She went to her knees beside the tree still bearing fruit, and she and Persephone carefully cultivated a tiny amount of fertilizer made of finely ground vegetable peelings, a bit of eggshell and herb stems into the soil at the base of the tree.

Bru took a dulled dagger and stirred the mix into the earth as Persephone poured it out of a small jar. Then she sat back on her heels as Persephone carefully poured water from a second jar into the earth.

The tree looked ever so much better than it had when Bru pointed out what was wrong. There were more leaves on it, and they were greener. By now there was just a single fruit, barely a third the size of Persephone's fist, and almost ripe. She thought about plucking it—then thought better of it. There was no telling what the effect would be if she took it when it was still a little green. Better to wait.

She put the water jar down as a breeze came up and dried Bru's yellow hair, sending little tendrils floating. She put both her hands, palm down, on the earth at the base of the tree; wearily, Bru did the same.

Persephone closed her eyes and concentrated with all her might on bringing more life to the little tree— not just for now, but for as long as it stood. She didn't want to just take the one fruit and abandon it; that felt wrong. The tree was giving her what she desperately needed; she wanted to sustain it and reward it.

She felt Bru doing something that was not quite the same—Bru seemed to concentrate on the earth itself, where Persephone concentrated on the tree. Strange, but perhaps this had something to do with how their two mothers' powers worked. When Demeter had blessed the fields, it had actually been the seeds that she placed her magic in—farmers brought their seeds to her temples, and representatives of their flocks and herds for her blessing. By contrast, from what Bru had said, her mother actually *was* the earth itself, she was made up of it, more like Gaia than Demeter. So, perhaps their magics reflected that.

The last of Bru's strength quickly ran out, however, and as they got to their feet, it was Persephone's narrow shoulder that Bru leaned on as they made their way down to Rhadamanthus's palace.

The king of Elysium was waiting there for them, with the usual nectar and ambrosia that was the common drink and food among the Olympian gods. Bru had made a face and complained after the first few days of this, saying she would have preferred mead and meat. Persephone couldn't blame her actually, for she was used to more "common" fare with her mother.

This time Bru didn't complain, and neither did Persephone. They were both in desperate need of restoration, Bru in particular. Yet beneath the exhaustion, Bru was clearly happy and triumphant, as always, because The Tradition was obviously working in their favor now. Persephone would get her pomegranate, and presumably a solution was being found for Bru and Leo's problem.

When they had rested a little, Rhadamanthus had Thanatos take them up in his chariot—nothing like as impressive as Hades's, of course—to bring them back to Hades's palace, where Bru, at least, would fall down onto a couch and sleep as if she would never wake again, until Persephone came to get her to do it all over again.

They were nearly done.

And if so, it would not be a moment too soon. Yesterday, Hecate had reported that the gods had gathered to confront Demeter in her own temple. Demeter would again demand the return of Persephone, and there could be only one answer to that, if they all wanted Olympia to be restored.

But as the two of them arrived from their daily battle, the sound of a gong shattered the silence of Hades's palace, a strangely penetrating sound that made the very walls ring.

Persephone paled. Bru put a steadying hand on her arm. "Is that what I think it is?" she asked. The girl nodded.

"All right then. Courage. We've done all we can do. No matter what happens, no one can have done more." Bru patted her shoulder. "You go take your place. I'll get myself cleaned up and wait in the courtyard, and we'll see what the Norns have in store for us."

Persephone was rattled enough that she didn't even ask what the Norns were.

Persephone felt cold all over. This was the day she had been dreading. And it was the one day of all days that she knew, deep in her heart, she had to be the strongest. The Tradition would not reward a weeper or despair.

And when she appeared to her mother, she would have to look, not like little Kore, but like a *woman,* and one capable of knowing her own mind and choosing her own destiny.

Steeling herself, with head high and wearing her best woman's gown—the long gown, not the little tunic that her mother preferred her to wear—she went to Hades's throne room and took her place on the new throne that had been placed at his side. There they waited for Zeus's messenger.

He was not long in coming; it was Hermes, and her heart sank because she knew that Zeus would only send Hermes, and not Hecate, if this was a command that had the force of all of the gods behind it.

Hermes would not look at her. Instead, he concentrated on Hades, and there was nothing of his usual playful nature as he addressed the lord of the dead. "Hear, Lord Hades, the command of Zeus, the king of the gods of Olympia, and master even of you, as you yourself have acknowledged."

Hades bowed his head, but his grip upon Persephone's hand tightened, even as her throat tightened. "Speak," Hades said, his voice dark with grief. "I hear the command of he who is overlord to us all."

"It is commanded that Persephone, daughter of Demeter, come up out of the Underworld and be restored to her mother, so that the good goddess will once more bring life to Olympia," Hermes said in flat tones that brooked absolutely no argument.

Persephone couldn't help herself; a single cry of anguish broke from her throat. Only Hades's hand on hers steadied her.

But his words almost undid her. "Let it be so," he said, and though his face was impassive, there were tears in his words. "But know that she does not look unkindly upon me. Know that I truly love her above all things. And know that I, who can make her a great Queen of the Kingdoms of the Olympians, am no unfit husband for Demeter's child."

"All this may be true," said Hermes, "yet still she must go. Make ready your chariot that I may take her to the Upper World."

"First let my husband and my love give me a last ride in his chariot," Persephone demanded. "Husband, I would bid farewell to the Fields of Elysium, the kindly realm where the worthy souls find their home, and to Rhadamanthus who is lord over it."

Hermes nodded; the chariot was brought, and Hades took the reins. Persephone stepped into the chariot beside him and he put his arm around her. Hermes crowded in with them.

"Is it ripe?" he whispered urgently to her. She could only shake her head.

"I don't know," she replied. His arm tightened and he said no more.

Hades had no need for doors or gates within his own realm. The horses had carried the chariot only a few paces when they broke through the mist and into the bright light of Elysium. Persephone recognized the path to her little tree immediately as the horses stepped onto it, and with a shiver of apprehension, she felt the chariot lurch as it headed up the slope. She hid her eyes in Hades's shoulder. She couldn't bear to look.

The chariot stopped, and she felt Hades—moving. Passing the reins to Hermes. Reaching out with the arm that was not holding her.

"Look up, my love," he whispered, and Persephone looked up to see him pulling the branch of her tree within her reach. And on that branch was a single, gloriously ripe fruit that glowed like a ruby in the sun.

Her heart soared. She plucked the fruit from the branch; it came away in her hand so easily it might not even have been attached.

"Will you share it with me?" he asked tenderly. With a nod, she broke the tiny fruit in half and handed half to him. Within her half were seven scarlet-pulped seeds. She ate them.

They were tart, very nearly bitter and dry—and she thought she had never tasted anything so good in her life, because the poor little tree had given her the best that it could, fully ripe. No one could say otherwise, and Hermes was the witness.

In fact, Hermes's eyes were as big as an owl's. He surely knew that nothing grew in the Underworld except the asphodel. Well, nothing had, until now.

Hades stepped down from the chariot then, his half of the pomegranate still untasted in his hand.

Demeter waited, impatiently, on the top of a hill just below Mount Olympus. Her stubbornness had cost the land dearly; the thin, brittle grass beneath her feet was brown and lifeless, the trees around her leafless, and nothing stirred on the wind but dust. There was not a bird or an insect in the air, and the only living things on the ground were the gods themselves, who waited with her.

Demeter felt a moment of guilt, but only a moment. All of this could have been prevented if Zeus had forced Hades to relinquish her daughter moons ago. Now her magic, pent up within her, stirred and pressed against her, threatening to burst out at any moment. And she could feel the great weight of The Tradition hovering over her, waiting.

She saw a plume of dust in the distance, a plume that soon became a trail, and beneath the trail, the black form of Hades's chariot. It was driven by Hermes, and beside bright Hermes—

Yes! It was Kore!

She flew like a bird to meet her daughter, love and magic bursting out of her, the grass literally greening at her feet as she ran. Everywhere that her footsteps fell, grass and flowers exploded out of the ground, and streaks of grass and flowers raced away from her. As those streaks of magic reached the trees, they, too, came to life; buds swelling on the branches, and unfurling to leaves and flowers in a moment.

But Demeter had no eyes for that, only for Kore, who leapt from the chariot and into her mother's arms.

"I didn't realize until now how much I missed you!" Kore cried, and for a long, long time, all they did was hold each other, kiss and weep.

But then, as the first sound of birdsong in moons echoed across the greening fields, and as the Otherfolk crept out of whatever places they had been keeping themselves until Demeter restored the land, Demeter's heart…felt a moment of doubt.

She held Kore at arm's length, and for the first time,

saw that she was wearing the long gown of a woman grown, that her face had grown grave and beautiful and—mature. Saw that the loose, flowing locks of the girl had been bound up into the hairdo of a woman. And knew that there was more going on with Kore than just the change in appearance.

"My dearest," she said, dreading the answer. "I know it should be impossible, for nothing but asphodel grows in the Underworld, but—has any food of Hades's realm passed your lips in the moons you were with him?"

Her daughter raised her head and regarded her with clear, blue eyes. "As we bid farewell, I plucked a pomegranate from a tree in Elysium, and Hades and I divided it between us. I ate seven seeds."

Demeter regarded her in horror. "Why would you do such a thing?" she gasped. "Was it some spell? Did Hades force you?"

She saw a strange expression on her daughter's face then. One that at first she could not identify. And when she did at last, she could hardly believe her eyes, for it was pity.

"Ah, my dearest," she cried, "if you had not eaten the pomegranate seeds you could have stayed with me, and always we should have been together. But now that you have eaten food in it, the Underworld has a claim upon you. You may not stay always with me here. Again you will have to go back and dwell in the dark places under the earth and sit upon Hades's throne."

"I grew that pomegranate myself so that I could eat it, Mother," the young woman said softly. "I know that you do not understand, but I love Hades. Not because of something he did to me, or some magic spell, but for himself. He is my beloved, and I am his and I could

not bear the thought of being unable to return to him."
Then her eyes filled with tears. "But now that I am
here, I know I cannot bear the thought of being unable
to return to you." Her lips trembled and she managed
a hesitant smile. "Can you not at least agree to share
me? What you call the 'dark places' hold so much joy
for me, because they hold my lord and my love."

And that was when Demeter realized that little Kore,
her baby girl, was gone.

As egg becomes chick, which becomes a bird that
must fly, as flower becomes fruit that must ripen and
fall or be plucked, so Kore had become Persephone. She
who was the goddess of fertility, knew this better than
anyone; and though it was bitter, it was something that
she had, in her heart, known would come.

Weeping, she bowed her head to the inevitable.

"As you ate seven seeds, so seven moons of the year
shall you be with Hades," she said. "And in that time,
I shall mourn, and Olympia will suffer winter as other
lands do. But not always you will be there. When the
flowers bloom upon the earth you shall come up from
the realm of darkness, and in great joy we shall go
through the world together, Demeter and Persephone."

When she said that last, Persephone's face lit up, for
she had used her daughter's adult name at last. "And
when I go beneath the earth again, let that be a season
of plenty and rejoicing, the Harvest Moon, when all
things ripen and the earth is glad, for though I go from
my beloved mother, I go *to* my beloved husband."

"So be it," Demeter said.

Leo stood before the throne of Hades, already exhausted. He had literally fought his way down into the

dark god's realm, step by step, guided by Hermes, but facing every sort of obstacle that could possibly have been placed in his path. He had climbed a cliff, picked his way across a field of jagged rocks that held unexpected pockets of fire, fought a one-eyed giant, tamed a three-headed dog with the help of Hermes and had to outrun a pack of hellhounds.

And now, at last, he saw Bru for the first time in months, and he wasn't allowed to go to her or touch her. They stood before Hades and Hecate with Hermes standing between them, preventing them even from looking at each other.

Hades sat on a tall throne carved of some black material, set in the middle of a courtyard in front of an enormous building that was the twin of the one Zeus called his home up on the mountain. But here there was no sun, no blue sky, only mist overhead, and more mist drifting across the courtyard, with a twilightlike light permeating everything.

The goddess was shrouded from head to foot in black material, and held a torch. Two dogs stood on either side of her—and Leo wondered, suddenly, what was the obsession that these gods had with dogs? Athena had dogs, Apollo had dogs, Hades had hellhounds and that three-headed thing, and now Hecate had these enormous beasts whose heads came up to her chest. "You have done well, outlanders, in all the trials that we have set you, but there is one task yet you must face, before we can reward you," Hecate said, her face absolutely still as a stone. "You must face yourselves."

Before either of them could ask what she meant, Hades spoke.

Now, Hades was impressive. Much more so than

Zeus, to tell the truth. There was a gravity about him, and a stillness, that were quite unnerving. Like his brother, he was dark, but unlike Zeus, every movement he made was slow and deliberate. "Within you both are monsters," Hades said, and gave Leo a penetrating look. "Your fears, your secrets, all the things you would never share with anyone, the things that will tempt you almost beyond bearing. Those monsters will take tangible form, and you must battle them—you will battle them alone, and yet bound together in faith. Leopold, you will lead the way, and Hermes will guide you. But you must never look back to see if Brunnhilde is following you. And you must never hope for her help in your battles, nor aid her in hers. These are yours to deal with alone." He turned his gaze to Brunnhilde. "Brunnhilde, you must follow him, but you may never give him any sign that you are there, nor interfere with what he does nor how his confrontations go in any way. And you must fight your own battles, with no help from him, nor ask for any."

Mist wreathed around Hades, emphasizing his distance. That was why Hades was more impressive than Zeus, Leo realized. Zeus was very human. Hades…wasn't.

Leo nodded; he assumed that over on the other side Bru did the same. Hades lifted his hand. "Then let the final trial begin."

Hermes turned and walked back in the direction they had come, into the mist that had suddenly billowed up behind them; Leo averted his eyes to avoid looking at Bru, and followed.

But of all the things his imagination had pictured for him to face, the first thing that appeared out of the mist and held up a hand to stop them was nothing he had expected.

"Leopold," Aphrodite said, and smiled. She seemed to have an inner glow that warmed the mist around her, and the delicate swath of cloth that clung to her body seemed held there by nothing more substantial than force of will. Her hair was unbound, and tumbled down her back in impossibly silky waves. "You know, you really don't need to go through all this." She waved her hand vaguely at Hermes and the mist, and gave him a smoldering look. Her lush sexuality left him feeling more than half stunned. "Why, after all, should you? If you were to simply give up here and now, you could come back to the Upper World and Olympia with me."

"And why would I do that?" Leo asked after clearing his throat.

Aphrodite pouted a little. "Why wouldn't you? You don't really think you'll be able to stay with Brunnhilde, do you? You've never been a man to be contented with only one woman, so how long do you think it will take before you are bored with someone who is as much man as woman, hmm?" One delicate eyebrow arched upward. "Think about it, and be honest. You could come with me right now, you know. I like you. I know you find me alluring and hard to resist. Why keep resisting? I could show you things, couch games your barbarian never dreamed of."

Leo felt himself growing hot and cold by turns, and his armored trews were suddenly much, much too tight. Her perfume wafted over to him, a combination of roses and musk.

"You wouldn't get immortality, of course," Aphrodite continued. "But why would you need it if you were leaving her to her own devices? And what I can offer you is worth so much more." She winked. "You wouldn't be the first mortal lover I've taken, so don't worry, I'll be gentle with you."

His mind spun in circles as he tried to sort his thoughts out. Aphrodite was right, it was as if she had read his past, and even some of his thoughts, for he had never thought of himself as the sort to settle down with a single woman. And even when he had been trying to find himself a Princess, or at least a fabulously wealthy wife, there had always been the vague surety that there would be a mistress or two on the side...

Of course, that had been before he met Bru. Somehow, the moment that he'd seen her asleep in that circle of fire, something inside him had changed forever. Or, perhaps, the change had come earlier than that, when he had passed out expecting that he was bleeding to death from a fatal wound, and awakened discovering that the death of a gentle unicorn had given him an undeserved second chance.

"I am the goddess of love, so I should be the expert on it," Aphrodite purred as the thin draperies she wore shifted as she moved, alternately concealing and revealing her body in ways that were far more erotic than being naked could have been. "What you mortals call love is a fleeting thing, fragile and quick to fade. Better to be honest now, come and enjoy the pleasures I offer, and we will part when we are both weary, without any vows that are impossible to keep."

Somehow, it was that last sentence that made his thoughts stop swimming, and settle. And he had been around Aphrodite enough the last several moons to have learned how to shake off the mesmerizing effect that her beauty and raw sexuality had on the susceptible.

"I know about you gods," he said, carefully choosing his words. "The funny thing about you is that you're a reflection of us mortals. A bigger reflection, like one in a mirror made to distort and exaggerate, but still, just a reflection of what we are."

Aphrodite took a small step back, blinking in confusion.

"You see, we made you. We saw you, we made up stories that we thought fit with what you were, and we *believed* in those stories so strongly that you became what we wanted you to become." He shrugged apologetically. "So, as the goddess of love, you're basically what we mortals want you to be, and most of us, I guess, want you to be the way you are now, beautiful, sensual and…" He paused to think of a diplomatic word. "Liberal with your favors. Only a goddess could possibly be that generous. That makes you the expert on *some* kinds of love, but not all of them. If I wanted to know how to seduce someone, you would be my first choice for advice and help. But for how to stay in love with someone for a very long time? Not so much."

Aphrodite's mouth actually fell open for a moment as she stared at him. But a moment later, her sense of humor caught up with her shock. "You're quite clever, Leopold. Perhaps not *wise,* to say such things to a goddess, but clever."

"I wouldn't have said something like that to a god who would get angry," he replied. "I hope you noticed that I didn't say 'stay in love with someone forever.' I don't even know if that's possible. I'm going to try, but I am not going to make any promises that are that, well, impulsive and inflexible. The Tradition loves those. It uses them to break people."

Aphrodite nodded. "Well said. And you have passed your first trial. Pass on—and—good luck."

"Thank you," he said, and meant it.

She stepped aside and vanished into the mist. Hermes had been waiting for him, and now continued to lead the way.

When that barely clad hussy had tried to seduce Leopold right under her nose, it had taken all of Bru's self-control to keep from running up to her and shield bashing her. "Goddess of love," was she? All well and good, she was as promiscuous as Freya, but Freya didn't go around trying to seduce other people's husbands!

Bru's hand tightened on the hilt of her sword, and she ground her teeth together.

And the way she was eyeing up Leo, like someone examining a particularly choice bit of roast she was about to devour—it just made Bru's blood boil!

And that very anger was what woke her up to the fact that this might very well be one of *her* trials, and the monster she was facing was her own jealousy.

So she stood, and seethed, and clamped her jaws shut on everything she wanted to shout, told her feet that they were not going anywhere just now, and waited.

And inside, besides the anger, she discovered a hard, cold core of fear. Because she *wasn't* anything like the lush, dark-haired Olympian beauty. Oh, she wasn't ugly, but she wasn't like *that*. Her body was muscular and hard, not soft and curved. She knew how to kill a man, but all she knew about how to please one, she had learned from Leo.

The more the woman spoke, with her dulcet voice and beguiling ways, the more her anger faded and her fear grew. She couldn't deny that most men wanted as many women as they could get. She couldn't deny that she herself was no great bargain unless you were looking for someone who could dispatch your enemies and then share a little bit of tickle-and-poke afterward.

But still, she did not move, or speak. How often had she seen her father running after some wench, and not anything Fricka could say or do would prevent him? In fact, her jealousy and railing seemed to make things worse. Whereas Freya, who actually led the Valkyria, could make virtually any male do her will in the same way that Aphrodite did. Why, she persuaded the gods to let her husband, Odr, enter Vallahalia even though he hadn't died in battle! None of the male gods, and few of the female, could resist her!

Bru was no Freya…but she was no Fricka, either. She would not rail at Leo like a fishwife. He would be himself, and though he might choose to change, she would not try to make him.

She was afraid to lose him, but if she could not keep him at her side and still be herself…had she ever really had him?

In the end, as her thoughts twisted and turned in confusion, all that she really knew was this: if she violated the terms of the trial, she *would* lose him, forever.

Just as she was about to close her eyes or look away, he said something that made Aphrodite step back a pace and blink. And both fear and jealousy fell away as she realized she had won.

At least, this time.

* * *

Leo could not recall a time when he had felt so battered in body and soul. He had thought that the fight to reach Hades's palace had been the hardest he had ever undertaken—harder than facing the Huntsman and Prince Desmond, harder than fighting off the Children of the Dragon's Teeth.

This…this was even harder.

It wasn't so much the *combat* by itself. It was the opponents.

One by one, he faced every fear, every humiliation and every defeat he had ever had. One by one, he was terrified, humiliated and defeated all over again. The first time it happened, he was petrified, thinking that to lose one of these battles was to lose Bru.

But as he picked himself up off the ground and his opponent faded away, he understood that winning wasn't the goal after all.

It didn't matter if he won or lost, only that he faced the things inside himself and survived. And, presumably, the same was true for Bru; he had heard nothing of her behind him, but that was the point, wasn't it?

But it was hard. Bad enough to have dealt with these over the course of a lifetime, but to face them one after another, but with no breaks? By this point his strength was just about run out; he kept his eyes fixed on Hermes's heels, and plodded along through the mist like an old man.

The one thing he didn't have to face again was the temptation to give up; evidently Aphrodite was deemed the most potent weapon in the rack on that score, and there was no point in bringing out anything else.

Just as he was thinking that, he almost ran into Hermes. He looked up.

Ahead of them was a solid wall of ebon blackness. Night was not this black. It oozed despair, dread and fear, and the end of hope. Hermes pointed.

"You must follow me through this," he said tonelessly. "This is your last trial. You must face the final darkness, the last fear, that of knowing that you are utterly, utterly alone. On the other side is the Upper World. This is your last chance to turn back and admit defeat."

Leo looked at the Void, and shuddered. He didn't want to go in there. He had never much liked being alone in the conventional sense, and to willingly plunge into *that?* Instinctively, he understood the import of Hermes's words. This wouldn't be merely being "lonely." This would be—being alone. He would find himself in there with nothing for company but all his faults and fallibilities, and he would be unable to escape them.

He didn't have a choice. Not if he ever wanted to be able to look at himself in the mirror again.

Hermes vanished into the black. Leo followed.

Five months since Persephone had returned to her mother and for the first time, spring and summer had come to the realm of Olympia, and now, on this the very first Harvest Moon of the Olympians, there was another occasion that would (hopefully) not be repeated. All of the gods and no few of the Godmothers had conferred and consulted; all agreed that Brunnhilde and Leopold had earned their respective rewards. As everyone had expected, for his reward, Leopold chose to have his beloved back, and Brunnhilde had chosen immortality for her love.

This was all agreed, and yet to make sure that The Tradition was properly satisfied, there was one more ordeal that they had to pass. The Harvest Moon, and the occasion for Persephone to return to the Underworld, seemed to be the most suitable moment. After all, there would be a trade of sorts—Brunnhilde for Persephone, one entering the Underworld, and one leaving. So now, as the Olympians gathered at one of the openings into Hades, Persephone among them, they waited and watched.

This would be a test of faith, in each other. Hades had decreed that Leopold could, indeed, fight his way down to the great palace and lead Brunnhilde out. But he had also decreed that once he began the journey back, he was neither to look back to see that she was following, nor speak to her, no matter what he saw or heard. And for her part, she was not to make a sound, nor touch him, nor give any sign that she was there—no matter what she might encounter.

And both of them would encounter a lot. Persephone, who knew her love very well, knew that he would not make this test a mere token.

What that long ordeal would be, what the two of them would face, no one knew, but since Hecate and Hades were the ones in charge of the obstacles Brunnhilde and Leo would encounter, they were bound to be very personal, and very dark. On the whole, Persephone reflected, she would rather face an ordeal created by any gods other than those two. Most of them would simply line up shades for a simple fight. Not Hades, and not Hecate.

Brunnhilde would have to trust that no matter what *she* saw, Leo wouldn't lead her astray. Leo would have to trust that, no matter how tempted she was, nor how terrified, Brunnhilde would follow him.

The gods waited with bated breath. Others had failed

this test before. Others would likely fail it in the future. As Hades had pointed out, this would set a precedent and he couldn't afford to make it anything less than the worst that anyone could bear. It could never be permitted to be easy to take a soul from Hades's realm, even when that soul wasn't actually dead.

Finally the door opened. A great stillness settled over the clearing.

First to emerge was Hermes, acting as Leo's guide. Then Leo, looking white and anguished. Then—nothing, and someone in the crowd groaned.

But then, stumbling and shaking so hard her armor rattled, Brunnhilde.

The assembled gods cheered, and Persephone ran from the crowd to meet them—

But she didn't reach them before Hermes signaled to Leo that he could turn, and the lovers fell into each other's arms.

Persephone stopped, right at the door into the Underworld, smiling so hard her mouth hurt. They clearly didn't need her.

And then she felt the presence she had ached for over the last five months, just behind her.

She turned to find Hades behind her, smiling down at her.

She had thought of all the things she would say to him when she finally saw him again, but now, when she saw him, she forgot all of them.

"Welcome back," said her love, and pulled her into his arms. And while the attention was on everyone else, she and he walked hand in hand into the darkness, and home.

Demeter had absolutely refused to make Leo immortal. She had flounced off to her temple to sulk for the seven months of winter, while the rest of the gods were still celebrating the Harvest Moon feast at the mouth of Hades's realm.

Once she was well gone, Hecate appeared in her customary puff of blue smoke, this time without her dogs, but with a large amphora dangling from one hand as if it weighed nothing. Bru greeted her with a grin, Leo with a matching one.

"Stubborn woman," Hecate muttered. "Well. As I told you both, thanks to Hades's helmet, I was able to watch her when she was working the magic to make that little mortal child an immortal. I tried it out on that little lad Zeus kidnapped for a cupbearer, so I know it works. This is why I was making sure you never ate anything but ambrosia for the last five months." She eyed Leo suspiciously. "Please tell me you obeyed my order to the letter."

"I swear!" Leo protested. "Lady, I know how The

Tradition works, and if you wanted me to eat nothing but ambrosia, then there had to be a good reason for it."

Hecate sighed with relief. "All right, the last part is this." She heaved the amphora at him. It definitely was much heavier than it had looked. Leo caught it with a grunt. "Come with me, we need privacy for this."

Without any preamble, the blue smoke enveloped all three of them, and when it cleared, they were in a windowless chamber that held a very comfortable-looking couch and a central hearth on which a fire burned. There was a good supply of firewood next to it. Leo smiled. Things were already improving.

"Now, Leo, you get completely undressed and bathe yourself in the nectar in that amphora."

He waited. Hecate showed no signs of vanishing.

"Ah—a little privacy?" he begged.

She snorted. "Mortal, you have absolutely nothing I haven't seen before, and nothing I am interested in. Strip. Bathe."

Feeling his manhood withering under her gaze, Leo meekly did as he was told, covering himself in the sticky nectar. Which would have been very, very nice if Bru was going to lick it off, but with Hecate standing there looking like the incarnation of his disapproving old nurse, was less than erotic.

"Now go sit down in the fire," Hecate ordered. "Or lie down, you might as well. You're going to be there all night."

"What?" Leo yelped.

"And every night for the next month."

"WHAT?"

She tapped her foot impatiently. "Do you want to be

immortal or not? By Kronos's severed goolies, I didn't get this much fuss and protest out of little Ganymede, and here you are a fully grown man! Bru will tend the fire, you'll toast in it all night long while I recite the spells. It will take thirty nights to burn the mortality out of you. That's how it is."

Leo's heart sank. It had been almost a whole year, and he had *not* wanted to spend his first night with his beloved separated by ten feet of pavement and a fire.

He certainly had not wanted to spend the first *thirty* nights with his beloved separated by ten feet of pavement and a fire.

But Bru was giving him the big-eyed pleading look. And after all she had gone through to get him this gift—

"Uh…question?" he said, wondering awkwardly where he ought to put his hands. And blushing enough for three.

"What?" Hecate glowered.

"Exactly what sort of immortality is this, anyway?" He'd learned quite a bit about "immortality" as the bargaining agent for the gods. "How does this work, exactly?"

Hecate stopped glowering and eyed him with speculation.

"I'd like to know too," Bru put in. "I'd like to know if you lot are going to try to fit us into your pantheon, or if your local mortals will. Because, if it's all the same to you, I'd rather not."

"Well." Hecate offered a small smile, which looked very odd on her usually dour face. "Intelligent questions. What a change! It's simple enough. It's relative immortality, just like the rest of the half-Fae. Ambrosia comes from the Fae realms, which is why you're supposed to eat only that for a set period of time. Then the spell takes the design, the 'half-Faeness,' from someone else and the ambrosia sets everything up. The fire is transformative. It doesn't really burn anything away, it's both a metaphoric and actual transformation. And the ambrosia coating you protects you from the very literal fire. In your case because, no, I do *not* want you two joining up with the Olympians, thank you, I'm using you, Brunnhilde, as the pattern. Demeter usually uses herself."

Leo scratched his head. The ambrosia itched. "How long is 'relative' immortality?"

"I don't have an answer for that. A very long time, unless you do something to get yourself killed. And if you do, your souls will go wherever you believe you'll go. Elysium wouldn't be too horrible, I suppose." Hecate shrugged. "From what Brunnhilde has told me, I wouldn't care for Vallahalia."

Leo and Bru exchanged a long look. There would be many discussions about this in the future, he was sure.

"Now, will you *please* step into the fire?" Hecate added. "I'd like to get this started in the proper time."

Leo sighed, and did as he was told. Although he had been expecting something painful, it wasn't. In fact, it was rather pleasant, if…weird. Then again, he had gotten used to weird. He did have a hill for a mother-in-law, after all.

He made a mental note *not* to mention the immortality when he and Bru visited *his* family. Things were already complicated enough.

He made himself a little hollow among the coals and curled up, giving Bru a longing look.

She smiled as Hecate began chanting. "Don't worry, husband," she said, with a wink that looked as if she had stolen it from Aphrodite. "I've never heard it said that sharing a couch could only be done between dusk and dawn. There are *many* hours in a day, and we have nowhere to go till the end of Harvest Moon."

He blinked. "Oh. Ha!" And the mere thought of what awaited him in the morning caused a great movement among the coals down around his nether regions.

"Worse than nymphs and satyrs, the two of you," Hecate muttered, and went on with her chanting.

Hades and Persephone paused by the edge of the Acheron. The unhomed souls were building up again. Persephone eyed them thoughtfully.

"Perhaps a temple?" she hazarded.

"Eh?" Hades's mind had clearly been elsewhere. Not that she blamed him. Five months was a very, very long time.

"A temple—no, several! Placed at caves or other places where mortals think entrances to your realm are. They can make offerings of coins for the spirits, and in return—" she thought quickly "—in return I will grant them guaranteed passage across the river. That way you remain the stern ruler, and—"

"And you are the sly little creature that works around my rules." He caught her up and kissed her soundly. "I like it. I believe you deserve a reward."

She giggled. "And what would that reward be?"

"Me, of course." He raised his voice in a bellow. "CHARON!"

"Coming, coming," came the lugubrious voice out

of the fog. "I'll be only too pleased to get you two to a room. You're scandalizing the spirits."

For the first time ever, Hades threw back his head and laughed, and laughed, and laughed until his sides ached.

* * * * *

For Brunnhilde and Leopold's meeting, look for Mercedes Lackey's
THE SLEEPING BEAUTY

And don't miss any of the other stories in
THE FIVE HUNDRED KINGDOMS

CAST IN MOONLIGHT

Michelle Sagara

CAST IN MOONLIGHT

The girl sat in a chair in the center of the highest point of the Tower of the Hawks. The aperture of the roof was open; moonlight touched her head and shoulders.

Lord Grammayre, Commander of the Hawks, one of the three bodies that enforced the Emperor's Law, faced her while she waited; her knees were drawn up to her chest and she'd tucked her chin behind them. She didn't look up.

She couldn't leave the Tower, but hadn't tried; the only time she had reacted at all was during his brief mirrored conversation with the Imperial Office. "You are familiar with the Tha'alani?" he'd asked.

She hadn't answered, but her tight, strained silence was enough; she knew. "I'll answer your questions," she finally said in a low, low voice. "I'll tell you anything you want to know. I've got no reason to lie."

"You will forgive me," he said in a voice that implied that if she didn't he wasn't concerned. "Your answers to my questions—any of them—will be suspect." The girl hadn't arrived as a guest; nor had she arrived as a messenger. She had arrived—through the roof—as an assassin, and it was clear that she understood the cost of failure. "The Tha'alani are best known for their ability to read thoughts, and they can approach memory clusters of events that you yourself might recall less clearly in a conscious fashion." He watched her closely. "If you do not resist his examination, it will pass quickly. There will be some minimal discomfort."

"And if I do?"

He didn't reply.

In the process of ascertaining that she wasn't armed, he had discovered marks that ran the length of her visible forearm and her lower legs; he was not certain how far they extended. They were a dark gray that was almost black, and they appeared to be writing, although not in a language that he recognized.

"How old are you, Kaylin?"

She didn't look up at the sound of her name. Since he assumed that the name she had given him was false, he wasn't surprised. But there was no defiance in her now. "Thirteen."

The Tower doors flashed a brief blue before they began to roll open. Standing between them was an older Tha'alani man. His expression was grim and set, and the single defining characteristic of his race—the stalks that occupied a third of his forehead—were weaving stiffly. He bowed.

"Lord Grammayre."

"Garadin."

"I apologize for my delay. I headed to the cells first, and was redirected."

"It is a slightly unusual case." Lord Grammayre

nodded to the girl who occupied the central portion of the Tower.

"This is the subject?"

"Yes."

"She is...young."

"Yes. I'm sorry."

Garadin hesitated. "May I suggest an alternate agent?"

"I have considered it carefully, but I do not have the luxury of time. I must make a decision, and it must be made with minimal knowledge and minimal paper-work."

"As you wish, Lord Grammayre."

The subject in question looked up. Her lips thinned and her body locked as if she were in sudden rigor. But once again, she made no attempt to flee. Her eyes and nostrils widened as Garadin approached. "What," he asked the Lord of Hawks, "am I to search for? What am I to determine?"

"I wish to know who sent her to the Tower. I wish to know," he added, "where she received the...tattoos...on her arms and legs, and if possible, the extent to which she understands them." He hesitated, and then added, "I wish to know, in the limited context of an informational search, what your opinions of her state of mind are."

Garadin nodded his graying head. He turned, reached for the girl's face, and drew it closer. She struggled, but it was minimal and visceral; she probably couldn't control the response. Garadin's thumbs pushed her matted hair out of the way, exposing skin; he touched her forehead with his stalks.

She screamed.

* * *

It was the screaming that echoed in the Tower long after Garadin had released the girl. Garadin himself was cool and remote. He had not, of course, physically harmed her at all; the Lord of Hawks bore witness, and in any case, that was not the Tha'alani way. Grammayre lifted one hand, and the circle in which the girl sat began to glow.

"Please," he said to Garadin. "My office."

"She is thirteen years of age," Garadin said. His voice, like his expression, was shuttered and would remain so, in Lord Grammayre's experience. "She knew her mother. She has never met her father. She lives in the fiefs."

"The fiefs."

Garadin nodded. "The marks cover her inner arms and legs. They are also found across most of her back, to her knowledge."

"And the marks themselves?"

Garadin said clearly, "She doesn't understand what they mean, and she fears them. She does not know how she received them."

"Did you notice that they were glowing while you were conducting your investigation?"

"No."

"Ah. They were. They were visible through the cloth of at least her shirt."

Garadin nodded again, as if the information signified little to him either way. "What do you intend for her?"

"What does she want?"

"That is not in the purview of the requested information."

"I ask only for your opinions."

"Grammayre, she is young. She is too young to be a Hawk. Short of remanding her into Imperial custody or the custody of the Foundling Halls—if they would take her—I fail to see why it is relevant."

"She attempted to kill me."

"Yes. And she failed. She is cognizant of both facts. She expects to die here, and she will not fight that fate. Will you have her executed?"

"Execution requires the usual run through the Imperial Courts."

"She is not a citizen of the Empire, as you are well aware."

The Lord of the Hawks was silent for a long moment. "She is not," he finally said, "similar to any of the assassins sent against me in the past."

Garadin waited.

"I have arrived at my exalted position," Lord Grammayre said, grimacing, "by instinct."

"And that?"

"The marks she bears are dangerous," he said softly.

"And she has attempted to kill you. I fail to see the significant difficulty."

"She failed to use them to stop you. Given her reaction otherwise, had she been able to, on a purely instinctive level, she would have."

The stalk jabbed air. "And had she?" was the slightly pointed question.

"You would—I believe—have been safe in the Tower. But more to the point, my second instinctive reaction is that she might, under the right circumstances, prove useful to the Halls of Law."

"At thirteen?"

"No. But she will not be thirteen forever. What is your opinion, Garadin?"

Garadin exhaled heavily. "It is my opinion," he finally said, with the enunciated care of his people, "that had she the capability, she would still have failed to kill you. She has killed, but so, Grammayre, have you. It is neither what she wants nor what she enjoys, and inasmuch as humans loathe their own 'secret' failings, she loathes herself for many of the deaths she has caused.

"But it is *also* my opinion that she is unsuited to a certain type of duty. If you ask—or force—her to kill, you will lose her. She will lose what very, very little sense of self or hope she now possesses." Garadin stood and began to pace in front of the desk in a tight circle. "Give her something to lose and she will fight with everything she has to defend it. But it must be the right thing. And there is the matter of her age. If she will not always be thirteen, she is thirteen *now*."

Lord Grammayre nodded. "It will present challenges," he finally said. "I will, however, petition the Imperial Court for leeway."

"And not the Emperor directly?"

"I feel this is…a trivial matter, and the Emperor values his time highly."

Garadin raised a brow. "An indirect petition will take time."

"Indeed." Lord Grammayre was silent for long enough that the interview was almost certainly at an end, but before Garadin could leave, he asked one last question. "What is her name?"

"Kaylin Neya."

"That is not the name she was known by."

"No. But inasmuch as you wish to change her circumstances, I feel that it is now the name she *should* be known by. The choice is, of course, yours."

After Garadin left, Lord Grammayre lifted his head. "Records."

The mirror on his desk was in no way the equivalent of the stately, full-length oval mirror that adorned his Tower room, but it was perfectly functional. The mirror's reflection—which consisted mostly of sparsely lined shelves and a very clean desk surface—shivered and fell away; what was left was a gray, blank slate.

"External case file. Time, six months past. Bodies— distinguishing marks. Inner arms. Approximate ages of victims. Cause of death."

The mirror began to flash as Records disgorged the requested information.

Sergeant Marcus Kassan looked up from the paperwork that covered most of the visible surface of his desk, butting in teetering stacks against the mirror that was used for personal communication and research. It was, at the moment, in its favorite state: blank. Mirrors had one of two base states: gray and featureless, or reflective. Sergeant Kassan didn't find reflective all that useful. He knew what he looked like, and anyone who didn't like it didn't make it his problem more than once. For the most part, he didn't have to deal with outsiders. This was a good thing because most of the outsiders who had cause to visit the Halls of Law were human, and Marcus Kassan was not. He was the sole

Leontine employed by the Halls of Law, and the racial fur and large fangs often caused humans less familiar with Leontines some distress.

His office, and therefore his job, was confined to investigations. The front office, which was known colloquially as Missing Persons, was the public face of the Halls. He'd only visited twice, which was one damn time too many.

Looking up, he saw two of his Barrani corporals. They looked, to the practiced eye, grim. Marcus had that practice. "Teela?"

"Three more for the morgue," she said, voice flat. "The building, except for corpses, was abandoned. Someone set off an Arcane bomb."

"An Arcane bomb?"

Her partner, Tain, nodded.

"Where was the bomb created?"

"We've got three distinct magical signatures," Teela replied. "We've run them through Records. You're not going to like it."

"How much less could I like it?"

"They're all Arcanists."

He swore. In his mother tongue, it was an impressive roar of sound. The office staff, jaded as they were, barely blinked.

He grimaced. "The corpses?"

"Best guess? They're human." This wasn't as sarcastic as it sounded; the Barrani were immortal and their comprehension of mortal age was often poor.

"Best guess," he growled. His lips had risen, exposing his fangs.

"Oldest would be ten. Two girls, one boy. Youngest estimate, eight."

"All three of the dead were children?"

She nodded. "One was missing a hand."

The growl replaced words, and claws knocked piles of paper off the desk.

"The bodies are being conveyed to Red now. We're here to pick up some of the magical heavy lifters, and we'll head back to the location."

"This is the third in the past six months. The Emperor is *not* going to be happy."

Teela grimaced. "Probably happier than the victims," she said under her breath. She was Barrani. Her hearing was as good as a Leontine's; what the humans in the office wouldn't pick up, she knew the Sergeant would. She turned away, and then turned back. "I don't think this is the last of it. I don't think we'll have another few months before we discover another half-burned-down building."

"Why?"

"Hunter's Moon." She said the words calmly.

He heard them, by dint of experience, differently. "This has something to do with the Barrani?"

She was silent for a moment. Exhaling, she finally said, "It may. On no previous occasion was an Arcane bomb used. On no previous occasion was magic used in any significant way. The rest of the setup is consistent with the first two sites—but not the bomb."

Magic implied, to Teela, Barrani involvement. Barrani involvement, to the Sergeant, implied ulcers. The Hawks enforced Imperial Law, and in *theory,* everyone who lived in the Empire was subject to that Law. In *practice,* where there was no interracial involvement claimed, the caste courts for each individual race could—and sometimes did—take precedence. The Barrani caste court would surrender Imperial Criminals to the regular courts when the world ended and there were none of them left standing. If then.

"Humans are perfectly capable when it comes to magic."

"Yes, sir. But the moon…"

"Yes?"

"It's a *Hunter's Moon*," she repeated softly.

He frowned. "Before I accept the possibility of Barrani involvement, I need something other than a hunch." Behind the backs of the two Hawks he could clearly see the wings of an Aerian.

The Hawklord's presence in the office immediately changed the flow of daily office bitching and gossip, because it was very, very seldom that the Lord descended from his Tower. Usually, if he wanted to give or relay orders, he summoned you up to the heights. Which made this instantly suspicious; if he came to Marcus in the office, it meant he *wanted* everyone to hear what he had to say.

Marcus glared, briefly, at Teela, who lifted one brow in response.

"We came straight here, Sergeant. If word of the latest disaster has reached the Tower, he's listening in on the mirror transmissions."

Not unheard of, but not likely. Marcus rose. "Lord Grammayre," he said as the Barrani Hawks slowly peeled away from the desk. They'd listen, of course, but they could listen while they pretended to be busy a desk or two away. The humans in the office didn't have that much grace.

"Sergeant Kassan," Lord Grammayre replied. "Please, be seated. This is not an emergency."

The simple sentence should have put Marcus at ease. It didn't. He waited, hoping his ears tufts weren't standing on end.

The Hawklord flexed his wings and then settled them tightly down his back. "I have an admittedly unusual request to make of your department."

What a surprise. Marcus folded his arms across his chest and continued to stand. "At the moment, we're working to capacity," he said in as neutral a tone as a territorial Leontine could muster.

"I expect no less from the Hawks," was the smooth reply.

"The last time you had a nonemergency favor, you stuck us with a Court scribe."

"Yes. And you survived."

"So did he."

"As you say. He is not likely to request a repeat, and you are now personally owed a favor by a junior member of the human caste court. But that is not the subject I wish to discuss at the moment."

Marcus waited. A low growl had set up shop in the back of his throat; it was quiet because his jaws were clamped shut.

Lord Grammayre's eyes were a pale shade of ash-gray, which was good. "I assure you that the current unusual request will cause vastly less difficulty than the previous one."

Marcus, still waiting, said nothing. It was, however, a loud nothing.

The Hawklord raised a brow. "Sergeant."

Marcus knew damn well that he couldn't say no. But his yes lacked grace and finesse, and he liked to draw it out for as long as possible. "What unusual request do you want us to handle in the middle of a possible disaster?"

"Do you remember the unusual investigation we participated in in the fief known as Nightshade half a year ago?"

Marcus stilled. The office held its collective breath, except for Joey, who showed his usual situational awareness and continued to chatter in the background. "The ritual serial killings?"

"Yes."

It would have been impossible to forget them; there was exactly one occasion in which the Hawks had lent any of their expertise to an investigation that was theoretically outside the bounds of their—or the Empire's—jurisdiction.

"One of the possible intended victims appears to have survived. She is currently in custody."

"The investigation was closed."

"It was. It is not being reopened now."

"You think the girl knows something—"

"No. I know for a fact she knows nothing about either the cause or the killers."

"Then why is she relevant?"

"As I said, she is currently in custody. She arrived voluntarily," he added.

"So did your scribe, as I recall." Before the Hawklord could reply, Marcus lifted one padded hand in surrender. Unfortunately, his claws were extended. The Hawklord noticed, of course, but failed to react. Given that one of his reactions could have been the Sergeant's instant demotion, that was for the best.

"You want my Hawks to escort her home?"

"That would be difficult," was the bland reply. "Since, at the moment, she has none. She was born— and raised—in the fiefs."

Marcus's eyes narrowed. "Oh, no. No. Absolutely not."

"No?"

"If she was a possible victim, that would make her what, twelve? Thirteen?"

"Indeed."

"You are not turning the Hawks into a babysitting service. The scribe was bad enough—but at least he was legal."

"I do not require babysitting, as you put it. Nor do I require that the Hawks provide that service, since they are undoubtedly poorly trained for it."

"Good."

"She is," Lord Grammayre continued, "thirteen, not three. She is capable of rudimentary self-defense. I think it highly doubtful that she will expire behind your capable backs when you're not paying attention."

"So you do want babysitting."

The Hawklord grimaced. "I want your observational skills. She is, in my opinion, highly unusual, and she may prove to be of significant benefit to the department."

"At *thirteen?*"

"Perhaps. She is not, however, well educated."

Had he been human, Sergeant Kassan would have groaned.

"She will require lessons in basic skills."

"*How* basic?"

"She is not, in my opinion, capable of reading at anything but street-sign level. Nor does she have the requisite skill in secondary languages."

"The requisite skill...for what?"

"To serve the Law, Sergeant Kassan."

The silence had managed to catch even Joey's attention by this point. The only person who broke it was the only person who dared.

"Consider this a progressive experiment on the benefits of early education, Sergeant. It will not be an onerous task. I wish you to introduce her to the duties—and the training—of the Hawks. If she is entirely unsuitable, we will review the attempt and decide at that point how to proceed."

"Where—exactly—did you intend her to stay?"

"Stay?"

"I note you said she's currently without a permanent residence."

"Ah, yes. She has had some experience in scrounging a meager living from the streets for herself. Some funding will, of course, be allocated should you decide that she would be better situated in an apartment with a known address. And while I would love to continue this discussion, the Lords of Law meet with the Emperor in an hour, and I believe today's meeting will be somewhat...sensitive."

The Halls of Law had been designed by a handful of architects who worked under the watchful eye of the Emperor. It had always been his stated intent to have his city policed by its citizens, and the Halls had therefore been built with an eye to the varying physical needs of the races that comprised Elantra. To date, only one of the three Towers had made any attempt to fulfill Imperial Intent: the Hawks. Lord Grammayre was, of course, Aerian, and it was expected that his rise to power would see an influx of fellow Aerians. What was less expected was the advent of a Leontine and a dozen Barrani. For the most part, the people who policed the streets of Elantra were human.

But it wasn't the humans who had been sent to the holding cells to retrieve one of its newest occupants, and the lone Aerian who now stood outside a locked door frankly begrudged the trip. While the halls were wide enough and tall enough to accommodate Aerian wings, they were very enclosed; none of the Aerians considered the cells a suitable jail.

Clint, of the Camaraan Flight, was that Aerian. In the pay of the Hawks he generally performed two services: he served as a guard at the doors, and he patrolled the skies above the sprawl of the city itself. He did not serve as a jail escort for children. On the other hand, he liked his work, and refusing the order was about the same as quitting outright, but with the added discomfort of ire thrown in.

He wasn't entirely certain what to expect, and his hand hovered over the door ward for just a second before he pressed his palm against the glowing rune. The door slid open. No one stepped out.

Clint grimaced. Dropping one hand to a small club, he stepped into the open doorway, spreading his wings slightly as they rose in a defensive arch at his back. Not all of the drunks thrown into the cells were friendly or docile when they woke, which is why two guards were usually assigned to escort them out.

The cells weren't large. Since all they usually contained were a single man or woman in the throes of a hangover, this wasn't considered an issue, and Clint was accustomed to seeing belligerence, embarrassment, and guilt on the faces of those he'd been sent to show the doors. True, he'd also seen fury and homicidal rage, but those were rarer, and led not to the streets, but to a different set of holding cells.

The occupant of this particular cell didn't rage; she also didn't weep. She sat, looking much smaller than she should have on a cot that size, her knees tucked under her chin, her arms wrapped around her shins. Only her chin rose as he stepped into the doorway. He waited for her to say something; she waited for him to speak.

He blinked. "Follow me."

After a listless moment, she did exactly that.

There was no defiance in the girl. Shame or guilt he could have handled, but instead there was a quiet—and deep—sense of gray despair that permeated her every movement. She noted almost immediately that he was carrying a truncheon, but it didn't surprise her; he noticed that she did a brief visual scan in the usual places for more lethal weapons as well. But her gaze, when it touched him at all, went straight past his eyes, and therefore his facial expression, to a point above his shoulders.

Whatever she saw there wasn't making her any happier, and it didn't make her any more talkative. She didn't even ask where she was being led. Clint wasn't certain what the Hawklord had told her; normally he didn't care. But halfway through the halls that led—

slowly—toward the inner office, he found himself wishing he'd asked, because halfway to the office skirted the edge of the Aerie, the tallest part of the Halls of Law. Here, the Aerians practiced drill and formation when the weather was truly crappy.

Aerians weren't birthed with a natural suit of armor, and they didn't learn first flight wearing it; the Aerians who were accepted into the Halls of Law therefore had to build some muscle and acclimatize themselves to the more exhausting rigors of long flights sporting extra weight. Their first laden flights were often practiced in the Aerie of the Halls as well, as the shouting in the heights above attested.

The girl looked up as they began to cross the floor and froze, tilting her head back far enough Clint was half-certain he'd have to catch her before she toppled over backward. She didn't, and something about her expression robbed him of the curt tone that orders were usually given in. The width of her eyes implied something like awe, but the turn of her lips, pain; the dichotomy was striking.

Humans were, among mortals, a singularly frustrating race, because so many of the subtle signs of mood were missing. The biggest of these was the color of the eyes: they had one. That one conveyed exactly nothing. Aerians, Leontines, and the slightly disturbing Tha'alani had the range of normal emotional color shifts, as did the Barrani and the Dragons. Humans were slightly defective. As a small child, Clint had once asked if they were really only intelligent animals, because animals had eyes that were exactly as unchanging. His father had snickered. His mother had been *very* unamused.

But watching the girl, he felt moved to words. Words, sadly, weren't his strength, but he tried anyway. "You've never met Aerians before, have you?"

"Lord Grammayre," she said, breaking away instantly and flushing slightly, as if caught in a criminal activity. Or a childish one. "I met Lord Grammayre." Her gaze immediately hit floor and clung there as if rooted.

"Lord Grammayre asked that I escort you to meet our Sergeant," he finally said. It was absurd to be talking this carefully to a street thief from the fiefs. Who said she was thirteen? Clint wasn't certain he believed it now; that kind of wonder was usually reserved for people who could afford to be naive and optimistic. He'd flown low patrols over parts of the fiefs, and he couldn't believe that this girl was one of those.

"What's your name?" he asked, because thinking of her as "the girl" was beginning to irritate him.

"Kaylin," she replied, with enough hesitance it was clearly a lie. "Kaylin Neya."

"I'm Clint of Camaraan."

"Camaraan? You're not from the City?"

"Home is the Southern Stretch," he replied. When her expression didn't change, he added, "Yes, I'm from the City—the mountains to the south are considered the City's outer boundary by the Emperor. Camaraan is my flight. The closest thing you'd have to it is family, although family is too small a word."

She fell silent, as if regretting the brief outburst of genuine curiosity. This time, her expression stiffened into a neutral mask; it added years to her face.

"Come on," he told her. "Or we'll be late."

* * *

A Leontine in the very best of moods often sent humans scuttling for the nearest cover. Leontines were taller than the average human, broader, more heavily built—without any fat or extra padding—and entirely covered in fur. They also had obvious fangs, and when annoyed, very obvious claws. Marcus was not in the best of moods.

Aware of this, and aware of why, Caitlin lingered by his desk. In part she could do this with a minimum of effort because the papers he'd accidentally sent flying still covered large parts of the floor, and they were important—for a value of important that screamed bureaucracy—so she had a reason to be there.

Caitlin was officially his aide. She was unofficially *everyone's* aide, as long as people didn't attempt to take advantage of her better nature and her inability to tell them all to drop dead when they tried to shift a crapload of their work onto her shoulders. Marcus had no difficulty with the latter, so things worked out, a few complaints and bruises aside. She was quiet, pleasant, sane, and sympathetic; she was *also* extremely well organized.

She looked up from a pile of paper she was collating, and Marcus caught a glimpse of her expression before she once again returned to work. It was enough to make him consider, briefly, strangling the Hawklord.

Clint escorted the experiment in early education to the business end of Marcus's desk; he then took up position one step back and to the girl's left. And she *was* a girl. If someone had told Marcus she was ten, he'd have believed it. She approached his desk as if she expected to have her throat ripped out—and deserved it. But she didn't weep or snivel or plead; he gave her that.

"Name?" he said brusquely.

"Kaylin. Kaylin Neya."

"Kaylin. You will look at me when I'm speaking to you. The floor isn't that interesting, and it's never going to be a threat." He turned to the mirror and barked for Records. "Record. Kaylin Neya, first interview."

Her eyes had widened as she watched the shifting swirl of color in the mirror resolve itself into her reflection—absent the rest of the clutter of the office and the Sergeant himself.

"Age?"

"Thirteen."

"Residence?"

She frowned and remained silent.

"NFA?"

This changed her frown, rather than dissolving it. "NFA?"

"No fixed address."

She nodded.

Caitlin, who'd been watching the very brief and businesslike exchange, now leaned slightly over the desk. "Kaylin," she said quietly, "when was your last meal?"

"P-pardon?"

"When did you last eat?"

The girl was clearly not one of nature's liars. Caitlin's question was not the one she'd expected, and she had no ready answer to offer. Which, of course, was answer enough for Caitlin.

"Yes," Marcus said, before she could ask his permission to leave to find something for the girl to eat. He didn't watch her go; the girl did. He gave her ten seconds, which was nine more than anyone else in the office would have gotten, before he barked her name in staccato syllables. "*What* did I tell you?"

"I look at you when you're speaking to me, sir."

"Good. Does Caitlin look like me?"

She flinched. "No, sir."

"Was she talking to you?"

"No, sir."

"Then pay attention!"

It was raining. Marcus hated rain. He entered his *pridlea* squelching through puddles of the runoff from his fur. The fact that he'd spent more time than the walk home required in the streets only made it worse, but he'd needed the time to think.

Kayala, the first and oldest of his five wives, took one look at him and, with a resigned but heated growl, helped him to towel dry. This was an act of great love, as she loathed the smell of wet fur. When she considered him dry enough, she dragged him toward the hearth; Graylin had started the fire burning and dimmed the lights with a curt growl that meant she was considering ripping out their vital organs. Some days, it was a pity that lights didn't have vital organs; Marcus would have removed a few of them himself.

"Marcus, why are you bringing work home with you?"

Marcus stretched out across the fur-strewn floor. His three daughters took this as an invitation—although they took pretty much anything as an invitation—to leap all over him. They gnawed at his arms and legs while he tossed them in the air. Reesa joined them, but given Kayala's expression, none of his other wives did.

He spoke over and around the yowling and the high growls, some of which were his own. Children only noticed tone at this time of night, not content. "We were right," he said grimly.

"There was a third house."

He nodded. "Teela and Tain almost managed to track them down, but some word must have gone out. They arrived to corpses and—" he spit "—an Arcane bomb."

Kayala frowned. "Why does the Emperor not deem them illegal? The only purpose they seem to serve is to throw off the magical scent."

"Gods know. His gods," was the careful reply. "We'll sift through the wreckage tomorrow. Red's doing an autopsy, but we don't expect to uncover anything. Or not anything good."

"How many dead this time?"

"Three. Two girls, one boy."

His wife began to growl, and the children, piqued, looked up; she shifted the tone of that growl into something playful, hooding the fangs she hadn't consciously exposed as she did. Marcus's years with the Hawks had taught them both many things. One: that people were strange. Two: that people were, regardless of race, racial characteristics, or longevity, still people. Except perhaps the Immortals.

Children were children. He cuffed one of his on the ear and she rolled away, exposing her throat and mewling helplessly, which caused Kayala to laugh and sniff the air for threats. This period of supposed helplessness didn't last long; the kit was back on his chest in a matter of minutes, her small pads and insignificant claws batting Marcus's face.

"There's more," Kayala said, because she knew him well.

"You mean besides the meeting Grammayre had with the other Lords of Law and the Emperor?" He curbed his tongue; Kayala preferred "clean" language around the children. "We look like incompetents and fools. The Imperial Guard is probably snorting in contempt." —

"The Imperial Guard is tasked with protecting the Emperor," was the dismissive reply. *No one* could, in her opinion, come close to killing the Emperor, so it was a pathetically easy job. "Your job is to protect the helpless, the defenseless."

"And the stupid. Don't forget the stupid." Marcus dropped his face into his hands, dislodging Leanndra in the process. "We're not doing our job at the moment. And we're not the ones who are paying for our incompetence."

Kayala slid an arm around his shoulders and gently bit his ears. "And?"

He growled at her; she held tight. "Grammayre decided that today, in the middle of this disaster, we're going to start a—a *progressive* early-education experiment."

"Pardon?"

"He's given us a fiefling. A child."

Her frown was more serious. "Marcus." She nodded pointedly at the children, who didn't appear to be listening. "The Hawklord is not, and has never been, a fool. What does he want from this child?"

"I don't know. He wants her to tag along underfoot and learn the ropes. Now. Maybe he wants us to protect her."

"From what?"

"Kayala—I don't know. She's scrawny. Underfed. She can't read. She can speak, but so far, not much— which is the only blessing. She's marked the same way the children who died in the fiefs were. Says she's thirteen, but she could be ten. She came to the Hawklord from the fiefs, and he intends her to stay."

"Where?"

That set up another growl, and Marcus had more difficulty squelching this one. "You can mirror Caitlin tomorrow and ask. I don't believe Caitlin was happy with my response either, and she's taken the situation in hand."

"I'm sorry, dear," Caitlin said as she opened her door into a dim apartment. "But we really had very little notice. I've sent messages to a number of possible landlords, but at this time of day, I don't expect to hear back until tomorrow." She nonetheless swept Kaylin into her home. The girl was quiet, and had been quiet for most of the walk from the Halls of Law. The workday had been long—and given the events reported by Teela and Tain, that wasn't likely to change any time in the near future.

In spite of her apologetic words, the first thing Caitlin did was check her mirror. It was in its reflective state, but no aurora of color blurred the image; no one had called. With a sigh, she turned back to the girl, who remained standing, shoulders slumped, in the small vestibule that served as a hall.

Caitlin was one of the few Hawks who had no desire to walk the beat or be in the thick of things. She *liked* the office, she tolerated the office squabbles, and she organized the paperwork required by the Imperial Palace.

She knew who everyone was; everyone knew who she was. She understood which rules were firm and which could be nudged or broken; inasmuch as an office could be, it was like a home—a family home. Her own apartment was her retreat.

But, like the office, she opened it up at need.

She tapped the lights and they began to glow, revealing the clutter of her home. It wasn't that Caitlin was messy; she wasn't. But she couldn't quite bring herself to part from gifts or other small tokens of affections, no matter how tacky they actually were. Still, her kitchen was clean, and the mess itself was mostly free of dust and cobwebs. She walked into the kitchen and then walked back out when she realized she wasn't being followed. Biting back a sigh, she said, "Kaylin?"

The girl moved hesitantly through the hall, pausing briefly to glance at the two framed paintings on the walls nearest the door. Caitlin waited until Kaylin moved into the larger sitting room in which guests were entertained, if *entertain* was the right word. "Please, take a seat."

The girl took a dubious look at clothing that had weathered a few unwashed days and a night in the cells, and then at the very clean upholstery. "I can stand," she finally said. "Or I can sit on the floor. We didn't have a lot of furniture—" She stopped speaking, swallowed, and said nothing.

"If you must sit on the floor," Caitlin told her, "come sit in the kitchen. I'll be making dinner, and I'd be happy for the company." It wasn't, strictly speaking, completely true, but it was true enough for the moment. Had she been opposed to company, she wouldn't have invited the girl home.

She took the cutting board off its place on the wall, and slid two knives from their block. No, she would have come home to the comfort and safety of her own apartment while the child wandered the streets in the dark, waiting for the Halls of Law to once again open its doors. She grimaced.

Kaylin came into the kitchen. "Can I help with anything?"

Caitlin raised a brow in surprise. She started to say no, and then thought better of it. "Yes, if you're all right handling knives. I've broth in the pot on the stove. It's cool now. If you'll take over the potatoes and carrots, I'll start the stove going."

She did start the fire, and thought with a grimace that she should have reversed the tasks, as the girl was young enough to be truly flexible, and the stove hadn't gotten less finicky or more easy to load with the passage of years. But when she was done, she watched Kaylin work. The girl was slow, deliberate, and focused; it was as if the task itself deserved or demanded all of her attention. Or as if it distracted her from her surroundings; she didn't want to be here. Caitlin wasn't offended.

She thanked Kaylin for her help, told her where to find dishes, and left the soup to boil.

Part of the reason for the girl's discomfort came up over dinner. "Look, I appreciate you trying to help me find a place," she said in a tone of voice that didn't exactly ooze gratitude, "but you have to know something—I can't afford one. I've got next to no money."

"You'll need a place to stay, dear."

Kaylin shrugged. "I'll find a place to stay."

"On this side of the river?"

The girl fell silent. She'd eaten a large meal and was still picking at the bread, but her gaze was on that unfocused elsewhere. "No," she finally said, the single word very low. "Probably one of the fiefs."

"Oh? Which one?"

She shrugged. "Does it matter?" The words were laced with enough bitterness that they added years to her.

"If I understood Lord Grammayre correctly, you're to work in some capacity for the Hawks."

Kaylin was silent.

"To do that, you'll need to live in the City. The Law doesn't extend—"

"To the fiefs? I know. Believe that I know."

Silence. Caitlin didn't let it get uncomfortable. "Were you born in the fiefs?"

"Yes. In Nightshade."

"You've never lived in the City."

"No—we had no way of getting here, and no way of affording it even if we did."

Since the fiefs were a footbridge away from the rest of the City, getting here, as Kaylin put it, wasn't the problem. But living here, with no job and no family, would be. "Do you want to go back?"

Kaylin stared at her as if she'd grown an extra head, which Caitlin assumed meant no. "No," she said, voice low. "But I have no idea what to do *here*." She threw one arm wide as if to take in the whole city.

"If I know the Sergeant, he'll find something. I won't guarantee that you'll like it," she added. "But he won't let you starve while you're working for him. He *is* a bit intimidating when you first meet him." She expected Kaylin to either agree or declare her Total Lack of Fear, but the girl did neither. She was watchful. "He's Leontine. Have you met a Leontine before?"

"No. Some Barrani, but mostly just humans."

"You won't see a lot of Leontines in the rest of Elantra, either. They tend to stay in the Leontine Quarter. You probably noticed his fangs."

Kaylin gave a vigorous nod.

"He doesn't use them except in exceptional circumstances. You will *never* be an exceptional circumstance. He does, on the other hand, forget about his claws. If you ever see the surface of his desk—and there's a chance you won't for a couple of months—it's heavily gouged. You said you've met Barrani?"

"Yes."

And clearly, she wasn't fond of the experience. "You'll have noticed their eyes change color depending on their mood?"

"Blue is death."

"Good. In Leontines, *red* is death. Gold is good. Orange is pushing your luck. Also, if he looks like he's gained thirty pounds in a minute? That's just his fur, but it's bad. If you've done something to cause a shift in eye color the best thing you can do is to expose your throat. Like this," she added, lifting her chin.

Kaylin's brow rippled toward the bridge of her nose in disbelief. "You said—"

"That he won't use his fangs, yes. But exposing your throat is a way of acknowledging—in Leontine terms—that *he's* the boss."

"Oh. And he won't try to tear it out?"

"He hasn't yet. What else is there? The Aerians mostly live in the Southern Stretch, but one or two do make their homes in the City itself—it requires more space and ceiling height than most of the buildings have."

"The Barrani?"

"They also live in the City. Some make their home in the High Halls, which is where the Barrani caste court reigns. There is no Barrani Quarter; there is no Aerian Quarter. Only the Leontines and the Tha'alani have a separate Quarter, but in the case of the Leontines, there are no walls to mark it." She hesitated again, and decided that she'd asked enough questions for the evening.

"Let me get some blankets. I'm sorry," she added, "but I don't have an extra bed. I've got the couch here, and bedrolls if you'd prefer the floor. I'm an early riser," she added a little apologetically, "so I might wake you."

"You're sure?"

"Sure?"

"It's okay for me to stay here?"

"I'm sure. It's a great deal safer than the streets at night."

"Here? There aren't even any Ferals. There's probably not much that can hurt me." She rose.

"I'm *sure*, dear. If you can sleep in the street, that's fine—but I won't be able to sleep knowing I sent you there. I'm not doing this for your sake, I'm doing it for my own. Can you live with that?"

Kaylin nodded. Caitlin brought her both blankets and bedroll and was not at all surprised that the girl chose to sleep on the floor.

She was slightly surprised that Kaylin was already awake in the morning. She'd folded the blankets and rolled up the bedroll and left them neatly beside one wall, and she sat on the floor, waiting. She was dressed. Dear gods.

Caitlin turned and began to root through her closet; she came up with a shirt and a set of trousers that she thought would definitely *need* a belt. But belts, she did have, and the clothing had the benefit of being clean and in good repair.

She handed these to Kaylin, who looked set to object—politely. "You can give them back when your own clothes are clean, but you cannot continue to go in to work in the clothing you're wearing now. It needs mending, and it needs patching as well, and for the next week or two, I won't have time to do either. Can you?"

"...a little."

"Good. I imagine you have no needles, no thread, and no scraps, to go along with the lack of a roof over your head. The needles, thread, and scraps I can supply now, and we're working on the problem of a roof."

"I could sleep in the cells at night," she offered.

"Absolutely not."

"They're warm, and they're safe."

"You will sleep in the cells," she replied firmly, "over my dead body."

They made it most of the way to the office before Kaylin spoke again, and it was in a much quieter voice. "Caitlin, what does he want from me?"

"Who, dear? Marcus?" Mostly, he wanted her gone, but Caitlin was not about to say this out loud.

"The Hawklord."

She started to answer—Caitlin could say a lot of words that meant precisely nothing in measured, even tones and very erudite words—and stopped herself. "I

don't know. I know the Sergeant far better than I know
Lord Grammayre, so anything I say here will be at best
a guess. I could be entirely wrong."

"What's your guess?"

"I think he wants you to learn about the Hawks because he thinks something about the Hawks will mean
something to you. Something more than just a job and
a roof over your head, although there is absolutely nothing wrong with those two things."

The girl was silent for half a block. "Why?"

"Why, dear?"

"Why do you think he thinks that?"

"It's just a hunch," was her quiet reply.

The arrival at the doors was poorly timed; they
weren't the only people who were on their way in, and
although it was early, they were made to wait. This in
itself wasn't unfortunate, but the reason they were made
to wait was: some of the Barrani Hawks were carrying
stretchers into the building. They'd make their way to
the morgue, where Red would be waiting to examine
them; Caitlin was pretty sure she knew which bodies
lay beneath the heavy sheeting that covered the stretchers.

She turned protectively to Kaylin, who watched in
silence. After a moment, Caitlin said, "You've seen
corpses before."

Kaylin, still watching as the Barrani conveyed the
dead up the stairs and through the open door, nodded
bleakly. "I thought it would be different here, across
the bridge." The whole of her expression was simulta-
neously hard and fragile, as if it were porcelain. "What
did they do?"

"Pardon?"

"Why did they kill them?"

A moment went by as Caitlin sorted through the words to figure out what they were actually asking. When she did, her brows rose into her hairline. "The Barrani did *not* kill them," she told the girl, a little more vehemently than she'd intended.

Kaylin glanced at Caitlin, and to her surprise, Caitlin caught the girl by her shoulders and pulled her around. "Kaylin, those Barrani are Hawks. They patrol the streets of the City in an attempt to enforce the Emperor's Laws. One of those laws prohibits murder, and the courts are especially harsh when the victims are children. The Hawks didn't kill whoever they're taking to the morgue—someone else did.

"And we are going to find out who it was."

"And then what?" was the bitter reply.

"And then he'll be brought to justice. Or she," Caitlin added, to be fair.

"Justice." The girl almost spit. The bodies disappeared through the open door as she watched. "I've seen justice like this all my life. I thought it would be different—"

Caitlin shook her. "You don't know what it's like. You haven't lived here for more than a day—at best. Don't judge. Watch. Learn. Do you want to see where the bodies are going, and why?"

Kaylin's eyes were wide, but she was almost mute; she managed a nod. Feeling slightly ashamed of her temper, Caitlin let go of the girl's arms, and instead caught her by one hand and marched her to the doors.

Clint and Navarre were on duty. They lowered their weapons to bar entrance, because it was actually part of their job; today it was not a part of their job Caitlin had any patience with. She didn't shout or raise her voice, however; she merely gave them a pointed look at her hand, and the child attached to it. The weapons rose sheepishly, although Clint looked faintly concerned.

"Is everything all right?" he asked. But he asked Kaylin, not Caitlin.

"She saw the bodies arrive," Caitlin replied, because it was absolutely clear to her that Kaylin wouldn't.

Clint's normally friendly face lost much of its warmth.

"We're heading to the morgue," Caitlin added.

The morgue was run by a man known to the Hawks as Red. It wasn't his legal name, but he had a severe dislike for that—why, Caitlin honestly didn't know—and was therefore called Red by anyone who wanted him to do any work for them again, ever. Except for his dislike of his name, he was an even-tempered, serious man, and like most of the Hawks, spent far too many hours at work when the situation demanded it.

Kaylin entered the room behind Caitlin and stopped just inside the doorway. The bodies had already been moved from stretchers to tables, although they remained covered. Red was speaking in low tones to the Barrani Hawks who'd stayed behind. There were two. He looked up as Caitlin cleared her throat. So did the Barrani.

"Caitlin?" Red said as he headed toward her. "What brings you here?"

Caitlin smiled and nodded toward Kaylin. "Kaylin, this is Red. Red, this is Kaylin."

Red held out a hand, which Kaylin immediately took.

"Pleased to meet you." He turned to Caitlin again and raised a brow.

"Kaylin, by request of Lord Grammayre, is to spend some time in the company of the Hawks."

"She's a bit young to be a recruit, isn't she?" was his dubious reply.

"She is."

"And possibly a bit young to see the inside of a working morgue."

"That, I doubt." She looked toward Kaylin. "Do you want to leave?"

Kaylin frowned, but shook her head. "What is this place?"

"The morgue."

"Yes, I heard that—I mean, what's it for?"

Red shrugged. "This is where the dead are brought, but only in two cases. If a person has died in suspicious circumstances, their body is brought here, where they're examined for traces of magic and chemical interference. If we find either, we log it as a murder, and the Hawks are sent to investigate."

"And these?" She looked at the three covered corpses.

He was silent for a long moment. "These," he finally said, "there's no question. They were murdered. We're not looking for proof of a murder versus natural causes, we're looking for anything about the death itself that might give us information about the killers."

Kaylin glanced pointedly at the two Barrani who were lounging—there really wasn't another word for it—by the far wall, looking bored. One of them peeled herself off the wall as she noticed the look Kaylin was giving them. She sauntered over to Red. Her eyes were a shade of green that had a lot of blue in it, but at the moment, given the surroundings, that was fair.

The younger girl stood her ground, but she bent into her knees and her hands reached for air before she realized she wasn't actually armed. Teela raised a dark brow.

"You don't have daggers," she said conversationally. "And even if you did, you'd be committing suicide if you drew one on me."

Kaylin said nothing.

"You think we killed them," was Teela's flat comment.

"And you didn't?"

Red looked slightly shocked.

"As it happens, no, we didn't." She lifted a brow in Caitlin's direction; Caitlin, however, had her expression on lockdown. "Not that we've got anything against a little violence, but we like a bit of fight." Her smile was distinctly unfriendly.

Kaylin's was entirely absent. After a minute, she looked at Red and said, clearly, "You believe them?"

Tain—and it was Tain—whistled. "You are not here to make any friends, are you?"

Red, however, raised both his hands and said, "Of course I believe them!"

"Why?"

Even Teela looked surprised.

"I've seen Barrani on the streets for most of my life," Kaylin told him. "They could do more damage than Ferals."

"Ferals?" Teela frowned. Oddly enough, the frown broke the tension that had been growing in her expression. "Wait, you grew up in the fiefs?"

"I did." After a small pause, she added, "Night-shade."

"Nightshade," was the cool reply, "is outcaste."

Kaylin's expression didn't change.

Looking over Kaylin's head, Teela met Caitlin's steady gaze. "You're *certain* the Hawklord insisted that she learn the ropes?"

"You were there, Teela. You heard every word, and Barrani memory is pretty much perfect."

"Yes, but mortal memory isn't," Teela replied, grinning. "All right, we'll take her."

"P-pardon?"

"You heard me. Mortal hearing is inferior, but not *that* inferior."

"I'm not certain that's what Lord Grammayre had in mind," Caitlin said stiffly.

"He probably doesn't know what he had in mind, either. Look, she doesn't even know what an outcaste is. She's certainly got no clue about what the Hawks do—and what they don't, which is more germane at the moment. I'm guessing she has very rudimentary fighting skills, and she can probably handle herself if things get ugly."

"Teela, may I point out that she's underage?"

Teela shrugged as if to say it was irrelevant. From a Barrani view, the difference between thirteen and eighteen was probably inconsequential, but then again, the Barrani didn't write the laws. "We're not asking her to fight. We're not asking her to take statements. We're not asking her to deliver the bad news to parents or the families of the deceased. We're not asking her to do anything, Caitlin, except hang around and observe.

"We can keep her alive," she added.

"And what protects her from you?"

"Ironjaw."

Caitlin cleared her throat. "Please keep in mind that we have—"

"Ironjaw is what the Sergeant is called behind his back," Tain told Kaylin. "I'm Tain," he added. "And this is Teela. How strong is your stomach?"

"Depends. What am I eating?"

"Oh, not eating," was the slightly evil reply. "Watching."

"Tain," Red began. The door ward's high-pitched scree saved him from giving the rest of the possible lecture.

"Mage is here," Teela told Caitlin. "We're up. If you want to head back to the office to prevent the use of reports as kitty litter, we'll keep an eye on Kaylin."

Kaylin looked close to panic.

"...unless she's too afraid to watch."

"Teela," Caitlin said, "be nice, dear."

"I'm not afraid," was the defiant—and expected—reply. Caitlin sighed and handed over the reins. "I'll expect her back at my desk at closing," she warned the two Barrani.

"We'll have her there. In one piece, even."

Kaylin stayed as close to Red as she could without hiding behind him. She didn't trust the Barrani, but she was already kicking herself—mentally—for antagonizing them. She would *never* have done anything that stupid in Nightshade. But Nightshade was gone. She would never go back there, not alive—and dead, she wouldn't care, because she wouldn't feel a thing.

She looked around the room. It was practically

empty; there was one stool, unoccupied, against a wall; there was one long counter with a couple of jars pushed back against the wall beneath some cupboards. There was a heavy basin in the center of the counter, and a couple of buckets to one side on the floor. And there were tables. A lot of tables. Across from the cupboards was the longest mirror Kaylin had ever seen in her life; it stretched from one end of the wall to the other. It had no frame to speak of, which was also something she'd never seen.

In it, she watched the two Barrani. Teela. Tain. They had the long, dark hair of Barrani everywhere, and they also had the flawless skin, the perfect beauty, that made them seem so dangerously aloof. Except when Tain had smiled, she'd noticed that one of his teeth was chipped. It made her vindictively happy for just a moment, but that kind of happiness never lasted.

Case in point: the doors opened and an older man stepped into the room. His hair was that streaked dark that people called gray, and his eyes were a very cool blue; he had a beard. He was wearing a dress, several rings, and an expression that could have frozen water. It thawed slightly when Red approached.

"Ceridath Morlanne," the man said, "from the Imperial Order of Mages. I was informed that my services were *urgently* required." He glanced at the bodies.

Red nodded. "It's not pretty," he added, "but we won't start our work until yours is done."

"Very well. Let's get to work on this, shall we?" He approached the first of the blanketed corpses. "You wish me to scan all three?"

"Yes. Records," he added, looking over his shoulder at, as far as Kaylin could tell, his own reflection. She was wrong, and she understood the minute she also looked at his reflection just how wrong. The mirror—like the small one on the Sergeant's desk—began to glow. The light it emitted was an ugly, harsh blue—it washed everything out, made it seem almost gray. She didn't like it.

"Recording." She liked the voice even less. But Red didn't seem alarmed by either light or voice, although his expression was now more focused, more intent.

The Barrani also looked less bored. It didn't make them look less dangerous.

The mage, who no one had bothered to introduce, glanced at both the Barrani and Kaylin; he frowned at Kaylin, but said nothing. Red motioned to Kaylin, and Kaylin moved away from the mage and the table in front of which he was standing.

The mage pulled the blanket back, and Red took it out of his hands.

On the slab was a girl's body. She was maybe ten years old.

Kaylin couldn't breathe. Didn't want to. She was holding on to air with two fists and clenched jaws. The girl was missing one eye. Her face was a patchwork of crossed cuts, some deeper than others; the incisions ran the length of her jaw and her throat. She was clothed, but not well, and the clothing itself had also been cut and torn. Her arm—one of her arms—was burned.

Kaylin didn't want to look; she couldn't look away. Mute, silent, she watched as the mage began to gesture. The gestures were open-palmed and slow.

Teela sidled over to where she stood. Bending close

enough that her hair brushed the side of Kaylin's face, she said, "Have you seen much magic before?"

Swallowing, Kaylin shook her head.

"Do you know what he's doing?"

She shook her head again. No. But even as she did, she felt her arms and her legs begin to tingle, and her eyes widened as she stared at the mage's back. She wore—she *always* wore—long sleeves. If she'd been alone, she would have opened the wrist-cuffs and peeled the sleeves back to her elbows so she could look at the marks that adorned all of the skin on her inner arms. She wasn't.

But the tingling grew worse as the mage continued to move; it passed from something on the edge of pleasant to something on the edge of painful when he began to speak. She drew breath because she had to breathe, and the pain got worse, as if breathing at all had reminded it she was here.

And then, as her hair began to stand on end—she would have sworn it was standing on end—she saw the girl's corpse begin to glow. She cursed under her breath.

"Kaylin?" Teela whispered, voice tickling her ear. She was way too damn close, and Kaylin wanted to elbow her—sharply—out of the way. But the magic was worse than the fact that a Barrani was standing over her shoulder.

"What—what is he doing to her?" She managed to force the words between her teeth.

"He's a mage. An Imperial mage, meaning he works for the Eternal Emperor, however indirectly." She paused, and then added, "Magic can't bring the dead back to life, if that's what's bothering you. It can't cause them more pain, they're already dead. Nothing will ever hurt them again."

She heard the words as if at a great distance—and as if they came from someone else's mouth, because she could never have imagined they could have come from a *Barrani*. Her arms and legs ached, and her borrowed shirt felt as if it were rubbing the skin off the back of her neck. She couldn't tell them that, of course. She *never* talked about the marks.

So she concentrated, instead, on the mage, and the ravaged, small body beneath his hands. For a long moment, nothing changed. The girl was still dead, the gaping wounds no longer bleeding. Her eyes had been closed by whoever had brought her here, or maybe Red himself, because he seemed kind enough to actually care about the dead.

The mage turned to Red, sweat beading his forehead. "Records—there is no evidence of any trace of magic within or upon the corpse. In the considered opinion of Ceridath Morlanne, the cause of death was not magical in nature, although it is possible that the physical injuries were caused indirectly by magical devices."

Kaylin sucked in air so sharply it should have cut her mouth.

"Hold a moment." Teela spoke in a crisp, clear voice that was aimed over Kaylin's head at the mage. "Do not drop the scan." She'd never looked friendly, but at this moment, she sounded much more like the Barrani that Kaylin expected: the implied *or I will kill you* hung, unsaid, in the air.

Turning to Kaylin, she said, "Tell me what you see." The tone of voice had softened, but not by much. It didn't matter. From out of the closed eyelids of the dead girl, rising as if they were made of golden smoke, were the shapes and forms of something that reminded Kaylin very much of the hidden marks that adorned her skin.

"Kaylin," Teela said again, her voice sharper and harder.

Kaylin shook herself and pointed.

"No, *describe* it."

"I must object," the mage said coldly. "Is the Corporal accusing me of lying?"

Red was staring at Teela. It was, however, Tain who answered. "Not yet," he said in a voice as cold as the mage's. "Although, if there's anything you'd like to say in your own defense, now would perhaps be advisable." As the mage lifted his chin, Tain reached out and touched the surface of the mirror. "Lord Grammayre, code three. Red?"

The coroner nodded slowly, and there was a sharp *snap* of sound that came from the doors. "Ceridath?"

The mage was furious, and the fury began to unfold in a series of very polite, very layered threats. Kaylin listened with half an ear, but there weren't any interesting or useful words there, and she still had Teela standing over her shoulder like a very bad nightmare.

"There are…runes…" Kaylin finally said. "They're gold, and sort of smoky, not solid. They're floating *right above her eyes,* Teela."

"Not for me, they're not. Red, Tain?"

Tain shook his head. Red, however, said, "I can't see anything out of the ordinary for a morgue."

Ceridath now turned to Kaylin. "Are you claiming," he said with obvious disbelief, "to be a *mage?*"

She shook her head.

"Have you had *any* experience in the Imperial Halls, any tutoring *whatsoever?*"

"No."

"Red," the mage said, "I have no idea when the Hawks began to employ children, but this one is clearly lying."

The coroner looked exceptionally uncomfortable. "Kaylin, if this is a game of some sort, stop playing it now. It's already going to cause more trouble than you can imagine with the Imperial Order, and we rely on the Imperial Order for most of the magical work the Halls require."

"I don't think she's playing a game," Teela said. "But if she is, she'll have the Hawklord to deal with. Or the Sergeant. I wouldn't personally have called it a code three, Tain."

He shrugged and then grinned. "I was bored."

"Let this be a lesson to you," Teela told Kaylin under her breath. "There's nothing more dangerous and unpredictable than a bored immortal—we've had several centuries to perfect the art."

"What's a code three?"

"No one can enter or leave this room except the Hawklord and anyone he chooses to bring with him."

"That's bad?"

"You try keeping an angry mage contained in a room he doesn't want to stay in. It gets ugly real fast."

"You've tried?"

"I've got several centuries on you. Yeah, I've tried."

"Did it work?"

"I'm still here."

"What do you think he's going to do?"

"Him? Probably nothing." She glanced at Kaylin's empty hands. "We're going to need to get you some kind of dagger. That grasping at empty air is going to get old really fast. If things start to look tricky, stand behind me. Directly behind me," she added. "Not somewhere near the wall."

The mage now drew himself up to his full height; his cheeks were red. "Reginald," he said in a cold, clear voice. "The Imperial Order will hear about this blatant lack of respect for one of its senior members."

Teela whistled under her breath. "Pretend you didn't hear that name."

"It's not up to me," was the cold reply. "It's up to Lord Grammayre."

"Very well. I will play out this charade with as much patience as a busy mage can muster. But I think the scans of the other two corpses are now on permanent hold."

Kaylin wasn't sure what to expect. To her eyes, both Tain and Teela looked…bored. They certainly didn't seem to consider the robed man a threat. She knew better than to trust them, but…Red and Caitlin weren't afraid of them. It would take a much greater depth of suspicion than Kaylin had ever possessed to be suspicious of Caitlin, because even in the fiefs, people like Caitlin existed.

The door opened. In its frame stood the man who ruled the Hawks. His gaze narrowed the minute it touched Kaylin, who resisted the urge to hide behind Teela.

"Lord Grammayre," Ceridath began.

The Hawklord lifted one hand. "Ceridath," he said.

His voice was as smooth as the surface of the mirror, and he offered the mage a very unusual bow. This seemed to mollify the mage somewhat.

"Red, you summoned me?"

"I did," Tain said before Red could speak.

"I...see. There was of a course a very good reason for the summons."

Tain nodded, unfazed by the sudden ice in the Hawklord's voice. "The Imperial mage—on record—stated uncategorically that there was no magic to be found on the first of the corpses he examined."

"That was not the unexpected result," the Hawklord replied. "Since none of the other victims have shown any signs of magical abuse."

Tain nodded. "We have, however, done the scans under the auspices of a single mage."

"Corporal, Ceridath is *not* the only mage who has been part of the investigation of this particular ring."

"No, indeed. He is one of three."

"Corporal—"

"Your Corporal is accusing me of falsifying my reports. Of, essentially, lying," Ceridath said.

Lord Grammayre raised one hand to his forehead, where he pinched the bridge of his nose. "On what grounds, Corporal?" he demanded in a tone that made clear the answer had better be bloody good.

The answer, sadly, was now shuffling slightly behind Teela in spite of her earlier intentions. She did not consider herself bloody good evidence of anything.

"The latest addition to the Hawks," Tain replied.

Lord Grammayre turned to Kaylin and she froze on the spot. "Kaylin," he said quietly, "come here immediately." He glanced at the open door and it closed. He hadn't spoken a word.

"Grammayre, I warn you—" Ceridath began.

The Hawklord ignored him. He waited for Kaylin, and Kaylin—with an unexpected shove between the shoulder blades, stumbled more or less in the right direction. When she reached him, he lifted his wings, stretching them, for a moment, to their full span. Flight feathers longer than her arm cut light and cast shadow as they began to fold—slowly—over her upturned face.

She startled, and he reached out and caught her shoulders, but his grip was gentle and steadying as his wings came down around them both.

"What," he said quietly, in this privacy of wings and his voice, "did you see?"

She told him.

"You are certain?"

"I don't know—I've never seen anything like it before, and I don't understand what it means—"

"Nor is your understanding required. But this is very, very unfortunate news. Go to Teela when I release you. Stay behind her, should things become difficult."

It was almost exactly what Teela had said. "Wait."

His wings stopped moving. "Yes?"

"The Barrani—do you trust them?"

"Yes."

"And you're certain they didn't kill these children?"

His eyes widened in surprise, and then they narrowed in something that looked unpleasantly like pity. "Yes, Kaylin. If I can be certain of nothing else about them, I'm certain of that." He lifted his wings and folded them once again behind his back. "Ceridath," he said. "If you have anything of import that you wish to tell us, now is the time."

Ceridath's eyes widened enough they were almost entirely round. "You cannot be serious."

"I can. Mirror," he added, "Magister Dreury of the Imperial Order of Mages."

The mirror went gray. It stayed gray for at least five minutes, and judging from the expression on Red's face, the delay was unusual. But the Hawklord stood as if he could wait all day—or year. When the mirror at last lost the flat, impenetrable gray, it opened into what looked like a very, very rich man's office. There were shelves in the background, and books lined every single one of them; there were glass cabinets that reflected a light whose source she couldn't see.

But in the centre of the mirror was a man who sat behind a large, almost shiny, desk. Unlike the desk of the Hawks's Sergeant, this one had a visible surface; it was, in fact, all surface.

"Lord Grammayre," the man said, frowning. "My apologies for the delay."

The Hawklord inclined his head and waited while the man behind the desk surveyed the room. At least that's what Kaylin assumed he was doing. "Ceridath," he said, as if to confirm her suspicion.

"Lord Dreury," Ceridath replied, executing a much more human bow.

"Is there some difficulty, Lord Grammayre?"

"There is a possible misunderstanding," the Hawk-lord replied. "And I require a member of the Imperial Order to attend us."

"You have one."

"Indeed. I would like a second opinion. I would further request that that second opinion come from a mage who does not normally work within the Halls of Law, and who is senior enough to make no mistakes—at all."

Lord Dreury's frown deepened. He wasn't a young man, so the frown only shifted the lines of his face, rather than adding any. He began to speak, but this time, Kaylin didn't understand a word he was saying.

Nor did she understand a single word of the Hawklord's reply, but clearly the shift in language wasn't a sign that either man was happy. She glanced at Teela, Tain, and Red—who all appeared to be able to follow what was actually being said. As did Lord Dreury.

It wasn't short. The syllables sounded soft and extended, but the tones in which they were spoken implied the exact opposite. Ten minutes passed. Fifteen. Teela's back looked a lot less impressive than it had when anyone had been paying attention to her.

She glanced at the exposed body that lay on the table, and the conversation—or argument—faded into the background. Without thinking, she walked to the corpse of the young girl whose closed eyes had revealed golden words—words that Kaylin couldn't read. Red noticed when she reached the body and moved toward her, although his gaze was still riveted on the mirror and the increasingly chilly voice of the man it contained.

Kaylin reached for the sheet that had covered the girl's body and face. She took care not to touch anything besides the blanket. Starting at the girl's feet—at her shoeless feet, at the bruised ring around her right ankle—she set one edge of the blanket down, taking care to cover everything. The blanket was heavier than the ones Kaylin was used to, but she'd often had to do without.

She knew what she was doing was stupid and pointless. Teela was right: the girl was dead. Nothing could be done to change that, and nothing worse could happen to her: she was beyond pain or fear.

But pointless or no, she did it anyway: she pulled the blanket up the dead girl's body, covering her torn and bloody clothing. Only when it reached her chin did she stop. She hesitated for a moment, and then tucked the edge of the blanket under the girl's chin, as if she were sleeping, or ever would again.

Red placed a hand on her shoulder, and she startled and turned, pulling away, her hands reaching for air again. He lifted his hand—both hands—in the air, palms toward her in an exaggerated gesture of surrender, before he drew away from Lord Grammayre and the mage.

"You can't leave yet," he told her quietly. "But when you can—"

"When'll that be?"

"Probably not more than a couple of hours." He grimaced. "I don't know what you did, but it's going to be costly if you're wrong." Shaking his head, he added, "This isn't the place for you. The morgue, I mean. In a couple of weeks, come back, I'll show you what I do. But this'll be hard, even for me. It's not something you should have to see."

"Why?"

He frowned. Reaching past her, he unfolded the blanket's upper edge and pulled it over the girl's face. "This doesn't bother you?"

"I've seen worse," she replied, meaning it. She bit

her lip and turned away, not from the corpse, but from his gaze. "Who killed them?"

"We don't know. But if what you said was true, we'll be a lot closer to getting an answer." He hesitated, and then said, "These aren't the first victims."

"There are more?" It wasn't the stupidest question she'd asked in her life, but it was close. She turned away. Turned back. "Are they all this young?"

"Or younger, yes."

"But—but *why?* Why are they doing this?"

"Because they want to and they can, for now."

"Why here?"

He frowned. "Pardon?"

"Why here, on this side of the river? I thought everything like this happened across the bridge. In the fiefs," she added with bewildered bitterness.

"Kaylin, people live on either side of the bridge. And people are people, no matter where they live, and no matter how much they have. Some are Caitlin—they give what they can, and they keep the rest of us in line. Some are…not."

"But—but on the other side of the river, no one *cares.*"

"Really?"

She stared at him.

"No one cares? No one's bothered? No one's afraid?"

"Of course people are afraid! We have no one there but the fieflord—and if the fieflord takes you or sells you, that's it, that's the only law! There are—there are supposed to be—laws *here.* There are supposed to be Hawks and Swords, and they're supposed to keep people *safe.* People like her," she added.

He stared at her for a minute, and she thought if he could have opened the doors, he would have thrown her out. But when he spoke, his voice was calm and quiet. "Who do you think those Hawks and Swords are?" he asked softly. "Do you think they're perfect, Kaylin? Do you think they have flawless days without a single error, ever? Do you think they have eyes in the back and the sides of their heads?

"Do you think they're not afraid?" He turned to the corpse. "This is the price of failure, yes. We don't pay it. The most we can do—and what we always try to do—is to make sure it doesn't happen again the same way. But we're human—"

Teela cleared her throat loudly.

Red frowned. "We're human," he repeated. "We're never going to be perfect. Best we can do is learn from our mistakes, and keep trying."

She stared at him.

"Perhaps," Lord Grammayre said in distinctly chilly and entirely comprehensible words, "this philosophical discussion about the nature of humanity and the purpose of the Hawks could wait for a more suitable time?"

Red flushed. Kaylin looked at her feet.

Three hours later, the doors were finally opened to admit another stranger in dark robes. He was older than Ceridath, and he wore a very thick gold chain, from which an equally thick gold medallion hung. He didn't look friendly—but at this point, no one in the room did. His beard was long and thin at the ends, and his hair was sparse, but what made him instantly unusual were two things: the color of his eyes and the way both of the Barrani lost any look of boredom.

His eyes were almost the same gold that the Sergeant's had been. But he was definitely *not* covered in fur and claws or fangs.

"Lord Grammayre," he said. "Ceridath."

Ceridath bowed.

"The Magister evinced some concern at your request, Lord Grammayre. It is highly unusual, and it was not done through the proper—and more germane, discreet—channels."

"I did not think we had the luxury of time. Forgive me," he added. "I did not realize they would appoint such an important member to the task."

"Ah. They did not. I am fond of my Imperial Order, and when I realized that the Magister was…flustered… I undertook the task on my own recognizance. Three candidates were proposed, but I felt, at this juncture, that absolute certainty—swift certainty—was essential." He spoke to no one but Lord Grammayre; everyone else might have been furniture. Or worse.

"I do not, however, have all day. Please, proceed."

Red, still invisible, walked over to the body that he had just covered. He removed the blanket himself.

"Ceridath, you were responsible for the scan?"

"Yes, Lord."

"And the analysis?"

"Mine."

"Very well. If I recall correctly, your sensitivity to magical residual effects has always been considered your strength. It is among the strongest in the Imperial Order."

Ceridath nodded.

"Is there anything you would like to say before I begin?"

If there was, he couldn't even manage a single syllable. It was the first time he'd looked less than icily composed or civilly furious. The new mage frowned, and his eyes began to shift color, moving from gold to bronze. "Ceridath," he said, and this time his voice was a low rumble.

Ceridath remained silent.

The older mage turned to the exposed corpse. "Lord Grammayre, with your permission?"

"Granted."

"Records. Secondary autopsy scan by Sanabalis of the Imperial Order of Mages. Note time and date."

"Noted."

Just as Ceridath had, Sanabalis began to cast. The movements he used were different; less fluid, to Kaylin's eye. He didn't speak, either. But he was doing something similar, because she felt the marks on her arms and legs begin to tingle. She braced herself, bit her lip, and remained silent when the tingling became painful. What failed to emerge this time were the runes that had risen like golden ghosts from the dead girl's eyes.

Teela walked over to where Kaylin stood, knees bent, lower lip between her teeth. "Well?"

Kaylin shook her head as the older mage said, "I do not find anything remiss, Lord Grammayre."

Teela grimaced and said something almost incomprehensible under her breath. The tone, however, made it clear that it was a curse—just not in a language that Kaylin understood. The Barrani Hawk lifted her head. "Lord Sanabalis," she said quietly, "is Ceridath's grasp of the particulars of the spell greater than yours?"

The older mage frowned. "Why do you ask?"

"The results of his spell, and the results of yours, differ."

"They do not," Ceridath began.

But Sanabalis lifted a hand. "In what way?"

"I would have you cast either a different spell, or a more centralized one," Teela replied, avoiding a direct answer.

"Centralized where?"

"The girl's eyes."

He frowned. "What about her eyes?"

"There is some residual magic there, and it is defined."

"I did not realize that you had spent any time in the Imperial Order, Corporal."

"Ah. I did not, of course. I spent some time dabbling in the early Arcanum, but I was not considered a promising student, and after some political turmoil, I was allowed to retire. But in my studies, there were different spells of detection; some required subtlety, and some did not. In this case, I believe that any spell was not cast to kill the child, and it was not cast on her corpse, which would make any traces hard to detect."

"Indeed. It is why the three mages seconded to the coroner are those who specifically specialize in such subtleties. But the request was made for a mage who does not regularly attend the Halls."

"The child was mortal," Teela continued. "It is possible that your detections are not finely tuned toward things that change and decay even in life. Neither you nor I are mortal, after all."

The mage simply nodded. If he wasn't mortal, Kaylin thought, what *was* he? "Your point is taken." He turned back to the body and this time his spell—if this is what a spell looked like—took longer. The accompanying motion of hands was subtle and slow.

Lord Grammayre glanced at Teela, and then at Kaylin, but he didn't choose to speak. Teela, however, gently guided Kaylin closer to the corpse over which the mage labored. She kept herself between Kaylin and the mage, but she left a line of sight open.

This time, after a much longer period of lip-biting pain, Kaylin saw the words begin to rise from the girl's closed eyes. They weren't solid, but they weren't so complicated she couldn't begin to see a shape and a pattern to them; the two glyphs were the same.

Teela touched her shoulder lightly, and Kaylin nodded emphatically. But it wasn't necessary; the mage's eyes suddenly widened—and they went from bronze to a very fiery orange almost instantly.

"There is something, then," Lord Grammayre said softly, and with just a hint of relief.

"There is," was the low, low reply.

"Is it strong enough to trace?"

"It is strong enough for Ceridath to trace." The words managed to be both heated and deathly cold at the same time. "Or he would have felt no need to lie about his findings." He turned to Ceridath. "I believe your tenure here will not be as short as you planned. Lord Grammayre, place Ceridath under arrest."

The Hawklord nodded.

"I will send for the Tha'alani."

Ceridath lifted an ashen face. "That won't be necessary," he said softly, and without much hope. Without the ice of defiance, he looked much older.

"Given your actions here, any information you now

willingly surrender will be suspect. I am disappointed, Ceridath."

"Yes. And I will pay for my treachery." He straightened his shoulders; his breath was ragged, and when he exhaled, his shoulders once again sunk. He hadn't otherwise moved.

"Why did you lie?" Kaylin demanded.

The Hawklord lifted a hand. "Kaylin, that will be enough."

"No—no it *won't*. Look at him—he has everything. He obviously has money, he's obviously respected. They had nothing, and even if he does die for this, it'll be a *clean* death. None of these three got that. And you said there were more—"

"Kaylin."

She knew it was stupid. It was more than stupid—it was dangerous. She didn't know Elantra. She couldn't trust the Hawks. She had no weapons, and even if she had, there were *two Barrani* here; she didn't have a hope in a direct confrontation with even one. But all of her life—all of the life she could remember—she'd dreamed of crossing the bridge over the Ablayne River, of leaving the fiefs and arriving in the City, where things were *safe.*

"Why?"

Where it was safe to have friends and safe to love people because none of them would die. Not this way. Not this way, again. And maybe, a dark thought said, this is what *she* deserved; the life that she'd lived was hers no matter *where* she lived it. She shouted once, wordless, in fury and denial and found herself a foot away from Ceridath.

Ceridath met her eyes, his own as human and unchanging as hers, and said, "Because they have my granddaughter." And he raised shaking hands to cover those eyes and his face.

She stared at the fine, jade veins in those hands and the fury was instantly guttered. It left her feeling cold and empty, but that—she was used to that. His words were the only spoken words for several minutes.

Lord Grammayre broke the silence. "Why," he said softly, "did you not come to us?"

The hands fell away. Ceridath looked at him, and then from him to the dead, and he said, "You couldn't save them. How could I count on you to save her? She's eight years old," he added, closing his eyes again. "She's eight, she's been so sheltered—"

"Do you know who has her?"

"No. I know the message came keyed to my personal mirror—at home—and I haven't been able to trace it. I didn't try very hard. The first attempt was detected, and they—" He flinched. "She's eight," he said again.

"What were you told to do?"

"I was to make certain I would be sent to the Halls of Law today because they knew someone would be sent. I was to falsify reports *if* there was anything to be reported. I have a spotless record," he added bitterly, "and my report would not be questioned."

"Did you recognize the signature you saw on the dead girl?"

He shook his head. "No."

The other mage lifted a hand; his eyes had dimmed from the fiery orange to something that was almost gold. "Have you been to any of the three sites?"

"No. I was scheduled," he added, "to attend the investigation into the third site this afternoon."

"At your request?"

"Yes."

"Good. It means there's something to be detected there. I will send Farris."

"A fine choice. He has no family. No wife, no children. His mother is up the coast." He hesitated again, and then squared his shoulders. "I have forfeited all rights, but nonetheless I ask that you allow me to communicate with my daughter."

"It's her child?"

"Yes."

Kaylin surprised herself now. "If you don't go," she told Ceridath, "they'll kill her. If she's even alive now."

"She's alive for the moment."

"But they'll kill—"

"Yes."

Kaylin swallowed, wanting the anger and the confusion that had fled. Turning to Lord Grammayre, she said, "Let him come with us. Please."

He raised a brow. "With 'us'?"

Teela cleared her throat. "We're due on-site this afternoon. I thought we'd take her with us. She could see some of the work the Hawks do, and it would keep her out of Caitlin's hair. And frankly, a first introduction to the Hawks shouldn't be a face full of angry Leontine, and he's going to be in a mood when he hears about this."

The Hawklord frowned. "This was not exactly what I had in mind for Kaylin," he finally said. "But you are correct in at least one thing—the Sergeant will be ill-pleased. Very well. But Teela? While I have no objections to her presence in this particular part of the investigation, you are to return her to—"

"Caitlin at the end of the day in one piece."

He raised a pale brow.

"She already handed us the memo when she dropped Kaylin off at the morgue." She bent and whispered, "Caitlin is scarier, in the end."

Kaylin looked at the Barrani as if she were insane, which caused Tain to chuckle.

"When you're old enough, you'll understand the joys of paperwork and reports. Caitlin can either expedite them or accidentally lose them. Or see that they're sent to the wrong department entirely. If you need to piss off anyone in the department, avoid pissing off Caitlin."

"You are *also* to return Kaylin to the Halls if there is *any* sign of unforeseen difficulty, Teela. She hasn't been trained, and even I am not willing to throw an untrained, unschooled girl into a conflict that involves magic and far too much money. Do I make myself clear?"

"As glass, sir."

"Good." He turned.

"Wait!" Kaylin said, taking an anxious step forward. Teela caught her by the shoulder, and she shrugged the hand off.

"While you are in transit, Corporal, I would appreciate if you explain explicitly the allowable forms of address, and the proper occasions for them." The Hawklord's voice defined the word *icy*.

Ice clearly didn't stop Kaylin. "What about the mage? Will you let him come—"

The Hawklord now turned his back—which was basically large folded wings—toward her.

"Lord Sanabalis. My apologies for the disruption of

your day, and if you feel he will accept them, my apologies for my curt words with Magister Dreury."

This time, when Teela grabbed Kaylin's shoulders, she held tightly; it'd leave bruises. "Hush, and listen," she whispered.

"I feel," the Hawklord continued, as if there had been no interruption, "if we are to even attempt a facade for the sake of the mage's grandchild, it is best that the results of your visit are not openly known. Whether or not you feel Ceridath deserves mercy or leeway, I must leave up to you. The addition of the second mage, however, is not optional." He gestured and the doors slid open.

Before Kaylin could hear the reply, Teela dragged her out of the room.

"I absolutely forbid it."

Sergeant Kassan was not, as Teela had implied, happy. His eyes were a shade of unpleasant orange, but even if Caitlin hadn't given warning, Kaylin would have known he was in a foul mood. The office was a *lot* quieter than it had been the previous day. But the silence was different. People were grimmer. The conversations that occurred were hushed, but not in a furtive way; there was no laughter. There were no smiles.

"Word got here before we did," Teela said to Tain.

He shrugged. "I told you the Quartermaster was going to give you a hassle. She's thirteen, Teela. He hates to equip half the Hawks on a good day, and they're the Imperial version of legal."

"The Quartermaster mirrored," the Sergeant added. "And it took five minutes to talk him off the ceiling. He has no intention of arming a child."

The child in question bristled, but managed to keep quiet, even though she knew how to wield a dagger.

"We didn't intend for him to arm her," Teela explained. "But some sort of rudimentary armor—"

"Which she would have *no use for* anywhere she's going?"

Teela grimaced. It looked lovely. "I don't know how much Lord Grammayre told you, but...she was helpful, Marcus. She was even, in my opinion, necessary. No, she didn't have to fight a mage, and no, she's not expected to storm a blockade, but she didn't have to do either."

"What, exactly, are you claiming she did?"

"She saw something that the mage missed."

"Probably the nose in front of his damn face." The Sergeant followed this with something that had a lot of *r*'s in it. "I don't care if she saw the end of the world, Teela. I forbid it. She is not going on-site with you."

"What is she going to do instead? Shuffle paper? File? You know if she touches the files, Caitlin's going to pull all her hair out, and human hair doesn't grow back so easily. They won't take her in Missing Persons—she's too young, and the visitors who come there are already spooked enough they *want* authority figures." She leaned over his desk, somehow avoiding the piles of paper there. "She'll be with us. Nothing we're likely to encounter is going through two Barrani to get to a child."

"Did I give the impression there was room for argument?"

"No, sir."

"Then why are you still here?"

Teela nodded sharply and stepped away from the desk.

Kaylin, silent until this moment, stepped forward. She couldn't lean over the desk without sending the papers flying, and didn't try—instead, she walked around its side to stand to the right of the chair the Sergeant was now filling. He watched her, his eyes bronze, his brows scrunched over them in recognizable confusion. "Yes?"

"I want to go with them."

One brow rose, changing the lines of his facial fur. "And some people want to jump off high buildings."

"Yes, but they want to die. Or try flying, which is about the same thing if you don't have wings. I *don't* want to die."

"Then you *don't* want to tag along with Barrani. Trust me."

She swallowed. "I don't want to be with Barrani, no. But I want to go where they're going."

A low growl began in his throat; she was afraid he'd open his mouth and it would emerge as a roar. But she stood her ground, lifting her chin as Caitlin had showed her, although it made it harder to talk. "I was in the morgue today. I was there when they uncovered one of the—the victims. Someone is killing them, and if I can help at all, even by accident, I *want to help.*"

"Why?"

She almost didn't answer. Almost couldn't. But silence wouldn't help her here, and it certainly wouldn't help anyone else. "Because helping is not what I did in my old life. And I want this life to be different."

He stared at her. His eyes hadn't changed color, but

he hadn't roared yet either. "Go on." He did fold his arms across his very broad chest, and she noticed that his claws were extended.

"I couldn't save anyone in the fiefs. I thought here no one would *need* saving." She swallowed again, mouth dry. "So I was wrong about that, too. But..." She turned to look at Teela, who was waiting in silence. "I did help. No, I didn't fight, and I wasn't muscle. I didn't make any threats. I couldn't even understand half of what was *said* in the damn room. But I helped.

"Teela thinks I'll be useful at the site. She's probably wrong. But I want to try. Because if you don't find enough information, whoever's been doing this will keep on doing it. More people will die."

"That's not going to change one way or the other. You can be here or you can be there and it's still true."

"Yes, but if I'm *there,* I might see something, somehow, that gives that little bit more information. If I'm here, I won't see anything."

"And if there's danger? If you do, in fact, have to fight?"

Teela snorted, but otherwise said nothing.

"It won't be the first time," Kaylin replied. "It might be the first time I fight with backup." He was still silent, and she thought it was hesitation. "I'm not stupid. I know when to cut my losses. I know when to run."

"You know when to obey a direct order?"

"Yeah. Didn't get many of those that were physically possible," she added.

He stared at her for what felt like a long damn time. "You understand that if anything happens to *you,* my neck is on the block. You are thirteen years old. If either

Corporal gives you an order, you obey it before you breathe. Is that understood?"

"Yes, sir."

He growled. "I *do not* like this," he finally said.

She waited.

"Fine. *Fine.* Teela, if anything happens to her, my neck is not going to be the only neck at risk. Understood?"

"Yes, sir."

"Tain?"

"Yes, sir."

"Good. Get out of here."

"Well, that could have gone worse," Tain said to Teela when they were well out of the Sergeant's earshot.

Teela raised a dark brow. Her eyes were a stunning, deep emerald, as were Tain's. She headed down a hall Kaylin hadn't seen yet. "Come and see the glory of the locker room. If you stick around for long enough, one of these lockers will be yours."

Kaylin followed Teela while Tain peeled off.

Locker room described a room with a bunch of what looked like tiny closets with things written on them. Those things, Teela said, were the names of their various owners. One had been scratched out. "Locker names are low on the list of priorities."

"Why are we here?"

"In theory? We're getting changed. In practice, you've got nothing to change into, and I'm already ready for street duty."

"Then—"

Teela opened one of the small closets. She pulled out

two sheathed daggers that hung on a small belt. "These are for you."

"But—"

"He said the Quartermaster wasn't going to arm you. He didn't specifically say I couldn't."

"But—"

"And frankly, it gets on my nerves when you flail around at your hip for a nonexistent weapon. Dealing with the mortals is hard enough as is—I don't need more irritants." She smiled, and once again Kaylin was struck by how absolutely gorgeous she was. "There's a trick you'll need to learn. Don't ask permission for anything unless it's serious. It's too damn easy for your superior officers to say no, and it's usually the first thing that comes out of their mouth. I can't do anything about your lack of armor, though."

Kaylin took the daggers. "You think I'll need them?"

"You'd better not," was the cheerful reply. "I can take any human I've ever met in a fight, but a Leontine is less certain. We don't have all day," she added.

Kaylin took the hint, slid the belt around her waist, and readjusted it. "Where are we going?"

"We're going to what's left of the building. The mages will meet us there. If you can, fail to speak. The Imperial mages are big on appropriate respect. Ceridath has reason to tolerate you now. The other mage won't."

"Got it."

Teela shook her head. "You're going to have to learn to speak High Barrani."

"What? Why?"

"Because it's a lot harder to show obvious disrespect in High Barrani than it is in your mother tongue. That, and most of our laws were written in it."

"Why?"

"Because the Emperor is a Dragon, and he considers Barrani the language of bureaucracy?" Teela chuckled.

Kaylin didn't even ask what she meant by bureaucracy; she figured she could pick it up on her own.

Kaylin eyed the carriage dubiously. "We can't walk?"

"No. What's wrong? You've never been in a carriage before?"

"There aren't many carriages in the fief, and if you get into one, you don't have a lot of choice about where you go or when you get out."

"Fair enough." Teela opened the door and climbed into the carriage's interior. Kaylin joined her, although the door was high enough up it took longer. "You ever run into the Ferals there?"

Kaylin laughed. It was a slightly wild laugh. "Yes." The carriage lurched forward and began to jump up and down as it moved. Kaylin grabbed the window's edge to steady herself. It didn't really work.

Teela, on the other hand, might have spent her entire life in a cramped, moving box. "See them a lot?"

"Hear them a lot. It's not considered safe to actually see them." She shrugged and added, "I don't think Nightshade's Barrani guards were bothered by them."

"No, they wouldn't be. But a pack of Ferals would still be a challenge if you wanted to escape unscratched. It's a pity they don't cross the bridge."

Kaylin gaped at her. It was a pity that a bunch of large, fanged predators who killed anything that moved didn't *cross the bridge?*

"There'd be a lot less nighttime traffic, and a lot less crime," Teela offered. She was grinning.

Kaylin, who had run from the *sound* of Ferals in her time, failed to see the humor.

"Kaylin, whether or not you find amusement in the situation doesn't change the situation itself—so you might as well dredge up something to laugh at. If you can't, life is pretty much all tears."

Kaylin said nothing. Instead, she turned to stare out the window because the world was moving past. It wasn't moving quickly, but it was a lot closer to the ground than she currently was, and she found it fascinating. She'd seen the streets of the city closest to the Ablayne, and the buildings there were obviously in better repair than the buildings in the fiefs; the people who walked the roads nearest the bridge were better fed and better dressed, especially in the winter, when falling asleep in the wrong place meant you'd never wake up.

But she'd never seen the streets the carriage now took, winding away from the river and toward the city's outer circle. The closest she had come was her trek to the Halls of Law itself, but the buildings that surrounded the Halls weren't homes; they were merchant shops, two inns, and a guild building. Farther away from the Halls were the larger, taller buildings that housed many families, but these buildings were actually in decent repair, with doors that worked and actual locks, as Kaylin had discovered on her first night across the bridge. They weren't *great* locks, but some training would be required to actually get around them.

Here, however, the large buildings with their rows and columns of almost identical windows gave way to shorter, flatter, and wider buildings. These buildings moved farther away from the streets in which the carriage traveled. The people who lived in them must be rich.

Teela's brows rose into her hairline and almost disappeared. "What, here?" She began to chuckle.

Kaylin grimaced and waited for the amusement to die out. It took too damn long.

"Apologies, Kaylin. This would not be considered the more expensive part of the City. If you ever see that, you'll know. But we're almost there now."

"Caitlin lives—"

"Caitlin lives in a modest apartment in a very safe part of town, yes. But it's Caitlin. As far as I can tell there's not much she spends money on, and not much she wants. She loves her job, she has no family in the City, and she spends some time on days off at the Foundling Halls. Some of her money goes there. We have no idea where the rest of it goes. But she doesn't want the bother of taking care of a house, as she calls it. We're reasonably certain she could afford to live here— it would be a longer walk to work, but that's about it."

"And you?"

"I live where I want to live."

"With Tain?"

Teela laughed. "Sometimes," she said with genuine amusement. She got out of the carriage before it rolled to a stop, which annoyed the driver, judging from his pinched expression. She didn't offer to help Kaylin down, and Kaylin jumped out of the coach, landing less than gracefully on her feet, knees bent.

"This way," Teela said.

It wasn't necessary. The contrast between the house that the carriage had stopped in front of and the houses to either side was marked: the house in the middle was scored black, missing glass in the windows, and missing a front door. The roof looked shaky as well; Kaylin wasn't certain how much weight it would support if someone were stupid enough to try to climb up on it.

"Is it safe?" she asked as she joined Teela.

"More or less."

"What does that mean?"

"The fire ate some of the structural beams; the explosion ate some of the floor. We've got scaffolding on the interior that's built from the basement up. If you don't wander far off that, you should avoid breaking a limb."

Tain was waiting inside. From the inside, things looked worse, and the uncertainty about the stability of the roof hardened. But there was, as Teela had said, some scaffolding and planking set up. Ceridath and another man in long robes were standing on some of it.

"Pretend," Teela whispered, "you're certain either one of these two men could kill you—or anyone you care about—if you breathe the wrong way around them."

Kaylin nodded. She looked at blackened walls, blackened and questionable stairs leading up, and a large hole in the floor that indicated there was a down. "They were discovered here?"

Teela nodded. The almost smug amusement that seemed her most frequent expression was entirely absent. *So,* Kaylin thought, *there are some things that aren't funny, even for you.* She found it oddly comforting. "Where?"

"In the basement. There were a series of small rooms in the basement." Her lips thinned.

"You think magic was used here."

"Yes. The neighbors are close enough that they would have heard something if the zone hadn't been magically silenced. You could centralize the magic over the children's virtual prisons—but depending on how long they lasted, and how long they were kept here, the magic would have to be either recast, in which case a mage was on-site, or extended, in which case the permanence would leave, or should leave, some mark. Understand?"

Kaylin nodded. "How did you get down to the basement?"

"There are ladders. None of the scaffolding is magical in nature, which is important at the moment. The basement floor is solid—it's this one that's questionable. We've had people downstairs for our first rough sweep."

"Mages?"

"Sort of." She grimaced. "No one as skilled as Ceridath. Ceridath is actually considered one of a handful of experts, but most mages will detect something. The mage we did bring wasn't hopeful."

"Why?"

"How much do you know about magic?"

Kaylin pinched her fingers together, and Teela winced.

"What you saw in the morgue was what we call a signature or an imprint. Any strong magic theoretically leaves one—but not all mages are sensitive enough to individuate what they see or read. Rudimentary magic makes clear that magic was done…a more subtle form of magic is required to actually tell someone by whom."

"And you had reasons—besides the wreckage—to suspect magic?"

"When magic is done and the mage isn't a fool, he

knows that it's possible that he might be traced. If he can detonate a large amount of magic that is *not* his, it will overwhelm any traces he might leave behind. Welcome to the Arcane bomb."

"One was used here?"

Teela nodded. "Which of course means there was something to hide. Welcome," she grimaced, "to most of our job. Heads up," she added.

Kaylin looked in the direction of Teela's glance. Ceridath was starting to cast. "I'd've noticed without the warning," she whispered.

Teela frowned. "Keep that to yourself for now. Tap my shoulder or arm if you notice anything. That's it."

Kaylin watched Ceridath. His movements were broader and wider; he spoke softly, and in an almost cajoling tone of voice. The man at his side, to whom she hadn't been introduced, nodded once, and then began to cast himself.

Kaylin had never been exposed to much magic, and was now very, very grateful for the lack. But...there'd been worse pain, and nothing was either broken or bleeding; she endured in a silence of drawn and held breath and heavy exhales.

Ceridath met her eyes only once, but the expression on his face made her want to cry. She recognized it. She thought she'd even felt it herself. She looked away, then. But there was no safety in shifting her gaze, because as his spell continued, her vision wobbled. Mindful of Teela's quiet warning, she remained silent—but it was difficult. Along one of the walls, she could see faint, blue light resolve itself into one large rune. It was more circular in shape than the marks on her arms, although it looked like some sort of writing. Except huge and *solid*. What had drifted up from the dead girl's eyes had been wispy, slight; there was nothing slight about this mark.

She frowned and leaned forward on the scaffolding, catching a beam to anchor her weight and getting splinters as well as stability. There was a second rune farther down the wall; it was as large, and it, too, was an even, glowing blue. As Ceridath continued to cast, both runes grew brighter, until they made the rest of the building look shadowed and dim in comparison.

Teela poked her sharply, and Kaylin looked up. She nodded.

"What do you see?"

"You told me I wasn't supposed to say—"

"Say it quietly. They're only human, they won't catch it."

Tain chuckled.

Kaylin frowned. "Can you ask Ceridath to stop?"

"Stop?"

"Or go back?"

"That's even less clear, Kaylin."

"When he first started, I could see runes, but they were fainter. And about the height of the wall."

"The whole wall?"

"Between what's left of the floor and what's left of the ceiling."

"And now?"

"They're really, really bright."

"Which is why you're squinting so badly?"

Kaylin nodded. "I think—I think if there *were* anything else to see, he's not going to see it now."

"But you think you might."

"No, not now. I can barely make out the gaping hole

in the floor anymore. But…at the beginning, I think maybe."

Teela asked a few more questions, and then squared her shoulders. "There is one problem."

"Only one?"

This earned a brief grin. "Are you certain it's Ceridath's spell and not Farris's?"

"No."

"Farris is here to confirm the accuracy of Ceridath's findings."

Kaylin nodded.

"It's going to be difficult to tell *him* to 'turn off' his spell, if it's him. And I'm not sure how easy it is to tell them to turn it down, either. From my understanding of magic, that's not the way it works. Wait here."

It wasn't Teela who returned; it was Ceridath. Teela was deep in discussion with Farris. Farris was, as Ceridath had promised, younger, but like Ceridath, being an Imperial mage seemed to put a chip on his shoulder the size of a small fief. Tain had come to stand by Teela's side, which made their area on the scaffolding very crowded.

Ceridath knelt by Kaylin. He looked old and tired. He still looked arrogant, but it wasn't as offensive somehow. "I do not understand how you can do what you do," he said quietly, "but I understand that it *is* you. What Teela is asking is…unusual."

"What's she asking?" Kaylin said, keeping her voice low.

"She is asking for an extension of the casting period, rather than its completion."

"So, make the beginning part longer and skip the end?"

"Something very like that, but with perhaps more polished words."

"Can you do it?"

"It would be—in very different circumstances—a very interesting theoretical endeavor." He took one look at her expression and grimaced. "I may be able to do what you ask—but I'm not sure it will have the results you hope for. Tell me what you saw, from beginning to end."

She hesitated and glanced at Teela, but no help was forthcoming from that quarter. "Does it matter? You're going to have to say you saw nothing, aren't you?"

The momentary shine left his eyes. "Without some intervention on the part of the Magister, this may be the last act of magic I am legally allowed to perform. It is my specialty, and until my grandchild was kidnapped, I was extremely proud of my skill. If I am never to practice it again, I will use it now to my full abilities. Yes, I will lie. Farris, however, will not.

"Tell me, Kaylin."

She began to describe not the runes themselves but rather the changing quality of the light they emitted as the spell progressed. His brows rose and he shook his head. "You are wasted, wherever you are now."

Her snort was brief and bitter, and she turned her face away.

"My apologies. I did not mean to offend."

She swallowed and turned back. "I didn't see anything but the large, blue runes—those are from the Arcane bomb?"

"Yes. It is not the way I see them," he added.

"Oh?" In spite of herself, she asked, "What do you see?"

"I see the manifestation of power's trace as if it were a mosaic or a textile tapestry. The colors are not singular, and they don't form as literal runes or sigils, although I *call* what I see a 'signature.'"

"Did you see—her eyes—"

He flinched, but nodded. "It was very, very subtle. I feel that if I had not been sent, it might have gone entirely unnoticed. It looked almost like a mask, a half mask that's meant to rest on the bridge of the nose."

"Her whole upper face?"

He nodded. "But as I said, it's the visualization of a paradigm—it is not exact. Your visualization adds information to mine, and I would say your visualization implies that the exact location of the magical connection was, in fact, her eyes. But mine—" He frowned. "Are you certain you have no desire to study the magical arts?"

Kaylin stared at him, and he reddened slightly. "One day," he said, "you'll have the privilege of doing something you love for a living." His face fell. "And I hope when you do, you are never in a position where you are forced to betray it."

Kaylin, who had been so angry, also lowered her head. "You were trying to save your granddaughter," she whispered. "I think—I think I'd do the same."

"Then do that now." His reply was firmer and stronger. "I will…experiment. I can't help but notice that the Corporal failed to mention your part in uncovering my duplicity to Lord Sanabalis. Even now she fails to mention it to young Farris. Do you know why?"

"No."

"I will attempt a similar discretion. Cough if you think I'm casting…too quickly." He started to speak, looked down at her, and shook his head. "You are not so much older than she is."

"I'm not your blood."

"No, you are not that." He made his way back to the argument in progress, because it had become an argument, and like the previous argument-with-mages, had shifted into a language that Kaylin couldn't understand. It frustrated her. But Teela didn't pull a weapon, and the mage didn't call down lightning or fire—if they even could. She realized she didn't know a lot about either Hawks or mages.

Ceridath's presence dumped figurative water on the heat. He looked old, forbidding, and unamused; Kaylin could practically feel the disgust he radiated. She almost couldn't believe he was the same man who had come to talk to her—the man who loved his magic and his theories just a little bit less than he loved his granddaughter.

Teela and Tain withdrew, exchanging a glance that was both chagrined and amused. "I don't know what you said to him," Teela whispered, "but don't say it again."

"He's going to try it."

"I didn't get that impression from what he said."

"What did he say?"

"Never mind. Do you need to get closer to the ground?"

Kaylin shook her head. Her skin was beginning its unpleasant tingle, and as far as she could tell, Ceridath hadn't even started to cast. But the marks on the walls began to glow again. She leaned over the edge of the planking and looked toward the floor, where she saw a similar mark; it was squarer in shape and it was the same pale blue. Shaking her head, she said, "I think we're going to need to go downstairs."

Downstairs in this case meant ladders. Teela didn't trust the look of the main floor; Kaylin did—she was certain it would collapse if she tried to walk across it. The ladders, on the other hand, were solid. She made her way down into a darkness alleviated by lamplight. A lot of lamplight. They weren't the only people in the basement, but the other three were Hawks, not mages. They didn't wear the tabards that Teela and Tain wore, but their jackets had the same Hawk embroidered across either shoulder.

"Teela," one of the men said.

"You talked to the neighbors?"

He nodded. "They didn't see anything unusual. The house was apparently being rented."

"Did they see or speak with the tenant?"

"Not often. He was apparently friendly and not particularly suspicious."

"Age, height?"

"Thirty-five to forty, about six-three. Reasonably well dressed, apparently well educated, although not in Elantra."

"Human?"

"What else in this part of town?"

Teela frowned, and the man grimaced. "Yes, sir. He apparently went out during the day, came back around dinnertime. He wasn't covered in blood, didn't entertain any obvious mages, and had the usual number of friends."

"Which would be?"

"A few couples who would arrive around dinner and leave afterward. That's it. He wasn't fat, wasn't fit, wasn't bald, wasn't striking—very, very nondescript."

"Name?"

"Luivide."

"Is that his first name or his family name?"

"Family name. Garron is his first name."

"You ran a check?"

The man nodded. "We've got nothing in Records."

"How surprising. Has he been seen since?"

"No. They assume he died in the, er, fire."

Kaylin peered around Teela. She'd been listening to the conversation and looking at everything that the lamplight touched, her brow furrowed. "Is that the same description of the guys at the other places? Teela said this was the third."

The man raised both brows. "What's this, Teela? You've got a trainee? Seems a little on the young side."

"Shut up and answer her question."

The man chuckled. "No. All of the buildings were rented, but one of them was rented by a woman, the other by an older man. Hey, don't touch anything— Teela, keep an eye on her!"

"Kaylin, listen to him. We haven't finished sifting through the wreckage yet."

But Kaylin barely heard her. The glowing blue runes that dominated the floor above had worked their way down to the basement, but they were fainter and more diffuse; they lay not across the walls, but across the packed dirt of the floor itself. She edged through them, searching.

Teela followed quietly, moving like a cat, her steps

light and deliberate. After a moment, she said, "This way."

Kaylin allowed herself to be led. Ceridath had started to speak—when, she wasn't certain—and his voice was now a steady, slow drone. The large runes began to shift in place, their patterns blurring—but they didn't get any brighter.

Teela led her to what remained of a small room. Here, of all the space in the basement so far, the blue light from the large runes was strongest; it lay pulsing against the three walls that didn't contain what was left of a door. Kaylin squinted, frowned, and began to cough. She'd never been a good liar, and her cough—while loud—was so badly staged it wouldn't have passed as a cough to anyone who wasn't listening for it.

Teela stared at her when she'd finished, one brow lifted. "Are you *quite* finished?"

Kaylin mumbled something that she hoped would pass as an apology and waited to see if Ceridath had heard. The light from the runes softened slowly—although it might have been her imagination. She wondered, if he saw this light as something textile, if he could *lift* it to see what might be underneath.

She couldn't. And what was underneath the light at the moment was a lot of porous rock that sat above more packed dirt. The ground was scorched, but even scorched, the smell of rotting flesh was strong. Kaylin started to kneel, but Teela caught her shoulders. "Not here," she said firmly. "We're not done here yet."

"There's nothing to touch," Kaylin pointed out.

Teela didn't reply.

Kaylin coughed again. This time, Teela cuffed the side of her head.

"*What* are you doing?"

Kaylin squinted. "It's too—it's too bright. I think there's something—" She pointed at the ground.

The Barrani Hawk was at her elbow instantly.

Kaylin knelt. She placed her palm against the porous stone, aware that as she did she was probably touching layers of dried blood.

"I told you not to *touch anything,*" the Barrani said in a chilly whisper.

"There's something here, Teela," she whispered. "I can almost see a smudge of different color. It's not like the last time. I think it's a wider area, almost like a circle."

Teela stiffened, and Kaylin looked up.

"A circle." The Hawk's eyes were sapphire-blue; Kaylin rocked back on her heels. She did not, however, reach for her daggers. Or breathe.

"Are you absolutely certain?"

"No."

"I'll get the mages."

It took longer to bring the mages down than it had to get any of the Hawks to the basement. Ceridath was slow to stop his casting, and Farris was clearly used to being in charge when he was brought into an "ongoing investigation." Being told how and where to work irritated him.

His irritation clearly amused Teela, which *also* irritated him; Kaylin half suspected that the Barrani was doing it on purpose. But they did come down the ladders, something their very fine robes didn't help, and Teela led them to the room. Ceridath looked slightly queasy; Farris, clearly, had spent more time on-site.

"Corporal," he said coldly, "they were *children*. I hardly think magic was necessary to either contain or confine them."

"I'm not implying that that was the point of the magic," was the cold reply. "You're not here to deduce on our behalf, you're here to provide information."

Farris slipped into what Kaylin could now recognize as High Barrani. She had to admire his courage—or his insanity—because he appeared to be unleashing it on a visibly annoyed Barrani. If he'd been just a little more friendly, she'd've tried to warn him. As it was, she sucked air through her teeth as Ceridath once again started to cast. This time, the spell was different, the focus different; Kaylin couldn't see the spell itself, but she could see the effects of it.

She coughed, but this time she coughed quietly. Ceridath's head snapped up in obvious annoyance—but not at her.

"If," he said in Elantran, "the two of you *wouldn't mind,* some of us are trying to do work that requires *concentration.*" He offered the brunt of his icy glare to Teela, stopped casting, and folded his arms.

Teela grimaced, but took the hint; she moved the argument. Farris came with it as if attached by chains. Frowning, Ceridath then waved Kaylin over.

His tone was curt and condescending—but his expression was not; she understood that he was once again attempting to hear what she had to say without looking like he was listening or asking. His knees bent slowly, and he grimaced, shifting his robes to avoid as much of the debris as it was possible to while kneeling in it.

"Farris is right," he murmured. "It makes no sense for magic to be used here, not directly on the children.

But…it was. It undoubtedly was." He looked at her. "You saw something here?"

"Yes. But not very clearly—it was like a smudge of different color."

He grimaced. "The entire floor is polluted."

She nodded. "I was thinking—if you see things as textiles, can you, you know, *lift* them to see what might be underneath?"

He raised one brow and then his lips curved in a very faint smile. But he didn't say she was wasted where she was, and he didn't ask her to study magic. "Let me look now. Farris will come when he's finished arguing with the Corporal. I have no idea why he does it—or where he gets the energy…it doesn't matter if she's only a lowly Hawk. She's Barrani. The Barrani could clean garbage off the street convinced of their innate superiority to mortals."

Kaylin, on the other hand, suddenly thought she understood why Teela was deliberately trying to annoy the younger mage, and she felt grateful. She also felt her skin begin to tingle. It wasn't as immediately painful as it had been the first time, which meant he was using a different spell or she was getting used to his magic.

She watched as the blue marks began to emerge. They weren't runic in the way they had been across the walls; it was as if the runes or sigils were so large they couldn't be contained in shape and form by something as small as the patch of floor.

She coughed gently; he grimaced. "I *am* trying," was the curt reply. It was strained, and if she looked carefully, she could see sweat beading his forehead. The blue didn't get any brighter, but it didn't dim. She began to examine the floor as carefully as he appeared to be examining it. "There," she said.

"I see it. I'm surprised you could. Well, more surprised."

"Does it look like cloth to you?"

"Very much, but fine, fine cloth. Its color?"

"The same color as—as the magic on the dead girl. But it looks like it's circular."

"Keep watching. Watch *closely*. You will not have much time."

She nodded. The blue light moved. It *rose*. As it rose, she could see that it was attached by threads, or trails of sharp light, to the floor itself. But beneath it she could see her golden smudge: it was not as bright as the blue light—she thought, when cast, it had never been as bright—but it was infinitely more complicated: it had the shape of the runes on her skin, but the lines, the strokes, the rounded curves, were finer and more dense. She recognized it, although it seemed more solid: it was the same mark as those that had risen from a dead girl's eyes in the morgue, but written over and over again until it comprised a closed circle, surrounding the blackened rock.

Looking up, she met Ceridath's eyes; he was watching her intently.

"It's the same," she said softly.

He nodded, and then said, "Corporal?"

Teela crossed the damp floor. Farris was behind her, and behind Farris, Tain. "Well?"

"I find evidence of the Arcane bomb here. It's likely that at least one was detonated *in* the holding cell. It obviates any possibility of any other magic. This was not unexpected," he added. "Farris?"

"I do not feel it is a good use of either our time or our power," was the clipped, curt reply.

"Then please, feel free to tell the Emperor that," Teela snapped.

Farris was silent; he met and held her gaze. Her gaze was now very blue, with very little green in it.

"You are the only person in the Imperial Order who is likely to find something I cannot," Ceridath pointed out. "And the Magister made clear that the Emperor is now almost...angry...with the lack of progress in this case."

Farris nodded.

Kaylin waited for the familiar bite of magic. She kept her expression neutral and concentrated on keeping her breathing even, but she didn't move to stand behind either Teela or Ceridath; instead, she watched Farris. His casting was not the slow, steady cast of the older mage; it was quick and sharp. The effects were instant; the blue light that adorned the ground grew by degrees, and the quality of it looked different, to Kaylin's eye. She glanced at Ceridath, who was absorbed in the manifestation of the spell's progress. This time, Kaylin could see the faint smudge that marred the otherwise solid blue, distorting its edges. She watched, waiting for Farris's reaction.

It was a long time in coming, but the smudge never got any clearer; it was lost entirely to the blue light at the end. Farris turned to Teela. "There is nothing here that I can detect. The magic from the Arcane bomb is too strong. Ceridath?"

Ceridath hesitated for just a fraction of a second, and then nodded. "If that will satisfy you, Corporal, our work here is done."

Teela didn't look satisfied. But she nodded. "Do you gentlemen require an escort, or can you find your own way home to the ivory tower?"

"Oh, given Imperial concern and the amount of work you'll no doubt have to do here, I'm sure we can find our own way," Farris replied coldly. "Ceridath?"

"I am fatigued, and I would like to leave this place as soon as possible."

"Good. Have a good day, Corporal."

Teela waited in silence for five minutes after the mages had departed. It was exactly the wrong kind of silence, and Kaylin backed away from it as if it were an unsheathed sword. Tain, who knew her better, did the same.

"She's not fond of mages," he told Kaylin.

"Is anyone? I don't think the Sergeant likes them much either."

"He doesn't. Our line of work is seldom as interesting—to mages—as their own. It is also work they feel any undereducated idiot could manage. Being put under our command annoys them, as it devalues their time. I don't care one way or the other," he added. "Teela doesn't appreciate it."

No kidding.

"But that's not what's made her angry at the moment."

"No?"

"No. Come on, we're heading back to the office."

Teela was angry enough that she didn't go to the office by way of the locker room, which meant Kaylin was still wearing two daggers—and a layer of dirt and dust—when they marched past the board with the

Hawks' duty roster toward the Sergeant, who was still sitting behind two large stacks of paper looking like an embattled, giant cat. Caitlin raised her head when Teela stormed by. She quietly did something to the mirror on her desk, and then rose; no one else appeared stupid enough to dare.

The Sergeant looked up as Teela reached the business end of his desk. Something about the Barrani caused his golden eyes to shade to an instant orange. "You found something."

"Yes and no," Teela replied. "We're about to head up to the Tower. I thought you might as well join us because you're going to get called there anyway, and it gives you a break from the paperwork."

"Hawklord?"

She nodded.

"How serious is this?"

"Very."

The Sergeant left his desk. When he joined Teela he stopped and looked at Kaylin, who'd been quietly standing behind Tain. "Wait with Caitlin," he told her.

Teela, however, shook her head. "We'll need her upstairs."

"I don't like it."

"Doesn't matter. You'll have enough to worry about after the meeting. You won't remember that you didn't want her there later."

Lord Grammayre was in the Tower. Kaylin had seen the inside of the Tower once, and once was enough; she approached it with dread. Dread, however, didn't make her walk slowly; she couldn't. Teela all but flew up the stairs, setting the pace. Teela also pressed her hand against the door ward—if you could call pounding it so hard they could probably hear it a Tower away "pressing." The doors rolled open immediately.

The man everyone called the Hawklord was standing in the center of his Tower, facing a tall, oval mirror. Kaylin had never seen so many mirrors in her life, but even if she had, she would never have seen so many that offered no reflection to the person standing—or sitting—in front of it.

Teela saluted. It was crisp, sharp, and absolute. Tain did likewise, but it didn't have the intensity of Teela's gesture.

The Hawklord nodded. "How did the site investigation go?"

"We had two mages. Ceridath and Farris, the latter of whom is every bit as irritating as you'd expect a much older mage to be, without the excuse of age."

The description, while accurate, didn't seem to amuse the Hawklord. "What occurred?"

"Our initial sweep was correct—Arcane bombs were used."

The Hawklord waited.

Teela turned to Kaylin and very treacherously nudged her toward the man who commanded them all. "Kaylin can tell you," she said.

The Hawklord's wings shifted slightly as he resettled them across his back. "Very well. Kaylin?"

She stared at him, mouth dry, aware that this was the man to whom she had to prove herself. And prove herself in order to do *what?*

"Kaylin?" he said again.

"Magic was used there before the Arcane bombs, sir."

"You saw evidence of its use?"

She nodded.

"How clearly?"

"Not very clearly at first. Ceridath did something that made it clear enough that I could see the trace of it as a rune or a sigil."

"Ceridath did?"

"He was trying to get the information," she said quietly. "While trying to hide that fact that I was helping him. But he did something—I think it was hard—he looked a lot more tired after he'd finished. That made it clear to both of us."

"Both?"

"Ceridath and me."

"You are certain Ceridath saw what you saw."

"I'm certain he saw what he saw."

The Hawklord raised a brow. "I see you *have* been speaking with a mage. You are certain, then, that you are interpreting the same trace?"

She nodded firmly.

"I fail to see how this is a difficulty."

"There are two," Teela cut in. "The first is relatively minor—it's the same sigil as the sigil found on one of the victims. It's more cohesive because the tissue is not organic and not decaying. In and of itself, it gives us no new information. We knew a mage was involved, and it, in fact, seems to be the *same* mage."

"I fail to see why this is a difficulty."

Teela glanced at Tain; Tain glanced at the wall. "You'll note the moon's position."

When the Hawklord failed to reply, she spoke a sharp word, and the long, oval mirror to one side of the Hawklord began to glow, as if it were a window into the clearest of nighttime skies. In its center, too large for the oval to contain, was the moon; it was tinged a pale red.

"Noted," the Hawklord said. "Why is this significant?"

"The mortals call it the Harvest Moon. The Barrani call it the Hunter's Moon. But when the *Barrani* call it the Harvest Moon, it has significantly different meaning—the Barrani do not till fields."

"The previous deaths on record did not occur during a particular phase of the moon. With the exception of magic—a magic that might well have gone undetected—there is no obvious difference in the operation. We are, in my opinion, clearly dealing with the same criminal element."

Teela fell silent. It was not a comfortable silence.

"I require some proof, Teela. Interracial crimes, especially those that concern the Barrani, are difficult in ways you of all people should understand. What is your second difficulty?"

"Ceridath, as expected, lied about his findings."

The Hawklord nodded.

"I had some doubts about the usefulness of that lie in preserving his granddaughter's life. Those doubts are significantly reduced now."

"Oh?"

"He had a known reason to lie. The second mage, to our knowledge, did not."

Both wings now rose as flight feathers expanded outward. "You are saying that the second mage lied."

"I am."

"Do you think he's aware of Ceridath's difficulty?"

"Oh, I'm certain he is. But not through Ceridath. I'm certain Ceridath was surprised."

"You did not confront the second mage."

"No."

"Good. Dismissed. Sergeant Kassan excepted. Corporal, put a *quiet* alert out to the Barrani Hawks. I may have need of their services on very short notice." He turned to the mirror and said something that Kaylin didn't understand—again!—and the gray in the mirror folded in on itself to reveal a man in what looked like armor.

Teela's brows rose, and she caught Kaylin by the shoulder. "Time to leave," she said.

"But—"

"You heard the Corporal," the Sergeant literally growled. "Go with her to Caitlin's desk and *stay there*."

"I don't understand," Kaylin said as they made their way down the stairs. The Barrani could walk quietly so naturally hers sounded like the only footsteps, and they echoed all the way up the spiral staircase.

Teela stopped walking so quickly Kaylin ran into her back. It was, notably, Kaylin who bounced. Teela turned to her; the Hawk's eyes weren't quite green, but they weren't quite blue, either.

"You may have indirectly given us the only break we've had in this case. All joking at your expense aside, we needed you there. We thought the Hawklord had lost one too many flight feathers when he dumped you on the Sergeant. Now we're wondering what the Hawklord knew that we didn't."

"Yeah, me too."

Tain chuckled. "Come on. If we don't get you down to Caitlin's desk, Ironjaw will sharpen his teeth on us."

"Or try," Teela added.

"But what's going to happen? And who was that guy?"

"That guy in the mirror, as you call him, is the Lord of Wolves. There aren't as many Wolves in the Halls as there are either Swords or Hawks, and with some reason. But they're good at a couple of things. Ground hunts. Surveillance. I bet someone's heading over to the Imperial Order now—or as soon as their conversation is finished. The Lord of Wolves isn't a very chatty man, but he's rumored to be hideously efficient."

"Wait," Kaylin said as they began to walk again.

"What?"

"You bet?"

"Pardon?"

"You just said 'I bet.'"

"It's a human turn of phrase. It means I'm fairly certain—"

"No, it doesn't."

"Really? And what do *you* think it means?"

Kaylin, at home for a moment in a subject she understood, began to explain.

"I really do not think that's a good idea, dear," Caitlin said firmly. She had folded her arms across her chest and was looking pointedly at Teela and Tain, while ostensibly talking to Kaylin.

"What, people don't make bets here?"

"They do—but *not* in the office. I don't think it's entirely appropriate."

"But—but why not?"

"Yes, Caitlin," Tain added, smiling as he leaned over the back of a chair. "Why not?"

"Well, for one—"

"Incoming," Teela said, saving Caitlin from her explanation. They all turned to see Sergeant Kassan—whose fur was notably fluffier—enter the office. "Fur standing on end, eyes orange," Kaylin murmured to Caitlin.

"Yes, dear. Come sit on my side of the desk. Teela, Tain, I believe he wants to speak with you. And I have some good news for Kaylin, so why don't you go and speak with the Sergeant somewhere else."

"Why?"

"I want her to be able to hear it."

"Kaylin, dear," Caitlin said in a tone of voice that suggested it wasn't the first time. "I realize the exit is interesting, but it hasn't changed in the last five minutes, and it's unlikely to change in the next five, either."

Kaylin reddened and turned back to Caitlin. "I'm sorry," she said morosely. "But—I want to know where they went. I want to know if they—if they found the people they're looking for. I want to know what happens."

"We all do. And whatever you did must have impressed Teela. I'd say she's actually fond of you, inasmuch as that's possible for the Barrani. But there are other things you have to think about first. Two of the landlords did mirror me while you were out, and we now have two possible apartments."

Kaylin looked at the floor between her feet. "I can't *afford* a place. I thought I told you that?"

"And I told you that there would be some budgetary room to help you with the cost of accommodations," was the firm reply. "If there's no emergency, we'll leave a bit early tonight, and we'll go to look at the two places."

Kaylin nodded.

"In the meantime, what have you eaten today?"

Kaylin was quiet as they left the building. If there'd been an emergency, it wasn't the kind that required Caitlin's immediate attention; she didn't leave early, but she didn't stay very late, as she put it. She led Kaylin through much, much quieter halls toward the exit, which was still manned by guards. Kaylin recognized one as Clint, the first Hawk she'd actually laid eyes on, if you didn't include the Hawklord.

She stopped in front of him, and turned.

He raised one brow. He was tall, although not as tall as the wingless human who stood to his right. It was the Aerian who had her attention.

"Kaylin?" Caitlin said over her shoulder. "We don't want to be late, dear."

She startled, nodded, and turned to join Caitlin. Then she turned back. "Clint?"

He raised a brow.

"How much weight can you carry?"

"Pardon?"

"When you fly—how much weight can you take with you?"

His look of confusion cleared, but it was replaced by suspicion. "Why?"

The man to his right had begun to chuckle.

"Kaylin—" Caitlin said, and gently touched her shoulder.

Kaylin's shoulder's dropped slightly, and she reddened. "Never mind," she murmured. "It was—it was just a question." She turned what she hoped looked like a genuine smile on Caitlin and climbed down the stairs.

Tanner waited until they were far enough down the street—although still visible—before he burst into laughter, which was, strictly speaking, frowned on for door guards. Clint glared at him.

"You know what she wanted to ask."

Clint considered accidentally dropping his weapon somewhere in the vicinity of Tanner's foot, which was also frowned on. The Hawks were expected to have *some* dignity in public. "Yes, I *know* what she wanted to ask."

It was one of the few hazards the Aerian Hawks faced at public events and in public places. For some reason that wasn't immediately obvious to Clint, human children were fascinated by Aerian wings. And the Aerian ability to fly. But Kaylin wasn't exactly a *child*...

Tanner was almost finished laughing when Clint glared at him. The glare apparently reset the period of the laughter. "It makes me feel like a pony," the Aerian grumbled.

"You could always say no."

"Easy for you to say—they're not asking you. I don't notice you telling the little rats to get lost when they ask you to carry them on your shoulders."

Tanner shrugged as Clint looked pointedly toward the interior of the Halls. "Yeah, but I know I have the words *big sucker* tattooed across my forehead. What's your excuse? What are you looking for?"

"Who," Clint replied. "We're about to be relieved. Shift's up five minutes ago."

"And you're so anxious to get home?"

"Where else?"

Tanner laughed again. "They're not walking quickly," he offered.

Clint told him where he could go.

Kaylin was embarrassed enough to be silent for a couple of blocks. But Caitlin was so mild and so friendly it was hard to *remain* silent. "It's just—it's their wings. It's that they can fly," she said, shoving her thumbs into her belt loops. "They're not trapped on the ground."

"They still have to eat and sleep, which means they still have to work."

Kaylin nodded. "I know they're mortal. I know they're probably just like normal people, but—" she shrugged "—they can fly." As if that explained anything. "I don't weigh much," she added anxiously. "And I wasn't going to—" She reddened.

"You won't be the first person who's asked, dear. I'm sure he wasn't offended."

"He probably thinks I'm an idiot."

"Oh, I doubt it." She stopped walking. "Do you see that building? The one with the coral roof?"

"What, the pink one?"

Caitlin nodded. "Except it's not quite pink."

It looked pink enough to Kaylin.

"There's an apartment available there. It's not apparently very large. We'll see it, of course. But it's a modern building, and it would be quite safe."

"What do you mean, modern?"

What she meant by modern became clear the instant they approached the front doors. It wasn't the windows—although there were glass windows in the door which looked in on a large, well-lit foyer—and it wasn't the walk, which was smooth, flat stone; nor was it the plants that had been dropped in the front of the building, near the walkway. It was the door itself.

There was a sigil on the door that glowed faintly.

Caitlin reached out to touch it; nothing happened. "See?" she said. "It's warded. Someone will come to open the door in a minute—we're expected—but no one can enter the building if they don't live here."

Kaylin was staring with growing unease at the ward itself. "It's magic, isn't it?"

"Well, yes, dear, but so are the mirrors in the office. Most of the doors in the Halls have wards, if you hadn't noticed."

"I don't—I don't want to touch it," Kaylin finally said. "Not every day. The other building—is it *as* modern?"

"No. But I do think this is a safer building for a young lady your age."

Kaylin folded her arms across her chest and tried to dredge up the gratitude she knew she should be feeling. Grimacing, she lifted her hand and placed her palm against the door.

She bit her lip hard enough that it started to bleed when she felt the magic suddenly surge—painfully— up her palm.

Caitlin, watching her, frowned and sighed. "I'll explain things to the landlord."

"I'm sorry." Kaylin meant it; she felt awful.

Caitlin had been not angry, which would have been bad; she'd been *disappointed*, which was infinitely worse. "You're going to have to live in whichever apartment we choose," was the reasonable reply. "You shouldn't feel bad about choosing one that suits you."

This didn't make Kaylin feel all that much better. She knew she didn't deserve the help she'd been offered, and she didn't understand *why* Caitlin had taken her under her wing. But she didn't want her to stop, either, and only in part because she was a free roof and food. Kaylin had watched her at work, and she'd watched the way the other Hawks reacted to her—even at a distance. It was like she was…family. Their family.

Kaylin could live without family. She'd proved that. She could live with family as well. But losing family was the hardest thing she'd survived, and she never wanted to do it again.

Then why find one at all? her inner voice said. *What you don't have, you can't lose. It's safer.*

But safety was cold.

As if the words were thoughts and some nebulous— and vindictive—god had picked them out of the air, she heard a loud shout from above.

"Kaylin, move!"

It wasn't *all* children that had this effect on Clint. It really wasn't.

It was the orphans. The foundlings. The children whose expression screamed *homeless* even if they never said a word. Seeing her in the holding cell that first time, he should have recognized instantly that she was trouble. Well, okay, he'd recognized that—but he should have clearly seen what *kind* of trouble. It was her eyes. Her unchanging human eyes. Yes, there was no varia- tion of color to indicate the shift in her mood—but she was one human who didn't need it. The width of her eyes was enough.

He flew lower over the City than he usually did while on sky patrol, but he'd lost the armor and the visible signs of his profession. He knew she was with Caitlin, and if the girl wasn't familiar enough to be recognized at a distance, Caitlin certainly was.

But it wasn't Kaylin or Caitlin that Clint saw first, and the person he did see he didn't recognize. It didn't matter. He recognized the position the man had taken on the flat of a roof; he lay flush with it, propped up on his elbows, his hands positioned beneath him as if he was sitting. Clint glanced at the street just below the building, and he almost froze.

There, coming into view, were the two women he had set out from the Halls to find: Caitlin. Kaylin. The man on the roof shifted, tightening his position. With a growing sense of certainty and horror, Clint understood who his target was.

"Kaylin, move!"

He folded wings as the assassin on the roof fired and then rolled to his feet to face an Aerian who was hurtling from the air to meet him.

Kaylin threw herself forward, tucking her chin and rolling as if she were still in the fiefs and that shouted warning was the very thin divide between life and death. She heard the beating of wings, heard a sudden, sharp whistle of air—and worse, heard the grunt of surprise and pain just behind and above where she'd come to her feet, knees bent. She drew her daggers while turning, and then almost dropped them.

Caitlin was clutching her arm, her eyes wide. Blood

seeped between her fingers. Kaylin glanced quickly around the street; it was empty. She jammed her knives back into her sheath and ran the few steps to Caitlin, where she caught the older woman by the arms and drew her as quickly as possible into the nearest gap between two buildings.

The bolt had winged Caitlin's upper arm. Kaylin hadn't seen the assassin. She hadn't seen him—or her— because she hadn't even been *looking*. "Caitlin?" she whispered.

Caitlin nodded, looking dazed. "I'm fine."

"Wait here," Kaylin told her. "I'll run and get help— we're not far—" She stopped speaking for just a minute. She was afraid to leave Caitlin here; she was afraid that they wouldn't make it back if she didn't. She had no sense of the lay of the land anywhere except directly around the Halls of Law themselves.

"Kaylin, I'm fine. It's just my arm," Caitlin whispered.

But she was white, she was bleeding, and she was trembling. Kaylin held her. Beyond the mouth of the alley she could hear the clash of steel, the sound of raised voices, as if they were a world away. What mattered was here, now.

"I never told you," Kaylin said.

This understandably confused the older woman, who was still clutching her arm. "Told me what, dear?"

"I—" Kaylin unbuttoned one sleeve and yanked it up to the crook of her elbow, exposing the marks that she always kept hidden. "These," she said.

Caitlin looked at them. She was still confused. "Tattoos?"

"No. They started to appear on my skin months ago.

On the insides of my arms—both arms, and the insides of my legs. On my back, as well. They all look like this. Like writing. But I can't read them. No one could."

"No one?"

No one I could show them to. Kaylin simply nodded. "I didn't understand what they meant. I still don't. But… after they appeared I discovered I could do one useful thing with them that I'd never been able to do without them."

As if she were talking about the weather, the office, or tea, Caitlin nodded. "Was it a useful or helpful thing?"

Kaylin swallowed. "Let me show you." The exposed marks on her arm began to glow. In the fading evening light, they looked like some combination of blue and gold; it wasn't enough to see by. But Caitlin looked at the runes as if hypnotized.

"Your hands are very warm," the older woman said.

Kaylin nodded. "They are." She reached out and gently pried Caitlin's hand from the wound. Caitlin winced, but didn't struggle or argue; she watched as Kaylin placed her own hand there in its stead. Her eyes rounded.

"Kaylin, what are you doing?"

"I'm—I'm closing it. The wound, I mean."

Caitlin was silent for a long moment. When she spoke again, her voice was hushed. "You need to speak with Lord Grammayre."

"I think he already knows," was the bitter reply. She knew Caitlin wanted to hear more, and she'd even started to try to find the words, when Clint rescued her. He landed at the mouth of the alley. His left arm was bleeding, but not a lot more than Caitlin's had been. It seemed to bother him a lot less, on the other hand.

"Thank the gods," he said. His wings were high and rigid. In the poorer light, Kaylin couldn't tell what color his eyes were. "You're both all right."

"Yes, dear," Caitlin replied. "Did you catch the person who attempted to fire?"

"Yes. Or rather, the ground did. His leg is broken. His right arm is broken. It's possible a few of his ribs are also cracked."

Caitlin winced, which caused Clint to roll his eyes— and even in the poor light, *that* was obvious. "Try to remember he was aiming to kill?"

Caitlin glanced at her arm and managed a wry smile. "That might not be as hard as it should be." She gently removed Kaylin's hand, and they both got to their feet. When Clint saw her bloodied sleeve, his expression changed.

When Caitlin saw *his* expression, hers changed as well. She lifted both her hands. "I'm fine, Clint. I wasn't hurt." Frowning, she added, "But you were. I think, as we're close enough to the Halls, we should head to the infirmary. I need to use the mirror," she added. "I think we're going to have to miss the apartment viewing."

As they walked back to the Halls, Caitlin said, "It's a very good thing you were there, Clint."

His expression could have been carved out of stone, there was so little give in it.

Caitlin raised a brow. "Why *were* you there?"

Kaylin had been wondering the same thing, but given the grimness of Clint's expression, and the definite pres-

ence of his blood, would never have had the courage
to ask.

For his part, Clint pretended he hadn't heard the
question—and maybe he hadn't. His gaze was focused
in a sweep above the ground, at window—or roof—
height. Kaylin joined him as the buildings grew more
familiar; it was a pretty silent walk, and even Caitlin
had given up on small talk by the time they reached the
Halls of Law. The guards on the door were two men
Kaylin didn't recognize. Clint and Caitlin clearly did,
but more important, the guards recognized them—and
were expecting them.

There was more grim on those steps than she'd seen
anywhere but at the wreckage of the house.

"Sergeant's waiting for you in the infirmary," one
of the men told Caitlin.

Caitlin winced.

"I can wait here," Kaylin told her.

"No, dear, I really don't think that's an option."

"I can wait in the office?"

"A better choice, but I still don't think that's an
option. And Clint does need to get to the infirmary.
Arguing will only delay—"

"I'm fine," the Aerian Hawk barked.

"You're bleeding."

Clint eyed the torn remnant of her sleeve. "And
you're not? Oh, wait—I'm somehow less hardy than the
office den mother, a woman who doesn't train, doesn't
work out, and doesn't—*ever*—join ground or air patrols."

"The air patrols would be a bit difficult."

Clint snorted, but that was infinitely better than his
rigid silence. Kaylin glanced at his wings; they were

fuller and slightly higher than they usually were, but even so, they looked soft and lovely. She flushed when he suddenly turned on her.

"They're *just wings*. They're like arms or legs."

Kaylin nodded, and Clint smacked his own forehead. "Here," he said, extending one. When she didn't move, he did, stepping toward her. He lowered the wing, but kept it extended. "This is not a comfortable position," he told her.

She understood that he meant her to actually *touch his wing,* and she stood there like an idiot, her mouth half-open. "Can I—can I hurt it?"

Both of his brows rose. "What, you?" Before she could answer, he continued. "The day you can accidentally hurt *my* wings is the day I retire. At the very least. Just be careful of the flight feathers."

It wasn't flight. He wasn't offering her the skies. It was—it was really a handshake. And she *knew* it was stupid…but she reached out anyway, her hands trembling.

"See?" he said, voice gruff. "Solid. Not as soft as they look. Not the stuff of dreams."

She smiled, eyes wide. "Not the stuff of dreams," she repeated quietly. He was wavering in her vision, and he lifted his wings to gently brush her cheek.

"Come on," he said, voice gruffer. "If Morlan lets me out of the infirmary without her usual hour-long lecture on wound care, I'll take you up over the City. Just don't tell everyone."

Sergeant Kassan was, indeed, waiting in the infirmary. He wasn't the only one. The infirmary, like the morgue, was a large room with a wall full of cupboards, a lot of counter space cluttered by a bunch of lidded jars. But instead of the morgue's tables, it contained beds with thin sheets, and there was no intimidating wall-size mirror anywhere in sight. There were standing screens shoved toward one wall; Kaylin guessed they could be pulled and moved anywhere a modicum of privacy was needed.

At the moment, they probably wouldn't have fit.

The Sergeant was standing in the center of a pack of Hawks who looked identical. They wore the Hawks' tabard, and they had the long, flowing hair that characterized the Barrani. She knew that Teela and Tain must be among them, and was embarrassed to admit—even to herself—that she couldn't tell which ones they were.

They saved her the humiliation of asking. Teela separated herself from the pack and approached. Her usual elegant saunter was gone, and if Kaylin had thought she'd never looked friendly before, she repented. Before she could speak, however, someone intercepted her.

"Caitlin!"

"Morlan," Caitlin replied with a tired smile.

Morlan was an Aerian with spotted wings, and one of the only female Aerians Kaylin had seen in the Halls. The infirmary was, as Caitlin quietly pointed out, her roost. She was happy to see Caitlin—for all of five seconds. But the torn and bloodied sleeve caught her attention on the sixth second, and all Caitlin's protestations aside, there was instant worry—and instant rage, but the rage was channeled into something productive. She made Caitlin sit down.

The Sergeant came over to the bedside, and Morlan also made him leave it, which caused his fur to stand on end. "Caitlin?"

"I am *honestly* fine, Marcus. You'll note that Clint is still bleeding, on the other hand."

"That? That's not bleeding, it's a kitten scratch."

Only when she'd pulled back the sleeve to see Caitlin's arm did Morlan stop.

"I told you," Caitlin began.

Morlan frowned. "Whose blood is this?"

Caitlin was silent.

"It's hers," Clint said.

"It can't be," Morlan replied in an equally flat voice. "You can look if you want, Sergeant. There's no wound."

The Sergeant, however, was looking at Kaylin, and after a minute, so was everyone else in the room. They were all angry, and Kaylin couldn't figure out why, but she felt her throat tighten. She could use anger as a defense or a shield, but she was tired and confused; she let it be.

Caitlin reached out and caught one of Kaylin's hands. "You don't understand. They're not angry *at* you," she said, as if every emotion Kaylin felt had been put into loud, screaming words.

"They're angry." Kaylin looked at Caitlin. She understood in that moment why almost everyone did. There was nothing threatening about Caitlin, but there was something about her that suggested a spine that would neither bow nor break.

The Sergeant growled. His eyes were classic orange, and his fur had not, in fact, come back down. *"Kitling,"* he said, "They're angry *for* Caitlin. She was lucky."

Kaylin felt herself relaxing. That anger made sense to her.

"It wasn't luck," Caitlin told him. "Whoever it was, he wasn't aiming at me."

Teela didn't look surprised. She placed a hand on Kaylin's shoulder. "They were aiming for our trainee?"

Caitlin nodded. "Clint?"

"It was Kaylin."

This should have calmed people down. It didn't. The Sergeant's eyes had gone from orange to a peculiar shade that wasn't *quite* red, and his lips had curled, exposing the length of his fangs. Teeth that long wouldn't have fit in Kaylin's mouth, even when it was fully open.

"We need to have a chat with the Wolflord," Teela said, heading for the door.

"Corporal," the Sergeant growled.

"What?" She spun, her hair gleaming as it followed her movement.

"Wait for me." He stalked out the door first, and Teela signaled to Tain, who broke away from the Barrani pack to join them. Kaylin started to follow, and Caitlin's hand tightened.

"Not you, dear."

"But—"

"You don't like hostility, and that is *not* going to be a friendly meeting."

"Should we wait?"

"Yes. I don't think the Sergeant is going to let us leave without an escort. Not tonight." She sighed, and added, "There's also the matter of the injured assassin."

Morlan lifted a wing. "The Hawklord's with him now," she said grimly. "And the Tha'alani are on their way to meet him as we speak. If he knows anything, we'll know it before Marcus gets out of his meeting. But yes, I think you should stay in the office until things have settled down a bit."

The mirror flashed enough of a warning that Caitlin could tell Kaylin to put the chair back, as people were often territorial about their chairs, their desks, or their square feet of cubicle. Kaylin was therefore sitting on the floor at Caitlin's feet when an angry Leontine and a small host of Barrani swept in. They had been joined by two Aerians, both of whom were familiar to Kaylin: Clint and Lord Grammayre.

They had also been joined by three men Kaylin didn't recognize. Given the sheer size of the Halls, this wasn't surprising—but none of the three wore the now-familiar Hawk. "We're not going to have much time," one of the strangers was telling the angry Leontine. "We'll have two hours from start to finish tomorrow. That's it. If we find what you hope we'll find, all bets are off."

"If we don't?"

"A member of the Imperial Dragon Court takes a personal interest in the well-being of the Imperial Order," was the reply. It seemed to mean something to everyone there. "You've got one man on the inside, but he's almost certainly under constant surveillance. We're not going in that way."

Kaylin started to rise, and Caitlin caught her hand and pressed it firmly.

The movement, however, caught the attention of the man. "You are Kaylin Neya?" he asked, one brow rising just that little bit too high.

She nodded.

"Captain Neall," he said, and held out a hand. She shook it with only a trace of hesitation. "I'm with the Wolves."

"She's with the Hawks," one of the Barrani said curtly.

The Captain raised his brow again. He was tall, slim, and younger than Caitlin; he had one scar across his forehead, and a nose that suggested a fistfight, but he was impeccably dressed and his posture was perfect. "Lord Grammayre?"

"She is, indeed, with the Hawks, if the poor display of manners does not already make that clear."

"How much does she know?"

"She was not present for the interrogation of the prisoner. She does, however, have a clear understanding of the methods used."

Kaylin froze for just a minute, but the Hawklord's expression was neutral.

"Very well." Captain Neall turned to Kaylin and then turned back to Lord Grammayre. "How old is she?"

"Kaylin?"

"Thirteen," Kaylin replied. "Almost fourteen."

Captain Neall grimaced. "Let's stick with thirteen."

Kaylin reddened, and once again, one of the Barrani spoke. "From our perspective she's almost fourteen. She's also almost eighteen."

This time, the Captain ignored the comment. "The man on the roof had a crossbow. I assume you are aware of this fact."

She nodded.

"The crossbow itself is of local make, and it is not of particularly high quality. Nor is that entirely relevant. Had the Corporal not interfered, he would have hit— and in all likelihood killed—his target. His target, we are informed, was you. Do you have any idea why?"

Someone coughed.

"I assume someone was paying him," Kaylin said.

This caused a different type of coughing.

"Very clever. Yes, someone was paying him."

"Who?"

"Less clear. A human woman, roughly forty, possibly fifty. Well dressed, slender. We have a memory crystal with a functional image."

"Where did she meet him?"

He raised a brow. "Young lady, I believe I'm the one asking the questions." He glanced at Lord Grammayre and shook his head. "The woman in question is not connected in any way with the Imperial Order of Mages. It is through the Imperial Order, however, that the information was conveyed."

"How do you know that?"

"Kaylin," the Hawklord said. "Answer the Captain's questions *without* posing your own, or we will be here until morning."

"There are only two points of origin we consider probable."

Kaylin nodded.

"And I am informed by the Corporal that we will require your assistance on-site to evaluate the two possibilities."

The Sergeant growled.

"We've already agreed to take some of the Barrani Hawks," the Captain said in a smooth, no-nonsense tone. "If they cannot protect her, given the circumstances, very little can. If we do not apprehend the criminals, it's likely that Barrani or no, she won't survive. For some reason, someone considered her a very grave threat."

Kaylin looked at Teela, recognizable because she,

too, was almost growling. "What am I supposed to do?" she asked quietly.

"Exactly what you did on-site. No more and no less. If Ceridath was behind this, I will kill him slowly."

But Kaylin shook her head. "I'd bet money it wasn't him—and even if it was, they have his granddaughter and he *knows* what they've done to their other victims."

"That's not the way it works, kitling."

"Maybe it should be."

The Hawklord cleared his throat. "Kaylin, you will go with Teela and Tain tomorrow afternoon. You will obey them if they give orders. They are subordinate in all situations to the Wolves in charge of the surveillance unless they feel your life is in danger."

Kaylin nodded.

It was Marcus who said, "You don't have to do this. You're not a Hawk. You've made no pledge and taken no oaths. You're not even getting paid. You've been here for a day—"

"Two," she said.

He growled; she lifted her chin.

"Nobody likes a pedant. You've been here for a day, and you've got assassins on you. At your age. In *my* department. They are *asking* you to do this, not ordering you to do it. You can refuse without breaking any laws, and frankly *I'll* sleep tonight if you do." He glared at her for a long, silent minute. "None of this is getting through, is it?"

She nodded.

"You want to go."

She nodded again.

"Why?"

"Because there's a chance we can save Ceridath's

granddaughter. And the other children they must have gathered somewhere in this city. Because I *won't* just be underfoot."

"You understand the risks, after tonight?"

She almost laughed, but it would have been the wrong laugh. "We couldn't even *walk* outside at this time of night without taking our lives in our hands. We had Ferals hunting by sundown. I think I can live with a little risk—and it's a risk I get to *choose*. I want to help. My reasons haven't changed. I've seen what happened to those children, too—I understand the risks." She folded her arms tightly across her chest.

"Fine." He turned to Teela. "Escort Caitlin and Kaylin home. Clint will fly scout."

Clint nodded.

As they left the office—still occupied by the rest of the Barrani, the Captain, and the Hawklord, Clint said, "Kaylin, you are going to age most of the department prematurely by the end of tomorrow. Swear to god I can see my hair graying."

"Speak for yourself," Teela laughed.

"Fine. Most of the department who *can* age. Have you really only been here two days?"

Kaylin nodded. She hesitated, and then said, "Did you mean it? About the flying?"

He raised a brow and then laughed. "Yeah, I meant it. I know where Caitlin lives. I'll take you there the long way. No one's targeting Caitlin directly, so it'll even be practical."

Teela and Tain came to Caitlin's in the morning as well, and Kaylin caught a glimpse of Aerian shadow across the early-morning streets when they left the building. The two Barrani Hawks were silent and their

expressions kept people away. They would have kept
Kaylin away had she not known they were there for her
benefit; even given the tabards, they looked like walking death wishes.

They made it to the Halls of Law without incident,
which seemed to disappoint at least Teela. Caitlin took
Kaylin to one side and, to the shock of many, asked
for help sorting through the reports in her in-pile. This
lasted only as long as it took Kaylin to admit that she
couldn't read the necessary précis of what the reports
contained, never mind the reports themselves. The older
woman pursed her lips and said, "That will have to
change. If you mean to work here at all, you'll actually
need to write some reports, and you'll need to be able
to read—and understand—a lot of them as well.

"I'll speak to the Hawklord about that. The new re-
cruits are expected to take classes in a number of different subjects, because some of the knowledge the Hawks
have isn't considered general knowledge. You'll probably be asked to join those."

Kaylin nodded, only half listening. "I want to learn
High Barrani."

"You'll *need* to learn High Barrani—but without the
ability to read and write, that's going to be very difficult. You can take these down the hall to the morgue,
though. I'm afraid until you start classes, there'll be a
lot of errand running. Most days will not be as eventful
as yesterday."

Kaylin carried messages until Teela came to get her.
"Here," she said, tossing a bundle of cloth at Kaylin.
"Just put it on over whatever you're wearing. It's going
to be a bit on the long side, but hopefully not much."

"What is it?"

"Just put it on."

With a little help from Caitlin, she did just that—and discovered that it was a cut-down version of the tabard Teela and Tain wore when they left the Halls. The embroidered Hawk figured prominently across its chest. She was silent for a long moment, running her fingers over its stylized wings.

Teela gave her that moment, no more. "Come on, kitling. If we're late to meet up with the Wolves, the Sergeant will have what's left of our hides."

"Be careful, Kaylin," Caitlin called out at her retreating back.

"It's like they don't trust us," Teela murmured.

"There's a reason they don't generally partner the Barrani Hawks with the fragile ones," Tain pointed out. "And given everyone's obsession with a handful of mortal years, they've classified Kaylin as *exceptionally* fragile."

"Yes, but we weren't supposed to be watching over the other ones. Heads up," she added as they turned a corner and almost ran into Captain Neall and two of his Wolves. He nodded as if he'd expected the near collision and turned neatly on heel.

"The carriages are waiting."

Kaylin winced, but said nothing; instead, in silence, she followed Teela and Tain. The Wolves weren't particularly friendly or chatty, but at this point, she didn't expect it; she expected the tension that had gripped the two Barrani, so she wasn't disappointed.

There was something almost dreamlike about the carriage ride. The streets moved past, framed by the window, and jostling as the wheels moved up and down;

she watched the buildings change, caught glimpses of other carriages on the wider roads, and saw people moving out of the way—or pointing—as they drove past. They drove quickly, and at last came to a stop. Teela was first out of the carriage.

"You're sure the direct route is the one we want?" Eyeing the building dubiously, Kaylin climbed out and looked at it; the building, while not as tall as the Halls of Law, was still pretty damn tall. It had two towers, shorter but somehow more majestic, at either end. Between those towers lay an expanse of pale stone, with windows—glass windows—and wide arches for various doors. Of course, to *get* to any of the doors, they had to get through the fences, or over them.

Captain Neall, on the other hand, didn't look like the type of man who was prepared to climb them. He walked to a small break in the fence—it looked like a small hut—and waited until someone came out. That someone was armed, large, and not particularly friendly—but while Kaylin preferred friendly, she'd long since given up on actually finding much of it.

The Captain handed the man some rolled-up paper, and the man unrolled it, read it—Kaylin had never wanted to read so badly in her life—and handed it back. Then he walked back into the small hut, and after a moment, the gates opened. They creaked.

"Let the Captain do the talking," Teela told Kaylin quietly. "Even if they ask you a direct question."

"This is your entire crew?" the guard asked Captain Neall.The Captain nodded, and added more impatiently, "The composition of the crew is detailed in the directive."

Kaylin frowned. "We're the Law, right?"

Teela nodded.

"We need permission to visit?"

"It's the Imperial Order of Mages. You probably need permission to sneeze."

"But...we're investigating something illegal."

"Yes. And apparently we're required to remain within the boundaries of the law, regardless. Funny thing that. No one mortal likes a hypocrite, except perhaps the hypocrite himself."

"And the Barrani don't care?"

"The Barrani," she said with a slender, edged smile, "don't bother with the hypocrisy. If they have the power, and they're certain of it, they do pretty much whatever they want. If there's uncertainty, they resort to diplomacy, but no one believes a word the other person is saying."

"So why are you working for the Hawks?"

Tain stepped on Kaylin's foot, and that was all the reply she got. They followed the guards down the walk and toward the large front doors, where more guards stood waiting. These guards, however, didn't stop them, as they already had two as escorts.

The building itself was very, very fine; it was bright, the halls were tall—although not so tall as the Aerie in the Halls of Law—and everything was well lit; the floors gleamed, where they could be clearly seen. Long rugs covered the center stretch of floor, absorbing noise. There was very little noise that wasn't footsteps. She was beginning to feel comfortable in this silent anonymity, when a man approached from the other end of the hall. She recognized him: It was Magister Dreury.

Kaylin wasn't too proud to hide behind Teela. Teela,

on the other hand, didn't appear to be concerned; she looked pointedly at Captain Neall.

"Captain," the Magister said in a cold, autocratic voice. "This is a highly unusual visit."

"It is, indeed, Magister. I'm certain you appreciate our concerns, and the reasons for a *private*, congenial visit. I was informed by the Lord of Wolves that any public investigation would be considered an insult to the fine members of the Imperial Order, and that such an extreme of accusation and possible *public* panic would be undesirable both for the Halls and for the Imperial Order itself.

"It is, however, possible—"

The Magister lifted a multiringed hand. "Enough," he said curtly. "I am far too old to play games of this nature for more than a few hours a day, and I've served my few hours. The meeting is in progress. You will have the run of the two areas you've requested for the duration. You will *leave* before the meeting itself is adjourned."

"Of course."

"Good. I myself am somewhat late, and as the meeting will not commence without my presence, I will lead you to the rooms."

The areas, as the Magister had called them, weren't completely empty. There was one man lounging in a chair, his feet on a desk, his hands folded in a steeple across his chest. He appeared to be sleeping, although he opened one eye as they crossed the threshold. The man was not, however, human; he was Barrani.

Teela's eyes went to an instant, cold blue; Tain's also

lost all green, but Tain, of the two, seemed less likely to overreact.

"Neall," Teela began, forgetting his rank. "You go too damn far."

The Barrani stranger stood, straightening the fall of his robes. His eyes were completely emerald-green, and his smile, while stunning, was also like a dagger's edge. "I see that rumors have some substance in this regard. You *are* with the Hawks." He offered Teela what Kaylin assumed was a very sarcastic bow; she ignored it.

"Corporal." The Captain's voice was cold. "At the moment we cannot afford entanglement with Imperial mages. At least the Arcanists work, aboveboard, for money."

"For *significant* amounts of money," Teela snapped.

"Oh, not always," the Barrani interjected. "Sometimes we do it because we're…bored. This sounded like it had the possibility of amusement."

"Given the price you're charging," Captain Neall said, "it had better provide the Wolves with more than just the dubious pleasure of amusing you."

The man smiled. He glanced at Teela and Tain, and then at Kaylin—but her age didn't seem to immediately trigger any condescension. Or, Kaylin amended, any unnatural condescension, given he was Barrani. "I'm certain it will provide the necessary information."

Teela was frowning; Captain Neall noticed—Kaylin thought he'd miss something when they put out his eyes, if then. He nodded to the man he'd identified as an Arcanist, but hadn't bothered to introduce. Kaylin, mindful of Barrani hearing, didn't ask what an Arcanist was, or what the difference between an Arcanist and a mage was. Instead, when Captain Neall led them out of the room—through a different door—she trailed behind Teela and Tain.

She wasn't certain what she'd expected. What she hadn't expected was the *mess*. The desk made Sergeant Kassan's desk look tidy.

"This," the Captain said, "is Ceridath's. Both rooms— the outer and the inner—are his. It is in this second room that he is reputed to do most of his study."

Kaylin honestly couldn't see how. Then again, she'd never owned so much raw *stuff* in her life; she had no idea if she'd be as messy, otherwise. There were *layers* of mess. She started to say something, remembered she wasn't supposed to speak, and then bit her lip as her arms and legs began the slow burn that clearly indicated the presence of magic in the room.

What was disturbing was the fact that the Arcanist hadn't bothered to gesture or speak at all. Looking at him, he appeared to be reading the spines of the several hundred books that formed a bastion along the shelves of the wall opposite the door, his hands clasped loosely behind his back. He did walk, he did move, but he was—like Teela or Tain—completely graceful and entirely unselfconscious as he did.

Kaylin wasn't. She walked slowly because it felt like her skin was being rubbed off every time anything came into contact with it—like, say, her clothing. But as the spell grew stronger, the room began to shift, very slightly, in her view. There were some spells on the books themselves, but not all of the books, and the spells were almost ethereal; there was very little obvious light cast. The color wasn't the gold of the other spells; it wasn't the blue of the Arcane bombs. It was a shadowy slate, which was probably why it was easy to miss.

She examined other parts of the room as the spell continued to grow in power, and again, some objects seemed to have been somehow magically enspelled, but the color was a theme; it was gray, or a gray-blue at its brightest, and it never quite emerged into something strongly runic. The last place she turned was the desk, and there she froze.

Teela came to her instantly, and touched her shoulder without speaking. Kaylin pointed toward the mirror on his desk. It was rectangular, with a metal frame that had small claws for legs; at the height of the frame, in the center of the bar, was one bright, golden sigil.

It was the *same* sigil.

"Thank you," the Captain said to the Arcanist. "If we can now move to the second set of rooms?"

The Arcanist nodded. "He is not a terribly significant power," he said dismissively of Ceridath. "But possessed of some subtlety."

"Wait, can you tell what the spell is supposed to do?"

"I?" The Arcanist glanced from the desk to Kaylin for the first time. "Not immediately, although were I given a week, yes."

"*Without* triggering it," Teela added.

"Oh, well."

The second set of rooms was a study in contrasts. Although the exterior room was very similar to Ceridath's, the interior was almost spotless. It gleamed. It was possessed of at least as many books, at least as many shelves, and to Kaylin's eye, the shelves were finer; the surface of the unoccupied desk was almost spotless. A mirror rested on the corner nearest the door. It was an oval, not a rectangle, and it seemed to be made of silver; the frame was not simple; the height of the oval was a carved figure with spread arms and the hint of wings, and the arms seemed to be more highly polished than the rest, because they seemed to reflect more light.

"This," the Arcanist said, with a critical eye, "was a costly piece."

"We're not concerned with the piece, per se," was Captain Neall's terse reply. "But rather the possibility of external enchantment."

But Teela said, "That was not crafted by mortal hands."

"No?"

"Oh no," the Arcanist said softly.

He began to cast, again with no outward display at all of his gathering—and spreading—power. Kaylin was almost surprised when no similar golden glyph appeared anywhere on the mirror. Which wasn't to say that there were no glyphs; there were. They were ice-blue and forest-green; there was one that defined the color yellow. They worked in concert, and they were so intricate she couldn't have traced their pattern; they were also compelling.

But she turned toward the rest of the study as the Arcanist did, and followed him as he began to examine the books on the shelves.

She didn't get very far. What was missing on the mirror, she found on the books; the enchantments were not as subtle, not as hard to see, as the enchantments in Ceridath's study. But every single one of them was, in Kaylin's vision, a radiant gold, and in that light, she could see a very familiar sigil.

* * *

She looked to Teela who was watching her like, well, a Hawk. Something must have caught Captain Neall's attention, because he said, "Thank you. We have the information we need," to the Arcanist.

The Arcanist's spell did not, however, fade or drop, although he did move away from the Captain toward Farris's desk. Kaylin watched him as he sauntered over to the chair behind the desk. Seating himself as if he owned it, he leaned toward the mirror and gestured; the sigils that Kaylin now knew meant a spell had been cast began to move. They danced in the air just above the frame as if they were performing for his benefit.

Teela shook Kaylin by the shoulder and Kaylin dragged her attention back to the attentive Captain of the Wolves.

"He'll hear everything we say," Teela told the Captain.

The Captain glanced at the Arcanist and shrugged. "He is not a fool. Whether he hears it or not, he will deduce."

Teela stiffened. "We will speak elsewhere," she finally said, "Or we will not speak." Turning—and still holding Kaylin's shoulder, she began to leave the room.

The Arcanist, however, lifted his voice. "Teela, if you are not still caught up in your present passion of attempting to blend in with the mortals—or perhaps, more interestingly, if you are—you will find this particular spell of interest."

Teela's grip tightened suddenly; Kaylin wondered, briefly, if she'd keep the collarbone. Then the Barrani Hawk let go and turned to Tain. "Take her out of earshot before you allow Neall his questions. I will speak with the Arcanist."

Tain frowned; his eyes had shaded to blue. They weren't as dark a blue as Teela's, though. "I don't like it."

"No. I am not in danger, here. Remember."

Tain nodded slowly, and withdrew; he also caught Kaylin by the shoulder, but only to break her stare, which had gone back to the sigils above Farris's mirror as if anchored. He was less physical than Teela, or perhaps more willing to allow her some dignity.

Only when Tain judged the distance sufficient—which was when they were once again in Ceridath's outer office—did he relinquish all command to Captain Neall. Neall was brusque; he was clearly not pleased, but he'd obviously been told when to make his compromises with the men of an entirely different division, even if he outranked them.

"Ceridath's mirror was enchanted," Kaylin said quietly. "By whoever cast the spell on both the dead girl and the holding room at the—at the site." She glanced at Tain, who nodded.

"You are certain of this?"

"I'm not a mage, but…if what Ceridath said was true, yes. Mages leave signatures. The signatures are unique."

"And Farris's mirror?"

She shook her head. "It wasn't his mirror—"

"The Arcanist seemed fascinated by it."

"There were other spells on the mirror—just not one cast by the mage who enchanted the child." Kaylin shrugged. "I don't know more than Ceridath told me. I don't even know if I understood it all."

"I *highly* doubt that."

Kaylin decided then and there that she didn't like the man. "The mirror *didn't* have the enchantment we were looking for—or maybe you couldn't see that for yourself?"

Captain Neall raised one brow. "Indeed, I cannot. Nor have I made any claim of competence in that area."

"Neither have I."

Tain cleared his throat. "Kaylin."

She turned, flushed, to glare, and he said, "The children will die soon. Any chance we have to save them is slipping by as minutes pass. Decide how much this display of ego is worth to you." He spoke so mildly and so carelessly he might have been talking about a midday snack—on a day when she wasn't almost starving.

The anger left her in a rush. She swallowed, thinking of the one corpse she'd briefly glimpsed. Of the empty holding cell, and the blood on the floor. Lifting her chin, meeting the gaze of the Captain—which hadn't changed at all, the heartless bastard—she said, "Farris's books, like Ceridath's books, were enchanted. Not all of them, only a few—but on Farris's books, the signature matched the signature on the corpses and on the site. They matched the spell on Ceridath's mirror as well." She frowned. "Ceridath said that he only made one attempt to investigate—"

Words fled and she turned in a panic toward his inner office. She slid between both Hawks and Wolves in a desperate attempt to reach the mirror. Only when she saw its flat, lifeless surface did she begin to breathe again.

"Kaylin," Captain Neall said, more of an edge to his voice.

She turned to him almost wildly. "Ceridath said—he tried to find out who was communicating with him, and how—and it went badly. I think they must have hurt his granddaughter. He stopped. But we *don't know* how they know or what they detected, and if he—"

The door to the outer office slammed open. There wasn't any need to find out who had entered because whoever it was ran straight from the entrance of the outer office to the door of the inner sanctum.

In it, hair slightly wild and eyes very wide, chest heaving as if from a great exertion, stood Ceridath.

They hadn't been close to two hours; even Kaylin, caught up in her observations, knew that. But Ceridath was here, regardless. She wondered if anyone had noticed his absence, and wondered what it would cost him if they had. But he seemed to feel he'd already lost everything, so maybe it didn't matter to him anymore.

He made it to the mirror, just as Kaylin had done, and saw its flat surface. Only then did his shoulders and brows fall. She looked up at him. "I'm sorry," she whispered.

He glanced at Captain Neall, the other two Wolves, and Tain. "I hardly think you have anything to apologize for," he told her. "Given that the Captain of the Wolves is undoubtedly in charge here. Captain?"

"As you surmise, we are investigating you. We are almost done," he added. "But our investigations also encompass a colleague."

"Farris?"

The Captain nodded. "Our expert has identified—"

Ceridath turned to Kaylin, which obviously surprised the Captain. Kaylin said, "Unless someone else was enchanting his books, the mage who cast the magic on the girl and the one who cast the magic on the floor was Farris. He also did something to your mirror," she added.

"My granddaughter—"

"We'll find out," Captain Neall replied. His smile— the first he'd offered—made Kaylin take a step back. It also made her wonder what the Wolves did in the service of the Emperor's Law. "We have enough information now to confront Farris directly. Lord Sanabalis will be on his way shortly, as will the Interrogators."

"Tha'alani?"

Captain Neall nodded. He started to say something else, when they were interrupted by a very loud *bang*. Neall lifted his head and said something extremely rude about Arcanists before he gestured and everyone filed out of the room toward where they'd left Teela.

All professional calm had left the Captain's face, and although it was petty, Kaylin felt a little satisfaction at seeing him behave like a human being. He moved, dragging his Wolves, a Hawk, and a mage in his wake, until he reached Farris's rooms. The door to Farris's outer office was shut. Kaylin looked at the door ward that adorned its center and grimaced; it was glowing very brightly.

"Do not touch the door," Ceridath said as the Captain lifted his palm. "The chamber was initially opened by Farris?"

"By the Magister," the Captain replied.

"The Magister will not easily be able to open the door again." He began to gesture, and Kaylin watched as the door's rune slowly transformed itself into a now-familiar sigil. "Who did you leave in the room?" Ceridath asked softly, his forehead creased, his brows slightly gathered in concentration.

"A Barrani Hawk," the Captain replied. Then, after a pause, "And a Barrani Arcanist."

The spell faltered a moment—or at least the brightness of Farris's signature did. Ceridath's eyes rounded so much it was a wonder they stayed in his head. "You *led an Arcanist here?*"

"The Magister was aware of his presence, and while he did not fully approve, he acceded to the request. Why is the door closed?"

"You would mostly likely have to ask Farris if you want an exact answer—but it is not at all uncommon for contingency spells to be placed upon the doors of *any* experienced mage. If something has triggered a contingency, the doors often lock. Sometimes they…resist… attempts to open them. If, however, you are not attached to your hand, you may attempt to use the ward."

"If I do?"

"In the very best case, it will merely alert Farris of your presence, as I was alerted."

"And in the worst?"

"It will still alert Farris to your presence. The likelihood of his ignorance, given the activation, is small, however."

Kaylin could see an argument brewing—or at least a lengthy and heated discussion—and she started to tell them both that they didn't have the time for it. But the door came to her rescue, in a fashion: it disintegrated.

Both the mage and the Captain seemed to forget how to speak as the Barrani Arcanist stepped into the hall, dusting ash off his robes. "Gentlemen." He turned back toward the empty frame and offered Teela a hand. She glanced at it, and then offered the Captain of the Wolves a very sharp salute.

The Arcanist snorted.

"Captain," Teela said without preamble, "we have a problem."

The Captain looked past her shoulder into the room. So did Kaylin; the outer office—at least—seemed to be untouched. Except for the now-absent door.

"Is it a problem that involves the political fury of the Magister?"

"No, sir."

His eyes narrowed into slits. "Is it a problem that involves the political ire of the *Barrani?*"

She didn't answer.

"Does it *matter?*" Kaylin finally demanded. Everyone in the hall looked down at her, in more ways than one. "The children—"

The Arcanist glanced at Teela. "I leave this in your hands," he told her. "In order to fulfill the terms of a *very* tedious contract, I must now retire to write—and submit—a report to the Captain."

As the Captain turned, Teela caught his arm. "Captain Neall," she said, voice low, "we have two important pieces of information. The first, the location of the current intended victims. The second, very little time."

"How did you obtain that information?"

"I did not obtain it. The Arcanist did. It will no doubt be costly, but it amused him. Unfortunately, it did not amuse the source of the information—the mirror was destroyed in the midst of the discussion."

"The Arcanist destroyed—"

"No. The person on the other end."

Ceridath's brows rose. "That would be impossible—" He stopped.

"Yes. If the person on the other end were not in some part responsible for the creation of the mirror itself, it would be. The mirror was not created by mortals, or even mortal mages."

Captain Neall wanted to say more; that was clear. What he did say, however, was, "The location, Corporal."

"It's on Vaturcroft. The fourth house."

Captain Neall grimaced. "I'll mirror the Wolflord."

"Not from Farris's office you won't," Teela replied in a perfectly matter-of-fact voice. "Tain."

"Where are you going?" the Captain asked.

"To Vaturcroft. We're under your orders while we investigate within the Imperial Order's confines. We're beholden to no such thing now, and we can't afford to wait. Farris, should he still be here, is your problem." Turning, she began to jog down the long hall. Tain followed on her heels, and so did Kaylin. She wasn't surprised to see Ceridath join her as well.

"We'll take a carriage," he said when they were almost at the exit. He was breathing heavily, and it hadn't been that much of a run. Teela and Tain had been stopped by the guards, which allowed Ceridath the chance to catch up.

He looked at one of those guards and said, "We need a carriage *now.*"

Kaylin didn't even notice how uncomfortable the carriage was. She didn't notice the buildings that passed by the windows, and only briefly noticed the people scrambling to get out of the way. What she noticed was the silence in the cabin; the silence and the sense that everything—*everything*—was taking too damn long.

Teela glanced once at Ceridath and opened her mouth; she closed it again before words could escape.

When the carriage lurched to a stop, she checked to see that Kaylin still had the daggers she'd been given. "We're one building down from where we'll need to be. I have no idea how many children they have, but that's the house. There are guards. They're not visible, and there shouldn't be many."

The house was far larger than the previous house had been, and it was separated from its neighbors by a lot more land and a stretch of fence.

"Farris won't be there, not yet. We don't know whether or not he sent a message, or if his contingency did we might be too late. If we're not, there'll be fighting. We can't afford to keep an eye on you and an eye out for their victims—you're not chained, you're not hobbled. You can use those," she added. No question. "Use them." She looked up at the mage. "I don't know much about your specialty—"

"I can get you in safely. I can—unless Farris was exceptionally cautious—get you in quietly. I am not remaining behind," he added.

Teela took a deep breath, nodded, expelled. "Good. We'll head to the back and hope the neighbors gape from the windows for a while before they think of doing anything sensible."

The back door—which was really a small side door—had a mark on its upper center which clearly indicated a door ward. Ceridath grimaced briefly and began to cast; Teela and Tain waited. "Simple ward," the mage finally said. "Hold." He cast again, and this time when he was done, he told them, "Now."

Kaylin assumed they meant to pick the lock.

They broke through the door instead; she wasn't certain it wasn't faster. But if she'd wondered what Ceridath was doing, she understood it then: they made no noise at all. But noisy or no, Ceridath continued to cast the minute he cleared the door's frame, yanking his robes free of splintered wood. Kaylin knew why: the other children had been hidden, probably with the aid of magic, from view. If it was there, he'd find it.

So would she.

Teela and Tain paid no attention to either mage or trainee; they were alert and focused. Since nothing made any sound, everything was visual. It was eerie, to Kaylin. Teela didn't appear to like it much either, but if she cursed, none of it reached Kaylin's ears. Ceridath motioned them forward into what looked like a long galley; it was mostly counter, and mostly clean. It was also empty.

There were stairs leading down almost across from the entrance. Teela looked to the mage, and he frowned. Kaylin felt no magic that wasn't his, and she saw nothing at all that implied magic had been done anywhere near this room.

Down, Ceridath mouthed, as if remembering something suddenly.

They nodded; they didn't have to break the door down.

They did have to deal with the men coming up the stairs. The men weren't dressed for fighting; if they were the type of thugs the fieflords kept, the thugs here dressed better.

Maybe the law was different, Kaylin thought. Maybe there were rules that weren't meant to be broken, and the Hawks had to follow those because they also upheld them. But one of the men's hands were red with blood; his clothing was spotted with it. Kaylin *screamed* in the silence as part of the floor fell out from under her feet.

It wasn't the literal floor; she knew this because Teela and Tain were already in motion. She drew her own daggers and as the men fell down the stairs—being kicked suddenly in the midsection helped—she leapt down the stairs as if she were their shadow.

Too late too late toolatetoolate.

Sound did not return. In silence, they moved into the basement. It wasn't well lit, but light was here—Ceridath's light, and the lights on the walls in tarnished sconces. The shadows they cast flickered, warped and stretched or thickened as they moved. They came across two more men, but these men *were* armed.

Not for long, though. They were human, and they obviously weren't trained to deal with a faceful of deadly Barrani. They went down, again in silence. The Barrani were already on the move. There were doors here, solid doors, not cell doors; nothing from the outside could see in, and nothing from the inside could look out. Here, though, the Barrani stopped; one door was ajar.

Kaylin ran toward it; Teela caught her shoulder. Sound returned to the world in an ugly rush although magic didn't leave it; her arms and legs hurt so much she thought her skin was peeling off. And she *didn't care*. It *didn't matter*. What mattered was the door. The blood on the floor, visible in the crappy light.

She reached the door before Teela—a feat she could never manage to repeat—and threw it open as the men on the floor began to groan. She heard steel against stone, but didn't move, didn't look, didn't even try to draw her own daggers. There was a child on the floor, facedown; blood pooled around her upper body, but it was wet, red; it wasn't sticky yet.

Someone was screaming and screaming and screaming—a child, a high voice, a terrible voice. She couldn't stop. But she *moved*.

"Kaylin, *no!*" Teela shouted.

Kaylin ran to the side of the girl, knelt, and pulled her off the ground.

As she did, the floor began to *burn*.

It burned in a thin circle, a barrier of flickering light. Although it had taken the shape and the form of fire, it was *cold*. Its flame was the color of silver moon washed in a red that, no matter how pale it became, would never be pink. *Coral?* Kaylin thought, but it was brief, a flash of Caitlin. Through the flames, she rolled the girl over onto her lap and saw that the child's throat had been cut. She screamed for them both, and her cheeks were hot and wet. The child's face bore cuts.

But these cuts, unlike the cuts on the corpse in the morgue, were precise strokes, like…writing. Her face was the color of wax, this child. Her blood was still running, and Kaylin's tabard absorbed it. She drew the child into her arms, and her voice died at last into a raw silence.

"Kaylin!"

She didn't even look. Her arms, her legs, her back— they were burning, yes. But…it wasn't the burn that Ceridath's magic, or Farris's, or even the unnamed Arcanist had caused. She *knew* this warmth, this heat, this burning, even if she had never *ever* felt it so strongly. Her arms, what little of them were exposed, given her chosen burden, were so incandescent a white that they could easily be seen through her sleeves.

Through Caitlin's sleeves.

Fear hit. Relief. Terror. Hope. They tore at her, but they held her aloft at the same time. She reached out, palm against the gaping wound as if by one hand she could hold the child's throat together. She didn't *know* if this girl was Ceridath's granddaughter; she didn't care. She could do something. She could banish some memories. She could—at last—arrive *in time*.

She felt the heat in her hands, and she felt it leave; she felt the girl's throat, and she felt—as she held breath, in silence—the faintest of pulses. She touched the girl's cheeks with her palms, which was difficult given the difference in their sizes and their positions; she touched the girl's eyes, her forehead, the brief gashes in her stomach.

The girl's eyes opened.

They were the wrong shade of green.

What is this? a voice said. It was neither young nor female. The flames in the circle rose higher, lapping at her feet.

Kaylin looked through them to meet the *very* blue eyes of Teela. "Teela!" she shouted.

Teela took a step toward her and went down as Tain tackled her, full on. Behind them, jaw slack, stood Ceridath, his expression heartbreaking.

Teela rose. She kicked one of the groaning men in the face; it was vicious but short. She would have kicked Tain, but Tain was too fast for her; he got out of the way.

"Kitling!" she shouted.

Kaylin nodded. "It's—something's wrong with her—"

"It's a Harvest Circle." Teela actually punched the wall closest to the doorway. Kaylin heard it, but didn't see it. "If we'd waited until it was dark, you'd—"

"I got here *in time*. I—she's speaking," Kaylin said. "But—in a man's voice."

Teela said a whole lot of what sounded like Leontine, then, and turned to the mage. She spoke in Barrani. The mage's eyes widened and he answered—in Barrani. If it was the last thing she ever did on this earth, Kaylin was going to learn how to speak that damn language like a native.

This time, Teela approached the circle with care, but made no attempt to cross it. "The circle isn't at full power."

It doesn't need to be, the strange voice said. Kaylin realized, then, that it wasn't the girl speaking; her lips didn't move. *Tell her that, since she seems to care for you. It doesn't need to be.*

"The bastard is gloating," Kaylin translated.

"Tell him I will kill him slowly. Far, far more slowly than anyone his pathetic circle has devoured." Her eyes were now so dark a blue they were almost all black. Beauty, Kaylin realized, was death. Because Teela had never looked more beautiful than she did at this moment. She spoke, and she spoke clearly in the lilting, lovely words that were High Barrani.

Kaylin would have been terrified into a run that wouldn't have ended while she could still breathe— if then. The man—if he was that—*laughed*. At the same time, the girl stirred in Kaylin's arms. She was a stranger, a stranger's child, someone who Kaylin didn't

know and might never see again. She was also, for just
that moment, the most precious gift that Kaylin had
ever been given.

"Teela—if there are others in the other rooms, get
them out!"

"Tain is working on it," Teela replied. "They're not
in danger now. You are."

Tell her I am not here, was the whispered reply.
*I have broken none of her coveted Laws. All of the
damage and death has been caused by her mortals. It
has been a glorious Harvest, and it is not* yet *finished.*

"I think—I think he thinks he knows you."

The circle of flames grew taller and brighter. Kaylin
could still see through them.

Teela said something to Ceridath, and Ceridath shook
his head; he looked…broken.

"Try. Try, damn you."

The man laughed. *Do you understand the significance of Harvest, little one?* he asked Kaylin. *Do you
understand the significance of the lunar circle in which
you now stand? You have…surprised me. You have
taken my Harvest from me; she will not now die without my direct intervention.*

"You wanted to kill her."

*Ah, no. I merely wanted the experience of her death.
I saw it all so clearly, if briefly; she was anointed.*

"Why? *Why?*"

He laughed. It was his laughter, in the end—his
laughter, not Teela's anger or fear, not the mage's horrible despair—that pushed Kaylin over an edge she had
never realized she'd been walking. Her arms tightened
around the girl, as this man—this monster, this worse-than-vulture—continued to speak.

Death is not a given for my people. Life is, and it is endless. There is no variation; there is gain, there is loss, there is the gathering of power, the brief flower of love.

She hated that he could even use the word. Her arms were still glowing, but…they were, like the circle, burning. They were burning hot to his cold, and the cloth that covered the marks began to thin. It didn't turn to ash, though; it turned to…thought. To memory. It faded, like so many intangibles could fade: hope. Trust. Love. Even love.

But we can *experience what we have not been given; it is a gift of the Harvest Moon, for those who are willing to risk it. There is power of a different kind to be found in its ice; power, knowledge. You are born to, and of, flesh; our kind was first carved of stone, the bones of earth. The seasons shift and we are touched by their changes in a way mortals could never be. Let me tell you. Let me tell you while you give me what the circle requires before it releases us both.*

The marks on her leg were also burning, and the cloth that hid them thinned, becoming translucent. But the girl in her arms didn't burn. She began to struggle, but her struggles were as weak as she was. Her eyes were still green—and they were Barrani green, a color Kaylin should have recognized.

"Let her go," she said, voice low.

He laughed. He laughed again. *You're worried about her when* you *are here?*

"Let. Her. Go."

The fires began to bend toward her, although the boundary of the circle itself didn't change; it wouldn't.

It was clearly writ in stone. Stone, she thought, and blood.

Moon gives us the cold fire; it does not burn, but it consumes nonetheless. You can leave the circle—you can try. It may consume you. She, however, cannot. We are bound until the last of her life slips away. You have extended the offering; you cannot end it. The sun is falling; bring your mages, bring your Dragons; it matters not. She bears the marks.

"No," Kaylin said, withdrawing her hands from the girl's face. "She doesn't." The cuts were gone. Her skin was pale except where it was red-brown with her own blood, but her cheeks were entirely unblemished.

The green of only one of the girl's eyes began to fade as Kaylin watched in the light of the heightened flames. "Ceridath!" She shouted. *"Cast!"*

He looked up, looked through the fires that everyone could see, and blinked.

"Cast what?" he shouted, his hands becoming trembling fists.

"Help me see!"

His eyes widened in confusion, but he understood what she was asking; he didn't understand why. It didn't matter. She felt the familiar, comfortable pain of his spell begin to take hold, even though her marks were visible and glaring in their brilliance. She looked down at the girl's eye. At the green eye. She remembered, sickened, that the body in the morgue had been missing one eye. As Ceridath's spell heightened her own ability to see magic, she saw two signatures: one was familiar.

One was not. The unfamiliar signature was an icy-blue, a sky-blue, and it shone entirely from the iris of the emerald eye.

She'd done many things in her life. None of them had included gouging out the eyes of a child. Her stomach rebelled; her conscious thought overrode it. This *wasn't* the child's eye. Kaylin didn't even know if she could see anything through it; she was pretty certain someone—someone Barrani—did.

The flames bent in and touched Kaylin; some of the heat went out of the marks on her arms as she raised them. She felt no cold, but the child in her lap screamed as the flames also touched her.

"I'm sorry," she whispered to the girl. She looked up in helpless fear and saw that Teela and Ceridath were no longer alone; Tain had joined them. Tain, and three other children, only one of whom was now clutched in the arms of a man who loved her more than he loved, in the end, the thing that made him what he was.

The girl didn't hear her hoarse apology; the other children *did* hear the girl's screams.

What are you doing, child?

Sickened, hand shaking, Kaylin took a breath so sharp it almost cut. But her hand was steady as she reached down and plucked out the child's emerald eye.

It rested in her palm, and the worst thing about it was the fact that it seemed to be turning, as if the gaze, absent the rest of a face, was trying to see. The child stopped screaming the instant the eye was gone, and she looked up at Kaylin, her face whole except for the empty socket, her arms shaking as she stilled. The fire closed over them both, and Kaylin's marks once again lost heat; the fire, however, touched nothing. It didn't burn, any more than moonlight could.

She rose. She helped the girl to her feet, gazing at

the cut and bloody dress she now wore, at her matted hair, the things that healing could never fix—and didn't need to. But when she tried to step over the circle, she bounced. "Teela," she cried.

Teela said nothing, but she came to the circle's edge.

"Help her," Kaylin whispered. Her hand became a fist around the eye as she pushed the girl *through* the circular blanketing flames.

She then walked back to the center of the circle and opened her palm. Brilliant, and a little less green, a little more blue, the eye observed her. She could almost see the ghost of a Barrani face imposed over it, and as she concentrated, it grew stronger. It wasn't a distinctive face; to Kaylin, unaccustomed to any contact with Barrani that running could avoid, the Barrani all looked too similar.

But this face filled her not with fear, but rage.

"What are you doing?" he said. This time, his transparent lips moved as he spoke. She could see his other eye now, could see the shift, the total loss of green; his eyes weren't the blue she was accustomed to seeing in Teela, and she was grateful for that.

"If I could," she said, voice low, "I would show you mortality. You only live forever if *no one kills you*. I can't." She felt the runes on her arms and legs once again begin to burn, and this time she burned with them. "I don't care about your Harvest. I don't care about your moon. I don't care about your *boredom*."

"Is it really me that angers you?" His voice grew softer. "These children would have died anyway. They were prey to mortals, very much like themselves. I did not arrange for their deaths, and I did not offer those deaths for sale. I was aware of them, and I made my accommodations with their jailers. That is all."

"You *didn't help them*. You *knew*."

One brow rose. "I do not help cows or the sheep led to slaughter to feed your endless, messy hungers, either. Nor do you eat what is slaughtered although you raise no hand yourself. If you choose to visit the slaughterhouse, what crime do you commit? You watch, you do not affect the fate of the slaughtered one way or the other."

Her body tightened until it was hard and stiff; until she could feel—she could only feel—two things: the marks on her skin and the anger beneath it that had become everything for just a moment. She opened her mouth, but words failed her entirely; her voice did not. She screamed her rage and her pain and her helplessness, and as she did, she lifted the eye. It widened, and she closed the fist, crushing it.

She heard his scream.

She had never heard a Barrani scream before. It was *almost* enough.

Oh, but it wasn't. It *wasn't*. Because she knew as she stood, screaming and shaking, that every word he had spoken was true. Hate the Barrani, fear them—as anyone who'd lived in the fief of Nightshade learned quickly—it didn't matter: it was the *humans* who had started this. It was *men* and *women* who had taken these children and offered them gods only knew where *for sale*. The fires that had surrounded her had guttered; she didn't even know when.

But absent that cold, cold fire, there was *nothing* that could quench the flames, the rage.

"Kaylin, *no!*" Teela shouted. Tinny, tiny voice, lost in the maelstrom.

There were two men here, two men who'd had weapons, two men who had been jailers for death. For horrible, painful death. The power was still strong in her and she gestured and they rose, and their eyes widened; she *felt* their confusion give way to fear. They opened their mouths on screams and blood and the marks burned and she saw red—only red—and some of it was theirs; their blood, their skin. She peeled them open as they screamed.

But their screams weren't the only screams, and she choked, stepped, stumbled, her hand still clutching something cold and hard, her throat raw.

The children were screaming.

They were *screaming* in terror. She'd come *in time.* She'd *saved them.* And…she was terrifying them now.

No, gods, no. She wanted to tell them that she was doing this for them—or for the children who had died, or the children who wouldn't have to—but it *wasn't* the truth, and she knew it.

Teela caught her arms. Teela, Barrani, beautiful and immortal; Teela, easily bored, blue-eyed and so graceful. It was Teela who shook her; Teela who raised a hand to *slap* her, and Teela who lowered that hand when she finally met her eyes.

Kaylin turned back to the room with its fading circle of fire, shrugging at least one arm free to do it. There, her knees buckled; there, she began to retch and cough and weep.

She wasn't sure how long it took the rest of the Hawks to arrive; she wasn't sure how much time had

passed. But the marks on her arms and legs no longer
burned; they no longer glowed. They were spent, and
perhaps they were as disgusted with Kaylin as she herself was. The children—even the girl whose life she had
barely saved—avoided her; they held on to Tain or his
shadow. One girl had buried herself in Ceridath's arms,
and Ceridath held her.

But his gaze, when Kaylin rose unsteadily and joined
Teela and Tain—staying as far from the children as she
could—was full of something suspiciously like pity.
Pity was better, far better, than horror.

"Your granddaughter?" she whispered. Her throat
hurt; she wasn't sure she could speak in anything louder.

He nodded. "Meredith," he said into her hair as she refused to turn to Kaylin. Her hair, which was almost black,
and was so ratty, so tangled, so dirty. "I know. But…
Kaylin saved you, in the end. If it were not for Kaylin—"

But the child wouldn't look at Kaylin. And Kaylin,
looking at what remained of the men she had killed—
horribly, brutally killed—couldn't blame her.

Marcus was there. Somehow. Marcus, four Barrani
Hawks, and—of all people—Clint, his wing ridges
high, his eyes a blue that was, as he saw Kaylin, shad-
ing to gray. Marcus said something to Teela and Tain—
his eyes were orange, and the orange didn't fade.

But Ceridath understood what was said, even if Kaylin
couldn't. He lifted his chin from its messy, beloved perch,
and he spoke in soft, modulated High Barrani.

Teela and Tain exchanged a glance, but said nothing
as they looked at Ceridath.

"What did he say?" Kaylin asked sharply, her voice
rough and low. "Teela—tell me. Did he—did he tell the
Sergeant that *he* killed those men?"

Ceridath looked at her over his granddaughter's head. "I have nothing left to lose," he told Kaylin softly. "Everything that I could possibly hope to preserve is safe, now."

But she shook her head, in pain. She looked at the blood-soaked Hawk that rested on her chest—well, more on her stomach, really, because the tabard was just too damn large, even cut down—and she wanted to cry. She lifted her chin instead, exposing her throat, and exposing everything else as well. "I killed them," she told Sergeant Kassan. "He didn't."

"Kaylin," Ceridath shook his head. "Let me—"

Marcus flexed claws; he had no further glance to spare the mage. "How?"

Clint's eyes had now stopped their shift to gray.

"I don't know," was her quiet reply. "I don't know *how*. Does it matter? They'd been disarmed. They couldn't do anything else." She lowered her chin because she lowered her head. "I was just *so angry*. I couldn't reach the other. I wanted them to suffer. I wanted them to die. I wanted them to understand what it felt like to be a helpless victim." She raised her head again, trying not to cry. "Are you going to arrest me now?"

His eyes were an odd shade of gold. When they'd become gold, she didn't know; she hadn't been looking at him.

"Kitling," he said. "Come here."

She didn't. Instead, she began to remove the tabard. She stopped when he growled.

"Did I or did I not give you an order?"

"You did," Teela said. "I heard it."

"Half the block heard it," Tain muttered.

Kaylin stared at him in confusion.

"Did I?" He barked.

"Yes?"

"Yes, what?"

"Yes, sir."

"Good. Then *why are you still standing there?"*

She looked back at Teela, Tain, and the children who huddled directly behind them. Teela nudged her forward.

She walked like a condemned person to where the Leontine Sergeant stood, and lifted her chin again. But he caught it, and she discovered that the pads of his paws were very, very soft—or at least they could be. He didn't speak; he met her eyes and held her gaze for what seemed like minutes. And then he cuffed the side of her head gently.

"Go with Clint," he told her. "He'll take you back to Caitlin. We've got a few hours of work to do here; wait with her. I'll need to speak with Lord Grammayre after the debriefing." He growled, and added, "Stay out of trouble. If Teela and Tain make it back to the office in one piece," and he glanced at them and growled again, "keep *away* from them."

Teela raised a brow, but was wise enough—or amused enough—to make no comment.

Kaylin looked at Clint, who was watching her, arms folded across his broad chest. He didn't smile, but he didn't frown, either; he just nodded.

"Go *straight* there."

The moon was full and low; the sky was the type of clear only the coldest of winter sees. But it wasn't cold. Kaylin knew because she was *in* it. Clint had made clear that holding on as tightly as she wanted to was just one side of strangulation—the wrong side—and she'd done her best to relax her grip; to let him do the work.

To trust him to carry her.

"He's not mad at me?" She raised her voice when the wind grew louder.

"The Sergeant? No. He *will* be when the paperwork hits his desk, but you've got the brains to hide behind Caitlin." His arms tightened briefly. "He's Leontine. He's practical. There's no way those men would have survived the end of their trial." He was quiet for a moment, and his eyes were a soft shade of ash-gray. They looked odd; the rest of his face was so dark and so warm. "I don't know what's going to happen to you," he added, because he knew she was afraid. "But I know it won't happen without a fight. You're too damn young to be a Hawk.

"But without you, there'd be four more corpses in the morgue. Teela won't let anyone forget, and Barrani memory is perfect. Just remember when you start basic training: you *wanted* to be here."

Directly to the Halls took an hour, and it passed over parts of the City the carriage hadn't. She pointed at things. She asked him a hundred questions. He answered them all, his voice low and deep, coming somewhere from his chest. She didn't want to land, but landing—like waking—was going to happen anyway, so she tried to remember everything, because memory, no one could steal.

It was late, and the office should have been empty, but Caitlin was there, at her desk, her mirror blank. She looked up when she saw Kaylin, and stood. Kaylin, still

covered in blood—although it was mostly dry now—
hesitated, and Caitlin walked around the desk toward
her, where she engulfed her in a fierce hug. When she let
go, she said, "I have food, dear. I'm certain you haven't
eaten.

"And I've got some news."

"The landlord?"

"We're scheduled to see the apartment in two days."

"But the money—"

Caitlin smiled, although it seemed like a nervous
smile. "We do have the funds, but it was a little more
complicated to get at them than I'd expected. The rules
with regard to non-casual labor are actually quite strict,
and you are, unfortunately, very underage."

Kaylin wilted.

"But as I said, the funding is available."

"How?"

"I'm not sure you'll like it, dear."

How bad could it be? "As long as I don't have to kill
anyone, I don't care."

Caitlin looked shocked the way only Caitlin could.
And mildly disapproving. Kaylin slid around her to the
food that she'd promised. "You most certainly will not
have to kill anyone. But…the department *has* funds set
aside, in principle, for a departmental mascot."

"A what?"

"A mascot, dear. You've never heard of them?"

Kaylin, mouth full of bread, shook her head.

"Ah. Well. A mascot is supposed to bring good luck
to, ah, an organization. It's also thought to be a symbol
of something the organization stands for."

"So what part won't I like?"

Caitlin just shook her head and smiled. "You'll find

out, dear. Chew before you swallow. You'll be good for the department," she added. "I don't think I've ever seen Teela quite so…human. Don't repeat that where she can hear it, and do remember the Barrani have much better hearing than ours.

"Give me the tabard. I'll make sure it's cleaned. You'll need it. It's large," she added, "but I'm certain you'll grow into it."

* * * * *

And so Kaylin begins her time with the Hawks. Chronologically, look for CAST IN SHADOW to continue her story.

But don't miss her new adventure in **CAST IN RUINS**

RETRIBUTION

Cameron Haley

For Mashenka

⦾⦾ RETRIBUTION

Author's Note: This takes place several months before MOB RULES

I was twelve years old the first time I killed a man. It stayed with me a long time. Literally. The guy haunted me for more than two years until Shanar Rashan, my mentor and the boss of my outfit, taught me how to exorcise a ghost.

I learned a lot from that experience. I learned I didn't have to feel helpless, because I wasn't. Turns out, a twelve-year-old budding sorceress is a poor choice of victim for a child predator. It was a powerful lesson for a fatherless girl coming up in the barrio.

But I also learned that killing a guy is the easy part—it's what comes after that's difficult. You gotta take care of the body, and you gotta ditch the ghost.

Crossroads are happening places in the supernatural underworld. Magic flows through the skin of the world, but its course is directed by the landscape, both natural and manmade. A crossroads is a place where these flows converge. That's one reason large cities are so rich in magic—they're full of crossroads.

A crossroads is also an excellent place to kill a man, because these same properties disorient and confuse his ghost. Of course, while the city streets are rich in magic, there are better choices when a guy needs killing. The corner of Hollywood and Vine may be a good spot to ditch a vengeful spirit, but you run the risk that the murder will show up on YouTube.

So that's how I found myself at the intersection of two dirt roads in the Mojave Desert under the light of a gibbous moon, looking down at the disabled form of Benny Ben-Reuven. Benny was an Israeli gangster in my outfit who'd recently attempted to secure a promotion by putting a bullet in my skull. The fact that he'd tried to shoot me should have clued him in that he wasn't ready. If he couldn't take me out with sorcery, what made him think he was more qualified to be Shanar Rashan's lieutenant?

Benny's wrists and ankles were bound to stakes driven into the earth, more for effect than necessity. I'd used a binding spell on him before we left the city that pretty much guaranteed he wouldn't be any trouble. But gangsters are creatures of habit and tradition, and we don't call them ritual executions for nothing.

"I hate to kill someone as stupid as you, Benny," I said.

"You don't have to do it, Domino. You don't have to do this. We could—"

"Benny, please," I said, shaking my head. "It's just a figure of speech. I don't really mind killing you. No reason to be unpleasant about it, though."

Benny fell silent. His eyes were wide, and he started

shaking. Maybe I was telling the truth. Maybe I didn't hate it. I guess that's another lesson I learned when I was twelve. Murder isn't pleasant, but it's not horrific, either, when the victim has it coming. More often than not, it's just pathetic.

"Thing is, I need to know if someone was behind you." I shrugged. "I can take what I need to know, if I have to. But it'll hurt. Easier if you just tell me."

Benny jerked his head from side to side. "No one knew, Domino. It was just me. I didn't come to this country to be some woman's dog."

I nodded and started pulling juice from the wasteland. "You got anything else you want to say, Benny?"

Benny did. He said it in a language I didn't understand, presumably his native Hebrew. I didn't know the words, but I recognized the cadence and I could sense the magic pouring into him from the desert, crashing over the metaphysical levy I'd created with my binding ritual. Benny was spinning a spell—a big one—and never mind that he shouldn't have been able to draw any juice through my ritual.

There's no percentage in allowing a guy to complete a death curse. I spun my own spell, chanting the words I'd memorized when I learned the invocation. "It is easy to go down into Hell," I said. "Night and day, the gates of dark Death stand wide." I reached out with the black magic and ruptured the artery in Benny's brain. The death spell is quick and painless, though it needs too much juice and precision to make it effective in a real fight. It's the right way to execute a guy when you have to do it.

Benny died instantly, but that didn't shut him up. His corpse completed the curse. I heard my name, Dominica, and my mother's name, Gisele Maria Lopez Riley. Then blood frothed from Benny's mouth and his corpse fell silent.

Like I said, in the underworld, killing a guy is just the beginning.

My car died on the way back to the city. There was nothing suspicious about this in itself. I drive a 1965 Lincoln Continental convertible, and whatever points I get for style, there's a downside to owning a car that's older than I am.

I was cruising along Highway 62 surrounded by nothing but desert and moon-washed darkness when the Lincoln coughed a few times and gave it up. I wrestled the car to the shoulder and switched on the emergency lights. I spun my nightvision spell and popped the hood. I went around to the front of the car and stared at the engine. It popped and clicked as it cooled. No obvious wires or hoses had come loose, which was just as well since I wouldn't have known how to reconnect them anyway.

Some people just assume magic and technology don't mix. In fact, magic mixes with anything if you know how to do it. Unfortunately, I suck at fixing things in general, mechanical things in particular, and I didn't have any spells that would get the Lincoln running again.

I pulled out my cell to call Rafael Chavez. He was one of the more competent gangsters in my outfit and I'd known him since I was a kid. He'd send someone to pick me up. I activated the cell and looked at the screen.

No signal.

My magic isn't much use with a dead engine, but I'm

enough of a sorcerer to make a call. I pulled in some juice and cast my voice out toward the distant city.

"Chavez."

"Domino?" The voice was sleepy. "What is it? Did you—"

"I'm fine, Chavez. I finished that job we talked about." The Organized Crime Task Force isn't likely to eavesdrop on a magical conversation, but that's no reason to get sloppy. "My car died. I need you to send someone."

"No problem, *chola*. Where are you?"

"Hell if I know…the middle of the fucking desert, not far from Twentynine Palms, maybe. Follow the link." With a little effort, Chavez could use my calling spell to locate me.

"Okay, sit tight. I'll get someone there yesterday."

I broke the connection and returned to the car. My nightvision spell amplified the moonlight, but it was still dark. And quiet.

"Too quiet," I said, and snickered.

The problem with using magic in the wasteland is that the wasteland isn't empty, and the magic lights you up like a beacon. Something old and hungry moved out there in the night. I felt it, like a hot wind stirring more than anything solid.

I crossed myself. I was Catholic in the same way I was American—by birth. As a sorcerer, I had my own rituals, and the Church never held them in high regard. But unlike most Catholics in the modern world, I still believed in the spooky parts of the faith. So even though I had my own spells and protections if something went down, I crossed myself. I didn't know what was out there, but it was a pretty good bet that God had a beef with it. The *Signum Crucis* was just my way of giving Him a heads up on the off chance He wanted to lay down some smite.

It'd never actually worked, probably because God had a beef with me, too. This time was no different. To the naked eye, nothing much happened. By my witch sight, though, I saw a black fog roll in from the desert. It roiled onto the highway and coalesced into the form of a man who appeared in midstride and walked toward my car. I watched the figure approach until he stopped at the edge of the circle I'd put down with sand and as much juice as I could squeeze from the desert night.

The man looked down at the circle and laughed. He breathed in deep through his nose, like he was taking in some fresh air. He was young, early twenties, with dark wavy hair that fell to his shoulders and a trim build. He wore a leather motorcycle jacket, battered jeans and cowboy boots. He was attractive in a completely inhuman way that's not really my type.

"You've been a busy bee," he said as he began walking around the edge of the circle.

"Idle hands are the Devil's tools."

The man laughed again. "He makes good use of ambitious ones, too."

"Who are you?"

"Call me Sam," he said. He was behind me now, following the edge of the circle behind my car.

"What do you want, Sam?"

"Make a guess."

"Fix my car?"

"Guess again."

"Suck the marrow from my bones?"

"Warmer."

"Well, you're not going to breach that circle, so you might as well go away."

"I've got some time. Maybe we can get to know each other, Domino."

This was the part where I was supposed to ask how he knew my name, except I'd have been more surprised if he didn't know my name.

"I'm not in the mood."

"Humor me. You killed a man tonight."

"You looking to be number two?"

Sam laughed. He was in front of the car again, and the hazards bathed him intermittently in orange light. "I'm not a man."

"Insecurity isn't sexy."

"How did that feel?"

"Solid. You gave me a perfect opening, but the timing—"

"Not the line, I mean the murder you did. How did that feel?"

"It didn't." I regretted it as soon as the words came out of my mouth. I'd have been better off with the snark and nothing but the snark.

"Nothing at all? Oh, that's cold. Such a monster."

I shrugged. "He tried to kill me. He made a play and came up short. Nothing to feel bad about."

Sam nodded. "I know just what you mean."

"So why do you want to kill me?"

"I don't *want* to, necessarily. There's a contract. I'm the guy they sent. You know how it is."

I suppose I should have been expecting it, but I was surprised. I'd been certain Sam was some sleepy old spirit my calling spell had woken up. I didn't think Benny had the chops for a real summoning. "The curse? You came on account of Benny?"

Sam shrugged. "Not at liberty, et cetera, et cetera."

I hadn't been able to understand the words of Benny's death curse, but there'd been enough juice to power a summoning. If that's what it was, there were certain rules I might be able to turn to my advantage.

"Maybe we can make a deal."

Sam arched an eyebrow. "What kind of deal?"

I hate making deals with spirits, mainly because it's damned hard to make a *good* one. Still, I didn't really want Sam hanging around when my ride showed. I might be protected from him, but whoever Chavez sent to pick me up wouldn't be.

"I could buy out your contract."

Sam shook his head, smiling sadly. "The contract is binding." His face brightened and he laughed. "Besides, it's what I do."

"Well, like I said, you're not getting through that circle, so I guess we can just sit here until the sun comes up."

"Yeah, about that…" Sam extended his arm across the plane of my circle and waved his hand at me. Then he stuck his foot across the line and shook it. "Hokey-pokey," he said.

Despite the shock, my training and a survival instinct bred on the streets took over and I reached for the juice. I started to spin a combat spell, but suddenly there was no air in my lungs. I couldn't speak, couldn't think, and the juice bled away into the night.

I was suffocating.

Sam vanished and reappeared beside me in the car. I reached for the forty-five holstered under my left arm, but he shook his head and I was pinned back in the driver's seat by an unseen force.

He took the pack of Camels from my dash, tapped one out and rolled the end between his thumb and forefinger until it lit. He took a long drag and blew it out in a thin stream. "Good news or bad news first?" he asked.

I still couldn't speak, so I made choking sounds instead.

Sam nodded at me.

"Bad news," I gasped.

"No power of this world can save you from me. Not your magic and not your gun. Your life has been given over to me and I will take it."

"Good news?"

"You've got three days," he said, leaning back in the seat and gazing up into the moonlit sky. "I'll take you when the moon is full."

"That's the good news?"

Sam laughed. "Yeah, and I'll be honest, it's not even that good. They're going to be the last three days of your life, but they won't be your best."

"So why wait? Why not get it over with?"

"Don't be impatient. As bad as the coming days will be, you're going to like what comes after even less."

"That's bullshit. You think you got the juice, take your best shot."

"It's in the contract. Three days of torment, then you die. It's a Jewish death curse." Sam shrugged apologetically. "The Jews are good at curses."

"That's anti-Semitic."

"No, it's a compliment. The Israelites are my peeps. We go way back. But an astonishing variety of people have been trying to kill them for millennia, and they've had a lot of practice with death curses."

"So, what…plagues, frogs, the life of my firstborn?"

"You have a child?"

"Not that I know of."

He nodded, grinning. "Anyway, that stuff is culturally specific. But I'll come up with something."

"Good. I fucking hate frogs."

"Thanks for the smoke, Domino. See you soon."

"Not if I see you first," I muttered, but I was alone in the car.

A wrecker out of Palm Springs showed up about half an hour later. I paid the guy a small fortune to tow the Lincoln all the way back into L.A. I wasn't sure how long it would be in the shop, but I was sure I didn't want to leave my car to the tender mercies of some high-desert redneck.

The wrecker left the Lincoln with my favorite mechanic and dropped me at my condo. I was hungry and there was nothing but beer and frozen burritos in my fridge. I welcomed the beer, but I couldn't face a burrito that late at night. I ordered chicken fried rice and a couple egg rolls from the all-night Chinese joint around the corner.

When the delivery guy arrived, I discovered I didn't have my wallet. I had some cash in a drawer in the kitchen, so I was able to pay for the food. But I'd lost my wallet.

Gangsters often prided themselves on living off the

grid and outside the normal rules of society. I was no different, I guess, but it only goes so far. Yeah, technically, I could put the hoodoo on anyone who asked for ID, but it's usually a lot easier to make with the driver's license or dry-cleaning receipt, as the case may be. So never mind that I'm a gangster and a sorcerer—losing my wallet was as big a pain in the ass for me as it would have been for any civilian.

Mentally retracing my steps, I remembered I'd had my wallet in the tow truck when I paid the driver. I couldn't remember having it after that, so there was a good chance I left it in the truck. I remembered the driver had given me a business card in case I ever broke down in the middle of the desert again. I was pretty sure I'd put the card in my wallet.

The tow service had been…Mike's Towing. Or Mack's Garage. Maybe Moe's Wrecker Service. Something like that. The chances were pretty good that Mike, Mack, or Moe would discover my wallet and give me a call. Failing that, Chavez had called the guy and he'd probably remember the name.

I ate my late-night dinner and caught a couple hours of fitful sleep. I woke to loud, insistent pounding on my door. I opened it to find a couple of detectives calling on me. There was a black woman with intelligent eyes and an interesting face in her mid-forties, and an older guy, the one with gray hair and bushy mustache who's riding out his last days on the job before retirement.

"I didn't do it," I said, and made to close the door. The old guy blocked it with his forearm and glared at me.

"Dominica Riley?" the woman asked.

"Maybe."

"Detective Meadows and Detective Sullivan. We'd like to ask you a few questions. Can we come in?"

"What kind of questions?"

The old guy, Detective Sullivan, produced a plastic bag from his jacket pocket. My wallet was inside. "We found something that belongs to you," he said.

"Oh, cool," I said, and reached for it. "You could have just dropped it in the mail, but thanks for stopping by."

Sullivan jerked the bag away from me. "Your wallet was found at a crime scene, Ms. Riley," Meadows said. "Now, can we come in, or should we come back with a warrant?"

"Give me the wallet and I'll answer your questions," I said. I put some juice into it, not a real spell but just enough spontaneous magic to make the suggestion stick.

"Sure," Sullivan said, and handed me the bag. Then he frowned. "We'll need that back at some point. It's evidence."

"Yeah, whatever." I showed them in and closed the door. I took the wallet out of the bag and tucked it in the pocket of my robe. I pointed to the sofa and the cops sat.

"Nice place," said Meadows. She seemed to be watching me a little too closely. Her attention was fixated on my talismans—I didn't take them off, even when I slept. The talismans—jewelry and such—stored protective spells I could trigger in an emergency. They had juice, but a civilian wouldn't notice. "What did you say you do, again?" the detective asked.

"I didn't."

"I know what you are," Meadows said. "You work for Shanar Rashan, don't you?"

I did my best to keep the shock off my face and took a closer look at the detective. She didn't have much more juice than the average civilian, but she was obviously a sensitive. She couldn't flow any juice or spin a spell, but she could feel it, maybe even see it, like a crude form of my witch sight.

"Oh, for Christ's sake, not this shit again," Sullivan said. "There's no Shanar Rashan. He doesn't exist. Can't we just stick to the real criminals?"

"You want some coffee?" I asked.

"Sure," Sullivan said. Meadows kept watching me.

"I don't have any. Beer?"

"We're on duty and it's eight-thirty in the morning."

"No beer, then." I went to sit in the armchair by the French doors that open onto the balcony, but Sam was already sitting there, grinning at me.

"What the fuck are you doing here?"

"Excuse me, Ms. Riley?" Detective Meadows frowned. "As we explained, we have some questions…" She obviously wasn't sensitive enough to see Sam.

"I'm just for you," said Sam, laughing.

I shook my head and dropped into the recliner. "Sorry, still asleep. What do you want to know?"

"Where were you last night?" Meadows asked.

"I stayed in and had Chinese," I said, pointing to the cartons on the coffee table.

"You don't really have any friends, do you?" Sam asked. "And you can't even trust most of the people you work with. You're completely alone."

I glared at him and started to respond, then looked quickly back to the detectives and faked a yawn.

"What time was that?" asked Meadows.

"Late."

"Where were you earlier?"

"In the desert."

"What were you doing in the desert?"

"Murder," said Sam.

"Getting some air," I said.

"That's it?"

"Yeah. I thought about a mud bath, but I don't really see the point."

"And later?"

"Tell them about how you nuked Benny's corpse with a fire spell," Sam suggested.

"I had some car trouble. Hired a wrecker service to tow my car back to the city."

"And what time was that?"

"Maybe two, two-thirty."

"And this wrecker service, it was Mark's Garage out of Palm Springs?"

"Yeah, that sounds right. Or Mike's Garage. Maybe Mack's."

"It was Mark's," Sullivan growled.

"Okay."

"And what happened when you got back to the city?"

"Nothing. He took my car to a mechanic and dropped me off here."

"Was there an argument? Maybe there was a disagreement about the charges?"

"Why don't you ask Mark?"

"He's dead," Sullivan said. "He was the victim of an apparent homicide last night. That's the crime scene I mentioned. Speaking of which, we're going to need that wallet back. It's evidence."

"I took his heart," Sam said. "There was a lot of blood, but I tucked your wallet under the body—that's why it's clean. 'Course, they're probably wondering how it got under the body."

I sighed. "Look, I'm sorry to hear that. But I don't know anything that will help you and you're not going to pin it on me, so maybe we can just wrap this up."

Sam appeared beside me suddenly, sitting on the recliner's armrest. I jumped and then tried to make like I was stretching. I glanced guiltily at the detectives. They seemed to be losing their patience.

"Maybe you'd like to go downtown to answer our questions," Sullivan said.

Even when you tried to cooperate, cops always got around to the threats. They have their rituals just like gangsters do. Sorcery wasn't an easy solution in a case like this. I could juice them and make them go away. I could make them forget about me completely. But they wouldn't be working the case alone and their blind spot about me would eventually attract the attention and suspicion of others. My boss used a lot of juice to keep himself and our outfit off the radar, and I didn't want to screw it up.

"You could rat me out," Sam said. "Go ahead—tell them I'm their guy. I don't mind if you give me up. The woman might even believe you."

"Tell you what," I said to Meadows. "Give me a card. If I think of anything else, I'll call you. I'm not going to leave town or anything. Promise."

They looked at each other and Sullivan shrugged. Meadows nodded and handed me her card. "Do that, Ms. Riley. And if we need anything from you in the meantime, we'll be back with paper."

Sam was waiting by the door. "I believe I'll kill one of them. Which one should I choose? Detective Sullivan can already smell his pension…that would either be horribly clichéd or deliciously ironic. What do you think, Domino?"

I opened the door for the detectives and forced a smile onto my face. "Look, thanks for coming by. I know you're just doing your job. If I can help, I will."

"Goodbye, Ms. Riley," said Meadows. She held my gaze a long time, as if to remind me she was onto my game.

"Yeah, we're going to need to get that wallet back," said Sullivan, "it's evi—"

I closed the door and pressed my back against it.

"I told you it wouldn't be your best three days," Sam said. He winked at me and disappeared.

In the old days, a sorcerer who needed to solve an arcane mystery might sift through dusty tomes of occult lore. I didn't have any dusty tomes, but I did have Wikipedia. The site itself wasn't much use—for real lore, I mean—but I could use it as a focus for divination magic.

I powered up the laptop in my office and brought the search window up on the screen. I typed *Sam* in the box and conjured an image of the spirit in my mind. Tapping the ley line running under my condo, I hit the enter key and triggered the divination ritual.

THERE WERE NO RESULTS
MATCHING YOUR QUERY.

This was disappointing but not entirely surprising. It just meant that, whatever he was, Sam had enough mojo to block my efforts to invade his privacy. Fortunately, I had a backup plan. Unfortunately, I'd really been hoping I wouldn't have to use it.

I went over to a low table by the window and flipped the power switch on a thirteen-inch black-and-white TV I'd had since I was a kid. It's where I kept my familiar, a jinn whose name was Abishanizad. I called him Mr. Clean. Long story.

It took a while for the tube to warm up, but the image of Mr. Clean's thick neck and bald, round head gradually materialized. Specifically, the back of his thick neck and bald, round head—Mr. Clean appeared to be sitting with his back to me. This was new, and I took a moment to consider it.

The interesting thing was that Mr. Clean was a spirit, and so he did not strictly exist in any physical sense. He didn't occupy any position in space by virtue of which his back would appear to me. He was merely an incorporeal entity magically bound to the television set.

Thus, by appearing with his back to me, Mr. Clean was making a statement, much like a gorilla at the zoo that sits with his back to the rubes come to gawk at him. I didn't know enough about either spirits or gorillas to be sure, but I figured the statement translated roughly as "Fuck off."

"You remind me of a gorilla at the zoo," I said.

"Fuck off," replied Mr. Clean in his rumbling baritone. He didn't turn around.

"Suit yourself," I said. "I need some information."

Mr. Clean's broad, muscular shoulders rose and fell as he sighed, but he didn't respond.

"Yeah, so, this spirit has been, I don't know, stalking me, I guess. I need to get the lowdown on him."

"Why is this spirit stalking you?"

"I don't know, for sure. It may be—"

"Maybe you imprisoned him in a box and he finally broke free, and now he wants to tear you limb from limb?"

"No, I just met this cat. He says it's a contract."

"What kind of contract?"

"The gangster kind. See, I had to kill this guy Benny Ben-Reuven, on account of he tried to kill me…"

"I'm not really interested in your desperate rationalizations," Mr. Clean interjected.

"…and I think he put a death curse on me. So this spirit—says his name is Sam—is stalking me, claims he's going to torment me for three days before killing me."

"And?"

"And, I want to know what you might have on this guy—the spirit, I mean."

Mr. Clean turned to face me, finally. "Tell me the curse."

"What do you mean?"

"I mean, recite the words, meathead."

"I can't. It was in Hebrew, I guess."

Mr. Clean chuckled. It was the kind of sound the universe might make if it was laughing at you. I didn't like it.

"What's so funny, gorilla-boy?"

"The murder victim, he was Jewish?"

"Yeah, Israeli."

"I believe I can identify the spirit," said Mr. Clean.

"Cool."

"This knowledge has a price."

It always does. Like I said, I hate dealing with spirits. I scored the grand prize in the familiar sweepstakes with Mr. Clean—he's powerful, ancient and knowledgeable. Where the supernatural is concerned, it's like having an informant on the inside. The downside is everything is quid pro quo: I have to offer the jinn some hypothetical future service if I want his help with anything. Really, it's more like a karmic debt I'm accumulating, and Mr. Clean is holding my marker. Someday I'll have to pay him off, plus the vig. So you could say the jinn is my familiar, but you could also say he's my loan shark.

"I could wash your car." I suppose I was thinking about the Lincoln. I'd been worrying about it all day.

"I don't drive," said Mr. Clean.

"What does it matter? It's just hypothetical anyway."

"Because this service is of no value to me, you could later claim that you'd only committed to perform an irrelevant service."

Good idea. Wish I'd thought of it.

"What then? I don't have time for this shit."

"I will require a massage."

I laughed. "Keep dreaming, genie. There's no way I do anything even hypothetically equivalent to giving you a massage."

"It's not sexual. It's therapeutic."

"It's not very therapeutic, either, because it's never going to happen. What else you got?"

"You can pick up my dry cleaning."

"You live in a Zenith."

"For the moment. When I gain my freedom, I'll be able to take physical form. I prefer my shirts starched and pressed."

"Okay, I can do that."

"Then we have a—"

"Wait! I'll pick up your dry cleaning *once*." Like a wireless provider, Mr. Clean is always angling to trap me in an open-ended service agreement.

Mr. Clean grunted. "What I've already told you is worth more than that. You will perform this service ten times, at my request."

"Three."

"Ten."

"Five."

"Ten."

"Done," I said, thankful there were no witnesses to my negotiating skills. "Give it to me. What is Sam?"

"His real name is Samael."

"Never heard of him."

"The Angel of Death."

I'd been wisecracking with the "life of my firstborn" bit, but it turned out I was right on the money. "Benny Ben-Reuven called in a fucking angel to hit me? He doesn't have the juice...didn't have the juice...whatever."

Mr. Clean shrugged. "Your victim believed this entity was Samael, the Angel of Death. Whether it actually is that being, or whether any such being actually exists...there may be a definitive answer to this question, but it is not one that hairless apes are given to know, even those who play at magic tricks."

"That was an insult, wasn't it?"

"Yeah."

"Sticks and stones, Smokey. Your theory still doesn't explain how Benny was able to bring in that kind of hitter. He wasn't much of a sorcerer. He tried to cap me, for fuck's sake. With a gun."

"This was a death curse."

"Yeah?"

"You were in the process of murdering this man. You were taking all he was and all he would ever be. That's a lot of juice, even for one with little talent for sorcery. He took that power, before you could, and he used it to summon this being."

"Damn, I need something like that."

"I could teach you a death curse. It would be costly."

"How costly?"

"The massage would have a Happy Ending."

"Oh, hell, no. Tell me how I get out from under this thing."

"You don't."

"I don't?"

"No. You can't weasel your way out of it. The contract was paid in blood. Ben-Reuven purchased your death with his own."

"What an asshole."

"You're hardly in a position to throw stones." Mr. Clean shrugged. "All's fair in love and black magic."

"Okay, I can't get away from the contract. What are my other options, assuming I'm not interested in dying?"

"What do you offer for this knowledge?"

"I'm already picking up your laundry five times."

"It's ten, and anyway, that was payment for the identity of your assassin. If you would know how to stop Samael, you must offer some further service. It had better be good."

My life was on the line and I figured it was time to make the jinn my best offer. "Rashan runs some massage parlors," I said, choking down the nausea that rose in my stomach. "I'll hook you up." The parlors were juice boxes, arcane dens fronting for sex-magic rituals. But despite this secret purpose—or rather because of it—they were also the place to go in L.A. for a world-class rub-and-tug.

"Done!" Mr. Clean said with an unwholesome gleam in his eye.

"Okay, Desperado, make with the knowledge. How do I stop Samael?"

"If this entity truly is Samael, the Angel of Death, you're boned, to use the popular vernacular."

"That vernacular really isn't popular anymore."

"Do you want to hear this?"

"Yeah."

"You do not have the power to defeat one of the Host, and Samael—the real Samael—is a badass even by the standards of the Seraphim."

"What if he's not a real angel?"

"Then you can simply kill him."

"But if he is a real angel, he'll wipe the floor with me."

Mr. Clean glowered. "Your surfeit of intellectual capacity is truly remarkable."

"I was smart enough to put you in that box."

"The point is," Mr. Clean growled, "if this entity is truly Samael, he must follow the rules. He will not take your life until three days have passed. Even if you try to kill him."

"So I get a free shot at him," I said, nodding. "If he's a poseur, maybe I take him out. If he's the real deal, no harm no foul. He still has to wait until the stars are right."

"The moon, actually."

"That's actually pretty clever, Snowball."

"It goes without saying."

"Fine, next time I won't say it. So what's my first move?"

Mr. Clean's eyes grew wide momentarily, and then he sighed. "I suggest you develop a plan of attack on your own. It would be a tactical error for me to advise you on this."

"Why's that? You want your Happy Ending or not?"

Sam's head popped up behind Mr. Clean and he grinned at me over the jinn's shoulder. "Because if you keep running that pretty mouth, I'll know exactly what you're planning to do."

I switched off the Zenith and unplugged it for good measure, and then I went into the bathroom to grab a shower. I didn't like the idea of Sam popping in for one of his unannounced visits, but I also didn't like the idea of spending the next three days with that not-so-fresh feeling. Besides, I do some of my best thinking in the shower.

Sam's appearance in Mr. Clean's TV didn't exactly inspire confidence in my plan. If nothing else, the stunt made it clear that even if he wasn't a real angel, Sam might still be able to take me to school. Hell, maybe he already had taken me to school when he introduced himself out in the desert. My circle hadn't seemed to bother him much. The truth was, I didn't know a lot about spirits or what they were capable of. I'd only ever summoned the one, Mr. Clean, and that had mostly been an accident. And besides, so far the results of that play were decidedly mixed.

Other than the jinn, I'd never given much thought to spirits. For that matter, even my own sorcery didn't involve a lot of knowledge. I'd always been able to use magic, and even though Rashan had showed me how to improve my command of it back in the day, I didn't really know how or why it worked. For a sorcerer, I knew fuck-all about the supernatural.

I did have my spellcraft, though, and I knew a fair amount of necromancy, including the spell that would return a dead soul to the Beyond, the one I'd used to deal with the pedophile I'd killed when I was a girl. Problem was, I didn't think Sam was a spirit of the dead. Whatever he was—assuming he wasn't the Angel of Death, I mean—he was probably something more akin to Mr. Clean.

I was a gangster, so I did know a thing or two about doing a hit. The key to doing it right was control. You control the situation, the environment, and the timing, and you control the target. Everything that happens or doesn't happen, it's because that's the way you want it. No surprises, no loose ends. The trick was going to be achieving that level of control when I didn't know exactly what Sam was or what he could do. They say a player can only play the cards she's dealt.

They only say that because they don't know how to cheat.

When I showed up at the shop, my mechanic told me he couldn't find anything wrong with the Lincoln. I paid him for his trouble, made a couple stops, and then drove east out of the city as the sun set in my rearview mirror.

If there's a list of common mistakes criminals make, returning to the scene of the crime is probably at the top of it. Right up there with leaving your wallet under the body. Still, I had work to do and you could say I was up against a deadline. The cops had a hard-on for me about Mark of Mark's Garage out of Palm Springs, but I doubted they knew anything about the late Benny Ben-Reuven. At least, I hoped Samael hadn't gotten around to telling them about it yet.

The Angel of Death—or whatever he was—joined me in the passenger seat after about an hour of highway time.

"This isn't going to work," he said.

"What isn't going to work?"

Samael turned around and looked at the TV sitting on the backseat. He grabbed the plastic bag and removed the item I'd picked up from the dollar store. It was a plastic angel statuette.

"This doesn't look anything like me," Samael said. The plastic angel had long blond hair, molded wings, white robes, and a yellow harp and halo.

"Why should it? That's an angel. You're just some wannabe bogeyman Benny juiced up out of the desert."

"Why do you need your pet devil?" Samael asked, jerking a thumb over his shoulder.

"Mr. Clean's not a devil. He's just some wannabe bogeyman *I* juiced up out of the desert."

Samael chuckled. "You're sure about that?"

"He's a jinn."

"You say jinn, I say devil…" Samael shrugged.

"Well, if you think he's a devil, I'll count that as a point in his favor."

Samael nodded. "So what's he for?"

"He keeps me company."

"You didn't need his company before, when you brought Benny out here to murder him."

"Well, I had Benny to keep me company that time, didn't I?"

"Only on the trip out," said Samael. "Speaking of Benny, who takes over his crew now that you've killed him?"

"I've got someone in mind. Don't worry your pretty little head about it."

"Carmen Leeds? You were planning to bring her in from Amy Chen's crew, weren't you?"

I looked over at Samael and scowled. "Like I said, don't worry about it."

"Thing is, I don't think that's going to work out." The frown of mock concern on his face made me want to shoot him. "See, someone must have tipped off Benny's crew, and I guess they didn't like the idea too much. Seems Jefferson Alexander figured he was next in line."

Jefferson Alexander was something of a minority in the underworld, in the sense that he wasn't a minority. He was a waspy Pasadena kid from old money—at least old by Southern California standards. People from privileged backgrounds didn't usually find their way into the underworld. I had no reason to think rich white kids couldn't have juice—it seemed to be completely random. But magic happened on the margins of society, and privilege had a way of keeping you safely away from the margins.

Whatever the case, Alexander had the sense of entitlement common to his ilk, so it didn't surprise me he felt he deserved a bump. The truth was, though, while he probably had at least as much juice as Benny, he didn't have much of a way with people. The guys in the outfit couldn't stand him, and that included most of his own crew. It also included me.

"Alexander maybe won't like it, but he'll accept it when I tell him how it is." I wasn't sure if I was saying this for Samael's benefit or my own.

"You think so? Then why did he put a bullet in Leeds's ear and leave her duct taped to an office chair in that chop shop on Edgehill?"

I slammed on the brakes and jerked the car to the side of the road. The Lincoln's tires squealed and it overshot the shoulder, raising a cloud of dust as it shuddered to a halt.

I turned and grabbed Samael by the throat. "What did you do, motherfucker?"

Samael grinned and didn't even try to escape my grip. "I didn't have to do much," he said. "Honestly, I could have done it myself and made it look like Alexander's work, but that wasn't necessary. He really wanted to do it. Ugly business. Murder comes so easily to you people."

I released my hold on Samael, for the time being, and called Chavez. This time, I got a signal. He hadn't heard anything about Leeds, so I told him to send some of his soldiers to the chop shop. Then I turned back to Samael. He'd gone back into the plastic bag and pulled out the book I'd bought at an occult store in Hollywood. It was titled *The Angel of Death*, by Friedrich von Junzt.

"You picked up a biography," he said, flipping through the pages. "I didn't know you were such a fan."

"Before, I was just planning to smoke you," I said. "But I can do a lot worse. If you've done something to Leeds, I'm going to let my imagination run wild."

Samael laughed. "What are you going to do? Put me in a TV and make me answer stupid questions?"

That hit a little too close to the mark. I slammed the

car into gear and left some rubber on the shoulder as I pulled back onto the highway.

"So what did you read about me?" Samael asked.

"Nothing much. Sometimes I have trouble falling asleep."

"Nightmares? I suppose that's one of the hazards of your line of work."

I wasn't real interested in therapy, but I figured it wouldn't hurt to see if I could get some information. Samael seemed like the kind of guy who wanted to talk about himself.

"Actually, I learned a lot. Too much. Seems there are a lot of contradictory stories about Samael."

"Such as?"

"Okay, so maybe he's the Angel of Death. But maybe he's Satan. Or maybe an archangel. Or a fallen angel, or...what was it you called Mr. Clean? Oh, yeah, a devil. Maybe he's just another small-time devil. Seems the ancient world was lousy with them."

Samael grinned. "And what's your theory?"

"In the stories, there's a lot of different takes on what he is. Sometimes good, sometimes evil, but always a pain in the ass."

"I've gotta be me."

"And the way I see it, none of it really matters. Whatever you are—whether or not you're really this cat in the stories—I'm still going to put you down."

"Your arrogance is magnificent."

I shrugged. "It's not arrogance if you can back it up."

"And you're convinced you can back it up."

"Oh, yeah. See, the scrub in the stories was a coward."

"A coward?" Samael grinned and bent an eyebrow at me.

"Yeah. He really only had two claims to fame. He slaughtered a bunch of Egyptian children—everyone knows that one. And he attacked Jacob when he was still a babe in his mother's womb—and he didn't even win *that* fight, by the way. So maybe he always wanted to be the badass they called in when a baby needed killing. But he never really amounted to more than a tale mothers told to frighten their children. Like I said, a bogeyman."

Samael's eyes flashed and his face darkened momentarily, and then the grin returned. "Ah, yes, the false bravado of the damned," he said. "No matter how many times I see it, it never fails to amuse me. I hope you can cling to it, at the end." Then he vanished, and the book he'd been holding toppled onto the floorboard.

I enjoyed the rest of my drive in blessed silence.

The place where I'd executed Benny looked much the same as I'd left it, including the glazed and blackened Benny-shaped scar at the center of the intersection.

It wasn't really necessary for me to do what I meant to do at the crossroads. But magic is ultimately all about patterns, about convergences, intersections, and associations. I'd be able to draw more power in this place, and as the site of Benny's death curse, it should be nicely attuned to Samael. It had other associations for me besides.

I left the Lincoln's headlights on to illuminate my work and gathered my supplies. I placed the TV in the middle of the road leading east from the intersection and switched it on. Electricity wasn't necessary—I only kept the set plugged in at my condo so Mr. Clean could watch the local channels. The jinn surveyed his surroundings, looking from side to side as if peering through a window.

"Have you decided to release me?"

"No such luck, Mr. Clean."

"My name is Abishanizad."

"Your parents must have hated you."

"Why have you brought me here?"

I momentarily considered asking the jinn to help with the manual labor, but finally decided it wouldn't be worth the negotiating.

"Hold on to your shorts," I said. "I'll let you know when I need you."

I began collecting stones from the desert, each about the size of a dinner plate. I didn't much care about shape or texture—some were round, some were flat, some were rough, and some were smooth. I placed them in four separate rows, each at a forty-five-degree angle between the roads. It took a lot of rocks, but the result was a kind of Paleolithic geomorph like the spokes of a giant wheel, with the hub at the intersection of the crossroads.

When I'd joined the outfit, my boss, Shanar Rashan, had brought me into the desert not far from this place to summon my familiar. That was the other association I could work with, and it's why the jinn had been hoping for an early parole when he saw where I'd taken him.

I had experience with exactly one spirit, Mr. Clean. I had a spell that had given me power over him. I had no idea if Samael was the same kind of entity as Mr. Clean, but I had no reason to think he wasn't. I was going to work with that.

I retrieved the plastic angel statuette and half buried it in the center of the crossroads, in the place where I'd killed Benny and burned his corpse. Then I went to stand in the middle of the west road, the same distance from the intersection as the spot where Mr. Clean was positioned. The moon hung low on the horizon, like a swollen yellow eye watching my preparations.

"Juice up, Mr. Clean," I called to the jinn. "I need all you can give me." One of the primary roles of any familiar is to flow a little extra juice for its master. A normal familiar could flow a little extra—Mr. Clean could flow a lot. I expected to need all of it. The real question was whether it would kill me.

When I'd summoned the jinn all those years before, I'd had no idea what to expect. It was my coming-out party as a young sorceress. It was a way of announcing myself to the unseen world, letting it take its measure of me and commanding its respect. I'd called out blindly to the darkness and Mr. Clean had answered.

This time, I'd be calling to Samael. That's why I was performing the ritual in the place where the death curse had manifested him. That was the purpose for the angel statuette. It wasn't just a subtle jab, though it was that, too—it was a way of crafting a connection, an association, between the entity, the magic, and me.

I began the chant at a whisper, just as I had when I was a girl. My mind emptied until it was a hollow chamber filled only with the words, and the pattern behind the words. I stretched out my arms and called the untamed magic of the wasteland to me, and it coursed along the four roads like a torrent. The stones of my geomorph began to glow with an orange radiance, like jack-o'-lanterns on Halloween.

"Tyger, Tyger, burning bright, in the forests of the night," I chanted. "What immortal hand or eye could frame thy fearful symmetry?" I'd never been much for poetry, but this verse had always held power for me, from the first time I'd heard it. When Rashan had taught me the summoning ritual, I'd known these were the words I would use to master it. When you're really on your game, magic feels *right*.

As the words gained volume, a hot wind blew in from the desert and lifted the hair from my shoulders. The wasteland itself awoke from its long slumber, and it *breathed*. Dark clouds rolled in and a bolt of lightning flashed down from the cloudless sky. It struck the center of the crossroads and the angel statuette was illuminated with electric-blue witch-light.

I took that power into me, all of it, and I reached out to Mr. Clean to take his as well. He screamed as I violated him, gorging myself on his magic like a vampire at a soft, wet throat.

"Tyger, Tyger, burning bright," I shouted into the roar of the wind and the maelstrom of magic.

And Samael came.

Black smoke roiled in along all four roads to converge in the center of the intersection. A form appeared, like a hard-edged darkness against the night, a hundred feet tall. I saw a ragged outline, snapping like the folds of a tattered robe, or maybe just a jagged tear in the world that opened onto another place, a place of unrelenting blackness.

The towering form gained solidity and details began to emerge. The figure held a massive iron sword and wore an iron crown. The face was in shadow, but I could tell that it looked upon me because the body was covered with hundreds, thousands, of eyes, each peering out at me from the darkness when the folds of the cloak shifted, never blinking.

The maelstrom I had created turned at the center of the crossroads, drawing this being down into the statuette. Like Abishanizad, a spirit of earth and air as old as the world, it would be caught in that relentless pull and be bound to the plastic angel. I would imprison it by my will and power and make it my slave.

Or not.

Samael spoke, and hearing his voice was like stroking out. My head exploded, my body lost all feeling, and I collapsed to the ground, utterly paralyzed.

"I am called Samael," he said. "I am sorrow and loss. I serve the God on the Mountain and you have no power over me." He lifted the iron sword and brought it down on the angel statuette. The blow didn't so much cleave it as vaporize it, and the dust was scattered on the raging wind.

The figure turned and a thousand eyes looked down at me where I lay prostrated in the dirt. And what I felt wasn't fear, it was despair. It was the abject hopelessness that one can only experience when death is inevitable and only oblivion awaits.

Samael was the Old Testament made manifest. My own faith, such as it was, was built upon that ancient foundation, but it was mostly about the possibility of salvation from it, through grace and redemption. There was no redemption here. There was only wrath and punishment. There was only retribution.

The towering figure of the Angel of Death vanished and was replaced by Samael's human form. The wind died as suddenly as it had risen and the night sky cleared. Samael walked over to me and crouched on his haunches. Strength gradually returned to my body and I struggled to sit up.

Samael grinned at me. "Let's hear it," he said.

"Hear what?" I gasped, fighting to pull the air back into my lungs.

"A snappy one-liner. A sarcastic gibe. You know, talk a little trash."

I laughed bitterly, shaking my head. "What do you call it? The 'bravado of the damned'? You've heard it a thousand times, and you still don't understand it."

"It's nothing more than impudence. It's pride." Samael paused, and then spat out a single word. "Sin."

I shook my head again. "No. You're stronger than I am. Fine. Maybe you'll kill me in a couple days and there's nothing I can do about it. Too bad for me."

"At least you've come to accept your fate."

"But why? Is it because you've earned your strength? Is it because you've worked for your power? Is it even the luck of the draw? Hell, no. The fucking game is rigged. Someone decided that you'd be stronger than me, that you'd have the power of life and death over me, so that's the way it is. Okay, no use crying about it. But don't expect me to be impressed. You haven't done anything to earn my respect. You're a fucking tool."

"It's the same in your world. You expected Benny to respect you, just because you had more power."

"Bullshit. *That's* the luck of the draw. Benny and I are the same. We're both human. So maybe I've got more juice than Benny, and maybe my boss has more than me. All men aren't created equal, at least in the underworld. We accept that. But at least the deck wasn't stacked ahead of the game."

Samael laughed. "You think it's random?"

"I know it is."

"And yet, you must know that magic is the pattern within the fabric. You must know this, or you would have no command over it."

"Yeah, sure," I said, and shrugged. I'd been philosophizing on precisely that subject as I set up the summoning ritual.

"So you know that magic is pattern, and yet you believe that the gift of it is random, without pattern? Do you not sense a contradiction in that? That everything else about magic is pattern, order, but those who are given to command it are not chosen, but are only a product of chance?"

That brought me up short. I'd never considered it because it just didn't fit my worldview. I didn't want to believe I was chosen for anything. I didn't want to believe anyone could make choices for me but me. If I wasn't the master of myself and my fate, what was I, really?

Samael nodded. "*That* is the question that should keep you up at night," he said. "It has haunted me since I was made. What if there is *only* the pattern, the purpose? What if 'I' am only an illusion, a trick of the light? You said I was a tool. What if the 'I' is just the by-product of a tool aware of itself?"

"No," I said, shaking my head. "There's no pattern or purpose behind everything, and even if there is, I don't figure in it. You want to know how I know that?"

Samael nodded, and I punched him in the nose. He reeled back, lost his balance, and toppled onto the sand.

"What the fuck?" he said, sitting up and gingerly prodding his nose. A trickle of blood ran down over his lip.

I laughed. "Didn't see that coming, did you? I believe in magic because I can see it. I can taste it and touch it. I can feel that pattern and weave it into a new one if I want to. I *don't* see that pattern in my life. I'm not feeling it. You want me to believe in it, show me. Until then, I'm not going to take the word of some spook with delusions of grandeur and an identity crisis to match."

Samael wiped the blood on the back of his hand and shook his head, smiling ruefully. We stood and faced each other. "I envy you," he said.

"Why? You've got the juice and the big-ass sword. I'm a mere mortal."

"That's exactly why I envy you. I *have* seen it, Domino. The pattern. I've seen more of it than you, anyway, enough that I can't just shut my eyes, wave my hand, and make it go away."

I looked at him closely. I'd gotten pretty good over the years at sensing when someone was holding out on me. "What else?" I asked. "That's not all of it."

He nodded. "I envy you because you may be right. I'm just a tool, but humans may not be. I don't know that you are, and I wish I had that. The rest of us are like insects caught in a spiderweb, but some of my kind believe that humans are free of it, for better or worse."

"Ignorance is bliss," I said.

"Amen," said Samael.

"Now that we've shared our existential angst, I don't suppose this changes anything?"

"It changes everything."

"Really?"

"Yes. I'm still going to kill you in two days. But up to the end, you'll believe you're dying free."

* * *

The next morning, I went to East L.A. to meet with Rafael Chavez. Carmen Leeds had been found dead, just as Samael had said she would be. Worse yet, Jefferson Alexander seemed determined to secede from the outfit, and it looked like his crew was behind him. Two murders in the organization in as many days was enough trouble—a civil war would be really bad for business.

I met Chavez in an outfit-controlled tattoo parlor. We had a lot of them all over our territory. Tattoos were powerful mojo, and the operation, though small in scale, worked on multiple levels. First, a lot of gangsters used tattoos to enhance their ability to flow and store juice. In theory, they worked just like any other kind of arcane symbology, from graffiti to old-school glyphs and runes. In fact, they were even more potent because they were permanently etched in the sorcerer's skin and paid for in blood and pain.

That blood and pain paid a dividend, too, even when the subject wasn't a sorcerer. The inking ritual had magic of its own, and we skimmed that juice from every customer that walked in the door for a tribal wrap or a tramp stamp.

And finally, human activity and emotion amplifies the potency of the juice that courses through our turf, and we can use the tattoos to augment that effect. Every patron that gets inked in one of our joints acts as a mobile amplifier wherever they go.

Chavez was in the back office talking on the phone. He hung up when I walked in. "Where you been, *chola?* We got a problem here."

"I went to fucking Disneyland, Chavez, what do you

think? It might be nice if I only had one problem at a time, but until that blessed day comes, you might have to handle some shit on your own."

"Okay, okay, D, chill out. We're doing the best we can."

"Tell me what's happening."

"I guess Alexander found out you were going to bump Carmen ahead of him. He disagreed with the decision, so he smoked Carmen. He says he's leaving the organization and I guess his crew likes the idea. Word is, he's been making contact with some other outfits, looking for a new team. This shit is going to get a lot bigger if someone takes him on."

"He's a fucking idiot," I said.

"Yeah, maybe, but he's got some juice and it's a good crew. They produce. There's some outfits that wouldn't mind laying down the welcome mat for him. Not friends of ours."

Gangsters could be prone to tunnel vision, and this was the kind of thing that happened when a guy didn't see the big picture. From where Alexander was standing, he had something to offer and plenty of interested buyers. What he apparently didn't realize was there was no fucking way I could let it happen.

Alexander himself was replaceable—everyone is— but the crew and its operation were real assets to the outfit. More importantly, you don't have an organization without rules, and we couldn't just stand back and let Alexander flaunt the rules. You give gangsters the idea they're independent contractors, and pretty soon you don't have an organization at all.

"I really hate this fucking guy," I said.

"I never liked him, either," Chavez said. "*Mi madre*

always told me not to trust white people whose first and last names were reversed."

"Jefferson Alexander?"

"She had a whole system worked out for evaluating white folks based on their names. Two first names or two last names were bad, but the reversed names were the worst."

"Jefferson Alexander could be two first names, or two last names, or it could be reversed names."

"Yeah, so he's triple fucking jeopardy, *chola*. Mama would never have brought him in."

"Well, he's gotta go now. No question about that."

"It's not that simple, *chola*. He's got his crew behind him, so you take him out you don't necessarily solve the real problem."

"Does Rashan know about this?"

"Yeah. He said you could handle it."

It would be nice if my boss got more personally involved from time to time. Then again, if he was interested in doing that I wouldn't have a job.

"So how do you isolate Alexander and still get his crew back on the reservation?" Chavez asked.

"I guess I've got to sit down with him. Convince him I'll consider his request. Thing is, no one likes the fucking guy. If I can buy enough time for his crew to remember that, they'll back me when I take him out. Hell, they might do it themselves."

"That could work," Chavez said. "The main thing is to make sure another outfit doesn't get behind him."

"Is there anyone in the crew we could give a bump once Alexander's out of the way?"

Chavez shrugged. "Well, you know, we looked at these guys before we decided to bring Leeds in. They're good, but none of them have upper-level management experience. Kelvin Zimmerman—they call him KZ— has potential. He runs a couple blocks in Baldwin Village, tight shop. But it's a big step from herding gangbangers to running a whole crew."

"Okay, I can work with potential. I want to know everything there is to know about this kid. And be ready to set up a meeting with him when it's time to move on Alexander. I want a smooth transition when the time comes."

Chavez nodded. "You want me to get you a sit-down with Alexander?"

"Yeah, soon as possible."

"Where you want it to be?"

"His choice."

"I don't think that's a good idea, *chola*. He already ganked Leeds, he might think he can make a move on you."

"God, I hope so. That would make this real easy, wouldn't it?"

Chavez laughed. "I like the way you think. Okay, I'll call you with the when and where."

I left the office and walked back through the tattoo parlor. Samael was sitting in one of the booths getting inked by a young Asian woman. She leaned over him, working on his left forearm with the needle gun.

"It's a flaming eyeball," he said, and grinned at me.

"Real original."

"Eyes are cool. I like eyes."

"If you say so."

"You think this thing with Alexander is going to work out?" he asked. "I'm not sure. If someone were to tip him off to your play, the whole plan could come apart."

The artist stopped working and sat up. She looked from me to Samael and back to me. She looked like a deer caught in the headlights.

I gave him a hard stare. "No idea what you're talking about," I said. "And even if I did, I wouldn't talk about it here."

Samael shrugged. "I don't see what the big secret is. Everyone here's got to know who they're working for." He looked at the girl and raised an eyebrow. "Right? You do know who owns this place, don't you?"

"I, uh, just work here, sir," she said. Smart girl. She *did* know, of course, and she wasn't just a tattoo artist. She had juice and enough of a brain not to talk about it.

"My mistake," Samael said. "Just a word to the wise, Domino. The clock is ticking."

"Yeah, it is," I said. "Enjoy it while you can."

Detectives Meadows and Sullivan were waiting for me at the door of my condo when I got home. I might have guessed.

"Ms. Riley, we'd like you to come downtown and answer some questions," Sullivan said.

"Why's that? I've still got your card. I'll give you a call if I remember anything that might help you."

"We have a witness who reports seeing you leaving the scene," Meadows said. "You're going to have to come with us."

"Let me guess, white male, early twenties, dark hair to his shoulders, nice build?"

Meadows frowned and glanced at Sullivan. "We can't divulge the identity of the witness, Ms. Riley."

"Yeah. This guy's lying to you. It's personal with him and me. You're going to find out he's not a very reliable witness. He's wasting your time."

"Maybe so," said Sullivan, "but you're still going to come with us."

"Am I under arrest?"

"Not yet," said Meadows. "But we can do it that way if you want."

I didn't have time for this shit. I tapped the ley line and flowed juice into a spell. "I have with me two gods," I said, "Persuasion and Compulsion." The magic would ensure the cops would buy just about anything I was selling.

"Excuse me, Ms. Riley?" said Meadows.

"The fuck are you talking about?" said Sullivan.

"You don't need me to come downtown," I said.

"The fuck we don't," said Sullivan.

"I'm not a suspect in this case."

"The fuck you're not."

I blinked and looked at the detectives with my witch sight. My compulsion had broken against them like waves against the rocks. Someone had warded them against my magic. The defenses were good—I'd eventually find a hole in them, but it would take a while.

Samael appeared behind the detectives, standing between them. He put his arms around their shoulders, but they didn't seem to notice. He smiled. "I did that," he said.

My mind raced as I ran through the options. I could get a lot tougher with the juice, but I didn't really want to go there with the cops, and anyway, I wasn't sure even combat magic could hammer through Samael's wards. I could force them to go get a warrant. I didn't know much about police procedure—I didn't need to when I could rely on magic to get me out of jams—but it seemed pretty likely they had more than enough on me to get one. And being arrested would just dig me in deeper.

In the end, I took a ride downtown. It was the first time since I was a juvenile delinquent I'd seen the inside of a police station. I spent a couple hours in an interview room stonewalling the detectives while I poked holes in the wards. Fortunately, Samael didn't show up to patch them or I might have been there all day.

Meadows managed to score some alone time with me, and she used it to press me on Shanar Rashan and the outfit. She knew there was more going on in the city than met the eye. She didn't have all of it, but she was just aware enough of the supernatural underworld that she couldn't let it go. Even if no one else in the department believed her, she was going to keep digging until she found the truth.

What she apparently didn't realize was that civilians—sensitive or not, cops or not—were never given a chance to find the truth. Eventually, she'd get too close, learn a little too much, and someone or something would make her go away.

When I'd weakened the wards sufficiently, I hit Meadows and Sullivan with the compulsion again. I told them to erase the interview tape and shred the paperwork, and then I walked out of there. It wasn't a perfect solution. Lots of other cops had seen me. I didn't know how much Meadows and Sullivan might have talked about me, or to whom, and I couldn't be sure how far the paper trail went. Maybe they'd get it all, or maybe there'd be a loose end someone would notice and start asking questions. Even with magic, cover-ups are complicated, which is why it's best to stay off Five-oh's radar in the first place.

I cabbed it back home and got a call from Chavez on the way. Alexander had agreed to meet with me… in a few days, maybe the weekend. It pissed me off that Alexander had such trouble working me into his schedule, and besides, I wasn't sure I'd be available in a few days. I told Chavez to politely request a more urgent fucking meeting.

I'd just gotten back to the condo when Chavez called again. He'd arranged the sit-down with Alexander for that evening. It was at a construction site in Baldwin Village, a low-income housing tract that would be the crack houses and shooting galleries of tomorrow. I had just enough time to grab a shower and a bite to eat.

In the past, the outfit didn't have any interest in construction, but we were trying something new. Build the right way—some creative geometry and the right symbology stamped into the foundations—and we'd be able to pull even more juice from the vice and sin for which these places would inevitably be used. Ordinarily, we had to convert a building—typically with graffiti magic—but that was a suboptimal solution if we could build our juice boxes from the ground up. Construction is all about efficiency and sustainability these days.

Alexander was waiting for me in a trailer at the construction site. Most of his crew was there, too. They were armed and juiced up, but that didn't necessarily mean Alexander was planning to take a shot at me. He might just be scared shitless. I still hoped he'd make a move and give me an excuse, but I wasn't counting on it, the way my luck had been running.

A gangster with an Uzi and nervous eyes opened the door for me and I climbed into the trailer. Alexander was sitting behind a battered metal desk with a Formica surface. He nodded to one of the folding chairs in front of the desk.

"Chavez said you wanted to sit down," he said. "Here I am."

I had to stifle a laugh as I took a seat. Alexander was trying to play the hard guy, but he didn't play it very well. It wasn't really his fault—a real hard guy is hard because life made him that way. You can take the rich white kid out of Pasadena, but you can't take Pasadena out of the rich white kid. Still, he didn't seem frightened or even concerned. He seemed confident, like he already knew what was going to happen. Given that he had no reason to feel confident, that made me curious.

"Yeah, real nice of you to meet with me, Jefferson. I was afraid we were going to lose you." I left it hanging there, and the look on Alexander's face told me he wasn't sure how to take it. Good. The same look told me it didn't bother him much, either way. Not good.

"Drink?" he asked, holding up a bottle.

"Cuervo?" I said, and shook my head. "I've already had my daily allowance of iguana piss." I admit, I'm a tequila snob. I can drink just about any hootch ever brewed or distilled and have a pretty good time, as long as you don't try to call it tequila. Alexander shrugged and poured a dirty drinking glass half-full.

"Well, say what you want to say. I got other people to see tonight."

Was that supposed to mean he was meeting with rival

outfits? Probably, and that meant I'd better do a really good job of changing his mind.

"What happened with Carmen Leeds was unfortunate," I said. "It wasn't sanctioned."

Alexander shrugged and took a drink.

"That said, strength demands respect. That's the way it is with our thing. I gotta recognize it. Makes it look like I picked the wrong guy to run this crew."

Alexander smirked and took another drink. "Yeah, I guess maybe you did."

I nodded and hoped he wouldn't see the way my jaw was clenching. "Okay, so you win. You run this crew."

"You're giving it to me?"

"No, you already took it. I can't give you what you've already taken, can I? I'm just signing off on it." If I had to pretend to eat shit, I could at least make it look good.

Alexander's eyes narrowed. "What's the catch?"

"No catch. The outfit is more important than any complaints I might have about your methods. We need this crew. The boss won't let it go."

Alexander nodded. "Okay, good," he said. "I'm cool with that."

That's because you're a fucking idiot. "Good, then, it's settled. Congratulations." I reached across the desk and shook his hand. "There's just one thing," I said and sat back down.

"What's that?"

"I got to be sure you haven't switched sides. It's a question of organizational security. I don't care what you might have been planning—that doesn't matter now. But if you've made any commitments, we need to know about it. If there are problems with another outfit, that'll have to be escalated up the chain of command."

"I haven't made any commitments. Not yet," he added.

No humility, no regret, no apparent concern that he may have put the outfit at risk. No apparent fear that I might lose my patience and melt his face. The guy was either more stupid than I gave him credit for—and I gave him credit for a lot—or he really liked his hole cards. What was his angle? Why did he feel so damn *safe?*

"Then we're good," I said, mentally adding, "Until I get around to killing you." I stood up and walked to the door.

"Thanks for coming by," Alexander said. "You made the right decision, this time." He smirked again.

I gave him a hard look. "I'll see you soon, Jefferson."

With the Alexander situation handled and the cops temporarily off my case, I had an opportunity to turn my attention back to Samael. The attempt to bind him with the ritual I'd used on Mr. Clean obviously hadn't worked out, and that pretty much exhausted my knowledge of spirit magic. I needed an expert.

Ismail Akeem was a Somali sorcerer who'd been with Shanar Rashan a lot longer than I had—longer, in fact, than any gangster I knew. Spirit magic was Akeem's specialty and his paranoia was legendary. His house in Koreatown was known to be well warded against spirits. I figured that gave me a decent shot of picking his brain without Samael eavesdropping on the conversation.

You meet enough freaks in the underworld to get

used to it after a while, but no one in the outfit creeped
me out like the Somali witch doctor. Akeem had a certain presence that seemed a little out of step with the rest
of the world. There was a light in his eyes that might be
knowledge the rest of us didn't possess, or that might
just be madness.

I parked my car on the street outside his house. The
grass in the front yard was dead and marred in places
by disturbing black splotches, like someone had spilled
crude oil on what was left of the lawn. I had no idea
what had caused the stains and quickly decided not to
think about it too much.

The light came on as I reached the porch and the
front door opened.

"Welcome, Domino," Akeem whispered. There
were conflicting stories in the outfit about the whispering. Some said it was caused by the ritual possessions
Akeem exposed himself to. Others said it was because
he ate spirits. Akeem himself always said he whispered
so the spirits wouldn't know what he was thinking. It
made me wonder if I should be whispering, too.

We went inside and I sat on the sofa. Akeem served
tea. He sat in an antique armchair and we drank the tea
in silence.

"You have troubles with the spirits," he said when
we'd finished. "Tell me about them."

"Just one spirit," I said. "And how did you know why
I wanted to see you?"

"How many times have you come to see me before?"
Akeem asked.

"Never, I guess."

Akeem nodded. "And why else would you be here
now? Most people find my company disturbing." I

shook my head, but he waved away my objections. "There are many of us in here," he said, tapping his temple. "Sometimes I find my own company disturbing." I'd bound Mr. Clean to an old TV set. Akeem had bound many more spirits to his service, but he didn't use a TV. He imprisoned them within his own body and bound them to his soul.

I told him about Benny Ben-Reuven and the death curse, about Samael and my failed attempt to bind him to the angel statuette. Akeem sat silently and listened without interruption or reaction.

"These spirits tell many stories about themselves," he said when I was finished. "In that, they are just like us. It doesn't mean the stories are true."

"So this Samael may not really be the Angel of Death?"

Akeem shrugged his thin shoulders. "There is no way to know. But what does it matter if it is true?"

"Well, if it's true, I'm fucked."

"What will be, will be," Akeem said. "Do not allow the stories this being tells about itself to defeat you before you have even begun to fight." That sounded a lot like Mr. Clean's advice. When I thought about it, that didn't really surprise me.

"So what can I do? He's proven that he's stronger than I am."

Akeem shook his head. "He's proven nothing. He's only shown you that you cannot bind him. This may be a matter of superior strength, yes, but it may also be a product of his nature, or of the magic that brought him here."

"Okay, that's good. What are some other ways I could get rid of him?"

"You could give him to me. He sounds…interesting. I believe I should like to eat him."

"No, Akeem. Thank you for the offer. But this is my problem. I can't put you at risk. You're too valuable to the outfit."

Akeem nodded. "When did you say he will make the attempt on your life?"

"Three days from when I killed Benny. When the moon is full."

"And this powerful spirit, this angel of death, why do you suppose he would need to wait? What does he care about the phases of the moon?"

"Yeah, I wondered about that, too. Why not just take me out? He said those were the rules—three days of torment, then he'd kill me."

"The answer is that he doesn't care about these things. Those are the rules, yes, but not his rules. They are merely the rules of the magic that called him and bound him to Benny Ben-Reuven's service."

"Okay, but what does that mean? How does that help me?"

"It helps you because these details are limitations. You see? It does not matter what this Samael is, or is not. The curse itself is limited, it has weaknesses, and you can attack those weaknesses. The spell is your enemy, not the spirit."

"Okay, that's real good. I may not have the juice to handle the Angel of Death, but I should be able to handle any spell Benny Ben-Reuven can throw at me."

"Yes," Akeem said.

"So this spell, how would it work?"

"As you say, Benny's death powered the summoning, initially. But this was only powerful enough to call the spirit and bind it here. The spell needs time to gain power, and it draws that power from the swelling moon. When the moon is full, the spell will have ripened sufficiently to compel the spirit to obey Benny's command."

"To kill me."

"Yes."

"But if I could stop the moon from becoming full, the spell wouldn't ripen and Samael wouldn't be compelled to kill me."

Akeem arched his eyebrows at me. "Is that within your power, to stop the moon from becoming full?"

"Not a chance."

"Indeed. The moon is beyond your reach, but the connection between you and the curse is not."

"Would I be able to see the connection?" I asked, giving myself a quick examination.

"You are marked."

"Where?" Whether the mark was physical or arcane, I should have been able to see it.

"Come," Akeem said. He stood and extended a hand. He led me over to where a mirror hung above a side table in the living room. He disappeared into another room and returned holding a hand mirror. "Lift your hair and look at the back of your neck," he said, and handed me the mirror.

I looked and didn't see anything. I looked again with my witch sight, and I saw it: a faintly glowing, lidless eye.

"Son of a bitch," I said.

"There is your mark," Akeem said.

"Why my fucking neck?"

Akeem shrugged. "It is the usual place. Some say it

is to place the mark nearest the seat of the soul. I don't believe such superstitions."

"Why then?"

"A hand or a foot, even an arm or leg—you could just cut it off."

I laughed. "Yeah, I guess that's not going to be an option here. So how do I get rid of this fucking thing?"

"Even on the neck, there are physical methods, depending how deep the mark is. It might be possible to remove the skin with fire or blade." He reached out and placed a cool, dry hand on the back of my neck. "Unfortunately, this mark is very deep."

"Yeah, that's too bad. What are the other options?"

"Your death would likely tear the mark free of its tether," Akeem suggested.

"On the other hand, I'd be dead."

"You could be revived, probably."

"Let's keep that one as a last resort. What else?"

"You could go to Rashan. He is old and very powerful. He might know a way to remove the mark."

"Okay, *that's* the last resort. I'll go to my boss if dying doesn't work." Rashan had made me his lieutenant because he believed I could take care of business on my own. I wasn't eager to undermine that belief. My job security depended on it.

"You could perform a cleansing ritual in a sacred river—the Ganges, the Jordan, the Nile..."

"Anything closer to home?"

"Aha Kwahwat."

"Never heard of it, but it doesn't sound that close."

"It's the Mojave name for the Colorado. Their name for themselves means 'people who live along the river.'"

"Cool. Can you teach me the ritual?"

"Yes, it isn't difficult, but I must warn you—it's very dangerous."

"Of course it is. Okay, what's so dangerous about it?"

"The ritual will create a physical manifestation of the magic that marks you. I do not know what form it will take, but you must defeat it to cleanse yourself of the mark."

"No problem, I prefer a stand-up fight to all this sneaking around."

Akeem looked at me blankly.

"You don't go to the movies much, do you?"

I drove through the Mojave Desert for the third time in two days, but this trip was taking me all the way to the Arizona border. It turned out some parts of the Colorado were more sacred than others, and the aqueduct that stretched from Lake Havasu to the Santa Ana Mountains didn't make the grade. I was looking for a spot near Needles where ancient petroglyphs adorned the rock formations along the river.

Akeem had showed me the cleansing ritual, and he'd been true to his word. The spell wasn't complicated and it didn't take long to learn. The real trick, I knew, would be dealing with the spell once it manifested and tried to kill me.

Now that I knew it was there, the mark on the back of my neck had started itching. I was pretty sure it was just my imagination, but that didn't make it itch any less. I drove through the desert night and smoked and itched.

Needles was the kind of town I wouldn't mind relocating to if I ever got tired of city life. It was a small, never-was kind of town in the middle of the desert, but it had juice. It perched on the western banks of the Colorado for starters, and as the petroglyphs I was looking for suggested, its history was ancient. It also straddled Route 66, which runs along one of the most potent ley lines on the continent. The town is full of the mid-century Americana that's kitschy at its worst but too cool for school at its best. Maybe it was a tourist trap and hotter than hell's attic, but Needles was still my kind of town.

I turned off I-40 and drove north for several miles on River Road. I parked the Lincoln at an RV park and campground near the river and set out on foot for the last leg of my journey. There wasn't much in the way of a canyon along this stretch of the Colorado, grand or otherwise. The ground was broken and rugged, but mostly flat. The area compensated for the general lack of canyons with a lot of interesting rock formations. After a couple hours, I found the cluster of reddish spires I was looking for.

I stopped at the edge of the water and examined the rocks with my witch sight. The petroglyphs were easy enough to find, and I could tell they were still altering the flow of magic in the area after who knew how many millennia. Just like the graffiti back home but built to last. I couldn't tell exactly what the symbols were meant to do, but I guessed I'd find a hollow or crevice that had once been a shaman's cave back in the rocks somewhere. A player had to carve out his turf and control his juice. Some things never change.

I stripped off my clothes and waded out into the water waist-deep. The flow wasn't too strong, maybe because of the ample width of the river and the gentle gradient, or maybe because of all the fucking dams humans had built along its course. The water wasn't cold—it was early summer, and even in the dead of night, the temperature must have been pushing seventy.

I bathed myself and then began the ritual. I opened myself to the river, and the rock, and the vast vault of stars overhead. The rush of magic that washed over me was so powerful, tapping it was effortless.

"If the doors of perception were cleansed," I chanted, "everything would appear to man as it is, infinite." The words were from a poem by William Blake, *The Marriage of Heaven and Hell*, and they flowed freely with the ancient magic that swept through this barren land.

The mark on my neck began to burn and the waters around me began to roil and churn. Gradually, a form began to take shape just below the surface, partially hidden from view by the white, moonlit froth. Slowly, the figure rose from the river, water streaming from its limbs and hair, until it stood before me. The figure was a familiar one.

It was me.

The chant died on my lips and I stared at my reflection. After the initial shock, I looked with a more critical eye. I thought I looked a bit wide in the hips. I wasn't getting any younger, and I supposed my metabolism was slowing down. I'd need to amp up the spells I used to keep the cellulite at bay, and it probably wouldn't hurt to skip the burritos for a while…

I noticed my doppelganger had a rather annoyed look on her face.

"Let me guess," I said, "evil twin?"

"I know you are," she said, "but what am I?"

"Huh?"

"You have it backward, sweetheart. You're the evil-doer. I'm the part of you that wants to be punished."

"That's a little twisted, don't you think?"

"You *would* say that."

"Uh, yeah, I just did…"

There was a moment of awkward silence. We stared at each other. We cleared our throats.

"So what happens now?"

"Now I punish you…us…whatever."

"Seems a little self-defeating. Can't we just go back to the way it was? You know, I'll do what I do, you can cry about it, and I'll mostly ignore you."

My self-righteous twin shrugged. "That's not going to work anymore. There's a contract."

"Yeah, but if you kill me, Samael won't be able to."

"I'm a manifestation of the curse. Maybe I *am* the way he kills you."

"It's not time yet."

"It won't be long. I can make it last a while."

"So make your move."

She sighed. "*You* summoned *me,* remember? You've got the idea you can kill me and make the curse go away. I can stand here all night." She laughed and shook her head.

I laughed, too, and then hit her with the force spell stored in the gangster ring on my pinkie finger. She triggered the magical shield in the ring on my—her—left ring finger, and my spell shattered against it like an arrow striking a steel door. We stared at each other some more.

"This really could take a while, huh?" I said.

"Yeah, I told you."

I pulled in juice from the river and started spinning

spontaneous attack spells. I hurled them at her, one after the other, as fast as I could flow the magic and twist it into lethal implements of my will. There was a lot of juice to be had and I brought a furious storm down upon her.

She easily deflected every attack as quickly as I could launch it. It was no mystery how she was doing it. I knew every move she was making and anticipated every defense. It didn't fucking help me, though, because she anticipated every attack no matter how hard I tried to juke her. Really, it was infuriating.

After a time, she got bored and began countering. This didn't exactly liven things up. Thrust, parry, thrust. Swing, block, feint, swing. Back and forth, going nowhere. I'm not sure how long we stayed at it, but eventually I could feel my toes pruning.

My toes were pruning. Because I was naked, standing in the river. I was naked. My self-righteous twin was naked. Only difference was, I had a pile of clothes waiting for me on the bank. I pretended to tire and began to give ground, retreating to the edge of the river. My adversary didn't seem to be buying it, but she pressed the attack anyway. When I gained solid ground, I ducked, rolled, and reached for my clothes.

And I came up holding the stainless-steel forty-five semiautomatic I'd placed in the pile under my jacket.

"Eat lead, bitch," I said, and squeezed the trigger.

My twin went to the crucifix at her neck, activating the physical shield stored in the amulet. There was an electric-blue discharge of magical energy as my shot ricocheted harmlessly into the night.

"Son of a bitch!" I took a couple hopping steps and threw the pistol as far out into the river as I could. It arced over the surface, end over end, and plopped into the water like a bullfrog going for a swim.

"Well, what did you expect?" my twin said. "You know about the shield, did you think I'd let you shoot me?"

"Shut the fuck up."

"I'm just saying, it wasn't very clever. You could have tried throwing rocks at me first, try to get me to discharge the shield. *Then* you shoot me." So helpful.

"You'd have thought of that, too," I said. "You could have used a telekinesis spell to throw the rocks back at me and still used the shield when I shot you."

"Yeah, good idea."

I threw up my hands and sat down on my clothes. "That's it," I said. "I surrender." I was all juiced out from the ridiculous duel, and the mark on my neck burned like a motherfucker. Besides, there's only so much frustration a girl can take.

My twin waded to shore and sat down by me, so close we were almost touching. "What did you think would happen, Domino?"

"I thought I could take you, obviously. You're not really me. You're just a spell."

"It's a really good spell," she said, "but that's not what I meant. How long did you think you could go around murdering people before you were called to answer for it?"

"I don't go around murdering people. If I have to kill a guy, he's got it coming—"

"Save it, Domino, I know the drill. It is what it is, no matter what you try to tell yourself. There are consequences."

"Oh, give me a fucking break. You're a spell, okay?

That's it—just a spell. Don't try to tell me this is about some absolute moral law handed down from on high. You can try to close the sale all you want, but I'm not buying."

She looked at me, and I thought there was a kind of desperation in her eyes. "Why, Domino. Why can't you see?"

I held her stare for a moment, then swallowed hard and looked down at my feet. I shrugged. "I'm a gangster," I said. "I'm not apologizing for it. Maybe you, or Samael, or God Almighty don't think much of what I am, but there's worse things I could be."

"There are better things, too."

I stood up and started getting dressed. "Says who? I like being a gangster. Beats an office job."

"Sarcasm and denial won't save you, Domino."

"Never failed me before," I said, and pulled on my boots. "I'm outta here. You coming, or what?"

"I can't go with you."

"You have to stay out here? What will happen to you?"

"I'm just a spell, remember? This manifestation will fade when you leave, and I'll be unmade when my purpose is fulfilled."

"When I'm dead."

"Yes."

My self-righteous twin was a manifestation of the curse condemning me to death. Maybe I could think of something more useful than trying to destroy it or talking a little smack. I sat back down.

"Tell me the curse," I said.

"What?"

"Tell me the words, in English."

"Angels of destruction will hit you," my twin recited. "You are damned wherever you go. Dark will be your path and God's angel will chase you. A disaster you have never experienced will befall you and all curses known in the Torah will apply to you. I deliver to you, the angels of wrath and ire, Dominica, the daughter of Gisele Maria Lopez Riley, that you may smother her and the specter of her, and cast her into hell, and dry up her wealth, and plague her thoughts, and scatter her mind that she may be steadily diminished until she reaches her death. Put to death the cursed Dominica. May she be damned, damned, damned!"

"Benny wasn't fucking around."

"Like I said, it's a really good spell."

"Samael isn't just going to kill me, he's going to drag me to hell? I won't even leave a ghost?"

My twin shook her head. "Samael can kill you, but he doesn't have the authority to judge you."

"So what's the bit about smothering the specter of me and casting me into hell?"

"It's a prayer for protection in the afterlife from the target of the death curse."

"And Benny needs protection because I'll be dead but that won't necessarily get rid of me?"

"Even with death curses," my twin said in a scolding tone, "violence never really solves anything."

"In the underworld, killing a man is just the beginning," I said.

"Right."

"Or a woman," I said and laughed. I stood up again and started making my way back along the river.

"What's so funny?" my twin called to me.

"I've got a plan," I said, turning back to her.

"What plan?"

"I'm going to make someone an offer he can't refuse."

Samael was waiting for me when I got back to the car. I ignored him and we drove in silence for a while. I thought about my next move. It was a gamble, but I was pretty sure it was the right play. The only other options Akeem had given me were dying and asking Shanar Rashan for help. Even with time running out, I wasn't real enthusiastic about either one. I was also thinking about Detectives Meadows and Sullivan. I'd gotten them off my back, but I wasn't convinced that was going to stick.

"I've been meaning to talk to you about that," Samael said.

I kept ignoring him.

"The cops, I mean. You'll be pleased to know they won't be bothering you anymore."

I glanced over at him with narrowed eyes. "Why's that?"

"There was another murder. Through shrewd police work," he said and winked, "they were able to connect it to the tow-truck driver. They have a new suspect."

"What kind of shrewd police work?"

He nodded, grinning. "A shoeprint with a distinctive wear pattern on the heel connected the two murders. Mud and fecal matter with a unique mineral, biological, and chemical composition connected the killer to the sewers below Chinatown. Maybe it was the MSG."

"You actually planted evidence at the first murder scene, the tow-truck guy?"

Samael tapped his forehead. "He who fails to plan,

plans to fail," he said. "Did you think I was winging this?"

"So who's the poor bastard you're pinning it on?"

"No need for you to worry—it's no one you know." Samael laughed. "I have to admit, I thought about framing up your boss, but we don't really have enough time to let that play out the way it deserves."

"Fuck you, who'd you pin it on?"

"A ghoul," Samael said, chuckling.

"Couldn't find a ghost or a goblin?"

"No, a real ghoul. Haven't you ever run across one?"

I hadn't, but I didn't feel like admitting it, so I just clamped my mouth shut and stared at the highway.

Samael nodded. "Well, there aren't that many of them, so it's not surprising. They're similar to vampires, except, instead of gaining power by drinking blood, they get it from eating human flesh."

"Like a zombie?" I couldn't help it—professional curiosity.

"No, they're not dead—or undead. At least, not at first. They start out human, as human as you or I. Well, you, I guess, not me so much. Anyway, they get some power from the cannibalism, like I said, but eventually it starts to change them."

"How?"

Samael shrugged. "They start looking a lot like a cadaver."

"How nice for them."

"Yeah, but here's the cool part. If they survive long enough, they begin another metamorphosis as their power continues to grow. They start to become incorporeal. Not completely, at first, but they can control it. Like maybe they can make parts of their body incorporeal. Then, later, they learn to phase out completely for a short time. Eventually, they become permanently incorporeal, like a wraith or something."

"And there's one of these things in L.A.?"

"More than one. Like I said, this one does most of his eating in Chinatown."

"And it murdered somebody?"

"Right. It can survive just fine eating corpses— you know, ones that are already dead—but this ghoul doesn't have any problem whipping up a fresh meal. It's old and hungry for power, pun intended. It'll soon be ready for its final metamorphosis."

"And you sent the detectives after this fucking thing?"

"Yeah. I told you, they won't be bothering you any-more."

I pressed the accelerator to the floor and kept it there. I made it back to the city just after dawn. Having screwed me again, Samael left me alone lying in the wet spot. Part of me said the detectives weren't my problem and I had enough shit on my plate. There was something more than a little absurd about a gangster going to bat for a couple of cops.

But I knew the detectives' lives were on my tab. Samael knew it, too, of course, which is why he set them up. It's not like he hadn't warned me. Even if I couldn't save myself, at least I could try to save Meadows and Sullivan before I checked out.

Samael had fed me enough information that I could probably have found the detectives without divination magic. Beyond the contractual three days of torment, he clearly wanted to keep me busy until it was time to die. For that reason, as well as the obvious one, I didn't want to waste any more time than necessary in the Chinatown sewage system, so I stopped by my condo and ran a standard finding spell.

For necromantic divinations, I use FriendTrace.com. I was hoping the detectives were still alive, though, so I went with a popular mapping site instead. I typed their names in the input box, pumped juice into the spell and clicked the search button.

"Gather up the fragments that remain," I said, "that nothing be lost." A bird's-eye view of Chinatown came up with a red arrow pointing at a location off North Main. That meant either that Meadows and Sullivan were together, or only one of them was still alive. I grabbed my backup forty-five from the hall closet on my way out.

In the movies, the sewers under any great city are vast, stinky catacombs of dark, claustrophobic, brick tunnels and chambers. The reality is that L.A.'s modern sewers are nothing more romantic than smooth-walled, concrete pipelines of varying sizes. Still, all but the largest interceptor lines are just as dark, claustrophobic, and stinky as the ones in the movies.

I entered through a maintenance cover in a back alley. When I dropped down into the muck, the stench hit me like a linebacker blindsiding a quarterback. I staggered and would have fallen if I hadn't caught myself on the slimy, curving wall. I bent double and retched. I'd been expecting a powerful stink, of refuse, and shit, and stagnant, filthy water. I hadn't been expecting the overpowering reek of dead, rotting flesh. Based on Samael's description of the ghoul, I supposed I should have been.

I dropped a protection on myself to keep the toxic

fumes at bay, and then I spun my nightvision spell. The magic seemed to penetrate the gloom well enough that I didn't think I'd need a light. There were sounds in the tunnel—the metallic groaning of distant valves, dripping water, the animal noises of small vermin. Nothing that sounded like a ghoul or a detective in distress. I picked a direction and crept down the tunnel.

As I advanced, the smell grew stronger. I had to flow more and more juice just to avoid adding the contents of my stomach to the sewage. Even with the juice, the hideous stench began to take its toll. My eyes, nose, and bare skin began to burn, as if from an extreme allergic reaction or exposure to toxic chemicals. My breathing became labored and fatigue numbed my limbs. I realized this wasn't just the mundane unpleasantness of the sewers. It was magic.

I'd gone maybe twenty feet when I stepped in the first pitfall. I dropped into the liquid filth, and though it was only about five feet deep, the fall plunged my head below the surface. I came up gasping and puking. I pulled myself out of the crude hole and hunched over, heaving until my stomach was empty. Then I heaved some more. Sludge clung to my skin and clothes and plastered my hair to my scalp.

The shakes had mostly subsided when I heard the noise, a horrible symphony of splashing and chittering growing louder as it approached. I knew what it was before I could see it. A massive horde of rats spilled down the tunnel toward me like a roiling, black flood. My nightvision resolved the amorphous, writhing mass, and the hundreds of tiny eyes shone like bright pinpoints of white light in the gloom.

I reached for the juice and it tasted foul as I drew

it in. "A great flame follows a little spark," I said, and a ball of fire exploded down the tunnel and burst over the horde of rats. The horrible smell of burned fur and flesh washed over me and drove me to my knees. Oily, noxious smoke filled the tunnel, choking me.

The rats kept coming. The survivors swarmed over me before I could spin another spell. I lost my balance under the weight of the scratching, biting horde and toppled backward into the hole. I went under again, submerged in filth and a squirming blanket of rats.

I'd drained all my combat talismans in the pointless duel with my evil twin. The rats pressed me down below the surface and tore at my flesh with their teeth and claws. With no air in my lungs and no strength in my body, I couldn't spin a spell. I beat at the rats with my fists, but my feeble attacks had no effect. I was dying.

Your life is supposed to flash before your eyes at the moment of death. Maybe it was delirium or a misfiring brain overloaded by abject terror, but I was spared the traditional recap. I simply panicked. I cast out mindlessly for the juice, sucking it in like fresh air, drawing into me all the magic I could hold, and then drawing more.

Magic awakens something primal in the human mind. In its presence, humans become agitated, paranoid, and aggressive, and particularly strong magic can cause them to degenerate into an almost animalistic state. Turns out, it can have an even more dramatic effect on a horde of frenzied rats.

There was a deep, electrical humming sound as the magic rushed into me, and my body began to blaze with an arcane radiance. I felt the smothering vermin freeze and begin to convulse, as if they were one organism.

They went mad. Some of them turned and began to devour each other, others began to devour themselves. Some flipped and twisted spasmodically as if in their death throes, and others flailed in the water, churning it to a disgusting froth. Still others simply fled, exploding away from me down the tunnel in either direction.

I crawled out of the hole and dragged myself to the side of the tunnel, smashing or swatting aside any of the repulsive creatures that came near. I sagged against the wall, struggling to breathe, still burning with the magical fire. I gradually regained control of myself and began spinning spells to bleed off the juice that threatened to consume me from the inside out. No fireballs this time—I wielded focused, precise force spells like hammer and scalpel, smashing and impaling the maddened rats one by one.

When it was finished, I sat in the sludge amidst the floating rat corpses. I threw my head back, looked up at the low ceiling of the tunnel, and screamed. I didn't care if the ghoul or anyone else heard me. The terror and revulsion felt like a living thing inside me, and I had to get it out.

Time passed. Eventually, I marshaled enough strength to climb to my feet and get moving. I stumbled through the sewer in a haze of pain and exhaustion. When the tunnels branched I followed the stench, forging onward as it grew stronger, backtracking if it began to subside. There were more pitfalls, and I avoided some of them. In one of those I didn't avoid, I discovered a crude tunnel leading away from its bottom perpendicular and several feet below the main line. I suspected there was a whole warren of tunnels down there that hadn't been excavated by the Public Works guys.

The tunnel brightened ahead of me and I saw that it opened up into a broad intersection of four trunk lines lit by an overhead electrical fixture. The ghoul had chosen this space for its lair. I might have expected a little decor, comparable to what a homeless person might cobble together. Some personal effects, maybe, or at least a pile of garbage for the ghoul to call its own. But the ghoul didn't have anything like that. Instead, its lair was littered with bones, which I discovered when they began shifting and snapping under my feet, and with the partially eaten carcasses of its victims.

I didn't have much time to soak in the ambience, because I was distracted by Meadows and Sullivan. The detectives hung suspended from chains anchored to the roof in the center of the tunnel intersection. It was a crossroads, I realized, and I wondered if the ghoul chose this place to do its killing for the same reason I chose mine.

Meadows was unconscious, beaten and bleeding, but I could see the rise and fall of her chest and hear her ragged breath. She was alive. Sullivan wasn't so lucky—the ghoul had gotten busy with him. His right leg had been gnawed off a few inches below his knee. His abdomen was torn open, and the organs and entrails were exposed. His face was a mask of blood and ruin.

Then his eyes snapped open and fluid sprayed from his mouth as he gasped. "Puhhh…"

"Jesus Christ!" I yelled, and spun a spell. A blade of force sliced through the chain suspending his body and he collapsed in my arms.

"Puhhh…" he groaned.

"Shut up, Sullivan," I hissed. "Don't talk." I wanted to help him—stop the bleeding, cover the open cavity where his abdomen was supposed to be, something, but I didn't even know where to start. Healing isn't exactly my specialty, and I didn't have any magic that could help him.

"Puhhh…" he said again. Then he clenched his jaw and forced out a word. "Partner…" He tried to turn his head toward Meadows, but he couldn't find the strength. He sank back and his eyes closed.

"She's okay, Sullivan," I whispered. "You protected her."

Detective Sullivan sighed. A bloody air bubble formed on his lips and popped. Then he died.

I released him and cut Meadows down. I cradled her, shaking her gently and patting her cheek. "Wake up," I said. "Please, Meadows, wake up. I don't think I have it in me to carry you out of here."

The lights went out.

It wasn't just the overhead fixture—the intersection was engulfed in a supernatural darkness. I could feel the magic in the air. I could taste it, as thick and nauseating as the stench. My nightvision was useless. I was blind.

I heard a splash to my left. Then I heard an airy, wheezing sound in the darkness that I couldn't identify at first. After a moment, I recognized it. Sniffing.

I spun up a light spell, hoping it would neutralize the magical darkness. It didn't. The spell came together like it should, but it didn't produce any light. The ghoul had some juice, and he was pumping more of it into his spell than I was. I could power up my spell, probably enough to overcome the darkness, but then I wouldn't be doing anything else. That didn't seem like a winning strategy.

I dropped the light spell and slowly stepped back,

away from the sniffing. Unfortunately, I'd forgotten about Meadows and I tripped over her unconscious body. I went down in the disgusting soup, again, and the ghoul seized the opportunity to attack.

There was no splashing to warn me, and I thought the creature must have leaped. One moment I was gathering my feet beneath me, and the next moment the ghoul was on me. We crashed into the water and rolled. My head plunged below the surface and smashed into the slimy concrete. I felt the thing's claws dig into my chest, pushing me under, and then its teeth bit deep into my shoulder, pain lancing through me like a hot knife.

I felt the ghoul's teeth grinding against bone. My lungs burned and white spots began to explode before my blinded eyes. I kicked and thrashed, struggling against the weight that pressed down on me, but the ghoul held me fast. I briefly managed to get my head above water and choked down a mixture of sewage and precious air before I went under again.

Abruptly, I could see. I looked up through the thin veil of foul water and saw the mottled gray form of the monster atop me. Its skin was loose and wrinkled, but the muscles that moved beneath it were lean and corded. I couldn't see its face because it was buried in my flesh, but the ghoul appeared to be completely hairless. Then it tore away from my shoulder and leaned back. It looked down at me with milky, dead eyes. A gobbet of my flesh hung from its withered lips, caught in a monstrous grinder of crooked, yellow fangs. The ghoul went incorporeal momentarily, flickering like a video image on the fritz.

The ghoul swallowed greedily, and then it opened its mouth wide, its lower jaw distending until I thought it would snap. It grabbed my head in both hands, immobilizing it, and I felt its claws sink into my scalp. The ghoul leaned down until its horrid maw filled my view.

Then I heard a muffled retort, another, and another. The ghoul's head snapped around, looking over its shoulder, and its grip on me loosened. It phased out again, shimmering and ephemeral as a mirage. I pushed my face out of the water and sucked in air. The ghoul became solid again, and a sharp crack followed instantly. The back of the ghoul's skull exploded, and a black, oily fluid sprayed from the ruin and spattered my face.

The ghoul screamed but it didn't die. It thrust away from me and launched itself at Detective Meadows, who was leaning against the tunnel wall and leveling her service revolver at the thing. She fired again as the ghoul rushed her, but it phased out and the bullet passed harmlessly through its center of mass, ricocheting off the far wall. When it was almost upon her, the ghoul became solid again.

"Vi Victa Vis!" I gasped, and struck the monster with a hammer of force in the small of its back. The spell hurled the ghoul over the detective's head and to her right, and slammed it into the concrete. There was a wet sound of pulped flesh and the crack of splintered bone, and the creature crumpled to the ground.

The ghoul twitched and jerked, phasing in and out, and its broken body crackled and snapped as it struggled to its feet. It turned and looked at me with those pale, soulless eyes, and it screamed again.

I looked at Meadows. "Run," I said. She looked once more from me to the ghoul. Then she ran, scrambling away as quickly as her injured body could move.

I looked back to the ghoul. "A great flame follows a little spark," I said, and the ball of blue-white fire spun into being above my upturned palm. The ghoul screamed again and flung out a gnarled claw at me. The force spell that struck my chest wasn't as powerful as mine had been, but the impact extinguished my fireball and hurled me backward, tumbling head over heels until I smashed into the opposite wall. The back of my head cracked painfully against the concrete.

"God*damn*it," I said, and slowly staggered upright, swaying momentarily until I caught my balance. I extended my hand and clenched it into a fist. "Man is born free," I said, "but everywhere he is in chains." Bands of force encircled the ghoul and began to constrict. The creature went incorporeal again, but I didn't release it. When the ghoul became physical, I flowed juice into the spell and tightened my grip, slowly compressing the creature's withered body as if I'd dragged it to the bottom of the sea. The ghoul's eyes popped and its internal organs were pulverized. Then a staccato snapping filled the tunnels as every bone in its body was ground to fragments.

When I was finished, the thing I held had all the structural integrity of a sack of jelly. I released it and it sank to the ground almost soundlessly. I walked a few paces down the tunnel Meadows had taken, and then turned. I spun up the fireball again and hurled it at the corpse. When the smoke cleared, there was nothing left of the ghoul except the stink.

After a few minutes, I found Meadows wandering lost through the sewers. "Detective," I called, and spun a light spell so she could see. Meadows whirled and leveled her revolver at me, then slowly lowered it until it hung at her side.

"I knew it," she said. "I was right all along—about you, about all of it."

"Yeah, you were right. What are you going to do now?"

"I can't do anything, can I? No one will believe it, and even if they did, you wouldn't let me do anything, would you? You could put a hex on me, make forget. You could make me disappear."

"I'm not going to do that," I said.

"And Shanar Rashan? He's real too, isn't he? He's not just an urban legend."

"That's a name you'd do best to forget."

"Meaning what?"

I shrugged. "I won't harm you, Meadows. But it isn't just about me." I might be disappearing myself, soon enough, and I wouldn't be able to protect her if she went poking her nose where it didn't belong. I wasn't going to press the point—Meadows was the kind of person who needed to figure it out for herself. I knew the type pretty well.

"So what now?"

"I guess you know Sullivan is dead. I leave and you call it in. You put down a serial killer tonight—there's plenty of evidence back there. They'll be able to identify some remains. I had to torch the ghoul, so you may have to get a little creative with the paperwork."

"Ghoul? Is that what it was?"

"I guess. This was my first one, so I'm not exactly an expert."

"Sweet Jesus," Meadows said, shaking her head. "You think you've seen the worst these streets have to offer, and then you find out there's a whole other world that's uglier than you ever imagined."

"Yeah," I said. "That's why it's better if people don't know."

"But I do know. Now I've got to figure out how to live with it."

"I could make you forget, if you want me to."

"No, Riley. No way. Don't do that to me. Please."

I nodded and turned to go. "Take care, Detective."

"See you around."

"I hope not," I said, and I left.

When I got back to the Lincoln, I pulled my cell out and saw I had seven missed calls from Chavez. I hit the speed dial without checking the voice mail and he answered on the first ring.

"What's the news?" I asked.

"*Chola*, we got a problem. Alexander grabbed KZ."

"What do you mean he grabbed him?"

"I mean, he took him fucking hostage or something. I don't understand it, D. Look, I was asking around about the kid, like we said, doing the due diligence in case we wanted to bump him up. But I was discreet about it, D—no way Alexander got wind."

"I think I know how he found out, Chavez, and it's not on you."

"You say so, *chola*. Thanks. What's our play?"

"Where is Alexander holding him?"

"The Paradise, that abandoned theater on South Broadway. Used to show porn there. The boss wants to reopen it, turn it into a juice box. I told him nobody goes to fucking porn theaters anymore, but he—"

"Okay, Chavez, I got it. What's Alexander doing? Has he made any demands?"

"He's not talking, *chola*. Far as I know, he hasn't got any demands. He went to the mattresses. He's got the rest of his crew in there—maybe they're backing him, maybe he took all of them hostage. I don't know. It's hard to tell, because he brought in some outside muscle."

"Who?"

"A crew from Pico Union, Salvadorans. Mean motherfuckers. Looks like he brought them in last week."

"Last week? What the hell?"

"Yeah, I been busy, D. I found out this motherfucker was planning to hit Leeds last week. That's when he brought in the Salvadorans."

Last week. *Before* I hit Benny Ben-Reuven. Even before Benny tried to hit me. Which meant…Alexander knew Benny was going to make a move on me. And he knew I'd kill Benny. And he knew Carmen Leeds would be the next in line. So he gets in front of the thing, sets up a hit on Leeds in advance.

It was a reasonably good theory, except for all the holes in it. Like, if Alexander was enough of a psychopath to murder everyone in his way—and I had no reason to doubt him—why not just murder Benny himself? Why wait for Benny to make a move against me and get himself killed? Plus, even if everything goes down the way he wants it to, he has to know I'd never let it stand. He has to know—he smokes Leeds, I smoke him. So why go to all the trouble?

All the bolts slid into place, neatly filling the holes in my theory. Alexander also had to know I'd be out of the way. He had to know Benny was packing a badass death curse. That's why he didn't do Benny himself and why he wasn't worried about retaliation from me. I kill Benny and get popped by the death curse, Alexander just has to stay alive a few days until the curse finishes me off. Maybe he even thought it would be immediate, didn't know about the mandatory three-day waiting period. Either way, he just has to buy some time. That's why the little cocksucker seemed so smug and agreeable at our sit-down.

I took a deep breath and exhaled slowly. "I got played, Chavez."

"Yeah, maybe we all did, but that don't matter. Let's go get this motherfucker."

"No, I mean I got played." I filled in the details for him—the death curse, Samael, everything.

"Jesus Christ, *chola*," Chavez said when I was finished. "That's one sneaky fucking white boy. Even *mi madre* wouldn't have seen that coming."

"Yeah."

"You should go to Rashan, D."

"And say what? That Alexander played me and would he please pull my ass out of the fire? Come on, Chavez, you know how this thing of ours works. Rashan will cancel my health insurance and give Alexander my job."

"No way, *chola*. He likes you. He wouldn't cut you loose."

"Fuck you, Chavez, he didn't make me lieutenant because he likes me. He gave me the job because he thought I could do it better than anyone else."

"So what are you going to do?"

"I'm working an angle." I looked at my watch. "But I've still got time to kill Jefferson Alexander."

* * *

The Paradise was one of those screen palaces from a different age, a time when going to the movies was still an event. That age was long dead by the seventies, and the Paradise reinvented itself as a joint where middle-aged guys in raincoats went to thoroughly enjoy the latest adult films. By the mid-eighties, home video had killed the porn-theater star and the Paradise became a drug haunt, just like every other derelict building the city hadn't gotten around to condemning. Now the ghosts of Bogie and Bacall, Chambers and Holmes mingled with those of junkies and crack whores, and the theater had become a kind of sorry-ass monument to urban decay.

In other words, the Paradise had juice. I could see why the boss wanted to bring it back online.

I parked down the street and walked cautiously along the sidewalk to the front of the theater. There was only one word spelled out on the marquee: CLOSED. The glass was long gone from the ticket booth and the entrance, replaced with sheets of plywood. The sheets were nearly hidden under a thick layer of graffiti, and I recognized our gang tags.

I placed my palm flat against the door and flowed a little juice, unlocking the wards. I pushed it open and stepped quietly inside. It was dark and I powered up my nightvision spell. The Paradise had probably had a grand, ornate entry when it opened. All that finery had been replaced by more utilitarian decor during the adult-film era, and now even the metal fixtures, linoleum, and stain-resistant carpet had been removed. The place was gutted, with exposed mechanicals in the ceiling and bare, cracked, and pitted concrete floors, also liberally adorned with graffiti. A rusting metal staircase led up to the projector room and balcony.

A shadowed figure appeared in the doorway at the top of the stairs. I felt the unmistakable electrical tingle and building pressure of magic gathering. The figure shouted something in a language I didn't understand but that sounded vaguely Asian, and a fiery lance streaked down at me.

It was solid spellcraft, accomplished even, and it reminded me this was a good crew, one the outfit needed. The spell also provided sufficient illumination with my nightvision that I could identify the gangster attacking me. It wasn't Alexander, it was a Vietnamese kid named Bobby Nguyen. He had some juice and he looked scared. He was backing up his boss, but he didn't seem happy about it.

I spun a spontaneous counter and caught his spell in midair. I reversed it and flicked my hand, hurling the spear back at Nguyen so fast it blurred to an indistinct, orange streak as it flew toward him. I froze the spell inches from his face.

"Get lost, Bobby," I said, and jerked my head in the direction of the door behind me.

Nguyen swallowed hard and nodded. He eased carefully around the fire spell and down the stairs. He gave me a kind of embarrassed wave, and then darted out the door.

I curled my hand into a fist, and the lance diminished to a tiny point of orange light and then vanished. I went up the stairs. I figured Alexander was in the main theater, but I didn't want to leave any of his crew at my back. I ducked my head into the projector room, but it was empty. I pushed through the swinging doors and stepped onto the balcony.

Two more of Benny's gangsters were waiting there, a guy and a girl, both young. I recognized them but couldn't remember their names. The guy was the one at the construction site who'd opened the trailer door for me, the one with the Uzi. He still had the Uzi, and he let loose with it when I came through the doors.

I triggered the crucifix—I'd charged all my talismans before coming to the theater—and bullets hammered the shield, setting off a miniature fireworks display as the sapphire energy discharged. Bullets chewed into the paneling of the doors and wall behind me in a blizzard of splintered wood.

"All movements go too far," I said, tearing the sub-machine gun from the gangbanger's grasp with the telekinesis spell and pulling it through the air into my own. *"Vi Victa Vis,"* I said, extending my hand toward him, palm out. The force spell hurled him backward and knocked him off the balcony. Fuck him, he tried to shoot me. Anyway, the balcony wasn't that high—he might live.

While I was dealing with the shooter, the girl was spinning a spell. I use famous quotations for my spell-craft, but the activity can be anything that helps you flow the juice and create the right pattern for the spell. She used finger tutting, which was new to me but made a lot of sense. On the downside, it required some really intricate hand gestures and positions. On the upside, it was nonverbal and looked really fucking cool.

I felt the magic well up in my mind, whispering to me inside my skull, calming me, encouraging me to throw down my weapon and give up the fight. I shook my head at the girl and smiled, flowing my own juice and washing out the hostile magic. Her eyes got a little wider and her shoulders slumped. She dropped to her knees and laced her fingers behind her head, like I was planning to read her Miranda rights. Good enough.

I moved to the edge of the balcony and looked down. There were half a dozen more gangsters in the theater, the big hitters in Benny's crew. At the front of the theater, on the raised platform where the screen had once been, KZ was bound to a wooden chair with a strip of duct tape covering his mouth. He was enclosed in a circle that had been laid down with red spray paint. By my witch sight, I could see the juice flowing through the circle and I could even get a sense of its purpose. It was a ward against my magic, but it was more than that. Alexander had also tied off a killing spell to the symbol. He'd be able to trigger it with little more than a thought.

I spun my levitation spell, floating over the banister and out into open space. I spread my arms dramatically and hung in the air above the gangsters below. Most of them started backing away, unwilling to attack me, but two of them cast halfhearted combat spells my way. I reached out with the juice, intercepting the spells and snuffing them out.

"Vi Victa Vis," I said, and hurled my force spell down at them, modifying the pattern in my mind and rearranging the magic in midcourse. The spell forked and struck both of my attackers at once, and they crashed through several rows of dilapidated seats before finally coming to rest, unmoving, on the theater floor. The others turned and ran.

I floated down from the balcony and landed in the

center aisle. I spun my eye in the sky spell and positioned it just below the ceiling. The spell would give me a three-hundred-and-sixty-degree view of anything in the theater. I walked down the aisle toward KZ.

Through the eye spell, I saw two of Alexander's Salvadorans step through the doors at the back of the theater, moving into position behind me. They must have followed me in from the street. So much for keeping the bad guys off my back. The Salvadorans' faces and heads were heavily tattooed and both were representing MS-13 colors. They'd probably come up in the gang, and I guessed old habits died hard.

The access door at the front of the theater opened, and two more of the Salvadorans came out and took positions on either side of KZ, just outside the circle. Finally, Jefferson Alexander made his appearance. He was dressed just as he'd been at our sit-down and looked a little crusty. He'd probably been too scared to leave his escort long enough to get a shower or a change of clothes. That made me happy.

Alexander walked over to stand closer to the Salvadorans. He spread his hands and sneered at me, as if daring me to make a move. "No one asked for you, bitch," he said. "Get the fuck out of here." He looked at the nearest Salvadoran and laughed, but got no reaction. Even his hired killers couldn't stand the fucking guy.

I kept walking. With the eye spell, I saw the Salvadorans by the door move up behind me. I stopped when I was about ten feet away from Alexander. I focused my attention on the two Salvadorans standing with him and spoke to them in Spanish.

"I'm Domino Riley," I said, "Shanar Rashan's lieutenant." The Salvadorans visibly flinched and glanced at each other. They already knew who I was, of course, but the boss's name had power. "That's who you've lined up against." I looked at Alexander and then back to the Salvadorans. "With him."

I had to give Alexander credit—there weren't many gangsters with some juice who were crazy enough to back him against me, not to mention my boss. But he'd found them. There was a moment in which no one moved and time itself seemed to take a coffee break. Then I felt magic being sucked from the room like air from a burning building, and the Salvadorans unleashed hell on my ass.

They'd obviously fought together before, because their attacks were coordinated. The two in front targeted my defenses. One went after my talismans with magic-eating juice while the other hit me with a chaos spell designed to short-circuit any active protections I might try to spin. The two in back went on the offensive, lashing out at me with elemental and kinetic energy.

All of this happened at once, in the space between breaths. In the moment before this malevolent magic crashed over me like a tsunami, my familiar appeared in the middle of the theater, standing like his namesake with his arms crossed over his barrel chest.

"Take it all, Mr. Clean," I said.

The jinn spun in place and became a whirlwind, and the maelstrom sucked the hostile magic from the air and devoured it. The wind howled and shrieked and I had to brace myself to keep from being taken by the vortex.

"Kill them," I said, and the jinn tore into the Salvadorans, smashing bone and tearing flesh in a frenzy born of years of imprisonment and syndicated reruns.

I turned to Alexander. He was watching the carnage

in stunned disbelief, slowly backing away toward the exit door. He saw me and a look of determination and defiance hardened his features.

"You do anything to me and KZ dies," he said, shouting to be heard above the roaring wind.

I smiled and hit Alexander's circle with my own chaos spell, overloading his weak-ass magic and pulling the deadly pattern apart at the seams. The wards collapsed in on themselves and the liberated juice was caught by the raging whirlwind and consumed. The wind died and Mr. Clean reappeared, standing with arms crossed once again at the back of the theater.

"Time to man up, Jefferson," I said. "I've really been looking forward to this."

Whether because he actually had some balls or he was up against the wall and knew it, Alexander came to play. He advanced and started spinning spontaneous combat spells, alternately pounding my defenses and exploring them for weaknesses in a sophisticated attack routine. The guy had some juice, even if he was a prick.

I backpedaled and countered his attacks. Alexander maintained the barrage, relentless, pulling more juice, hammering against my will with a power born of desperation. I had to admit, I'd probably underestimated the fucking guy.

I stayed with the rope-a-dope until I sensed Alexander tiring. I was just about to bring the pain when Detective Meadows appeared out of nowhere. "Police! Down on the ground!" she yelled, her revolver aimed at Alexander in a two-handed police grip. "Now!"

The conflagration of magic dissipated and died as Alexander and I both turned to look at her. He didn't turn his head from the detective, but I saw Alexander's eyes swivel to me.

"No fucking way," he said, and laughed. Alexander extended his arm toward Meadows. The gun quivered, and then shook. Slowly, her arm bent until the gun's barrel was pressed under her chin. Her body tensed and froze.

"Meadows, what the fuck are you doing here?" It was stupid, but I was too stunned to think straight.

"I followed you," she said, looking over at me out of the corner of her eye. "I thought you'd lead me to Rashan."

Alexander looked from the detective to me. "You two know each other? And she knows about the boss?" He laughed again and shook his head.

"Let her go," I said. "Don't dig yourself in any deeper, Jefferson."

"Fuck me, she's a cop, Domino! And you actually care, don't you?"

"Yeah, maybe I do." I flung out my hand and the revolver was torn from the detective's grip, tumbling through the air to clatter off the far wall. I flicked my wrist and Meadows was hurled backward, flipping over the first row of seats and out of sight.

I spun my chaining spell, and iron bands of force enfolded Alexander, wrapping him in a lethal embrace. I squeezed, forcing the air from his lungs. He couldn't move and couldn't speak. He couldn't flow any juice and couldn't spin a spell. He was at my mercy.

I approached until we were standing nose to nose. His eyes bulged and veins stood out on his forehead and temples. His face was turning a blotchy reddish-purple. I held the chaining spell steady and pulled in more juice. I'd made a mistake with Benny Ben-Reuven, and I didn't plan to make it twice.

"If you tell the truth you don't have to remember anything," I said. I thrust my own will deep inside Alexander's mind. A squeal escaped his lips and his body jerked and tensed. He fought me and I dug in deeper, the spell slicing through his consciousness like a lobotomist's knife.

The mistake I'd made with Benny is I'd believed him when he said no one else was behind him. I'd believed him because it was the simplest explanation for the attack. It hadn't been well planned. Benny had just waited for an opportunity when we were alone, and then he'd tried to shoot me in the head. It hadn't looked to me like he'd given it much thought at all, and that fit with what I knew about Benny.

Deep inside Alexander's mind, I found the truth. The hit *had* been planned, it just hadn't been planned by Benny. He'd learned about Benny's death curse and coveted it. Benny had insisted it wasn't for *goyim,* so Alexander came up with a way to use it for his own ends. He began planting suggestions in Benny's mind— some with juice and some without, but always with the idea that Benny had to make a play to move up in the organization. He found Benny's not-so-deep-seated misogyny, and he worked with that, too, worrying and picking at it until it nagged Benny like an angry boil that wouldn't go away.

Alexander had done all this with the idea that Benny would eventually take a shot at me. He didn't know how Benny would do it and didn't really care. He knew it wouldn't work, and he knew I'd kill Benny for it. Then the death curse would come down on me, and the organizational ladder would be open, two rungs ahead of Alexander.

If it had ended there, his hands would be clean—Benny and I would have done all his dirty work for him. But that wasn't enough for him. Alexander had to kill Carmen Leeds, and he couldn't make it look like anyone else was behind that murder. He hadn't realized he'd have to deal with me, however temporarily. He thought the curse would take me as soon as I smoked Benny, and that would give him a free shot at Leeds.

I probed around in all the dark corners of Alexander's ugly little mind until I was sure the scheme ended with him. His crew had come along with him, but mostly because they didn't know what he was up to. All they knew was that I'd killed their boss and brought in someone from the outside to replace him. Alexander convinced them I was trying to break up the crew because it had become too successful, too powerful. Alexander had brought in the Salvadorans as insurance, but that was just the beginning. After he took my job, his plan was to purge the ranks of any disloyal elements and replace them with more of the killers from Pico Union.

I dropped the spell and retreated inside my own head. I held the chaining spell on Alexander and cranked the vise a little tighter, just because. Then I balled my fist, took a step back, and punched him in the mouth. I put a little juice into it and his jaw shattered.

I turned to Detective Meadows. She'd peeled herself off the theater floor and was slouched in one of the seats in the first row. She saw the way I was looking at her and held up her hands.

"I know," she said. "Maybe I shouldn't have followed you."

"Yeah, maybe not. I told you, Meadows. You keep it up, you're going to get hurt."

"I'm a cop. What am I supposed to do, ignore my job?"

I shook my head. "This isn't your job. This is my job. Your job is out there with all the normal criminals."

Meadows shook her head. "None of that matters," she said. "What difference does it make if I get the bad guys off the street if I can't even touch the *really* bad guys?"

I looked at her for a moment before speaking. "When I was a little girl," I said, "a man tried to rape me." Meadows tried to speak, but I waved her off. "I had the power to stop him. I could protect myself. Most children can't. Most moms and dads can't, either. That's your job."

"Because you're not going to do it," Meadows said. It was an accusation.

"That's right," I said. "Because I'm a bad guy, too."

"You're not a bad guy, Riley. Maybe you need to think you are."

"Maybe. But I'm not one of the good guys, either."

Meadows nodded. She got up and went to retrieve her revolver, returning it to the holster clipped at her belt. She turned and looked at me once more, and then she left.

I dragged Alexander's unconscious body out to my car and threw him in the trunk. Then I banished Mr. Clean once again to the Zenith in the backseat. I got the idea the jinn had thoroughly enjoyed the evening's work. It wasn't in him to do a job for free, though, and his assistance in the fight had come at an unspeakable price. I'd need to brush up on my knowledge of essential oils.

I drove into the desert for what was likely to be the last time. Samael didn't appear to keep me company, which was just as well because I wasn't sure I had any of the bravado of the damned left in me.

I'd made arrangements with Chavez and he knew what to do if I didn't come back. I'd recommended him to take my place as lieutenant. He deserved it, but it would be Shanar Rashan's decision in the end. For his part, Chavez was ready to put together a posse and go after Samael the old-fashioned way. I vetoed that idea. I didn't want the death curse to decimate the outfit. I was all about organizational best practices, right up to the end.

When I reached the crossroads, I got out of the car and sat in the dirt in the middle of the intersection. The moon was full and the magic of that wild place was thick enough to raise the hair on my arms. Even the roads were transformed in the moonlight, appearing to my witch sight like ancient rivers rather than something carved from the desert by the hands of men. Before long, Benny's ghost appeared.

He turned a full circle, looking out at the desert. He looked up at the moon. "Has it really only been three days?" he asked. "There's no sense of time here. It could have been a hundred years."

"Just three days," I said. "But it was a long fucking three days."

"Why are you here? Have you come to beg for your life?"

I laughed. "No such luck, Benny. I'm here because this is where I want to die."

"Why? You'll be trapped here, just like I am."

I nodded. "Yeah, I'll be trapped here. With you. It'll be like a steel-cage death-match. We'll have a lot of time to work out our disagreement."

Benny's eyes widened and he shook his head. "No! I'm protected from you."

"No, Benny, you *prayed* for protection from me. That's not really the same thing, is it? Like they say, God always answers prayers, but sometimes the answer is no. You had enough juice to kill me—props for that— but you don't have enough juice to save yourself from the things I'll do to you once I'm dead."

The ghost started stumbling around in ragged circles, fading in and out of view as he searched futilely for a way to escape the crossroads. I just watched him and after a time he accepted the inevitable. He stood and faced me again.

"What do you want?"

"A sit-down, what else?"

Benny nodded. "Okay. I'm listening."

"We got played, Benny—both of us." I spelled out Alexander's scheme for him. Benny got angrier the longer I spoke. His spectral image flickered and faded in and out as he lost his grip on the world of the living.

"That motherfucker," Benny said when I'd finished. "He made me do it, Domino! He made me take a shot at you!"

"It's a little late to cover your ass, Benny. Alexander maybe gave you the idea, encouraged you a little, but it wouldn't have worked if you didn't want to do it." Benny started to protest, but I held up my hands, cutting him off. "It's on me, too, Benny. Like I said that night, I didn't really mind killing you. I just did what we do. I didn't think it through."

Benny's ghost stared up at the sky again and sighed. "You know the weirdest thing about being dead? I always heard ghosts hated the living, like they were jealous of them because they were still alive."

"You're not?"

"Fuck, no. Now that I'm dead, I don't see much point in being alive in the first place."

"That sucks, Benny."

"I mean, what's the difference? When you're alive, it seems like the most important thing in the world, but what does it matter, really? There was an inscription I heard about, it was on a Roman tomb or some shit. It said, 'I was not. I was. I am not. I care not.' I always thought, what kind of fucking attitude is that, you know? Turns out, that shit was proper wisdom, Domino."

"I don't know, Benny, maybe it's something only ghosts and Romans got figured out. I still care."

He looked at me and his image wavered again. "You do, don't you? You still want to live."

"Sure I do," I said, rubbing the back of my neck. "The last three days, I haven't been thinking about much else."

"You want me to pull the contract."

"Yeah, that's what I want," I said.

"What's in it for me?"

I shrugged. "Well, if you don't, I'm going to stay here and spend some time with you, Benny. I'm pretty sure I'll be able to convince you it's better to be alive."

Benny nodded. "What else you got?"

I stood and walked over to the car. I popped the trunk and dragged Alexander to the middle of the intersection. He was conscious, but I still had the chaining spell on him, so he couldn't move. With a broken jaw, he couldn't speak, either. I gathered the stones I'd used when I tried to bind Samael and rearranged them into a circle around the crossroads. The circle bisected the roads leading to the intersection. I'd only need to move one of the stones to open a way out.

"You'll release me?" Benny asked, looking at the stones.

"Yeah, you'll be free as a bird, Benny. Plus, I throw in Alexander to sweeten the pot."

"So either I spend eternity with you trapped at this fucking crossroads, or I'm free and I get to take out my frustration on Alexander?"

"Yeah, that's the deal." I looked at him and narrowed my eyes. "You ask me, it's a pretty fucking good deal."

Benny nodded. "Okay, we're straight, Domino. Hell, it wasn't really your fault anyway. Like you said, we both got played. And I did try to shoot you. Anyway, I'm not really doing you a favor, you know. So you live a little while longer—big fucking deal. Most of it will suck and you're still gonna die. That's what I've been trying to tell you, Domino. The Angel never stops chasing you."

"That's all it takes to lift the curse?"

"That's all it takes," Samael said, appearing beside Benny's shade. "No power of this world can save you, Domino, but there's an out clause for a dead man's forgiveness." He turned to Benny. "Is that your wish, Binyamin Ben-Reuven? You want to pull the contract?"

"About that," Benny said, "maybe we can renegotiate."

"On what terms?"

Benny pointed down at Alexander. "I want to put the hit on this sorry motherfucker," he said. "I never liked the fucking guy."

Detective Sullivan was planted with full honors by the Los Angeles Police Department. I knew it wasn't a good idea, but I stopped by to pay my respects when they put him in the ground. I didn't have any strong feelings about the guy, but he seemed like a decent sort and I felt I owed him that much. I stood alone by a tree a short distance from his grave and watched as the priest sent him on his way.

"I can't help but feel partly responsible for his death," Samael said. I'd been expecting him, but my heart still skipped a beat. My hand went reflexively to the back of my neck, even though I knew the mark was gone. Samael was leaning casually against the tree with his arms crossed, chewing a toothpick and watching the funeral.

"What are you doing here?" I asked. "Figured you'd gone back to whatever hole you crawled out of."

Samael laughed. "Why would I do that?"

I looked at him and grinned. "You didn't hear?"

"Hear what?"

"I put a contract on you, Sammy." I gestured to Sullivan's grave. "This shit here has consequences. You should know that better than anyone."

"You're bluffing, Domino. You don't have the juice."

I smiled. A car door slammed behind me, and I turned. A black Mercedes was parked on the side of the road that wound through the cemetery. Shanar Rashan nodded at me and started walking toward us.

Samael gave a low whistle. "Damn, you put the Turk on me?"

"He's not really Turkish. He's Sumerian."

"You sure he can handle me?"

"Word is, he taught Ismail Akeem how to eat spirits back in the day." I shrugged. "Worst case, a spot opens up at the top of the chain of command. I'm willing to see how it plays. What about you, Sammy? You in?"

Samael took a long look at Rashan, and then glared at me. "Another time, Domino. I'll be watching you." He winked and then he was gone.

My boss walked up beside me and looked at the mourners gathered at the graveside. "Is she the one?" he asked, nodding to Detective Meadows.

"Yeah," I said. "She could be a problem. She could also be a friend of ours."

"She has the sight, but no real juice."

"She's smart," I said, "and strong."

Rashan looked at me and smiled. "Okay, Dominica. Don't force it. If the detective's interest in us persists, make sure she becomes a friend and not a problem."

I nodded. "Thanks, boss."

"Anything else?"

I glanced over at the spot where Samael had been standing. "I think we're all good for a while."

Rashan nodded and returned to his car, and I watched as he drove away. I stayed at the cemetery until Sullivan's friends and family had all gone, and then I walked up to his grave. I pulled the book about Samael out of my jacket pocket and flipped through the pages. Then I closed it and tossed it on top of the casket.

"Sleep well, Detective," I said. "The bogeyman's gone away."

* * * * *

The UNDERWORLD CYCLE,
featuring Domino Riley,
continues with MOB RULES
available now and coming soon look for
SKELETON CREW

ACKNOWLEDGMENTS

A big thanks to my editor, Mary-Theresa Hussey, for bringing me this opportunity, and for the insightful work she did to make this a stronger story.

Orphan. Crusader. Angel. Thief.

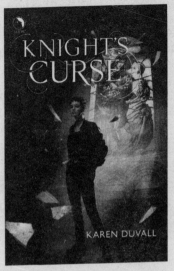

A skilled knife fighter since the age of nine, Chalice knows what it's
like to live life on the edge—precariously balanced between the dark
and the light. But the time has come to choose. The evil sorcerer who
kidnapped her over a decade ago requires her superhuman senses to
steal a precious magical artifact…or suffer the consequences.

Available now!

 HARLEQUIN®
www.Harlequin.com

LKD340

There's more to Kaylin Neya than meets the eye....
New York Times bestselling author

MICHELLE SAGARA

is back with two classic tales from her beloved
Chronicles of Elantra series.

Both available now!

And look for the latest volume in this darkly magical series:

Coming in October 2011.

www.Harlequin.com

LMS337

The end of the world was just the beginning.

Edgar-nominated and critically acclaimed author

SOPHIE LITTLEFIELD

delivers a fierce, haunting narrative of a brave new world.

Civilization has fallen, leaving California barren and broken.
Cass Dollar beat the odds and got her missing daughter
back—she and Ruthie will be happy. Still, flesh-eating Beaters
dominate the landscape, and soon Cass is thrust into the dark
heart of a group promising humanity's rebirth—at all costs.

Available now!

www.Harlequin.com

LSL339

Domino Riley hates zombies.

Bodies are hitting the pavement in L.A. as they always do, but this time they're getting right back up, death be damned. They may be strong, but even Domino's mobbed-up outfit of magicians isn't immune to the living dead.

If she doesn't team up with Adan Rashan, the boss's son, the pair could end up craving hearts and brains, as well as each other....

Pick up your copy today!

LCH326

ONE DATE WITH THE BOSS CAN GET COYOTE UGLY....

C.E. MURPHY

PRESENTS ANOTHER RIVETING INSTALLMENT IN THE WALKER PAPERS SERIES!

Seattle detective Joanne Walker has (mostly) mastered her shamanic abilities, and now she faces the biggest challenge of her career—attending a dance concert with her sexy boss, Captain Michael Morrison. But when the performance—billed as transformative—changes her into a coyote, she and Morrison have bigger problems to deal with. What's more, one ordinary homicide pushes Joanne to the very edge....

SPIRIT DANCES

Available now!

LUNA™

www.LUNA-Books.com

LCEM325